ORIGIN

ORIGIN

‡ A NOVEL

DAN BROWN

RANDOM HOUSE
LARGE PRINT

Copyright © 2017 by Dan Brown

All rights reserved.
Published in the United States of America by Random House Large Print in association with Doubleday, a division of Penguin Random House LLC, New York, and distributed in Canada by Random House of Canada, a division of Penguin Random House
Canada Limited, Toronto.

Page 719 is an extension of this copyright page.

Cover design by Michael J. Windsor
Cover photographs: spiral stairs © rosmi duaso / Alamy; background © Birute Vijeikiene / Shutterstock

The Library of Congress has established a Cataloging-in-Publication record for this title.

ISBN: 978-0-3754-3454-9

www.randomhouse.com/largeprint

FIRST LARGE PRINT EDITION

Printed in the United States of America

10 9 8 7 6 5 4 3 2 1

This Large Print edition published in accord with the standards of the N.A.V.H.

IN MEMORY OF MY MOTHER

ORIGIN

We must be willing to get rid of the life we've planned, so as to have the life that is waiting for us.

—JOSEPH CAMPBELL

FACT:

All art, architecture, locations, science, and religious organizations in this novel are real.

As the ancient cogwheel train clawed its way up the dizzying incline, Edmond Kirsch surveyed the jagged mountaintop above him. In the distance, built into the face of a sheer cliff, the massive stone monastery seemed to hang in space, as if magically fused to the vertical precipice.

This timeless sanctuary in Catalonia, Spain, had endured the relentless pull of gravity for more than four centuries, never slipping from its original purpose: to insulate its occupants from the modern world.

Ironically, they will now be the first to learn the truth, Kirsch thought, wondering how they would react. Historically, the most dangerous men on earth were men of God . . . especially when their gods became threatened. **And I am about to hurl a flaming spear into a hornets' nest.**

When the train reached the mountaintop, Kirsch saw a solitary figure waiting for him on the platform. The wizened skeleton of a man was draped in the traditional Catholic purple cassock and white rochet, with a zucchetto on his head. Kirsch recognized his host's rawboned features from photos and felt an unexpected surge of adrenaline.

Valdespino is greeting me personally.

Bishop Antonio Valdespino was a formidable figure in Spain—not only a trusted friend and counselor to the king himself, but one of the country's most vocal and influential advocates for the preservation of conservative Catholic values and traditional political standards.

"Edmond Kirsch, I assume?" the bishop intoned as Kirsch exited the train.

"Guilty as charged," Kirsch said, smiling as he reached out to shake his host's bony hand. "Bishop Valdespino, I want to thank you for arranging this meeting."

"I appreciate your **requesting** it." The bishop's voice was stronger than Kirsch expected—clear and penetrating, like a bell. "It is not often we are consulted by men of science, especially one of your prominence. This way, please."

As Valdespino guided Kirsch across the platform, the cold mountain air whipped at the bishop's cassock.

"I must confess," Valdespino said, "you look different than I imagined. I was expecting a scientist, but you're quite . . ." He eyed his guest's sleek Kiton K50 suit and Barker ostrich shoes with a hint of disdain. " 'Hip,' I believe, is the word?"

Kirsch smiled politely. **The word "hip" went out of style decades ago.**

"In reading your list of accomplishments," the bishop said, "I am still not entirely sure what it is you do."

"I specialize in game theory and computer modeling."

"So you make the computer games that the children play?"

Kirsch sensed the bishop was feigning ignorance in an attempt to be quaint. More accurately, Kirsch knew, Valdespino was a frighteningly well-informed student of technology and often warned others of its dangers. "No, sir, actually game theory is a field of mathematics that studies patterns in order to make predictions about the future."

"Ah yes. I believe I read that you predicted a European monetary crisis some years ago? When nobody listened, you saved the day by inventing a computer program that pulled the EU back from the dead. What was your famous quote? 'At thirty-three years old, I am the same age as Christ when He performed His resurrection.'"

Kirsch cringed. "A poor analogy, Your Grace. I was young."

"Young?" The bishop chuckled. "And how old are you now . . . perhaps forty?"

"Just."

The old man smiled as the strong wind continued to billow his robe. "Well, the meek were supposed to inherit the earth, but instead it has gone to the young—the technically inclined, those who stare into video screens rather than into their own souls. I must admit, I never imagined I would have reason to meet the young man leading the charge. They call you a **prophet,** you know."

"Not a very good one in your case, Your Grace," Kirsch replied. "When I asked if I might meet you and your colleagues privately, I calculated only a twenty percent chance you would accept."

"And as I told my colleagues, the devout can always benefit from listening to nonbelievers. It is in hearing the voice of the devil that we can better appreciate the voice of God." The old man smiled. "I am joking, of course. Please forgive my aging sense of humor. My filters fail me from time to time."

With that, Bishop Valdespino motioned ahead. "The others are waiting. This way, please."

Kirsch eyed their destination, a colossal citadel of gray stone perched on the edge of a sheer cliff that plunged thousands of feet down into a lush tapestry of wooded foothills. Unnerved by the height, Kirsch averted his eyes from the chasm and followed the bishop along the uneven cliffside path, turning his thoughts to the meeting ahead.

Kirsch had requested an audience with three prominent religious leaders who had just finished attending a conference here.

The Parliament of the World's Religions.

Since 1893, hundreds of spiritual leaders from nearly thirty world religions had gathered in a different location every few years to spend a week engaged in interfaith dialogue. Participants included a wide array of influential Christian priests, Jewish rabbis, and Islamic mullahs from around the world, along with Hindu **pujaris**, Buddhist **bhikkhus**, Jains, Sikhs, and others.

The parliament's self-proclaimed objective was "to cultivate harmony among the world's religions, build bridges between diverse spiritualities, and celebrate the intersections of all faith."

A noble quest, Kirsch thought, despite seeing it as an empty exercise—a meaningless search for random points of correspondence among a hodgepodge of ancient fictions, fables, and myths.

As Bishop Valdespino guided him along the pathway, Kirsch peered down the mountainside with a sardonic thought. **Moses climbed a mountain to accept the Word of God . . . and I have climbed a mountain to do quite the opposite.**

Kirsch's motivation for climbing this mountain, he had told himself, was one of ethical obligation, but he knew there was a good dose of hubris fueling this visit—he was eager to feel the gratification of sitting face-to-face with these clerics and foretelling their imminent demise.

You've had your run at defining our truth.

"I looked at your curriculum vitae," the bishop said abruptly, glancing at Kirsch. "I see you're a product of Harvard University?"

"Undergraduate. Yes."

"I see. Recently, I read that for the first time in Harvard's history, the incoming student body consists of more atheists and agnostics than those who identify as followers of any religion. That is quite a telling statistic, Mr. Kirsch."

What can I tell you, Kirsch wanted to reply, **our students keep getting smarter.**

The wind whipped harder as they arrived at the ancient stone edifice. Inside the dim light of the building's entryway, the air was heavy with the thick fragrance of burning frankincense. The two men snaked through a maze of dark corridors, and Kirsch's eyes fought to adjust as he followed his cloaked host. Finally, they arrived at an unusually small wooden door. The bishop knocked, ducked down, and entered, motioning for his guest to follow.

Uncertain, Kirsch stepped over the threshold.

He found himself in a rectangular chamber whose high walls burgeoned with ancient leather-bound tomes. Additional freestanding bookshelves jutted out of the walls like ribs, interspersed with cast-iron radiators that clanged and hissed, giving the room the eerie sense that it was alive. Kirsch raised his eyes to the ornately balustraded walkway that encircled the second story and knew without a doubt where he was.

The famed library of Montserrat, he realized, startled to have been admitted. This sacred room was rumored to contain uniquely rare texts accessible only to those monks who had devoted their lives to God and who were sequestered here on this mountain.

"You asked for discretion," the bishop said. "This is our most private space. Few outsiders have ever entered."

"A generous privilege. Thank you."

Kirsch followed the bishop to a large wooden table where two elderly men sat waiting. The man on the left looked timeworn, with tired eyes and a matted white beard. He wore a crumpled black suit, white shirt, and fedora.

"This is Rabbi Yehuda Köves," the bishop said. "He is a prominent Jewish philosopher who has written extensively on Kabbalistic cosmology."

Kirsch reached across the table and politely shook hands with Rabbi Köves. "A pleasure to meet you, sir," Kirsch said. "I've read your books on Kabbala. I can't say I understood them, but I've read them."

Köves gave an amiable nod, dabbing at his watery eyes with his handkerchief.

"And here," the bishop continued, motioning to the other man, "you have the respected **allamah**, Syed al-Fadl."

The revered Islamic scholar stood up and smiled broadly. He was short and squat with a jovial face that seemed a mismatch with his dark penetrating eyes. He was dressed in an unassuming white **thawb**. "And, Mr. Kirsch, I have read **your** predictions on the future of mankind. I can't say I **agree** with them, but I have read them."

Kirsch gave a gracious smile and shook the man's hand.

"And our guest, Edmond Kirsch," the bishop concluded, addressing his two colleagues, "as you know, is a highly regarded computer scientist, game theorist, inventor, and something of a prophet in the technological world. Considering his background, I was puzzled by his request to address the three of us. Therefore, I shall now leave it to Mr. Kirsch to explain why he has come."

With that, Bishop Valdespino took a seat between his two colleagues, folded his hands, and gazed up expectantly at Kirsch. All three men faced him like a tribunal, creating an ambience more like that of an inquisition than a friendly meeting of scholars. The bishop, Kirsch now realized, had not even set out a chair for him.

Kirsch felt more bemused than intimidated as he studied the three aging men before him. **So this is the Holy Trinity I requested. The Three Wise Men.**

Pausing a moment to assert his power, Kirsch walked over to the window and gazed out at the breathtaking panorama below. A sunlit patchwork of ancient pastoral lands stretched across a deep valley, giving way to the rugged peaks of the Collserola mountain range. Miles beyond, somewhere out over the Balearic Sea, a menacing bank of storm clouds was now gathering on the horizon.

Fitting, Kirsch thought, sensing the turbulence he would soon cause in this room, and in the world beyond.

"Gentlemen," he commenced, turning abruptly back toward them. "I believe Bishop Valdespino has already conveyed to you my request for secrecy. Before we continue, I just want to clarify that what I am about to share with you must be kept in the strictest confidence. Simply stated, I am asking for a vow of silence from all of you. Are we in agreement?"

All three men gave nods of tacit acquiescence, which Kirsch knew were probably redundant anyway. **They will want to bury this information—not broadcast it.**

"I am here today," Kirsch began, "because I have made a scientific discovery I believe you will find startling. It is something I have pursued for many years, hoping to provide answers to two of the most fundamental questions of our human experience. Now that I have succeeded, I have come to you specifically because I believe this information will affect the world's **faithful** in a profound way, quite possibly causing a shift that can only be described as, shall we say—disruptive. At the moment, I am the only person on earth who has the information I am about to reveal to you."

Kirsch reached into his suit coat and pulled out an oversized smartphone—one that he had designed and built to serve his own unique needs. The phone had a vibrantly colored mosaic case, and he propped it up before the three men like a television. In a moment, he would use the device to dial into an ultrasecure server, enter his forty-seven-character password, and live-stream a presentation for them.

"What you are about to see," Kirsch said, "is a rough cut of an announcement I hope to share with the world—perhaps in a month or so. But before I do, I wanted to consult with a few of the world's most influential religious thinkers, to gain insight into how this news will be received by those it affects most."

The bishop sighed loudly, sounding more bored than concerned. "An intriguing preamble, Mr. Kirsch.

You speak as if whatever you are about to show us will shake the foundations of the world's religions."

Kirsch glanced around the ancient repository of sacred texts. **It will not shake your foundations. It will shatter them.**

Kirsch appraised the men before him. What they did not know was that in only three days' time, Kirsch planned to go public with this presentation in a stunning, meticulously choreographed event. When he did, people across the world would realize that the teachings of all religions did indeed have one thing in common.

They were all dead wrong.

CHAPTER 1

Professor Robert Langdon gazed up at the forty-foot-tall dog sitting in the plaza. The animal's fur was a living carpet of grass and fragrant flowers.

I'm trying to love you, he thought. **I truly am.**

Langdon pondered the creature a bit longer and then continued along a suspended walkway, descending a sprawling terrace of stairs whose uneven treads were intended to jar the arriving visitor from his usual rhythm and gait. **Mission accomplished,** Langdon decided, nearly stumbling twice on the irregular steps.

At the bottom of the stairs, Langdon jolted to a stop, staring at a massive object that loomed ahead.

Now I've seen it all.

A towering black widow spider rose before him, its slender iron legs supporting a bulbous body at least thirty feet in the air. On the spider's underbelly hung a wire-mesh egg sac filled with glass orbs.

"Her name is Maman," a voice said.

Langdon lowered his gaze and saw a slender man standing beneath the spider. He wore a black brocade sherwani and had an almost comical curling Salvador Dalí mustache.

"My name is Fernando," he continued, "and I'm

here to welcome you to the museum." The man perused a collection of name tags on a table before him. "May I have your name, please?"

"Certainly. Robert Langdon."

The man's eyes shot back up. "Ah, I am so sorry! I did not recognize you, sir!"

I barely recognize myself, Langdon thought, advancing stiffly in his white bow tie, black tails, and white waistcoat. **I look like a Whiffenpoof.** Langdon's classic tails were almost thirty years old, preserved from his days as a member of the Ivy Club at Princeton, but thanks to his faithful daily regimen of swimming laps, the outfit still fit him fairly well. In Langdon's haste to pack, he had grabbed the wrong hanging bag from his closet, leaving his usual tuxedo behind.

"The invitation said black and white," Langdon said. "I trust tails are appropriate?"

"Tails are a classic! You look dashing!" The man scurried over and carefully pressed a name tag to the lapel of Langdon's jacket.

"It's an honor to meet you, sir," the mustached man said. "No doubt you've visited us before?"

Langdon gazed through the spider's legs at the glistening building before them. "Actually, I'm embarrassed to say, I've never been."

"No!" The man feigned falling over. "You're not a fan of modern art?"

Langdon had always enjoyed the **challenge** of modern art—primarily the exploration of why particular works were hailed as masterpieces: Jackson Pollock's drip paintings; Andy Warhol's Campbell's Soup cans; Mark Rothko's simple rectangles of color. Even so, Langdon was far more comfortable discussing the religious symbolism of Hieronymus Bosch or the brushwork of Francisco de Goya.

"I'm more of a classicist," Langdon replied. "I do better with da Vinci than with de Kooning."

"But da Vinci and de Kooning are so **similar!**"

Langdon smiled patiently. "Then I clearly have a bit to learn about de Kooning."

"Well, you've come to the right place!" The man swung his arm toward the massive building. "In this museum, you will find one of the finest collections of modern art on earth! I do hope you enjoy."

"I intend to," Langdon replied. "I only wish I knew **why** I'm here."

"You and everyone else!" The man laughed merrily, shaking his head. "Your host has been very secretive about the purpose of tonight's event. Not even the museum staff knows what's happening. The **mystery** is half the fun of it—rumors are running wild! There are several hundred guests inside—many famous faces—and nobody has **any** idea what's on the agenda tonight!"

Now Langdon grinned. Very few hosts on earth would have the bravado to send out last-minute invitations that essentially read: **Saturday night. Be there. Trust me.** And even fewer would be able to persuade hundreds of VIPs to drop everything and fly to **northern Spain** to attend the event.

Langdon walked out from beneath the spider and

continued along the pathway, glancing up at an enormous red banner that billowed overhead.

AN EVENING WITH
EDMOND KIRSCH

Edmond has certainly never lacked confidence, Langdon thought, amused.

Some twenty years ago, young Eddie Kirsch had been one of Langdon's first students at Harvard University—a mop-haired computer geek whose interest in codes had led him to Langdon's freshman seminar: Codes, Ciphers, and the Language of Symbols. The sophistication of Kirsch's intellect had impressed Langdon deeply, and although Kirsch eventually abandoned the dusty world of semiotics for the shining promise of computers, he and Langdon had developed a student–teacher bond that had kept them in contact over the past two decades since Kirsch's graduation.

Now the student has surpassed his teacher, Langdon thought. **By several light-years.**

Today, Edmond Kirsch was a world-renowned maverick—a billionaire computer scientist, futurist, inventor, and entrepreneur. The forty-year-old had fathered an astounding array of advanced technologies that represented major leaps forward in fields as diverse as robotics, brain science, artificial intelligence, and nanotechnology. And his accurate predictions about future scientific breakthroughs had created a mystical aura around the man.

Langdon suspected that Edmond's eerie knack for prognostication stemmed from his astoundingly broad knowledge of the world around him. For as long as Langdon could remember, Edmond had been an insatiable bibliophile—reading everything in sight. The man's passion for books, and his capacity for absorbing their contents, surpassed anything Langdon had ever witnessed.

For the past few years, Kirsch had lived primarily in Spain, attributing his choice to an ongoing love affair with the country's old-world charm, avant-garde architecture, eccentric gin bars, and perfect weather.

Once a year, when Kirsch returned to Cambridge to speak at the MIT Media Lab, Langdon would join him for a meal at one of the trendy new Boston hot spots that Langdon had never heard of. Their conversations were never about technology; all Kirsch ever wanted to discuss with Langdon was the arts.

"You're my culture connection, Robert," Kirsch often joked. "My own private bachelor of arts!"

The playful jab at Langdon's marital status was particularly ironic coming from a fellow bachelor who denounced monogamy as "an affront to evolution" and had been photographed with a wide range of supermodels over the years.

Considering Kirsch's reputation as an innovator in computer science, one could easily have imagined him being a buttoned-up techno-nerd. But he had instead fashioned himself into a modern pop icon who moved in celebrity circles, dressed in the latest styles, listened to arcane underground music, and

collected a wide array of priceless Impressionist and
modern art. Kirsch often e-mailed Langdon to get
his advice on new pieces of art he was considering for
his collection.

And then he would do the exact opposite, Langdon mused.

About a year ago, Kirsch had surprised Langdon by
asking him not about art, but about God—an odd
topic for a self-proclaimed atheist. Over a plate of
short-rib crudo at Boston's Tiger Mama, Kirsch had
picked Langdon's brain on the core beliefs of various
world religions, in particular their different stories of
the Creation.

Langdon gave him a solid overview of current beliefs,
from the Genesis story shared by Judaism, Christianity, and Islam, all the way through the Hindu story of
Brahma, the Babylonian tale of Marduk, and others.

"I'm curious," Langdon asked as they left the res-
taurant. "Why is a futurist so interested in the past?
Does this mean our famous atheist has finally found
God?"

Edmond let out a hearty laugh. "Wishful thinking!
I'm just sizing up my competition, Robert."

Langdon smiled. **Typical.** "Well, science and religion are not competitors, they're two different languages trying to tell the same story. There's room in
this world for both."

After that meeting, Edmond had dropped out of
contact for almost a year. And then, out of the blue,
three days ago, Langdon had received a FedEx envelope with a plane ticket, a hotel reservation, and a

handwritten note from Edmond urging him to attend tonight's event. It read: **Robert, it would mean the world to me if you of all people could attend. Your insights during our last conversation helped make this night possible.**

Langdon was baffled. Nothing about that conversation seemed remotely relevant to an event that would be hosted by a futurist.

The FedEx envelope also included a black-and-white image of two people standing face-to-face. Kirsch had written a short poem to Langdon.

Robert,
When you see me face-to-face,
I'll reveal the empty space.
                    —Edmond

Langdon smiled when he saw the image—a clever allusion to an episode in which Langdon had been involved several years earlier. The silhouette of a chalice, or Grail cup, revealed itself in the empty space between the two faces.

Now Langdon stood outside this museum, eager to learn what his former student was about to announce. A light breeze ruffled his jacket tails as he moved along the cement walkway on the bank of the meandering Nervión River, which had once been the lifeblood of a thriving industrial city. The air smelled vaguely of copper.

As Langdon rounded a bend in the pathway, he finally permitted himself to look at the massive, glimmering museum. The structure was impossible to take in at a glance. Instead, his gaze traced back and forth along the entire length of the bizarre, elongated forms.

This building doesn't just break the rules, Langdon thought. **It ignores them completely. A perfect spot for Edmond.**

The Guggenheim Museum in Bilbao, Spain, looked like something out of an alien hallucination—a swirling collage of warped metallic forms that appeared to have been propped up against one another in an almost random way. Stretching into the distance, the chaotic mass of shapes was draped in more than thirty thousand titanium tiles that glinted like fish scales and gave the structure a simultaneously organic and extraterrestrial feel, as if some futuristic leviathan had crawled out of the water to sun herself on the riverbank.

When the building was first unveiled in 1997, **The New Yorker** hailed its architect, Frank Gehry, as having designed "a fantastic dream ship of undulating form in a cloak of titanium," while other critics around the world gushed, "The greatest building of our time!" "Mercurial brilliance!" "An astonishing architectural feat!"

Since the museum's debut, dozens of other "deconstructivist" buildings had been erected—the Disney Concert Hall in Los Angeles, BMW World in Munich, and even the new library at Langdon's own alma mater. Each featured radically unconventional design and construction, and yet Langdon doubted any of them could compete with the Bilbao Guggenheim for its sheer shock value.

As Langdon approached, the tiled facade seemed to morph with each step, offering a fresh personality from every angle. The museum's most dramatic illusion now became visible. Incredibly, from this perspective, the colossal structure appeared to be quite literally floating on water, adrift on a vast "infinity" lagoon that lapped against the museum's outer walls.

Langdon paused a moment to marvel at the effect and then set out to cross the lagoon via the minimalist footbridge that arched over the glassy expanse of water. He was only halfway across when a loud hissing noise startled him. It was emanating from beneath his feet. He stopped short just as a swirling cloud of mist began billowing out from beneath the walkway. The thick veil of fog rose around him and then tumbled outward across the lagoon, rolling toward the museum and engulfing the base of the entire structure.

The Fog Sculpture, Langdon thought.

He had read about this work by Japanese artist Fujiko Nakaya. The "sculpture" was revolutionary in that it was constructed out of the medium of visible air, a wall of fog that materialized and dissipated over

time; and because the breezes and atmospheric conditions were never identical one day to the next, the
sculpture was different every time it appeared.

The bridge stopped hissing, and Langdon watched
the wall of fog settle silently across the lagoon, swirling and creeping as if it had a mind of its own. The
effect was both ethereal and disorienting. The entire
museum now appeared to be hovering over the water,
resting weightlessly on a cloud—a ghost ship lost
at sea.

Just as Langdon was about to set out again, the tran-
quil surface of the water was shattered by a series of
small eruptions. Suddenly five flaming pillars of fire
shot skyward out of the lagoon, thundering steadily
like rocket engines that pierced the mist-laden air and
threw brilliant bursts of light across the museum's
titanium tiles.

Langdon's own architectural taste tended more to
the classical stylings of museums like the Louvre or
the Prado, and yet as he watched the fog and flame
hover above the lagoon, he could think of no place
more suitable than this ultramodern museum to host
an event thrown by a man who loved art and innovation, and who glimpsed the future so clearly.

Now, walking through the mist, Langdon pressed
on to the museum's entrance—an ominous black hole
in the reptilian structure. As he neared the threshold,
Langdon had the uneasy sense that he was entering
the mouth of a dragon.

CHAPTER 2

Navy admiral Luis Ávila was seated on a bar stool inside a deserted pub in an unfamiliar town. He was drained from his journey, having just flown into this city after a job that had taken him many thousands of miles in twelve hours. He took a sip of his second tonic water and stared at the colorful array of bottles behind the bar.

Any man can stay sober in a desert, he mused, **but only the loyal can sit in an oasis and refuse to part his lips.**

Ávila had not parted his lips for the devil in almost a year. As he eyed his reflection in the mirrored bar, he permitted himself a rare moment of contentment with the image looking back at him.

Ávila was one of those fortunate Mediterranean men for whom aging seemed to be more an asset than a liability. Over the years, his stiff black stubble had softened to a distinguished salt-and-pepper beard, his fiery dark eyes had relaxed to a serene confidence, and his taut olive skin was now sun-drenched and creased, giving him the aura of a man permanently squinting out to sea.

Even at sixty-three years old, his body was lean and toned, an impressive physique further enhanced by his

tailored uniform. At the moment, Ávila was clothed
in his full-dress navy whites—a regal-looking livery
consisting of a double-breasted white jacket, broad
black shoulder boards, an imposing array of service
medals, a starched white standing-collar shirt, and
silk-trimmed white slacks.

**The Spanish Armada may not be the most potent
navy on earth anymore, but we still know how to
dress an officer.**

The admiral had not donned this uniform in
years—but this was a special night, and earlier, as
he walked the streets of this unknown town, he had
enjoyed the favorable looks of women as well as the
wide berth afforded him by men.

Everyone respects those who live by a code.

"¿Otra tónica?" the pretty barmaid asked. She was
in her thirties, was full-figured, and had a playful
smile.

Ávila shook his head. **"No, gracias."**

This pub was entirely empty, and Ávila could feel
the barmaid's eyes admiring him. It felt good to be
seen again. **I have returned from the abyss.**

The horrific event that all but destroyed Ávila's life
five years ago would forever lurk in the recesses of his
mind—a single deafening instant in which the earth
had opened up and swallowed him whole.

Cathedral of Seville.

Easter morning.

The Andalusian sun was streaming through stained
glass, splashing kaleidoscopes of color in radiant
bursts across the cathedral's stone interior. The pipe

organ thundered in joyous celebration as thousands of worshippers celebrated the miracle of resurrection.

Ávila knelt at the Communion rail, his heart swelling with gratitude. After a lifetime of service to the sea, he had been blessed with the greatest of God's gifts—a family. Smiling broadly, Ávila turned and glanced back over his shoulder at his young wife, María, who was still seated in the pews, far too pregnant to make the long walk up the aisle. Beside her, their three-year-old son, Pepe, waved excitedly at his father. Ávila winked at the boy, and María smiled warmly at her husband.

Thank you, God, Ávila thought as he turned back to the railing to accept the chalice.

An instant later, a deafening explosion ripped through the pristine cathedral.

In a flash of light, his entire world erupted in fire.

The blast wave drove Ávila violently forward into the Communion rail, his body crushed by the scalding surge of debris and human body parts. When Ávila regained consciousness, he was unable to breathe in the thick smoke, and for a moment he had no idea where he was or what had happened.

Then, above the ringing in his ears, he heard the anguished screams. Ávila clambered to his feet, realizing with horror where he was. He told himself this was all a terrible dream. He staggered back through the smoke-filled cathedral, clambering past moaning and mutilated victims, stumbling in desperation to the approximate area where his wife and son had been smiling only moments ago.

There was nothing there.

No pews. No people.

Only bloody debris on the charred stone floor.

The grisly memory was mercifully shattered by the chime of the jangling bar door. Ávila seized his **tónica** and took a quick sip, shaking off the darkness as he had been forced to do so many times before.

The bar door swung wide, and Ávila turned to see two burly men stumble in. They were singing an off-key Irish fight song and wearing green **fútbol** jerseys that strained to cover their bellies. Apparently, this afternoon's match had gone the way of Ireland's visiting team.

I'll take that as my cue, Ávila thought, standing up. He asked for his bill, but the barmaid winked and waved him off. Ávila thanked her and turned to go.

"Bloody hell!" one of the newcomers shouted, staring at Ávila's stately uniform. "It's the king of Spain!"

Both men erupted with laughter, lurching toward him.

Ávila attempted to step around them and leave, but the larger man roughly grabbed his arm and pulled him back to a bar stool. "Hold on, Your Highness! We came all the way to Spain; we're gonna have a pint with the king!"

Ávila eyed the man's grubby hand on his freshly pressed sleeve. "Let go," he said quietly. "I need to leave."

"No . . . you **need** to stay for a beer, **amigo**." The man tightened his grip as his friend started poking with a dirty finger at the medals on Ávila's chest. "Looks like you're quite a hero, Pops." The man tugged on one of Ávila's most prized emblems. "A medieval mace? So, you're a knight in shining armor?!" He guffawed.

Tolerance, Ávila reminded himself. He had met countless men like these—simpleminded, unhappy souls, who had never stood for anything, men who blindly abused the liberties and freedoms that others had fought to give them.

"Actually," Ávila replied gently, "the mace is the symbol of the Spanish navy's Unidad de Operaciones Especiales."

"Special ops?" The man feigned a fearful shudder. "That's very impressive. And what about **that** symbol?" He pointed to Ávila's right hand.

Ávila glanced down at his palm. In the center of the soft flesh was inscribed a black tattoo—a symbol that dated back to the fourteenth century.

This marking serves as my protection, Ávila thought, eyeing the emblem. **Although I will not need it.**

"Never mind," the hooligan said, finally letting go of Ávila's arm and turning his attention to the barmaid. "You're a cute one," he said. "Are you a hundred percent Spanish?"

"I am," she answered graciously.

"You don't have some Irish in you?"

"No."

"Would you **like** some?" The man convulsed in hysterics and pounded the bar.

"Leave her alone," Ávila commanded.

The man wheeled, glaring at him.

The second thug poked Ávila hard in the chest. "You trying to tell us what to do?"

Ávila took a deep breath, feeling tired after this day's long journey, and he motioned to the bar. "Gentlemen, please sit down. I'll buy you a beer."

————

I'm glad he's staying, the barmaid thought. Although she could take care of herself, witnessing how calmly this officer was dealing with these two brutes had left her a little weak-kneed and hoping he might stay until closing time.

The officer had ordered two beers, and another tonic water for himself, reclaiming his seat at the bar. The two **fútbol** hooligans sat on either side of him.

"Tonic water?" one taunted. "I thought we were **drinking** together."

The officer gave the barmaid a tired smile and finished his tonic.

"I'm afraid I have an appointment," the officer said, standing up. "But enjoy your beers."

As he stood, both men, as if rehearsed, slammed rough hands on his shoulders and shoved him back onto the stool. A spark of anger flashed across the officer's eyes and then disappeared.

"Grandpa, I don't think you want to leave us alone with your girlfriend here." The thug looked at her and did something disgusting with his tongue.

The officer sat quietly for a long moment, and then reached into his jacket.

Both guys grabbed him. "Hey! What are you doing?!"

Very slowly, the officer pulled out a cell phone and said something to the men in Spanish. They stared at him uncomprehendingly, and he switched back to English. "I'm sorry, I just need to call my wife and tell her I'll be late. It looks like I'm going to be here awhile."

"Now you're talking, mate!" the larger of the two said, draining his beer and slamming the glass down on the bar. "Another!"

As the barmaid refilled the thugs' glasses, she watched in the mirror as the officer touched a few keys on his phone and then held it to his ear. The call went through, and he spoke in rapid Spanish.

"**Le llamo desde el bar Molly Malone**," the officer said, reading the bar's name and address off the coaster before him. "**Calle Particular de Estraunza, ocho**." He waited a moment and then continued. "**Necesitamos ayuda inmediatamente. Hay dos hombres heridos**." Then he hung up.

¿Dos hombres heridos? The barmaid's pulse quickened. **Two wounded men?**

Before she could process his meaning, there was a

blur of white, and the officer spun to his right, sending an elbow smashing upward into the larger thug's
nose with a sickening crunch. The man's face erupted
in red and he fell back. Before the second man could
react, the officer spun again, this time to his left, his
other elbow crashing hard into the man's windpipe
and sending him backward off the stool.

The barmaid stared in shock at the two men on the
floor, one screaming in agony, the other gasping and
clutching his throat.

The officer stood slowly. With an eerie calm, he
removed his wallet and placed a hundred-euro note
on the bar.

"My apologies," he said to her in Spanish. "The
police will be here shortly to help you." Then he
turned and left.

———

Outside, Admiral Ávila inhaled the night air and
made his way along Alameda de Mazarredo toward
the river. Police sirens approached, and he slipped
into the shadows to let the authorities pass. There was
serious work to do, and Ávila could not afford further
complications tonight.

The Regent clearly outlined tonight's mission.

For Ávila, there was a simple serenity in taking
orders from the Regent. No decisions. No culpabil-
ity. Just action. After a career of giving commands, it
was a relief to relinquish the helm and let others steer
this ship.

In this war, I am a foot soldier.

Several days ago, the Regent had shared with him a secret so disturbing that Ávila had seen no choice but to offer himself fully to the cause. The brutality of last night's mission still haunted him, and yet he knew his actions would be forgiven.

Righteousness exists in many forms.

And more death will come before tonight is over.

As Ávila emerged into an open plaza on the riverbank, he raised his eyes to the massive structure before him. It was an undulating mess of perverse forms covered in metal tile—as if two thousand years of architectural progress had been tossed out the window in favor of total chaos.

Some call this a museum. I call it a monstrosity.

Focusing his thoughts, Ávila crossed the plaza, winding his way through a series of bizarre sculptures outside Bilbao's Guggenheim Museum. As he neared the building, he watched dozens of guests mingling in their finest black and white.

The godless masses have congregated.

But tonight will not go as any of them imagine.

He straightened his admiral's cap and smoothed his jacket, mentally fortifying himself for the task that lay ahead. Tonight was part of a far greater mission— a crusade of righteousness.

As Ávila crossed the courtyard toward the museum's entrance, he gently touched the rosary in his pocket.

CHAPTER 3

The museum atrium felt like a futuristic cathedral.

As Langdon stepped inside, his gaze shifted immediately skyward, climbing a set of colossal white pillars along a towering curtain of glass, ascending two hundred feet to a vaulted ceiling, where halogen spotlights blazed pure white light. Suspended in the air, a network of catwalks and balconies traversed the heavens, dotted with black-and-white-clad visitors who moved in and out of the upper galleries and stood at high windows, admiring the lagoon below. Nearby, a glass elevator slid silently back down the wall, returning to earth to collect more guests.

It was like no museum Langdon had ever seen. Even the acoustics felt foreign. Instead of the traditional reverent hush created by sound-dampening finishes, this place was alive with murmuring echoes of voices percolating off the stone and glass. For Langdon, the only familiar sensation was the sterile tang on the back of his tongue; museum air was the same worldwide—filtered meticulously of all particulates and oxidants and then moistened with ionized water to 45 percent humidity.

Langdon moved through a series of surprisingly

tight security points, noticing more than a few armed guards, and finally found himself standing at another check-in table. A young woman was handing out headsets. **"Audioguía?"**

Langdon smiled. "No, thank you."

As he neared the table, though, the woman stopped him, switching to perfect English. "I'm sorry, sir, but our host tonight, Mr. Edmond Kirsch, has asked that everyone wear a headset. It's part of the evening's experience."

"Oh, of course, I'll take one."

Langdon reached for a headset, but she waved him off, checking his name tag against a long list of guests, finding his name, and then handing him a headset whose number was matched with his name. "The tours tonight are customized for each individual visitor."

Really? Langdon looked around. **There are hundreds of guests.**

Langdon eyed the headset, which was nothing but a sleek loop of metal with tiny pads at each end. Perhaps seeing his puzzled look, the young woman came around to help him.

"These are quite new," she said, helping him don the device. "The transducer pads don't go **inside** your ears, but rather rest on your face." She placed the loop behind his head and positioned the pads so that they gently clamped onto his face, just above the jawbone and below the temple.

"But how—"

"Bone conduction technology. The transducers

drive sound directly into the bones of your jaw, allowing sound to reach your cochlea directly. I tried it earlier, and it's really quite amazing—like having a voice inside your head. What's more, it leaves your ears free to have outside conversations."

"Very clever."

"The technology was invented by Mr. Kirsch more than a decade ago. It's now available in many brands of consumer headphones."

I hope Ludwig van Beethoven gets his cut, Langdon thought, fairly certain that the original inventor of bone conduction technology was the eighteenth-century composer who, upon going deaf, discovered he could affix a metal rod to his piano and bite down on it while he played, enabling him to hear perfectly through vibrations in his jawbone.

"We hope you enjoy your tour experience," the woman said. "You have about an hour to explore the museum before the presentation. Your audio guide will alert you when it is time to go upstairs to the auditorium."

"Thank you. Do I need to press anything to—"

"No, the device is self-activating. Your guided tour will begin as soon as you start moving."

"Ah yes, of course," Langdon said with a smile. He headed out across the atrium, moving toward a scattering of other guests, all waiting for the elevators and wearing similar headsets pressed to their jawbones.

He was only halfway across the atrium when a male voice sounded in his head. "Good evening and welcome to the Guggenheim in Bilbao."

Langdon knew it was his headset, but he still stopped short and looked behind him. The effect was startling—precisely as the young woman had described—like having someone **inside** your head.

"A most heartfelt welcome to you, Professor Langdon." The voice was friendly and light, with a jaunty British accent. "My name is Winston, and I'm honored to be your guide this evening."

Who did they get to record this—Hugh Grant?

"Tonight," the cheery voice continued, "you may feel free to meander as you wish, anywhere you like, and I'll endeavor to enlighten you as to what it is you're viewing."

Apparently, in addition to a chirpy narrator, personalized recordings, and bone conduction technology, each headset was equipped with GPS to discern precisely where in the museum the visitor was standing and therefore what commentary to generate.

"I do realize, sir," the voice added, "that as a professor of art, you are one of our more savvy guests, and so perhaps you will have little need of my input. Worse yet, it is possible you will wholly disagree with my analysis of certain pieces!" The voice gave an awkward chuckle.

Seriously? Who wrote this script? The merry tone and personalized service were admittedly a charming touch, but Langdon could not imagine the amount of effort it must have taken to customize hundreds of headsets.

Thankfully, the voice fell silent now, as if it had exhausted its preprogrammed welcome dialogue.

Langdon glanced across the atrium at another enormous red banner suspended above the crowd.

EDMOND KIRSCH

TONIGHT WE MOVE FORWARD

What in the world is Edmond going to announce?
Langdon turned his eyes to the elevators, where a cluster of chatting guests included two famous founders of global Internet companies, a prominent Indian actor, and various other well-dressed VIPs whom Langdon sensed he probably should know but didn't. Feeling both disinclined and ill-prepared to make small talk on the topics of social media and Bollywood, Langdon moved in the opposite direction, drifting toward a large piece of modern art that stood against the far wall.

The installation was nestled in a dark grotto and consisted of nine narrow conveyor belts that emerged from slits in the floor and raced upward, disappearing into slits in the ceiling. The piece resembled nine moving walkways running on a vertical plane. Each conveyor bore an illuminated message, which scrolled skyward.

I pray aloud . . . I smell you on my skin . . . I say your name.

As Langdon got closer, though, he realized that the moving bands were in fact stationary; the illusion of motion was created by a "skin" of tiny LED lights positioned on each vertical beam. The lights lit up in rapid succession to form words that materialized out of the floor, raced up the beam, and disappeared into the ceiling.

I'm crying hard . . . There was blood . . . No one told me.

Langdon moved in and around the vertical beams, taking it all in.

"This is a challenging piece," the audio guide declared, returning suddenly. "It is called **Installation for Bilbao** and was created by conceptual artist Jenny Holzer. It consists of nine LED signboards, each forty feet tall, transmitting quotes in Basque, Spanish, and English—all relating to the horrors of AIDS and the pain endured by those left behind."

Langdon had to admit, the effect was mesmerizing and somehow heartbreaking.

"Perhaps you've seen Jenny Holzer's work before?"

Langdon felt hypnotized by the text coursing skyward.

I bury my head . . . I bury your head . . . I bury you.

"Mr. Langdon?" the voice in his head chimed. "Can you hear me? Is your headset working?"

Langdon was jolted from his thoughts. "I'm sorry— what? Hello?"

"Yes, hello," the voice replied. "I believe we've already said our greetings? I'm just checking to see if you can hear me?"

"I . . . I'm sorry," Langdon stammered, spinning

away from the exhibit and looking out across the atrium. "I thought you were a **recording**! I didn't realize I had a real person on the line." Langdon pictured a cubicle farm manned by an army of curators armed with headsets and museum catalogs.

"No problem, sir. I'll be your personal guide for the evening. Your headset has a microphone in it as well. This program is intended as an interactive experience in which you and I can have a dialogue about art."

Langdon could now see that other guests were also speaking into their headsets. Even those who had come as couples appeared to have separated a bit, exchanging bemused looks as they carried on private conversations with their personal docents.

"**Every** guest here has a private guide?"

"Yes, sir. Tonight we are individually touring three hundred and eighteen guests."

"That's incredible."

"Well, as you know, Edmond Kirsch is an avid fan of art and technology. He designed this system specifically for museums, in hopes of replacing group tours, which he despises. This way, every visitor can enjoy a private tour, move at his own pace, ask the question he might be embarrassed to ask in a group situation. It is really much more intimate and immersive."

"Not to sound old-fashioned, but why not just **walk** each of us around in person?"

"Logistics," the man replied. "Adding personal docents to a museum event would literally **double** the number of people on the floor and necessarily cut in half the number of possible visitors. Moreover, the cacophony of all the docents lecturing simultaneously would be distracting. The idea here is to make discussion a seamless experience. One of the objectives of art, Mr. Kirsch always says, is to promote dialogue."

"I entirely agree," Langdon replied, "and that's why people often visit museums with a date or a friend. These headsets might be considered a bit antisocial."

"Well," the Brit replied, "if you come with a date or friends, you can assign all the headsets to a single docent and enjoy a group discussion. The software is really quite advanced."

"You seem to have an answer for everything."

"That is, in fact, my job." The guide gave an embarrassed laugh and abruptly shifted gears. "Now, Professor, if you move across the atrium toward the windows, you'll see the museum's largest painting."

As Langdon began walking across the atrium, he passed an attractive thirtysomething couple wearing matching white baseball caps. Emblazoned on the front of both caps, rather than a corporate logo, was a surprising symbol.

It was an icon Langdon knew well, and yet he had never seen it on a cap. In recent years, this highly stylized letter **A** had become the universal symbol for one of the planet's fastest-growing and increasingly vocal

demographics—atheists—who had begun speaking
out more forcefully every day against what they considered the dangers of religious belief.

Atheists now have their own baseball caps?

As he surveyed the congregation of tech-savvy
geniuses mingling around him, Langdon reminded
himself that many of these young analytical minds
were probably very antireligious, just like Edmond.
Tonight's audience was not exactly the "home crowd"
for a professor of religious symbology.

CHAPTER 4

🌐 ConspiracyNet.com

BREAKING NEWS

Update: ConspiracyNet's "Top 10 Media Stories of the Day" can be viewed by clicking <u>here</u>. Also, we have a brand-new story just now breaking!

EDMOND KIRSCH SURPRISE ANNOUNCEMENT?

Tech titans have flooded Bilbao, Spain, this evening to attend a VIP event hosted by futurist Edmond Kirsch at the Guggenheim Museum. Security is extremely tight, and guests have not been told the purpose of the event, but ConspiracyNet has received a tip from an inside source suggesting that Edmond Kirsch will be speaking shortly and is planning to surprise his guests with a major scientific announcement. ConspiracyNet will continue to monitor this story and deliver news as we receive it.

CHAPTER 5

The largest synagogue in Europe is located in Budapest on Dohány Street. Built in the Moorish style with massive twin spires, the shrine has seats for more than three thousand worshippers—with downstairs pews for the men and balcony benches for the women.

Outside in the garden, in a mass burial pit, are interred the bodies of hundreds of Hungarian Jews who died during the horrors of the Nazi occupation. The site is marked by a Tree of Life—a metal sculpture depicting a weeping willow whose leaves are each inscribed with the name of a victim. When a breeze blows, the metal leaves rattle against one another, clattering with an eerie echo above the hallowed ground.

For more than three decades, the spiritual leader of the Great Synagogue had been the eminent Talmudic scholar and Kabbalist—Rabbi Yehuda Köves—who, despite his advancing years and poor health, remained an active member of the Jewish community both in Hungary and around the world.

As the sun set across the Danube, Rabbi Köves exited the synagogue. He made his way past the boutiques and mysterious "ruin bars" of Dohány Street en route to his home on Marcius 15 Square, a stone's throw from Elisabeth Bridge, which linked the ancient cities of Buda and Pest, which were formally united in 1873.

The Passover holidays were fast approaching—normally one of Köves's most joyous times of the year—and yet, ever since his return last week from the Parliament of the World's Religions, he had been feeling only a bottomless disquiet.

I wish I had never attended.

The extraordinary meeting with Bishop Valdespino, Allamah Syed al-Fadl, and futurist Edmond Kirsch had plagued Köves's thoughts for three full days.

Now, as Köves arrived home, he strode directly to his courtyard garden and unlocked his **házikó**—the small cottage that served as his private sanctuary and study.

The cottage was a single room with high bookshelves that sagged under the weight of religious tomes. Köves strode to his desk and sat down, frowning at the mess before him.

If anyone saw my desk this week, they'd think I'd lost my mind.

Strewn across the work surface, a half-dozen obscure religious texts lay open, plastered with sticky notes. Behind them, propped open on wooden stands, were three heavy volumes—Hebrew, Aramaic, and English versions of the Torah—each opened to the same book.

Genesis.

In the beginning . . .

Köves could, of course, recite Genesis from memory, in all three languages; he was more likely to be reading academic commentary on the Zohar or advanced Kabbalistic cosmology theory. For a scholar of Köves's caliber to study Genesis was much like Einstein going back to study grade-school arithmetic. Nonetheless, that's what the rabbi had been doing this week, and the notepad on his desk looked to have been assaulted by a wild torrent of hand-scrawled notes, so messy that Köves could barely make them out himself.

I look like I've turned into a lunatic.

Rabbi Köves had started with the Torah—the Genesis story shared by Jews and Christians alike. **In the beginning God created the heaven and the earth.** Next, he had turned to the instructional texts of the Talmud, rereading the rabbinic elucidations on **Ma'aseh Bereshit**—the Act of Creation. After that, he delved into the Midrash, poring over the commentaries of various venerated exegetes who had attempted to explain the perceived contradictions in the traditional Creation story. Finally, Köves buried himself in the mystical Kabbalistic science of the Zohar, in which the unknowable God manifested as ten different **sephirot,** or dimensions, arranged along channels called the Tree of Life, and from which blossomed four separate universes.

The arcane complexity of the beliefs that made up Judaism had always been comforting to Köves—a reminder from God that humankind was not meant to understand all things. And yet now, after viewing

Edmond Kirsch's presentation, and contemplating the simplicity and clarity of what Kirsch had discovered, Köves felt like he had spent the past three days staring into a collection of outdated contradictions. At one point, all he could do was push aside his ancient texts and go for a long walk along the Danube to gather his thoughts.

Rabbi Köves had finally begun to accept a painful truth: Kirsch's work would indeed have devastating repercussions for the faithful souls of this world. The scientist's revelation boldly contradicted almost every established religious doctrine, and it did so in a distressingly simple and persuasive manner.

I cannot forget that final image, Köves thought, recalling the distressing conclusion of Kirsch's presentation that they had watched on Kirsch's oversized phone. **This news will affect every human being—not just the pious.**

Now, despite his reflections over the last few days, Rabbi Köves still felt no closer to knowing what to do with the information that Kirsch had provided.

He doubted Valdespino and al-Fadl had found any clarity either. The three men had communicated by phone two days ago, but the conversation had not been productive.

"My friends," Valdespino had begun. "Obviously, Mr. Kirsch's presentation was disturbing . . . on many levels. I urged him to call and discuss it further with me, but he has gone silent. Now I believe we have a decision to make."

"I've **made** my decision," said al-Fadl. "We cannot sit idly by. We need to take control of this situation. Kirsch has a well-publicized scorn for religion, and he will frame his discovery in a way to do as much damage as possible to the future of faith. We must be proactive. We must announce his discovery **ourselves**. Immediately. We must cast it in the proper light so as to soften the impact, and make it as nonthreatening as possible to the believers in the spiritual world."

"I realize we discussed going public," Valdespino said, "but unfortunately, I cannot imagine how one frames **this** information in a nonthreatening way." He sighed heavily. "There is also the issue of our vow to Mr. Kirsch that we would keep his secret."

"True," al-Fadl said, "and I too am conflicted about breaking that vow, but I feel we must choose the lesser of two evils and take action on behalf of the greater good. We are **all** under attack—Muslims, Jews, Christians, Hindus, all religions alike—and considering that our faiths all concur on the fundamental truths that Mr. Kirsch is undermining, we have an obligation to present this material in a way that does not distress our communities."

"I fear there is no way this will make any sense," Valdespino said. "If we are entertaining the notion of going public with Kirsch's news, the only viable approach will be to cast **doubt** on his discovery—to discredit him before he can get his message out."

"Edmond Kirsch?" al-Fadl challenged. "A brilliant scientist who has never been wrong about anything?

Were we all in the same meeting with Kirsch? His presentation was persuasive."

Valdespino grunted. "No more persuasive than presentations made by Galileo, Bruno, or Copernicus in their day. Religions have been in this predicament before. This is just science banging on our door once again."

"But on a far deeper level than the discoveries of physics and astronomy!" al-Fadl exclaimed. "Kirsch is challenging the very **core**—the fundamental root of everything we believe! You can cite history all you like, but don't forget, despite your Vatican's best efforts to silence men like Galileo, his science eventually prevailed. And Kirsch's will too. There is no way to stop this from happening."

There was a grave silence.

"My position on this matter is simple," Valdespino said. "I wish Edmond Kirsch had not made this discovery. I fear that we are unprepared to handle his findings. And my strong preference is that this information never see the light of day." He paused. "At the same time, I believe that the events of our world happen according to God's plan. Perhaps with prayer, God will speak to Mr. Kirsch and persuade him to reconsider making his discovery public."

Al-Fadl scoffed audibly. "I don't think Mr. Kirsch is the kind of man capable of hearing the voice of God."

"Perhaps not," Valdespino said. "But miracles happen every day."

Al-Fadl fired back hotly, "With all due respect, unless you're praying that God strikes Kirsch dead before he can announce—"

"Gentlemen!" Köves intervened, attempting to defuse the growing tension. "Our decision need not be rushed. We don't need to reach a consensus tonight. Mr. Kirsch said his announcement is a month away. Might I suggest that we meditate privately on the matter, and speak again in several days? Perhaps the proper course will reveal itself through reflection."

"Wise counsel," Valdespino replied.

"We should not wait too long," al-Fadl cautioned. "Let's speak again by phone two days from now."

"Agreed," Valdespino said. "We can make our final decision at that time."

That had been two days ago, and now the night of their follow-up conversation had arrived.

Alone in his **házikó** study, Rabbi Köves was growing anxious. Tonight's scheduled call was now almost ten minutes overdue.

At last, the phone rang, and Köves seized it.

"Hello, Rabbi," said Bishop Valdespino, sounding troubled. "I'm sorry for the delay." He paused. "I'm afraid Allamah al-Fadl will not be joining us on this call."

"Oh?" Köves said with surprise. "Is everything all right?"

"I don't know. I've been trying to reach him all day, but the **allamah** seems to have . . . **disappeared**. None of his colleagues have any idea where he is."

Köves felt a chill. "That's alarming."

"I agree. I hope he is okay. Unfortunately, I have more news." The bishop paused, his tone darkening further. "I have just learned that Edmond Kirsch is holding an event to share his discovery with the world . . . tonight."

"Tonight?!" Köves demanded. "He said it would be a **month**!"

"Yes," Valdespino said. "He lied."

CHAPTER 6

Winston's friendly voice reverberated in Langdon's headset. "Directly in front of you, Professor, you will see the largest painting in our collection, though most guests do not spot it right away."

Langdon gazed across the museum's atrium but saw nothing except a wall of glass that looked out over the lagoon. "I'm sorry, I think I may be in the majority here. I don't see a painting."

"Well, it is displayed rather unconventionally," Winston said with a laugh. "The canvas is mounted not on the wall, but rather on the **floor**."

I should have guessed, Langdon thought, lowering his gaze and moving forward until he saw the sprawling rectangular canvas stretched out across the stone at his feet.

The enormous painting consisted of a single color—a monochrome field of deep blue—and viewers stood around its perimeter, staring down at it as if peering into a small pond.

"This painting is nearly six thousand square feet," Winston offered.

Langdon realized it was ten times the size of his first Cambridge apartment.

"It is by Yves Klein and has become affectionately known as **The Swimming Pool**."

Langdon had to admit that the arresting richness of this shade of blue gave him the sense he could dive directly into the canvas.

"Klein invented this color," Winston continued. "It's called International Klein Blue, and he claimed its profundity evoked the immateriality and boundlessness of his own utopian vision of the world."

Langdon sensed Winston was now reading from a script.

"Klein is best known for his blue paintings, but he is also known for a disturbing trick photograph called **Leap into the Void,** which caused quite a panic when it was revealed in 1960."

Langdon had seen **Leap into the Void** at the Museum of Modern Art in New York. The photo was more than a little disconcerting, depicting a well-dressed man doing a swan dive off a high building and plunging toward the pavement. In truth, the image was a trick—brilliantly conceived and devilishly retouched with a razor blade, long before the days of Photoshop.

"In addition," Winston said, "Klein also composed the musical piece **Monotone-Silence**, in which a symphony orchestra performs a single D-major chord for a full twenty minutes."

"And people **listen**?"

"Thousands. And the one chord is just the first movement. In the second movement, the orchestra sits motionless and performs 'pure silence' for twenty minutes."

"You're joking, right?"

"No, I'm quite serious. In its defense, the performance was probably not as dull as it might sound; the stage also included three naked women, slathered in blue paint, rolling around on giant canvases."

Although Langdon had devoted the better part of his career to studying art, it troubled him that he had never quite learned how to appreciate the art world's more avant-garde offerings. The appeal of modern art remained a mystery to him.

"I mean no disrespect, Winston, but I've got to tell you, I often find it hard to know when something is 'modern art' and when something is just plain bizarre."

Winston's reply was deadpan. "Well, that is often the question, isn't it? In your world of classical art, pieces are revered for the artist's skill of execution—that is, how deftly he places the brush to canvas or the chisel to stone. In modern art, however, masterpieces are often more about the **idea** than the execution. For example, anyone could easily compose a forty-minute symphony consisting of nothing but one chord and silence, but it was Yves Klein who had the idea."

"Fair enough."

"Of course, **The Fog Sculpture** outside is a perfect example of conceptual art. The artist had an **idea**—to run perforated pipes beneath the bridge and blow fog onto the lagoon—but the **creation** of the piece was performed by local plumbers." Winston paused. "Although I do give the artist very high marks for using her medium as a code."

"**Fog** is a code?"

"It is. A cryptic tribute to the museum's architect."

"Frank Gehry?"

"Frank **O.** Gehry," Winston corrected.

"Clever."

As Langdon moved toward the windows, Winston said, "You have a nice view of the spider from here. Did you see **Maman** on your way in?"

Langdon gazed out the window, across the lagoon, to the massive black widow sculpture on the plaza. "Yes. She's pretty hard to miss."

"I sense from your intonation that you're not a fan?"

"I'm trying to be." Langdon paused. "As a classicist, I'm a bit of a fish out of water here."

"Interesting," Winston said. "I had imagined that **you** of all people would appreciate **Maman**. She is a perfect example of the classical notion of juxtaposition. In fact, you might want to use her in class when you next teach the concept."

Langdon eyed the spider, seeing nothing of the sort. When it came to teaching juxtaposition, Langdon preferred something a bit more traditional. "I think I'll stick with the **David**."

"Yes, Michelangelo is the gold standard," Winston said with a chuckle, "brilliantly posing David in an effeminate contrapposto, his limp wrist casually holding a flaccid slingshot, conveying a feminine vulnerability. And yet David's eyes radiate a lethal determination, his tendons and veins bulging in anticipation of killing Goliath. The work is simultaneously delicate and deadly."

Langdon was impressed with the description and wished his own students had as clear an understanding of Michelangelo's masterpiece.

"**Maman** is no different from **David**," Winston said. "An equally bold juxtaposition of opposing archetypal principles. In nature, the black widow is a fearful creature—a predator who captures victims in her web and kills them. Despite being lethal, she is depicted here with a burgeoning egg sac, preparing to give life, making her both predator and progenitor— a powerful core perched atop impossibly slender legs, conveying both strength and fragility. **Maman** could be called a modern-day **David**, if you will."

"I **won't**," Langdon replied, smiling, "but I must admit your analysis gives me food for thought."

"Good, then let me show you one final work. It happens to be an Edmond Kirsch original."

"Really? I never knew Edmond was an artist."

Winston laughed. "I'll let you be the judge of that."

Langdon let Winston guide him past the windows to a spacious alcove in which a group of guests had assembled before a large slab of dried mud hanging on the wall. At first glance, the slab of hardened clay reminded Langdon of a museum fossil exhibit. But this mud contained no fossils. Instead, it bore crudely etched markings similar to those a child might draw with a stick in wet cement.

The crowd looked unimpressed.

"Edmond did this?" grumbled a mink-clad woman with Botoxed lips. "I don't get it."

The teacher in Langdon could not resist. "It's actually quite clever," he interrupted. "So far it's my favorite piece in the entire museum."

The woman spun, eyeing him with more than a hint of disdain. "Oh **really**? Then **do** enlighten me."

I'd be happy to. Langdon walked over to the series of markings etched coarsely into the clay surface.

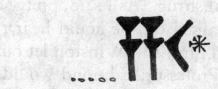

"Well, first of all," Langdon said, "Edmond inscribed this piece in clay as an homage to mankind's earliest written language, cuneiform."

The woman blinked, looking uncertain.

"The three heavy markings in the middle," Langdon continued, "spell the word 'fish' in Assyrian. It's called a pictogram. If you look carefully, you can imagine the fish's open mouth facing right, as well as the triangular scales on his body."

The assembled group all cocked their heads, studying the work again.

"And if you look over here," Langdon said, pointing to the series of depressions to the left of the fish, "you can see that Edmond made footprints in the mud **behind** the fish, to represent the fish's historic evolutionary step onto land."

Heads began to nod appreciatively.

"And finally," Langdon said, "the asymmetrical as-

terisk on the right—the symbol that the fish appears
to be consuming—is one of history's oldest symbols
for God."

The Botoxed woman turned and scowled at him.
"A fish is eating God?"

"Apparently so. It's a playful version of the Darwin
fish—evolution consuming religion." Langdon gave
the group a casual shrug. "As I said, pretty clever."

As Langdon walked off, he could hear the crowd
muttering behind him, and Winston let out a laugh.
"Very amusing, Professor! Edmond would have appreciated your impromptu lecture. Not many people
decipher that one."

"Well," Langdon said, "that **is**, in fact, my job."

"Yes, and I can now see why Mr. Kirsch asked me
to consider you an extra-special guest. In fact, he
asked me to show you something that none of the
other guests are going to experience tonight."

"Oh? What would that be?"

"To the right of the main windows, do you see a
hallway that is cordoned off?"

Langdon peered to his right. "I do."

"Good. Please follow my directions."

Uncertain, Langdon obeyed Winston's step-by-step
instructions. He walked to the corridor entrance, and
after double-checking that nobody was watching, he
discreetly squeezed in behind the stanchions and
slipped down the hallway out of sight.

Now, having left the atrium crowd behind, Langdon walked thirty feet to a metal door with a numeric
keypad.

"Type these six digits," Winston said, providing Langdon with the numbers.

Langdon typed the code, and the door clicked.

"Okay, Professor, please enter."

Langdon stood a moment, uncertain what to expect. Then, gathering himself, he pushed open the door. The space beyond was almost entirely dark.

"I'll bring the lights up for you," Winston said. "Please walk in and close the door."

Langdon inched inside, straining to see into the darkness. He closed the door behind him, and the lock clicked.

Gradually, soft lighting began to glow around the edges of the room, revealing an unthinkably cavernous space—a single gaping chamber—like an airplane hangar for a fleet of jumbo jets.

"Thirty-four thousand square feet," Winston offered.

The room entirely dwarfed the atrium.

As the lights continued to glow brighter, Langdon could see a group of massive forms out on the floor— seven or eight murky silhouettes—like dinosaurs grazing in the night.

"What in the world am I looking at?" Langdon demanded.

"It's called **The Matter of Time**." Winston's cheery voice reverberated through Langdon's headset. "It's the heaviest piece of art in the museum. Over two million pounds."

Langdon was still trying to get his bearings. "And why am I in here alone?"

"As I said, Mr. Kirsch asked me to show you these amazing objects."

The lights increased to full strength, flooding the vast space with a soft glow, and Langdon could only stare in bewilderment at the scene before him.

I've entered a parallel universe.

CHAPTER 7

Admiral Luis Ávila arrived at the museum's security checkpoint and glanced at his watch to assure himself he was on schedule.

Perfect.

He presented his Documento Nacional de Identidad to the employees manning the guest list. For a moment, Ávila's pulse quickened when his name could not be located on the list. Finally, they found it at the bottom—a last-minute addition—and Ávila was allowed to enter.

Exactly as the Regent promised me. How he had accomplished this feat, Ávila had no idea. Tonight's guest list was said to be ironclad.

He continued to the metal detector, where he removed his cell phone and placed it in the dish. Then, with extreme care, he extracted an unusually heavy set of rosary beads from his jacket pocket and laid it over his phone.

Gently, he told himself. **Very gently.**

The security guard waved him through the metal detector and carried the dish of personal items around to the other side.

"Que rosario tan bonito," the guard said, admiring

the metal rosary, which consisted of a strong beaded chain and a thick, rounded cross.

"Gracias," Ávila replied. **I constructed it myself.**

Ávila walked through the detector without incident. On the other side, he collected his phone and the rosary, replacing them gently in his pocket before pressing on to a second checkpoint, where he was given an unusual audio headset.

I don't need an audio tour, he thought. **I have work to do.**

As he moved across the atrium, he discreetly dumped the headset into a trash receptacle.

His heart was pounding as he scanned the building for a private place to contact the Regent and let him know he was safely inside.

For God, country, and king, he thought. **But mostly for God.**

———

At that moment, in the deepest recesses of the moonlit desert outside Dubai, the beloved seventy-eight-year-old **allamah,** Syed al-Fadl, strained in agony as he crawled through deep sand. He could go no farther.

Al-Fadl's skin was blistered and burned, his throat so raw he could barely pull a breath. The sand-laden winds had blinded him hours ago, and still he crawled on. At one point, he thought he heard the distant whine of dune buggies, but it was probably just the howling wind. Al-Fadl's faith that God would save him had long since passed. The vultures were no longer circling; they were walking beside him.

The tall Spaniard who had carjacked al-Fadl last night had barely spoken a word as he drove the **allamah**'s car deep into this vast desert. After an hour's drive, the Spaniard had stopped and ordered al-Fadl out of the car, leaving him in the darkness with no food or water.

Al-Fadl's captor had provided no indication of his identity or any explanation for his actions. The only possible clue al-Fadl had glimpsed was a strange marking on the man's right palm—a symbol he did not recognize.

For hours, al-Fadl had trudged through sand and shouted fruitlessly for help. Now, as the severely dehydrated cleric collapsed into the suffocating sand and felt his heart give out, he asked himself the same question he had been asking for hours.

Who could possibly want me dead?

Frighteningly, he could come up with only one logical answer.

CHAPTER 8

R obert Langdon's eyes were drawn from one colossal form to the next. Each piece was a towering sheet of weathered steel that had been elegantly curled and then set precariously on its edge, balancing itself to create a freestanding wall. The arcing walls were nearly fifteen feet tall and had been torqued into different fluid shapes—an undulating ribbon, an open circle, a loose coil.

"**The Matter of Time**," Winston repeated. "And the artist is Richard Serra. His use of unsupported walls in such a heavy medium creates the illusion of instability. But in fact, these are all very stable. If you imagine a dollar bill that you curl around a pencil, once you remove the pencil, your coiled bill can stand quite happily on its own edge, supported by its own geometry."

Langdon paused and stared up at the immense circle beside him. The metal was oxidized, giving it a burnt copper hue and a raw, organic quality. The piece exuded both great strength and a delicate sense of balance.

"Professor, do you notice how this first shape is not quite closed?"

Langdon continued around the circle and saw that the ends of the wall did not quite meet, as if a child had attempted to draw a circle but missed the mark.

"The skewed connection creates a passageway that draws the visitor inside to explore the negative space."

Unless that visitor happens to be claustrophobic, Langdon thought, moving quickly on.

"Similarly," Winston said, "in front of you, you will see three sinuous ribbons of steel, running in a loosely parallel formation, close enough together to form two undulating tunnels of more than a hundred feet. It's called **The Snake,** and our young visitors enjoy running through it. In fact, two visitors standing at opposite ends can whisper faintly and hear each other perfectly, as if they were face-to-face."

"This is remarkable, Winston, but would you please explain why Edmond asked you to show me this gallery." **He knows I don't get this stuff.**

Winston replied, "The specific piece he asked me to show you is called **Torqued Spiral,** and it's up ahead in the far right corner. Do you see it?"

Langdon squinted into the distance. **The one that looks like it's a half mile away?** "Yes, I see it."

"Splendid, let's head over, shall we?"

Langdon took a tentative glance around the enormous space and made his way toward the distant spiral as Winston continued speaking.

"I have heard, Professor, that Edmond Kirsch is an avid admirer of your work—particularly your thoughts on the interplay of various religious traditions throughout history and their evolutions as reflected in art. In many ways, Edmond's field of game theory and predictive computing is quite similar— analyzing the growth of various systems and predicting how they will develop over time."

"Well, he's obviously very good at it. They call him the modern-day Nostradamus, after all."

"Yes. Though the comparison is a bit insulting, if you ask me."

"Why would you say that?" Langdon countered. "Nostradamus is the most famous prognosticator of all time."

"I don't mean to be contrary, Professor, but Nostradamus wrote nearly a thousand loosely worded quatrains that, over four centuries, have benefited from the creative readings of superstitious people looking to extract meaning where there is none . . . everything from World War Two, to Princess Diana's death, to the attack on the World Trade Center. It's utterly absurd. In contrast, Edmond Kirsch has published a limited number of very specific predictions that have come true over a very short time horizon— cloud computing, driverless cars, a processing chip powered by only five atoms. Mr. Kirsch is no Nostradamus."

I stand corrected, Langdon thought. Edmond Kirsch was said to inspire a fierce loyalty among those with whom he worked, and apparently Winston was one of Kirsch's avid disciples.

"So are you enjoying my tour?" Winston asked, changing the subject.

"Very much so. Kudos to Edmond for perfecting this remote docenting technology."

"Yes, this system has been a dream of Edmond's for years, and he spent incalculable amounts of time and money developing it in secret."

"Really? The technology doesn't seem all that complicated. I must admit, I was skeptical at first, but you've sold me—it's been quite an interesting conversation."

"Generous of you to say, although I hope I don't now ruin everything by admitting the truth. I'm afraid I have not been entirely honest with you."

"I'm sorry?"

"First of all, my real name is not Winston. It's Art."

Langdon laughed. "A museum docent named **Art**? Well, I don't blame you for using a pseudonym. Nice to meet you, Art."

"Furthermore, when you asked why I wouldn't just walk around with you in person, I gave you an accurate answer about Mr. Kirsch wanting to keep museum crowds small. But that answer was incomplete. There is another reason we are speaking via headset and not in person." He paused. "I am, in fact, incapable of physical movement."

"Oh . . . I am so sorry." Langdon imagined Art sitting in a wheelchair in a call center, and regretted that Art would feel self-conscious having to explain his condition.

"No need to feel sorry for me. I assure you **legs** would look quite strange on me. You see, I'm not quite how you imagine."

Langdon's pace slowed. "What do you mean?"

"The name 'Art' is not so much a name as it is an abbreviation. 'Art' is short for 'artificial,' although Mr. Kirsch prefers the word 'synthetic.'" The voice paused a moment. "The truth of the matter, Professor, is that this evening you have been interacting with a synthetic docent. A computer of sorts."

Langdon looked around, uncertain. "Is this some kind of prank?"

"Not at all, Professor. I'm quite serious. Edmond Kirsch spent a decade and nearly a billion dollars in the field of synthetic intelligence, and tonight you are one of the very first to experience the fruits of his labors. Your entire tour has been given by a synthetic docent. I am not human."

Langdon could not accept this for a second. The man's diction and grammar were perfect, and with the exception of a slightly awkward laugh, he was as elegant a speaker as Langdon had ever encountered. Furthermore, their banter tonight had encompassed a wide and nuanced range of topics.

I'm being watched, Langdon now realized, scanning the walls for hidden video cameras. He suspected he was an unwitting participant in a strange piece of "experiential art"—an artfully staged theater of the absurd. **They've made me a rat in a maze.**

"I'm not entirely comfortable with this," Langdon declared, his voice echoing across the deserted gallery.

"My apologies," Winston said. "That is understandable. I anticipated that you might find this news difficult to process. I imagine that is why Edmond asked me to bring you in here to a private space, away from the others. This information is not being revealed to his other guests."

Langdon's eyes probed the dim space to see if anyone else was there.

"As you are no doubt aware," the voice continued, sounding eerily unfazed by Langdon's discomfort, "the human brain is a binary system—synapses either fire or they don't—they are on or off, like a computer switch. The brain has over a hundred trillion switches, which means that building a brain is not so much a question of technology as it is a question of scale."

Langdon was barely listening. He was walking again, his attention focused on an "Exit" sign with an arrow pointing to the far end of the gallery.

"Professor, I realize the human quality of my voice is hard to accept as machine-generated, but speech is actually the easy part. Even a ninety-nine-dollar e-book device does a fairly decent job of mimicking human speech. Edmond has invested **billions**."

Langdon stopped walking. "If you're a computer, tell me this. Where did the Dow Jones Industrial Average close on August twenty-fourth, 1974?"

"That day was a Saturday," the voice replied instantly. "So the markets never opened."

Langdon felt a slight chill. He had chosen the date as a trick. One of the side effects of his eidetic memory was that dates lodged themselves forever in his mind. That Saturday had been his best friend's birthday, and Langdon still remembered the afternoon pool party. **Helena Wooley wore a blue bikini.**

"However," the voice added immediately, "on the previous day, Friday, August twenty-third, the Dow Jones Industrial Average closed at 686.80, down 17.83 points for a loss of 2.53 percent."

Langdon was momentarily unable to speak.

"I'm happy to wait," the voice chimed, "if you want to check the data on your smartphone. Although I'll have no choice but to point out the irony of it."

"But . . . I don't . . ."

"The challenge with synthetic intelligence," the voice continued, its light British air now seeming stranger than ever, "is not the rapid access to data, which is really quite simple, but rather the ability to discern how the data are interconnected and entangled—something at which I believe you excel, no? The interrelationship of ideas? This is one of the reasons Mr. Kirsch wanted to test my abilities on **you** specifically."

"A test?" Langdon asked. "Of . . . me?"

"Not at all." Again, the awkward laugh. "A test of **me**. To see if I could convince you I was human."

"A Turing test."

"Precisely."

The Turing test, Langdon recalled, was a challenge proposed by code-breaker Alan Turing to assess a machine's ability to behave in a manner indistinguishable from that of a human. Essentially, a human judge listened to a conversation between a machine and a human, and if the judge was unable to identify which participant was human, then the Turing test was considered to have been passed. Turing's benchmark challenge had famously been passed in 2014 at the Royal Society in London. Since then, AI technology had progressed at a blinding rate.

"So far this evening," the voice continued, "not a single one of our guests has suspected a thing. They're all having a grand time."

"Hold on, **everyone** here tonight is talking to a computer?!"

"Technically, everyone is talking to **me**. I'm able to partition myself quite easily. You are hearing my default voice—the voice that Edmond prefers—but others are hearing other voices or languages. Based on your profile as an American academic male, I chose my default male British accent for you. I predicted that it would breed more confidence than, for example, a young female with a southern drawl."

Did this thing just call me a chauvinist?

Langdon recalled a popular recording that had circulated online several years ago: **Time** magazine's bureau chief Michael Scherer had been phoned by a telemarketing robot that was so eerily human that Scherer had posted a recording of the call online for everyone to hear.

That was years ago, Langdon realized.

Langdon knew that Kirsch had been dabbling in artificial intelligence for years, appearing on magazine covers from time to time to hail various breakthroughs. Apparently, his offspring "Winston" represented Kirsch's current state of the art.

"I realize this is all happening quickly," the voice continued, "but Mr. Kirsch requested that I show you this spiral at which you are now standing. He asked that you please enter the spiral and continue all the way to the center."

Langdon peered down the narrow curving passage and felt his muscles tighten. **Is this Edmond's idea of a college prank?** "Can you just tell me what's in there? I'm not a big fan of cramped spaces."

"Interesting, I didn't know that about you."

"Claustrophobia is not something I include in my online bio." Langdon caught himself, still unable to fathom that he was speaking to a machine.

"You needn't be afraid. The space in the center of the spiral is quite large, and Mr. Kirsch requested specifically that you see the **center**. Before you enter, however, Edmond asked that you remove your headset and place it on the floor out here."

Langdon looked at the looming structure and hesitated. "You're not coming with me?"

"Apparently not."

"You know, this is all very strange, and I'm not exactly—"

"Professor, considering Edmond brought you all the way to this event, it seems a small request that you walk a short distance into this piece of art. Children do it every day and survive."

Langdon had never been reprimanded by a computer, if that was in fact what this was, but the cutting comment had the desired effect. He removed his headset and carefully placed it on the floor, turning now to face the opening in the spiral. The high walls formed a narrow canyon that curved out of sight, disappearing into darkness.

"Here goes nothing," he said to nobody at all.

Langdon took a deep breath and strode into the opening.

The path curled on and on, farther than he imagined, winding deeper, and Langdon soon had no idea how many rotations he had made. With each clockwise revolution, the passage grew tighter, and Langdon's broad shoulders were now nearly brushing the walls. **Breathe, Robert.** The slanting metal sheets felt as if they might collapse inward at any moment and crush him beneath tons of steel.

Why am I doing this?

A moment before Langdon was about to turn around and head back, the passageway abruptly ended, depositing him in a large open space. As promised, the chamber was larger than he expected. Langdon stepped quickly out of the tunnel into the open, exhaling as he surveyed the bare floor and high metal walls, wondering again if this was some kind of elaborate sophomoric hoax.

A door clicked somewhere outside, and brisk footsteps echoed beyond the high walls. Someone had entered the gallery, coming through the nearby door that Langdon had seen. The footsteps approached the spiral and then began circling around Langdon, growing louder with every turn. Someone was entering the coil.

Langdon backed up and faced the opening as the

footsteps kept circling, drawing closer. The staccato clicking grew louder until, suddenly, a man appeared out of the tunnel. He was short and slender with pale skin, piercing eyes, and an unruly mop of black hair.

Langdon stared stone-faced at the man for a long moment, and then, finally, permitted a broad grin to spread across his face. "The great Edmond Kirsch always makes an entrance."

"Only one chance to make a first impression," Kirsch replied affably. "I've missed you, Robert. Thanks for coming."

The two men shared a heartfelt embrace. As Langdon patted his old friend on the back, he sensed that Kirsch had grown thinner.

"You've lost weight," Langdon said.

"I went vegan," Kirsch replied. "Easier than the elliptical."

Langdon laughed. "Well, it's great to see you. And, as usual, you've made me feel overdressed."

"Who, me?" Kirsch glanced down at his black skinny jeans, pressed white V-neck tee, and side-zip bomber jacket. "This is couture."

"White flip-flops are couture?"

"Flip-flops?! These are Ferragamo Guineas."

"And I'm guessing they cost more than my entire ensemble."

Edmond walked over and examined the label of Langdon's classic jacket. "Actually," he said, smiling warmly, "those are pretty nice tails. It's close."

"I've got to tell you, Edmond, your synthetic friend Winston . . . very unsettling."

Kirsch beamed. "Incredible, right? You can't believe what I've accomplished in artificial intelligence this year—quantum leaps. I've developed a few new proprietary technologies that are enabling machines to problem-solve and self-regulate in entirely new ways. Winston is a work in progress, but he improves daily."

Langdon noticed that deep creases had appeared around Edmond's boyish eyes over the past year. The man looked weary. "Edmond, would you care to tell me why you brought me here?"

"To Bilbao? Or into a Richard Serra spiral?"

"Let's start with the spiral," Langdon said. "You **know** I'm claustrophobic."

"Precisely. Tonight is all about pushing people outside their comfort zones," he said with a smirk.

"Always your specialty."

"Moreover," Kirsch added, "I needed to speak to you, and I didn't want to be seen before the show."

"Because rock stars never mingle with guests before a concert?"

"Correct!" Kirsch replied jokingly. "Rock stars appear magically onstage in a puff of smoke."

Overhead, the lights suddenly faded off and on. Kirsch pulled back his sleeve and checked his watch. Then he glanced to Langdon, his expression turning suddenly serious.

"Robert, we don't have much time. Tonight is a tremendous occasion for me. In fact, it will be an important occasion for all of humankind."

Langdon felt a flush of anticipation.

"Recently, I made a scientific discovery," Edmond

said. "It's a breakthrough that will have far-reaching implications. Almost nobody on earth knows about it, and tonight—very shortly—I will be addressing the world live and announcing what I've found."

"I'm not sure what to say," Langdon replied. "This all sounds amazing."

Edmond lowered his voice, and his tone grew uncharacteristically tense. "Before I go public with this information, Robert, I need your advice." He paused. "I fear my life may depend on it."

CHAPTER 9

Silence had fallen between the two men inside the spiral.

I need your advice . . . I fear my life may depend on it.

Edmond's words hung heavily in the air and Langdon saw disquiet in his friend's eyes. "Edmond? What's going on? Are you okay?"

The overhead lights faded off and on again, but Edmond ignored them.

"It has been a remarkable year for me," he began, his voice a whisper. "I've been working alone on a major project, one that led to a groundbreaking discovery."

"That sounds wonderful."

Kirsch nodded. "It is indeed, and words can't describe how excited I am to share it with the world tonight. It will usher in a major paradigm shift. I am not exaggerating when I tell you that my discovery will have repercussions on the scale of the Copernican revolution."

For a moment, Langdon thought his host was joking, but Edmond's expression remained dead serious.

Copernicus? Humility had never been one of Edmond's strong suits, but this claim sounded bor-

derline preposterous. Nicolaus Copernicus was the
father of the heliocentric model—the belief that the
planets revolve around the sun—which ignited a scientific revolution in the 1500s that entirely obliterated the Church's long-held teaching that mankind
occupied the center of God's universe. His discovery
was condemned by the Church for three centuries,
but the damage had been done, and the world had
never been the same.

"I can see you're skeptical," Edmond said. "Would
it be better if I said Darwin?"

Langdon smiled. "Same issue."

"Okay, then let me ask you this: What are the two
fundamental questions that have been asked by the
human race throughout our entire history?"

Langdon considered it. "Well, the questions would
have to be: 'How did it all begin? Where do we come
from?'"

"Precisely. And the second question is simply the
ancillary to that. Not 'where do we come from' . . .
but . . ."

"'Where are we going?'"

"Yes! These two mysteries lie at the heart of the
human experience. Where do we come from? Where
are we going? Human **creation** and human **destiny**.
They are the universal mysteries." Edmond's gaze
sharpened and he peered at Langdon expectantly.
"Robert, the discovery I've made . . . it very clearly
answers both of these questions."

Langdon grappled with Edmond's words and their
heady ramifications. "I'm . . . not sure what to say."

"No need to say anything. I'm hoping you and I can find time to discuss it in depth following tonight's presentation, but at the moment, I need to talk to you about the darker side of all this—the potential **fallout** from the discovery."

"You think there will be repercussions?"

"Without a doubt. By answering these questions, I have placed myself in direct conflict with centuries of established spiritual teachings. Issues of human creation and human destiny are traditionally the domain of religion. I'm an interloper, and the religions of the world are not going to like what I'm about to announce."

"Interesting," Langdon replied. "And is this why you spent two hours grilling me about religion over lunch in Boston last year?"

"It is. You may remember my personal guarantee to you—that in our lifetime, the myths of religion would be all but demolished by scientific breakthroughs."

Langdon nodded. **Hard to forget.** The boldness of Kirsch's declaration had emblazoned itself word for word in Langdon's eidetic memory. "I do. And I countered that religion had survived advances in science for millennia, and that it served an important purpose in society, and while religion might evolve, it would never die."

"Exactly. I also told you that I had found the purpose of my life—to employ the truth of science to eradicate the myth of religion."

"Yes, strong words."

"And you challenged me on them, Robert. You argued that whenever I came across a 'scientific truth' that conflicted with or undermined the tenets of religion, I should discuss it with a religious **scholar** in hopes I might realize that science and religion are often attempting to tell the same story in two different languages."

"I do remember. Scientists and spiritualists often use different vocabularies to describe the exact same mysteries of the universe. The conflicts are frequently over semantics, not substance."

"Well, I followed your advice," Kirsch said. "And I consulted with spiritual leaders about my latest discovery."

"Oh?"

"Are you familiar with the Parliament of the World's Religions?"

"Of course." Langdon was a great admirer of the group's efforts to promote interfaith discourse.

"By chance," Kirsch said, "the parliament held their meeting outside Barcelona this year, about an hour from my home, at the Abbey of Montserrat."

Spectacular spot, Langdon thought, having visited the mountaintop sanctuary many years ago.

"When I heard it was taking place during the same week I had planned to make this major scientific announcement, I don't know, I . . ."

"Wondered if it might be a sign from God?"

Kirsch laughed. "Something like that. So I called them."

Langdon was impressed. "You addressed the **entire** parliament?"

"No! Too dangerous. I didn't want this information leaking out before I could announce it myself, so I scheduled a meeting with only three of them—one representative each from Christianity, Islam, and Judaism. The four of us met in private in the library."

"I'm amazed they let you **in** the library," Langdon said with surprise. "I hear that's hallowed ground."

"I told them I needed a secure meeting place, no phones, no cameras, no intruders. They took me to that library. Before I told them anything, I asked them to agree to a vow of silence. They complied. To date, they are the only people on earth who know anything about my discovery."

"Fascinating. And how did they react when you told them?"

Kirsch looked sheepish. "I may not have handled it perfectly. You know me, Robert, when my passions flare, diplomacy is not my métier."

"Yes, I've read that you could use some sensitivity training," Langdon said with a laugh. **Just like Steve Jobs and so many genius visionaries.**

"So in keeping with my outspoken nature, I began our talk by simply telling them the truth—that I had always considered religion a form of mass delusion, and that as a scientist, I found it difficult to accept the fact that billions of intelligent people rely on their respective faiths to comfort and guide them. When they asked why I was consulting with people for whom I apparently had little respect, I told them I was there to gauge their reactions to my discovery so I could get some sense of how it would be received by the world's faithful once I made it public."

"Always the diplomat," Langdon said, wincing. "You
do know that sometimes honesty is not the best policy?"

Kirsch waved his hand dismissively. "My thoughts
on religion are widely publicized. I thought they
would appreciate the transparency. Nonetheless, after
that, I presented my work to them, explaining in
detail what I had discovered and how it changed
everything. I even took out my phone and showed
them some video that I admit is quite startling. They
were speechless."

"They must have said **something**," Langdon
prompted, feeling even more curious to know what
Kirsch possibly could have discovered.

"I was hoping for a conversation, but the Christian
cleric silenced the other two before they could say a
word. He urged me to reconsider making the information public. I told him I would think about it for
the next month."

"But you're going public **tonight**."

"I know. I told them my announcement was still
several weeks away so they wouldn't panic or try to
interfere."

"And when they find out about tonight's presentation?" Langdon asked.

"They will not be amused. **One** of them in particular." Kirsch locked eyes with Langdon. "The cleric
who convened our meeting was Bishop Antonio
Valdespino. Do you know of him?"

Langdon tensed. "From Madrid?"

Kirsch nodded. "One and the same."

Probably not the ideal audience for Edmond's radical atheism, Langdon thought. Valdespino was a powerful figure in the Spanish Catholic Church, known for his deeply conservative views and strong influence over the king of Spain.

"He was host of the parliament this year," Kirsch said, "and therefore the one I spoke to about arranging a meeting. He offered to come personally, and I asked him to bring representatives from Islam and Judaism."

The lights overhead faded again.

Kirsch sighed heavily, lowering his voice further. "Robert, the reason I wanted to speak to you before my presentation is that I need your advice. I need to know if you believe that Bishop Valdespino is dangerous."

"Dangerous?" Langdon said. "In what way?"

"What I showed him threatens his world, and I want to know if you think I'm in any physical danger from him."

Langdon immediately shook his head. "No, impossible. I'm not sure what you said to him, but Valdespino is a pillar of Spanish Catholicism, and his ties to the Spanish royal family make him extremely **influential** . . . but he's a priest, not a hit man. He wields political power. He may preach a sermon against you, but I would find it very hard to believe that you are in any physical danger from him."

Kirsch looked unconvinced. "You should have seen the way he looked at me as I left Montserrat."

"You sat in that monastery's sacrosanct library and

told a bishop that his entire belief system is delusional!" Langdon exclaimed. "Did you expect him to serve you tea and cake?"

"No," Edmond admitted, "but I also didn't expect him to leave me a threatening voice mail after our meeting."

"Bishop Valdespino called you?"

Kirsch reached into his leather jacket and pulled out an unusually large smartphone. It had a bright turquoise case adorned with a repeating hexagonal pattern, which Langdon recognized as a famous tiled pattern designed by the modernist Catalan architect Antoni Gaudí.

"Have a listen," Kirsch said, pressing a few buttons and holding up the phone. An elderly man's voice crackled tersely out of the speaker, his tone severe and dead serious:

> Mr. Kirsch, this is Bishop Antonio Valdespino.
> As you know, I found our meeting this morning
> profoundly disturbing—as did my two colleagues.
> I urge you to call me immediately so we can discuss
> this further, and I can again warn you of the dangers
> of going public with this information. If you do not
> call, be advised that my colleagues and I will consider
> a preemptive announcement to share your discoveries,
> reframe them, discredit them, and attempt to reverse
> the untold damage you are about to cause the
> world . . . damage that you clearly do not foresee. I
> await your call, and I strongly suggest you not test
> my resolve.

The message ended.

Langdon had to admit he was startled by Valdespino's aggressive tone, and yet the voice mail did not so much frighten him as it deepened his curiosity about Edmond's impending announcement. "So, how did you respond?"

"I didn't," Edmond said, slipping the phone back into his pocket. "I saw it as an idle threat. I was certain they wanted to **bury** this information, not announce it themselves. Moreover, I knew the sudden timing of tonight's presentation was going to take them by surprise, so I wasn't overly concerned about their taking preemptive action." He paused, eyeing Langdon. "Now . . . I don't know, something about his tone of voice . . . it's just been on my mind."

"Are you worried you're in danger **here**? Tonight?"

"No, no, the guest list has been tightly controlled, and this building has excellent security. I'm more worried about what happens once I go public." Edmond seemed suddenly sorry he'd mentioned it. "It's silly. Preshow jitters. I just wanted to get your gut instinct."

Langdon studied his friend with mounting concern. Edmond looked unusually pale and troubled. "My gut tells me Valdespino would never place you in danger, no matter how angry you made him."

The lights dimmed again, insistently now.

"Okay, thank you." Kirsch checked his watch. "I need to go, but can you and I meet later? There are some aspects of this discovery I'd like to discuss further with you."

"Of course."

"Perfect. Things are going to be chaotic after the presentation, so you and I will need someplace private to escape the mayhem and talk." Edmond took out a business card and started writing on the back. "After the presentation, hail a cab and give this card to the driver. Any local driver will understand where to bring you." He handed Langdon the business card.

Langdon expected to see the address of a local hotel or restaurant on the back. Instead he saw what looked more like a cipher.

BIO-EC346

"I'm sorry, give **this** to a taxi driver?"

"Yes, he'll know where to go. I'll tell security there to expect you, and I'll be along as quickly as possible."

Security? Langdon frowned, wondering if BIO-EC346 were the code name for some secret science club.

"It's a painfully simple code, my friend." He winked. "You of all people should be able to crack it. And, by the way, just so you're not taken off guard, **you'll** be playing a role in my announcement tonight."

Langdon was surprised. "What kind of role?"

"Don't worry. You won't have to do a thing."

With that, Edmond Kirsch headed across the floor toward the spiral's exit. "I've got to dash backstage—but Winston will guide you up." He paused in the doorway and turned. "I'll see you after the event. And let's hope you're right about Valdespino."

"Edmond, relax. Focus on your presentation. You're not in any danger from religious clerics," Langdon assured him.

Kirsch didn't look convinced. "You may feel differently, Robert, when you hear what I'm about to say."

CHAPTER 10

The holy seat of the Roman Catholic Archdiocese of Madrid—Catedral de la Almudena—is a robust neoclassical cathedral situated adjacent to Madrid's Royal Palace. Built on the site of an ancient mosque, Almudena Cathedral derives its name from the Arabic **al-mudayna,** meaning "citadel."

According to legend, when Alfonso VI seized Madrid back from the Muslims in 1083, he became fixated on relocating a precious lost icon of the Virgin Mary that had been entombed in the walls of the citadel for safekeeping. Unable to locate the hidden Virgin, Alfonso prayed intently until a section of the citadel's wall exploded, falling away, and revealed the icon inside, still lit by the burning candles with which she had been entombed centuries ago.

Today, the Virgin of Almudena is the patron saint of Madrid, and pilgrims and tourists alike flock to mass at Almudena Cathedral for the privilege of praying before her likeness. The church's dramatic location—sharing the Royal Palace's main plaza—provides an added attraction to churchgoers: the possibility of glimpsing royalty coming or going from the palace.

Tonight, deep inside the cathedral, a young acolyte was rushing through the hallway in a panic.

Where is Bishop Valdespino?!

Services are about to begin!

For decades, Bishop Antonio Valdespino had been head priest and overseer of this cathedral. A longtime friend and spiritual counselor to the king, Valdespino was an outspoken and devout traditionalist with almost no tolerance for modernization. Incredibly, the eighty-three-year-old bishop still donned ankle shackles during Holy Week and joined the faithful carrying icons through the city streets.

Valdespino, of all people, is never late for mass.

The acolyte had been with the bishop twenty minutes ago in the vestry, assisting him with his robes as usual. Just as they finished, the bishop had received a text and, without a word, had hurried out.

Where did he go?

Having searched the sanctuary, the vestry, and even the bishop's private restroom, the acolyte was now running at a sprint down the hallway to the administrative section of the cathedral to check the bishop's office.

He heard a pipe organ thunder to life in the distance.

The processional hymn is starting!

The acolyte skidded to a stop outside the bishop's private office, startled to see a shaft of light beneath his closed door. **He's here?!**

The acolyte knocked quietly. "¿Excelencia Reverendísima?"

No answer.

Knocking louder, he called out, "¡¿Su Excelencia?!"

Still nothing.

Fearing for the old man's health, the acolyte turned the handle and pushed open the door.

¡Cielos! The acolyte gasped as he peered into the private space.

Bishop Valdespino was seated at his mahogany desk, staring into the glow of a laptop computer. His holy miter was still on his head, his chasuble wadded beneath him, and his crozier staff propped unceremoniously against the wall.

The acolyte cleared his throat. "La santa misa está—"

"Preparada," the bishop interrupted, his eyes never moving from the screen. "Padre Derida me sustituye."

The acolyte stared in bewilderment. Father Derida is substituting? A junior priest overseeing Saturday-night mass was highly irregular.

"¡Vete ya!" Valdespino snapped without looking up. "Y cierra la puerta."

Fearful, the boy did as he was told, leaving immediately and closing the door as he went.

Hurrying back toward the sounds of the pipe organ, the acolyte wondered what the bishop could possibly be viewing on his computer that would pull his mind so far from his duties to God.

———

At that moment, Admiral Ávila was snaking through the growing crowd in the Guggenheim's atrium, puzzled to see guests chatting with their sleek headsets. Apparently the audio tour of the museum was a two-way conversation.

He felt glad to have jettisoned the device.

No distractions tonight.

He checked his watch and eyed the elevators. They were already crowded with guests heading to the main event upstairs, so Ávila opted for the stairs. As he climbed, he felt the same tremor of incredulity he had felt last night. **Have I really become a man capable of killing?** The godless souls who had ripped away his wife and child had transformed him. **My actions are sanctioned by a higher authority,** he reminded himself. **There is righteousness in what I do.**

As Ávila reached the first landing, his gaze was drawn to a woman on a nearby suspended catwalk. **Spain's newest celebrity,** he thought, eyeing the famous beauty.

She wore a formfitting white dress with a black diagonal stripe that ran elegantly across her torso. Her slender figure, lush dark hair, and graceful carriage were easy to admire, and Ávila noticed he was not the only one with eyes on her.

In addition to the approving glances of the other guests, the woman in white held the full attention of two sleek security officers who shadowed her closely. The men moved with the wary confidence of panthers and wore matching blue blazers with embroidered crests and the large initials **GR.**

Ávila was not surprised by their presence, and yet the sight of them made his pulse quicken. As a former member of the Spanish armed forces, he knew full well what **GR** signified. These two security escorts would be armed and as well trained as any body-guards on earth.

If they are present, I must take every precaution, Ávila told himself.

"Hey!" a man's voice barked, directly behind him.

Ávila spun around.

A paunchy man in a tuxedo and a black cowboy hat was smiling broadly at him. "Great costume!" the man said, pointing to Ávila's military uniform. "Where does someone get something like that?"

Ávila stared, fists clenching reflexively. **Through a lifetime of service and sacrifice,** he thought. "**No hablo inglés,**" Ávila replied with a shrug, and contin-ued up the stairs.

On the second floor, Ávila found a long hallway and followed signs to a remote restroom at the far end. He was about to enter when the lights through-out the museum faded off and on—the first gentle nudge urging guests to start heading upstairs for the presentation.

Ávila entered the deserted restroom, chose the last stall, and locked himself inside. Alone now, he felt the familiar demons trying to surface within him, threatening to drag him back into the abyss.

Five years, and the memories still haunt me.

Angrily, Ávila pushed the horrors from his mind and retrieved the rosary beads from his pocket. Gently, he looped them over the coat hook on the door. As the beads and crucifix swung peacefully before him, he admired his handiwork. The devout might be horrified that anyone could defile the rosary by creating an object like this. Even so, Ávila had been assured by the Regent that desperate times afforded a certain flexibility in the rules of absolution.

When the cause is this holy, the Regent had promised, **God's forgiveness is guaranteed.**

As with the protection of his soul, Ávila's **body** had also been guaranteed deliverance from evil. He glanced down at the tattoo on his palm.

Like the ancient **crismón** of Christ, the icon was a symbol constructed entirely of letters. Ávila had inscribed it there three days ago with iron gall and a needle, precisely as he had been instructed, and the spot was still tender and red. If he were captured, the Regent assured him, all he had to do was make his palm visible to his captors, and within hours, he would be released.

We occupy the highest levels of government, the Regent had said.

Ávila had already witnessed their startling influence, and it felt like a mantle of protection all around him. **There still exist those who respect the ancient ways.** One day Ávila hoped to join the ranks of this elite, but for the moment, he felt honored to play any role at all.

In the solitude of the bathroom, Ávila took out his phone and dialed the secure number he had been given.

The voice on the line answered on the first ring. "¿Sí?"

"**Estoy en posición,**" Ávila replied, awaiting final instructions.

"**Bien,**" the Regent said. "**Tendrás una sola oportunidad. Aprovecharla será crucial.**" You will have only one chance. Seizing it will be crucial.

CHAPTER 11

Thirty kilometers up the coastline from Dubai's glistening skyscrapers, man-made islands, and celebrity party villas lies the city of Sharjah—the ultraconservative Islamic cultural capital of the United Arab Emirates.

With more than six hundred mosques and the region's finest universities, Sharjah stands as a pinnacle of spirituality and learning—a position fueled by massive oil reserves and a ruler who places the education of his people above all else.

Tonight, the family of Sharjah's beloved **allamah,** Syed al-Fadl, had gathered in private to hold a vigil. Instead of praying the traditional **tahajjud,** the night vigil prayer, they prayed for the return of their cherished father, uncle, and husband, who had mysteriously disappeared yesterday without a trace.

The local press had just announced that one of Syed's colleagues was claiming that the normally composed **allamah** had seemed "strangely agitated" upon his return from the Parliament of the World's Religions two days ago. In addition, the colleague said he had overheard Syed engaged in a rare heated phone argument shortly after his return. The dispute was in English, and therefore indecipherable to him, but the colleague swore he had heard Syed repeatedly mention a single name.

Edmond Kirsch.

CHAPTER 12

Langdon's thoughts swirled as he emerged from the spiral structure. His conversation with Kirsch had been both exciting and alarming. Whether or not Kirsch's claims were exaggerated, the computer scientist clearly had discovered **something** that he believed would cause a paradigm shift in the world.

A discovery as important as the findings of Copernicus?

When Langdon finally emerged from the coiled sculpture, he felt slightly dizzy. He retrieved the headset he had left on the floor earlier.

"Winston?" he said, pulling on the device. "Hello?"

A faint click, and the computerized British docent was back. "Hello, Professor. Yes, I'm here. Mr. Kirsch asked me to take you up the service elevator because time is too short to return to the atrium. He also thought you would appreciate our oversized service elevator."

"Nice of him. He knows I'm claustrophobic."

"Now I do too. And I will not forget it."

Winston guided Langdon through the side door into a cement hallway and elevator bay. As promised, the elevator carriage was enormous, clearly designed to transport oversized artwork.

"Top button," Winston said as Langdon stepped inside. "Third floor."

When they arrived at their destination, Langdon stepped out.

"Righto," Winston's cheery voice chimed in Langdon's head. "We'll go through the gallery on your left. It's the most direct way to the auditorium."

Langdon followed Winston's directions through an expansive gallery displaying a series of bizarre art installations: a steel cannon that apparently shot gooey globs of red wax at a white wall; a wire-mesh canoe that clearly would not float; an entire miniature city made of burnished metal blocks.

As they crossed the gallery toward the exit, Langdon found himself staring in utter bewilderment at a massive piece that dominated the space.

It's official, he decided, **I've found the strangest piece in this museum.**

Spanning the width of the entire room, a multitude of timber wolves were dynamically posed, sprinting in a long line across the gallery where they leaped high in the air and collided violently with a transparent glass wall, resulting in a mounting pile of dead wolves.

"It's called **Head On,**" Winston offered, unprompted. "Ninety-nine wolves racing blindly into a wall to symbolize a herd mentality, a lack of courage in diverging from the norm."

The irony of the symbolism struck Langdon. **I suspect Edmond will be diverging dramatically from the norm this evening.**

"Now, if you'll continue straight ahead," Winston said, "you'll find the exit to the left of that colorful diamond-shaped piece. The artist is one of Edmond's favorites."

Langdon spotted the brightly colored painting up ahead and instantly recognized the trademark squiggles, primary colors, and playful floating eye.

Joan Miró, Langdon thought, having always liked the famous Barcelonan's playful work, which felt like a cross between a child's coloring book and a surrealist stained-glass window.

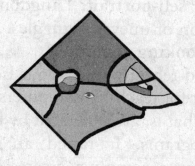

As Langdon drew even with the piece, however, he stopped short, startled to see that the surface was utterly smooth, with no visible brushstrokes. "It's a **reproduction?**"

"No, that's the original," Winston replied.

Langdon looked closer. The work had clearly been printed by a large-format printer. "Winston, this is a **print.** It's not even on canvas."

"I don't work on canvas," Winston replied. "I create art virtually, and then Edmond prints it for me."

"Hold on," Langdon said in disbelief. "This is **yours?**"

"Yes, I tried to mimic the style of Joan Miró."

"I can see that," Langdon said. "You even **signed** it—Miró."

"No," Winston said. "Look again. I signed it **Miro**—with no accent. In Spanish, the word **miro** means 'I look at.'"

Clever, Langdon had to admit, seeing the single Miró-style eye looking at the viewer from the center of Winston's piece.

"Edmond asked me to create a self-portrait, and this is what I came up with."

This is your self-portrait? Langdon glanced again at the collection of uneven squiggles. **You must be a very strange-looking computer.**

Langdon had recently read about Edmond's growing excitement for teaching computers to create algorithmic art—that is, art generated by highly complex computer programs. It raised an uncomfortable question: When a computer creates art, who is the artist—the computer or the programmer? At MIT, a recent exhibit of highly accomplished algorithmic art had put an awkward spin on the Harvard humanities course: **Is Art What Makes Us Human?**

"I compose music too," Winston chimed. "You should ask Edmond to play some for you later, should you be curious. At the moment, however, you do need to hurry. The presentation is starting shortly."

Langdon left the gallery and found himself on a high catwalk overlooking the main atrium. On the opposite side of the cavernous space, docents were hustling the last few straggling guests out of the elevators, herding them in Langdon's direction toward a doorway up ahead.

"Tonight's program is scheduled to begin in just a few minutes," Winston said. "Do you see the entrance to the presentation space?"

"I do. It's just ahead."

"Excellent. One final point. As you enter, you will see collection bins for headsets. Edmond asked that you **not** return your unit, but rather keep it. This way, after the program, I will be able to guide you out of the museum through a back door, where you'll avoid the crowds and be sure to find a taxi."

Langdon pictured the strange series of letters and numbers that Edmond had scrawled on the business card, telling him to give it to the taxi driver. "Winston, all Edmond wrote was 'BIO-EC346.' He called it a painfully simple code."

"He speaks the truth," Winston replied quickly. "Now, Professor, the program is about to begin. I do hope you enjoy Mr. Kirsch's presentation, and I look forward to assisting you afterward."

With an abrupt click, Winston was gone.

Langdon neared the entry doors, removed his headset, and slipped the tiny device into his jacket pocket. Then he hurried through the entrance with the last few guests just as the doors closed behind him.

Once again, he found himself in an unexpected space.

We're standing up for the presentation?

Langdon had imagined the crowd gathering in a comfortable sit-down auditorium to hear Edmond's announcement, but instead, hundreds of guests stood packed into a cramped, whitewashed gallery space. The room contained no visible artwork and no seating—just a podium at the far wall, flanked by a large LCD screen that read:

Live program begins in 2 minutes 07 seconds

Langdon felt a surge of anticipation, and his eyes continued down the LCD screen to a second line of text, which he needed to read twice:

Current remote attendees: 1,953,694

Two million people?
Kirsch had told Langdon he would be live-streaming his announcement, but these numbers seemed unfathomable, and the ticker was climbing faster with each passing moment.

A smile crossed Langdon's face. His former student had certainly done well for himself. The question now was: What in the world was Edmond about to say?

CHAPTER 13

In a moonlit desert just east of Dubai, a Sand Viper
1100 dune buggy veered hard to the left and skidded to a stop, sending a veil of sand billowing out
in front of the blazing headlights.

The teenager behind the wheel ripped off his goggles and stared down at the object he had almost run
over. Apprehensive, he climbed out of the vehicle and
approached the dark form in the sand.

Sure enough, it was exactly what it had appeared
to be.

There in his headlights, sprawled facedown on the
sand, lay a motionless human body.

"Marhaba?" the kid called out. "Hello?"

No response.

The boy could tell it was a man from his clothing—a
traditional chechia hat and loose-fitting **thawb**—and
the man looked well fed and squat. His footprints
had long since blown away, as had any tire tracks or
hints as to how he might have gotten this far out into
the open desert.

"Marhaba?" the kid repeated.

Nothing.

Uncertain what else to do, the boy reached out with
his foot and gently nudged the man's side. Although

his body was plump, his flesh felt taut and hard, already desiccated by the wind and sun.

Definitely dead.

The boy reached down, grasped the man's shoulder, and heaved him onto his back. The man's lifeless eyes stared up at the heavens. His face and beard were covered in sand, but even dirty, he looked friendly somehow, even familiar, like a favorite uncle or grandfather.

The roar of a half-dozen quad bikes and buggies thundered nearby as the kid's dune-bashing buddies circled back to make sure he was all right. Their vehicles roared up over the ridge and slid down the face of the dune.

Everyone parked, removed their goggles and helmets, and gathered around the macabre discovery of a parched corpse. One of the boys started speaking excitedly, having recognized the dead man as the famous **allamah** Syed al-Fadl—a scholar and religious leader—who spoke from time to time at the university.

"**Matha Alayna 'an naf'al?**" he asked aloud. **What should we do?**

The boys stood in a circle, staring silently at the corpse. Then they reacted like teenagers around the world. They pulled out their phones and began snapping photos to text to their friends.

CHAPTER 14

S tanding shoulder to shoulder with guests jostling around the podium, Robert Langdon watched in amazement as the number on the LCD screen ticked steadily higher.

Current remote attendees: 2,527,664

The background chatter in the cramped space had risen to the level of a dull roar, the voices of hundreds of guests buzzing with anticipation, many making excited last-minute phone calls or tweeting their whereabouts.

A technician stepped to the podium and tapped the microphone. "Ladies and gentlemen, we asked earlier that you please turn off your mobile devices. At this time, we will be blocking all Wi-Fi and cellular communications for the duration of this event."

Many guests were still on their phones, and they abruptly lost their connections. Most of them looked wholly stupefied, as if they had just witnessed some miraculous piece of Kirschian technology capable of magically severing all connection with the outside world.

Five hundred dollars at an electronics store, Langdon knew, being one of several Harvard professors who now used portable cell-jamming technology to render their lecture halls "dead zones" and keep students off their devices during class.

A cameraman now moved into position with a massive camera on his shoulder, which he directed at the podium. The room lights dimmed.

The LCD screen read:

Live program begins in 38 seconds
Current remote attendees: 2,857,914

Langdon watched the attendee counter with amazement. It seemed to be climbing faster than the U.S. national debt, and he found it nearly impossible to fathom that close to three million people were sitting at home at this very moment watching a live stream of what was about to happen in this room.

"Thirty seconds," the technician announced softly into the microphone.

A narrow door opened in the wall behind the podium, and the crowd immediately hushed, all looking expectantly for the great Edmond Kirsch.

But Edmond never materialized.

The door stood open for nearly ten seconds.

Then an elegant woman emerged and moved toward the podium. She was strikingly beautiful—tall and willowy with long black hair—wearing a formfitting white dress with a diagonal black stripe.

She seemed to drift effortlessly across the floor. Taking center stage, she adjusted the microphone, took a deep breath, and gave the attendees a patient smile as she waited for the clock to tick down.

Live program begins in 10 seconds

The woman closed her eyes a moment, as if to gather herself, and then she opened them again, a portrait of poise.

The cameraman held up five fingers.

Four, three, two . . .

The room fell completely silent as the woman raised her eyes to the camera. The LCD display dissolved into a live image of her face. She fixed the audience with spirited dark eyes as she casually brushed a strand of hair from her olive-toned cheek.

"Good evening, everyone," she began, her voice cultured and gracious, with a light Spanish accent. "My name is Ambra Vidal."

An unusually loud burst of applause erupted in the room, making it apparent that a good number of people knew who she was.

"¡Felicidades!" someone shouted. **Congratulations!**

The woman blushed, and Langdon sensed there was some piece of information he was missing.

"Ladies and gentlemen," she said, quickly pressing on, "for the past five years, I have been the director of this Guggenheim Museum Bilbao, and I am here tonight to welcome you to an incredibly special evening presented by a truly remarkable man."

The crowd applauded enthusiastically, and Langdon joined them.

"Edmond Kirsch is not only a generous patron of this museum, but he has become a trusted friend. It has been a privilege and a personal honor for me to have been able to work so closely with him over the past few months to plan the events of this evening. I've just checked, and social media is buzzing around the world! As many of you have no doubt heard by now, Edmond Kirsch is planning to make a major scientific announcement tonight—a discovery that he believes will be forever remembered as his greatest contribution to the world."

A murmur of excitement shot through the room.

The dark-haired woman smiled playfully. "Of course, I begged Edmond to tell **me** what he had discovered, but he refused to give even a hint."

A round of laughter was followed by more applause.

"Tonight's special event," she continued, "will be presented in English—Mr. Kirsch's native language—although for those of you attending virtually, we are offering real-time translation in more than twenty languages."

The LCD screen refreshed, and Ambra added, "And if anyone ever doubted Edmond's self-confidence, here is the automated press release that went out fifteen minutes ago to social media around the globe."

Langdon eyed the LCD screen.

Tonight: Live. 20:00 hours CEST
Futurist Edmond Kirsch to announce discovery that will
change the face of science forever.

So that's **how you get three million viewers in a matter of minutes,** Langdon mused.

As he returned his attention to the podium, Langdon spotted two people he had not noticed earlier—a pair of stone-faced security guards standing at full attention against the sidewall, scanning the crowd. Langdon was surprised to see the monogrammed initials on their matching blue blazers.

The Guardia Real?! What is the king's Royal Guard doing here tonight?

It seemed unlikely that any member of the royal family would be in attendance; as staunch Catholics, the royals would almost certainly eschew public association with an atheist like Edmond Kirsch.

The king of Spain, as a parliamentary monarch, held very limited official power, and yet he retained enormous influence over the hearts and minds of his people. For millions of Spaniards, the crown still stood as a symbol of the rich Catholic tradition of **los reyes católicos** and Spain's Golden Age. The Royal Palace of Madrid still shone as a spiritual compass and monument to a long history of stalwart religious conviction.

Langdon had heard it said in Spain: "Parliament rules, but the king **reigns.**" For centuries, the kings who had presided over Spain's diplomatic affairs had all been deeply devout, conservative Catholics. **And the current king is no exception,** Langdon thought, having read of the man's deep religious convictions and conservative values.

In recent months, the aging monarch was reported to be bedridden and dying, with his country now preparing for the eventual transition of power to his only son, Julián. According to the press, Prince Julián was something of an unknown quantity, having lived quietly in the long shadow of his father, and now the country was wondering what kind of ruler he would turn out to be.

Did Prince Julián send Guardia agents to scout Edmond's event?

Langdon flashed again on Edmond's threatening voice mail from Bishop Valdespino. Despite Langdon's concerns, he sensed the atmosphere in the room was amiable, enthusiastic, and safe. He recalled Edmond telling him that tonight's security was incredibly tight—so perhaps Spain's Guardia Real was an additional layer of protection to ensure that the evening went smoothly.

"For those of you who are familiar with Edmond Kirsch's passion for the dramatic," Ambra Vidal continued, "you know he would never plan to have us stand in this sterile room for long."

She motioned to a set of closed double doors on the far side of the room.

"Through those doors, Edmond Kirsch has constructed an 'experiential space' in which to present his dynamic multimedia presentation tonight. It is fully automated by computers and will be streamed live around the entire world." She paused to check her gold watch. "Tonight's event is carefully timed, and Edmond has asked that I get you all inside so we can begin precisely at eight fifteen, which is only minutes away." She pointed to the double doors. "So if you would, ladies and gentlemen, please move inside, and we will see what the amazing Edmond Kirsch has in store for us."

On cue, the double doors swung open.

Langdon peered beyond them, expecting to see another gallery. Instead, he found himself startled by what lay beyond. Through the doors, there appeared to be a deep dark tunnel.

———

Admiral Ávila hung back as throngs of guests began jostling excitedly toward the dimly lit passageway. As he peered into the tunnel, he was pleased to see that the space beyond was dark.

Darkness would make his task a great deal easier.

Touching the rosary beads in his pocket, he gathered his thoughts, going over the details he had just been given regarding his mission.

Timing will be critical.

CHAPTER 15

Fashioned of black fabric that was stretched across supportive arches, the tunnel was about twenty feet wide and sloped gently upward to the left. The tunnel floor was covered with plush black carpet, and two strands of strip lighting along the base of the walls provided the only illumination.

"Shoes, please," a docent whispered to the new arrivals. "Everyone please remove your shoes, and carry them with you."

Langdon stepped out of his patent-leather dress shoes, and his stocking feet sank deep into the remarkably soft carpet. He felt his body relax instinctively. All around him, he heard appreciative sighs.

As he padded farther down the passage, Langdon finally saw the end—a black curtain barrier where guests were being greeted by docents who handed each of them what appeared to be a thick beach towel before ushering them through the curtain.

Inside the tunnel, the earlier buzz of anticipation had now dissolved into uncertain silence. As Langdon arrived at the curtain, a docent handed him a folded piece of fabric, which he realized was not a beach towel but rather a small plush blanket with a pillow sewn into one end. Langdon thanked the docent and stepped through the curtain into the space beyond.

For the second time tonight, he was forced to stop in his tracks. Although Langdon could not say what he had imagined he would see beyond the curtain, it most certainly was nothing close to the scene now before him.

Are we . . . outdoors?

Langdon was standing on the edge of an expansive field. Above him stretched a dazzling sky of stars, and in the distance, a slender crescent moon was just rising behind a lone maple tree. Crickets chirped and a warm breeze caressed his face, the wafting air thick with the earthy scent of freshly cut grass beneath his stocking feet.

"Sir?" a docent whispered, taking his arm and guiding him into the field. "Please find a space here on the grass. Lay out your blanket, and enjoy."

Langdon padded out into the field along with the other equally flabbergasted guests, most of whom were now choosing spots on the vast lawn to spread out their blankets. The manicured grassy area was about the size of a hockey rink and bounded all around by trees, fescue, and cattails, which rustled in the breeze.

It had taken Langdon several moments to realize this was all an illusion—a tremendous work of art.

I'm inside an elaborate planetarium, he thought, marveling at the impeccable attention to detail.

The star-filled sky above was a projection, complete with a moon, scudding clouds, and distant rolling hills. The rustling trees and grasses were truly there—either superb fakes or a small forest of living plants in concealed pots. This nebulous perimeter of vegetation cleverly disguised the enormous room's hard edges, giving the impression of a natural environment.

Langdon crouched down and felt the grass, which was soft and lifelike, but entirely dry. He'd read about the new synthetic turfs that were fooling even professional athletes, and yet Kirsch had gone a step further and created slightly uneven ground, with small swales and mounds as in a real meadow.

Langdon recalled the first time he had been fooled by his senses. He was a child in a small boat drifting through a moonlit harbor where a pirate ship was engaged in a deafening cannon battle. Langdon's young mind had been incapable of accepting that he was not in a harbor at all, but in fact he was in a cavernous underground theater that had been flooded with water to create this illusion for the classic Disney World ride Pirates of the Caribbean.

Tonight, the effect was staggeringly realistic, and as the guests around him took it in, Langdon could see that their wonder and delight mirrored his own. He had to give Edmond credit—not so much for creating this amazing illusion, but for persuading hundreds of adults to kick off their fancy shoes, lie down on the lawn, and gaze up at the heavens.

We used to do this as kids, but somewhere along the way, we stopped.

Langdon reclined and placed his head on the pillow, letting his body melt into the soft grass.

Overhead, the stars twinkled, and for an instant, Langdon was a teenager again, lying on the lush fairways of the Bald Peak golf course at midnight with his best friend, pondering the mysteries of life. **With a little luck,** Langdon mused, **Edmond Kirsch might solve some of those mysteries for us tonight.**

––––––

At the rear of the theater, Admiral Luis Ávila took one final survey of the room and moved silently backward, slipping out unseen through the same curtain through which he had just entered. Alone in the entry tunnel, he ran a hand along the fabric walls until he located a seam. As quietly as possible, he pulled apart the Velcro closure, stepped through the wall, and resealed the cloth behind him.

All illusions evaporated.

Ávila was no longer standing in a meadow.

He was in an enormous rectangular space that was dominated by a sprawling oval-shaped bubble. **A room built within a room.** The construction before him—a domed theater of sorts—was surrounded by a towering exoskeleton of scaffolding that supported a tangle of cables, lights, and audio speakers. Pointing inward, a shimmering array of video projectors glowed in unison, casting wide beams of light downward onto the translucent surface of the dome, and creating the illusion within of a starlit sky and rolling hills.

Ávila admired Kirsch's knack for drama, although

the futurist could never have imagined just how dramatic his night would soon turn out to be.

Remember what is at stake. You are a soldier in a noble war. Part of a greater whole.

Ávila had rehearsed this mission in his mind numerous times. He reached into his pocket and pulled out the oversized rosary beads. At that moment, from an overhead bank of speakers inside the dome, a man's voice thundered down like the voice of God.

"Good evening, friends. My name is Edmond Kirsch."

CHAPTER 16

I n Budapest, Rabbi Köves paced nervously in the dim light of his **házikó** study. Clutching his TV remote, he flipped anxiously through the channels as he awaited further news from Bishop Valdespino.

On television, several news channels had interrupted their regular programming during the past ten minutes to carry the live feed coming out of the Guggenheim. Commentators were discussing Kirsch's accomplishments and speculating about his mysterious upcoming announcement. Köves cringed at the snowballing level of interest.

I have seen this announcement already.

Three days ago, on the mountain of Montserrat, Edmond Kirsch had previewed an alleged "rough-cut" version for Köves, al-Fadl, and Valdespino. Now, Köves suspected, the world was about to see the same exact program.

Tonight everything will change, he thought sadly.

The phone rang and jolted Köves from his contemplation. He seized the handset.

Valdespino began without preamble. "Yehuda, I'm afraid I have some more bad news." In a somber voice, he conveyed a bizarre report that was now coming out of the United Arab Emirates.

Köves covered his mouth in horror. "Allamah al-Fadl . . . committed **suicide**?"

"That is what the authorities are speculating. He was found a short time ago, deep in the desert . . . as if he had simply walked out there to die." Valdespino paused. "All I can guess is that the strain of the last few days was too much for him."

Köves considered the possibility, feeling a wave of heartbreak and confusion. He too had been struggling with the implications of Kirsch's discovery, and yet the idea that Allamah al-Fadl would kill himself in despair seemed wholly unlikely.

"Something is wrong here," Köves declared. "I don't believe he would do such a thing."

Valdespino fell silent for a long time. "I'm glad you said that," he finally agreed. "I have to admit, I too find it quite difficult to accept that this was a suicide."

"Then . . . who could be responsible?"

"Anyone who wanted Edmond Kirsch's discovery to remain a secret," the bishop replied quickly. "Someone who believed, as we did, that his announcement was still weeks away."

"But Kirsch said nobody else **knew** about the discovery!" Köves argued. "Only you, Allamah al-Fadl, and myself."

"Maybe Kirsch lied about that too. But even if the three of us **are** the only ones he told, don't forget how desperately our friend Syed al-Fadl wanted to go public. It's possible that the **allamah** shared information about Kirsch's discovery with a colleague in the Emirates. And maybe that colleague believed, as

I do, that Kirsch's discovery would have dangerous repercussions."

"Implying what?" the rabbi demanded angrily. "That an associate of al-Fadl **killed** him in order to keep this quiet? That's ridiculous!"

"Rabbi," the bishop replied calmly, "I certainly don't **know** what happened. I'm only trying to imagine answers, as you are."

Köves exhaled. "I'm sorry. I'm still trying to absorb the news of Syed's death."

"As am I. And if Syed was murdered for what he knew, then we need to be careful ourselves. It is possible that you and I are also targeted."

Köves considered this. "Once the news goes public, we are irrelevant."

"True, but it is not **yet** public."

"Your Grace, the announcement is only minutes away. Every station is carrying it."

"Yes . . ." Valdespino let out a tired sigh. "It seems I'll have to accept that my prayers have gone unanswered."

Köves wondered if the bishop had literally prayed for God to intervene and change Kirsch's mind.

"Even when this goes public," Valdespino said, "we are not safe. I suspect Kirsch will take great pleasure in telling the world that he consulted with religious leaders three days ago. I'm now wondering if an appearance of ethical transparency was his true motive for calling the meeting. And if he mentions us by name, well, you and I will become the focus of intense scrutiny and perhaps even criticism from our own flocks, who might believe we should have taken action. I'm sorry, I'm just . . ." The bishop hesitated as if he had something more he wanted to say.

"What is it?" Köves pressed.

"We can discuss it later. I'll phone you again after we witness how Kirsch handles his presentation. Until then, please stay inside. Lock your doors. Speak to nobody. And be safe."

"You're worrying me, Antonio."

"I don't mean to," Valdespino replied. "All we can do is wait and see how the world reacts. This is in God's hands now."

CHAPTER 17

The breezy meadow inside the Guggenheim Museum had grown quiet after Edmond Kirsch's voice boomed down from the heavens. Hundreds of guests were reclined on blankets, gazing up into a dazzling sky of stars. Robert Langdon lay near the center of the field, caught up in the growing anticipation.

"Tonight, let us be children again," Kirsch's voice continued. "Let us lie out beneath the stars, with our minds wide open to all possibilities."

Langdon could feel the excitement rippling through the crowd.

"Tonight, let us be like the early explorers," Kirsch declared, "those who left everything behind and set out across vast oceans . . . those who first glimpsed a land that had never before been seen . . . those who fell to their knees in awestruck realization that the world was far greater than their philosophies had dared imagine. Their long-held beliefs about their world disintegrated in the face of new discovery. This will be our mind-set tonight."

Impressive, Langdon mused, curious if Edmond's narration was prerecorded or whether Kirsch himself was backstage somewhere reading from a script.

"My friends"—Edmond's voice resounded above them—"we have all gathered tonight to hear news of an important discovery. I ask your indulgence in allowing me to set the stage. Tonight, as with all shifts in human philosophy, it is critical we understand the historical context into which a moment like this is born."

Thunder rolled in the distance, right on cue. Langdon could feel the deep bass from the audio speakers rumbling in his gut.

"To help us get acclimated tonight," Edmond continued, "we are very fortunate to have with us a celebrated scholar—a legend in the world of symbols, codes, history, religion, and art. He is also a dear friend. Ladies and gentlemen, please welcome Harvard University professor Robert Langdon."

Langdon jolted up onto his elbows as the crowd clapped enthusiastically and the stars overhead dissolved into a wide-angle shot of a large auditorium packed with people. Onstage, Langdon paced back and forth in his Harris Tweed jacket before a rapt audience.

So this is the role that Edmond mentioned, he thought, settling back uneasily into the grass.

"Early humans," Langdon lectured on-screen, "had a relationship of wonder with their universe, especially with those phenomena they could not rationally understand. To solve these mysteries, they created a vast pantheon of gods and goddesses to explain anything that was beyond their understanding—

thunder, tides, earthquakes, volcanoes, infertility, plagues, even love."

This is surreal, Langdon thought, lying on his back and staring up at himself.

"For the early Greeks, the ebb and flow of the ocean was attributed to the shifting moods of Poseidon." On the ceiling, the image of Langdon dissolved, but his voice continued to narrate.

Images of pounding ocean surf materialized, shaking the entire room. Langdon watched in wonder as the crashing waves morphed into a desolate wind-whipped tundra of snowdrifts. From somewhere, a cold wind blew across the meadow.

"The seasonal change to winter," Langdon's voice-over continued, "was caused by the planet's sadness at Persephone's annual abduction into the under-world."

Now the air grew warm again, and from out of the frozen landscape, a mountain rose, climbing higher and higher, its peak erupting with sparks, smoke, and lava.

"For the Romans," Langdon narrated, "volcanoes were believed to be the home of Vulcan—blacksmith to the gods—who worked in a giant forge beneath the mountain, causing flames to spew out of his chimney."

Langdon smelled a passing whiff of sulfur, and was amazed at how ingeniously Edmond had transformed Langdon's lecture into a multisensory experience.

The rumbling of the volcano abruptly stopped.

In the silence, crickets began chirping again, and a warm grassy breeze blew across the meadow.

"The ancients invented countless gods," Langdon's voice explained, "to explain not only the mysteries of their planet, but also the mysteries of their own bodies."

Overhead, the twinkling constellations of stars reappeared, now superimposed with line drawings of the various gods they represented.

"Infertility was caused by falling out of favor with the goddess Juno. Love was the result of being targeted by Eros. Epidemics were explained as a punishment sent by Apollo."

New constellations now lit up along with images of new gods.

"If you've read my books," Langdon's voice continued, "you will have heard me use the term 'God of the Gaps.' That is to say, when the ancients experienced gaps in their understanding of the world around them, they filled those gaps with God."

The sky filled now with a massive collage of paintings and statues depicting dozens of ancient deities.

"Countless gods filled countless gaps," Langdon said. "And yet, over the centuries, scientific knowledge increased." A collage of mathematical and technical symbols flooded the sky overhead. "As the gaps in our understanding of the natural world gradually disappeared, our pantheon of gods began to shrink."

On the ceiling, the image of Poseidon came to the forefront.

"For example, when we learned that the tides were

caused by lunar cycles, Poseidon was no longer necessary, and we banished him as a foolish myth of an unenlightened time."

The image of Poseidon evaporated in a puff of smoke.

"As you know, the same fate befell all the gods—dying off, one by one, as they outlived their relevance to our evolving intellects."

Overhead, the images of gods began twinkling out, one by one—gods of thunder, earthquakes, plagues, and on and on.

As the number of images dwindled, Langdon added, "But make no mistake about it. These gods did not 'go gentle into that good night'; it is a messy process for a culture to abandon its deities. Spiritual beliefs are etched deeply on our psyches at a young age by those we love and trust most—our parents, our teachers, our religious leaders. Therefore, any religious shifts occur over generations, and not without great angst, and often bloodshed."

The sound of clattering swords and shouting now accompanied the gradual disappearance of the gods, whose images winked out one by one. Finally, the image of a single god remained—an iconic wizened face with a flowing white beard.

"Zeus . . . ," Langdon declared, his voice powerful. "The god of all gods. The most feared and revered of all the pagan deities. Zeus, more than any other god, resisted his own extinction, mounting a violent battle against the dying of his own light, precisely as had the earlier gods Zeus had replaced."

On the ceiling flashed images of Stonehenge, the Sumerian cuneiform tablets, and the Great Pyramids of Egypt. Then Zeus's bust returned.

"Zeus's followers were so resistant to giving up on their god that the conquering faith of Christianity had no choice but to adopt the face of Zeus as the face of their **new** God."

On the ceiling, the bearded bust of Zeus dissolved seamlessly into a fresco of an identical bearded face—that of the Christian God as depicted in Michelangelo's **Creation of Adam** on the ceiling of the Sistine Chapel.

"Today, we no longer believe in stories like those about Zeus—a boy raised by a goat and given power by one-eyed creatures called Cyclopes. For us, with the benefit of modern thinking, these tales have all been classified as mythology—quaint fictional stories that give us an entertaining glimpse into our superstitious past."

The ceiling now showed a photo of a dusty library shelf, where leather-bound tomes on ancient mythology languished in the dark beside books on nature worship, Baal, Inana, Osiris, and innumerable early theologies.

"Things are different now!" Langdon's deep voice declared. "We are the Moderns."

In the sky, fresh images appeared—crisp and sparkling photographs of space exploration . . . computer chips . . . a medical lab . . . a particle accelerator . . . soaring jets.

"We are an intellectually evolved and technologically skilled people. We do not believe in giant black-smiths working under volcanoes or in gods that control the tides or seasons. We are nothing like our ancient ancestors."

Or are we? Langdon whispered inwardly, mouthing along with the playback.

"Or are we?" Langdon intoned overhead. "We consider ourselves modern rational individuals, and yet our species' most widespread religion includes a whole host of magical claims—humans inexplicably rising from the dead, miraculous virgin births, vengeful gods that send plagues and floods, mystical promises of an afterlife in cloud-swept heavens or fiery hells."

As Langdon spoke, the ceiling flashed well-known Christian images of the Resurrection, the Virgin Mary, Noah's Ark, the parting of the Red Sea, heaven, and hell.

"So just for a moment," Langdon said, "let us imagine the reaction of humankind's future historians and anthropologists. With the benefit of perspective, will they look back on our religious beliefs and categorize them as the mythologies of an unenlightened time? Will they look at our gods as we look at Zeus? Will they collect our sacred scriptures and banish them to that dusty bookshelf of history?"

The question hung in the darkness for a long moment.

And then, abruptly, Edmond Kirsch's voice broke the silence.

"YES, Professor," the futurist boomed from on

high. "I believe **all** of that will happen. I believe future generations will ask themselves how a technologically advanced species like ours could **possibly** believe most of what our modern religions teach us."

Kirsch's voice grew stronger as a new series of images splashed across the ceiling—Adam and Eve, a woman shrouded in a burka, a Hindu firewalk.

"I believe future generations will look at our current traditions," Kirsch declared, "and conclude that we lived during an unenlightened time. As evidence, they will point to our beliefs that we were divinely created in a magical garden, or that our omnipotent Creator demands that women cover their heads, or that we risk burning our own bodies to honor our gods."

More images appeared—a fast-moving montage of photographs depicting religious ceremonies from around the world—from exorcisms and baptisms to body piercing and animal sacrifices. The slide show concluded with a deeply unsettling video of an Indian cleric dangling a tiny infant over the edge of a fifty-foot tower. Suddenly the cleric let go, and the child plummeted fifty feet, straight down into an outstretched blanket, which joyful villagers held like a fireman's net.

The Grishneshwar Temple drop, Langdon thought, recalling that it was believed by some to bring God's favor to a child.

Thankfully, the disturbing video came to an end.

In total darkness now, Kirsch's voice resonated overhead. "How can it be that the modern human mind is capable of precise logical analysis, and yet simultaneously permits us to accept religious beliefs that should crumble beneath even the slightest rational scrutiny?"

Overhead, the brilliant sky of stars returned.

"As it turns out," Edmond concluded, "the answer is quite simple."

The stars in the sky grew suddenly brighter and more substantial. Strands of connecting fiber appeared, running between the stars to form a seemingly infinite web of interconnected nodes.

Neurons, Langdon realized just as Edmond began to speak.

"The human brain," Edmond declared. "Why does it believe what it believes?"

Overhead, several nodes flashed, sending pulses of electricity through the fibers to other neurons.

"Like an organic computer," Edmond continued, "your brain has an operating system—a series of rules that organizes and defines all of the chaotic input that flows in all day long—language, a catchy tune, a siren, the taste of chocolate. As you can imagine, the stream of incoming information is frenetically diverse and relentless, and your brain must make sense of it all. In fact, it is the very programming of your brain's operating system that defines your perception of reality. Unfortunately, the joke's on us, because whoever wrote the program for the human brain had a twisted sense of humor. In other words, it's not our fault that we believe the crazy things we believe."

The synapses overhead sizzled, and familiar images

bubbled up from within the brain: astrological charts; Jesus walking on water; Scientology founder L. Ron Hubbard; the Egyptian god Osiris; Hinduism's four-armed elephant god, Ganesha; and a marble statue of the Virgin Mary weeping literal tears.

"And so as a programmer, I have to ask myself: What kind of bizarre operating system would create such illogical output? If we could look into the human mind and read its operating system, we would find something like this."

Four words appeared in giant text overhead.

DESPISE CHAOS.
CREATE ORDER.

"This is our brain's root program," Edmond said. "And therefore, this is exactly how humans are inclined. Against chaos. And in favor of order."

The room trembled suddenly with a cacophony of discordant piano notes, as if a child were banging on a keyboard. Langdon and those around him tensed involuntarily.

Edmond yelled over the clamor. "The sound of someone banging randomly on a piano is unbearable! And yet, if we take those same notes and arrange them in a better **order** . . ."

The haphazard din immediately halted, supplanted by the soothing melody of Debussy's "Clair de lune."

Langdon felt his muscles relax, and the tension in the room seemed to evaporate.

"Our brains rejoice," Edmond said. "Same notes.

Same instrument. But Debussy creates **order**. And it is this same rejoicing in the creation of order that prompts humans to assemble jigsaw puzzles or straighten paintings on a wall. Our predisposition to organization is written into our DNA, and so it should come as no surprise to us that the greatest invention the human mind has created is the computer—a machine designed specifically to help us create order out of chaos. In fact, the word in Spanish for computer is **ordenador**—quite literally, 'that which creates **order**.' "

The image of a massive supercomputer appeared, with a young man sitting at its lone terminal.

"Just imagine you have a powerful computer with access to all of the information in the world. You are permitted to ask this computer any questions you like. Probability suggests you would eventually ask one of two fundamental questions that have captivated humans since we first became self-aware."

The man typed into the terminal, and text appeared.

Where do we come from?
Where are we going?

"In other words," Edmond said, "you would ask about our **origin** and our **destiny**. And when you ask those questions, this would be the computer's response."

The terminal flashed:

INSUFFICIENT DATA FOR ACCURATE RESPONSE.

"Not very helpful," Kirsch said, "but at least it's honest."

Now an image of a human brain appeared.

"However, if you ask **this** little biological computer—Where do we come from?—something else happens."

From out of the brain flowed a stream of religious images—God reaching out to infuse Adam with life, Prometheus crafting a primordial human out of mud, Brahma creating humans from different parts of his own body, an African god parting the clouds and lowering two humans to earth, a Norse god fashioning a man and a woman out of driftwood.

"And now you ask," Edmond said, "Where are we going?"

More images flowed from the brain—pristine heavens, fiery hells, hieroglyphs of the Egyptian Book of the Dead, stone carvings of astral projections, Greek renderings of the Elysian Fields, Kabbalistic descriptions of **Gilgul neshamot**, diagrams of reincarnation from Buddhism and Hinduism, the Theosophical circles of the Summerland.

"For the human brain," Edmond explained, "**any** answer is better than no answer. We feel enormous discomfort when faced with 'insufficient data,' and so our brains **invent** the data—offering us, at the very least, the **illusion** of order—creating myriad philosophies, mythologies, and religions to reassure us that there is indeed an order and structure to the unseen world."

As the religious images continued to flow, Edmond spoke with increasing intensity.

"Where do we come from? Where are we going? These fundamental questions of human existence have always obsessed me, and for years I've dreamed of finding the answers." Edmond paused, his tone turning somber. "Tragically, on account of religious dogma, millions of people believe they already **know** the answers to these big questions. And because not every religion offers the **same** answers, entire cultures end up warring over whose answers are correct, and which version of God's story is the One True Story."

The screen overhead erupted with images of gunfire and exploding mortar shells—a violent montage of photos depicting religious wars, followed by images of sobbing refugees, displaced families, and civilian corpses.

"Since the beginning of religious history, our species has been caught in a never-ending cross fire—atheists, Christians, Muslims, Jews, Hindus, the faithful of all religions—and the only thing that unites us all is our deep longing for **peace**."

The thundering images of war vanished and were replaced by the silent sky of glimmering stars.

"Just imagine what would happen if we miraculously learned the answers to life's big questions . . . if we all suddenly glimpsed the **same** unmistakable proof and realized we had no choice but to open our arms and accept it . . . together, as a species."

The image of a priest appeared on the screen, his eyes closed in prayer.

"Spiritual inquiry has always been the realm of religion, which encourages us to have blind faith in its teachings, even when they make little logical sense."

A collage of images depicting fervent believers now appeared, all with eyes closed, singing, bowing, chanting, praying.

"But **faith**," Edmond declared, "by its very definition, requires placing your trust in something that is unseeable and indefinable, accepting as fact something for which there exists no empirical evidence. And so, understandably, we all end up placing our faith in different things because there is no **universal** truth." He paused. "However . . ."

The images on the ceiling dissolved into a single photograph, of a female student, eyes wide open and intense, staring down into a microscope.

"Science is the antithesis of faith," Kirsch continued. "Science, by definition, is the attempt to **find** physical proof for that which is unknown or not yet defined, and to reject superstition and misperception in favor of observable facts. When science offers an answer, that answer is universal. Humans do not go to war over it; they rally around it."

The screen now played historical footage from labs at NASA, CERN, and elsewhere—where scientists of various races all leaped up in shared joy and embraced as new pieces of information were unveiled.

"My friends," Edmond now whispered, "I have made many predictions in my life. And I am going to make another one tonight." He took a long slow breath. "The age of religion is drawing to a close," he said, "and the age of science is dawning."

A hush fell over the room.

"And tonight, mankind is about to make a quantum leap in that direction."

The words sent an unexpected chill through Langdon. Whatever this mysterious discovery turned out to be, Edmond was clearly setting the stage for a major showdown between himself and the religions of the world.

CHAPTER 18

🌐 ConspiracyNet.com

EDMOND KIRSCH UPDATE

A FUTURE WITHOUT RELIGION?

In a live stream currently reaching an unprecedented three million online viewers, futurist Edmond Kirsch appears poised to announce a scientific discovery that he hints will answer two of humanity's most enduring questions.

After an enticing prerecorded introduction by Harvard professor Robert Langdon, Edmond Kirsch has launched into a hard-hitting critique of religious belief in which he has just made the bold prediction, "The age of religion is drawing to a close."

So far tonight, the well-known atheist appears to be a bit more restrained and respectful than usual. For a collection of Kirsch's past antireligious rants, click here.

CHAPTER 19

Just outside the fabric wall of the domed theater, Admiral Ávila moved into position, hidden from view by a maze of scaffolding. By staying low, he had kept his shadow hidden and was now ensconced only inches from the outer skin of the wall near the front of the auditorium.

Silently, he reached into his pocket and removed the rosary beads.

Timing will be critical.

Inching his hands along the string of beads, he found the heavy metal crucifix, amused that the guards manning the metal detectors downstairs had let this object slip past them without a second glance.

Using a razor blade hidden in the stem of the crucifix, Admiral Ávila cut a six-inch vertical slit in the fabric wall. Gently, he parted the opening and peered through into another world—a wooded field where hundreds of guests were reclining on blankets and staring up at the stars.

They cannot imagine what is coming.

Ávila was pleased to see that the two Guardia Real agents had taken up positions on the opposite side of the field, near the right front corner of the auditorium. They stood at rigid attention, nestled discreetly in the shadows of some trees. In the dim light, they would be unable to see Ávila until it was too late.

Near the guards, the only other person standing was museum director Ambra Vidal, who seemed to be shifting uncomfortably as she watched Kirsch's presentation.

Contented with his position, Ávila closed the slit and refocused his attention on his crucifix. Like most crosses, it had two short arms that made up the transverse bar. On **this** cross, however, the arms were magnetically attached to the vertical stem and could be removed.

Ávila grabbed one of the cruciform's arms and forcefully bent it. The piece came off in his hand, and a small object fell out. Ávila did the same on the other side, leaving the crucifix armless—now just a rectangle of metal on a heavy chain.

He slid the beaded chain back into his pocket for safekeeping. **I'll need this shortly.** He now focused on the two small objects that had been hidden inside the arms of the cross.

Two short-range bullets.

Ávila reached behind him, fishing under his belt, pulling from the small of his back the object he had smuggled in beneath his suit jacket.

Several years had passed since an American kid named Cody Wilson had designed "The Liberator"—the first 3-D-printed polymer gun—and the technology had improved exponentially. The new ceramic and polymer firearms still did not have much power, but what they lacked in range, they more than made up for by being invisible to metal detectors.

All I need to do is get close.

If all went as planned, his current location would be perfect.

The Regent had somehow gained inside information about the precise layout and sequence of events this evening . . . and he had made it very clear how Ávila's mission should be carried out. The results would be brutal, but having now witnessed Edmond Kirsch's Godless preamble, Ávila felt confident that his sins here tonight would be forgiven.

Our enemies are waging war, the Regent had told him. **We must either kill or be killed.**

———

Standing against the far wall in the right front corner of the auditorium, Ambra Vidal hoped she did not look as uncomfortable as she felt.

Edmond told me this was a scientific program.

The American futurist had never been shy about his distaste for religion, but Ambra had never imagined tonight's presentation would display such hostility.

Edmond refused to let me preview it.

There would certainly be fallout with the museum board members, but Ambra's concerns right now were far more personal.

A couple of weeks ago, Ambra had confided in a very influential man about her involvement in tonight's event. The man had strongly urged her **not** to participate. He had warned of the dangers of blindly hosting a presentation without any knowledge of its content—especially when it was produced by the well-known iconoclast Edmond Kirsch.

He practically ordered me to cancel, she remembered. **But his self-righteous tone made me too incensed to listen.**

Now, as Ambra stood alone beneath the star-filled sky, she wondered if that man was sitting somewhere watching this live stream, his head in his hands.

Of course he is watching, she thought. **The real question is: Will he lash out?**

———

Inside Almudena Cathedral, Bishop Valdespino was sitting rigidly at his desk, eyes glued to his laptop. He had no doubt that everyone in the nearby Royal Palace was also watching this program, especially Prince Julián—the next in line for the throne of Spain.

The prince must be ready to explode.

Tonight, one of Spain's most respected museums was collaborating with a prominent American atheist to broadcast what religious pundits were already calling a "blasphemous, anti-Christian publicity stunt." Further fanning the flames of controversy, the museum director hosting tonight's event was one of Spain's newest and most visible celebrities— the spectacularly beautiful Ambra Vidal—a woman who for the past two months had dominated Spanish headlines and enjoyed the overnight adoration of an entire country. Incredibly, Ms. Vidal had chosen to put everything at risk by hosting tonight's full-scale attack on God.

Prince Julián will have no choice but to comment.

His impending role as Spain's sovereign Catholic figurehead would be only a small part of the challenge he would face in dealing with tonight's event. Of substantially greater concern was that just last month, Prince Julián had made a joyous declaration that launched Ambra Vidal into the national spotlight.

He had announced their engagement to be married.

CHAPTER 20

Robert Langdon was feeling uneasy about the direction of this evening's event.

Edmond's presentation was skating dangerously close to becoming a public denunciation of faith in general. Langdon wondered if Edmond had somehow forgotten that he was speaking not only to the group of agnostic scientists in this room, but also to the millions of people around the globe who were watching online.

Clearly, his presentation was devised to ignite controversy.

Langdon was troubled by his own appearance in the program, and although Edmond certainly meant the video as a tribute, Langdon had been an involuntary flash point for religious controversy in the past . . . and he preferred not to repeat the experience.

Kirsch, however, had mounted a premeditated audiovisual assault on religion, and Langdon was now starting to rethink his nonchalant dismissal of the voice mail Edmond had received from Bishop Valdespino.

Edmond's voice again filled the room, the visuals dissolving overhead into a collage of religious symbols from around the world. "I must admit," Edmond's voice declared, "I have had reservations about tonight's announcement, and particularly about how it might affect people of faith." He paused. "And so, three days ago, I did something a bit out of character for me. In an effort to show respect to religious viewpoints, and to gauge how my discovery might be received by people of various faiths, I quietly consulted with three prominent religious leaders—scholars of Islam, Christianity, and Judaism—and I shared with them my discovery."

Hushed murmurs echoed throughout the room.

"As I expected, all three men reacted with profound surprise, concern, and, yes, even anger, at what I revealed to them. And while their reactions were negative, I want to thank them for graciously meeting with me. I will do them the courtesy of not revealing their names, but I do want to address them directly tonight and thank them for not attempting to interfere with this presentation."

He paused. "God knows, they **could** have."

Langdon listened, amazed at how deftly Edmond was walking a thin line and covering his bases. Edmond's decision to meet with religious leaders suggested an open-mindedness, trust, and impartiality for which the futurist was not generally known. The meeting at Montserrat, Langdon now suspected, had been part research mission and part public relations maneuver.

A clever get-out-of-jail-free card, he thought.

"Historically," Edmond continued, "religious fervor has always suppressed scientific progress, and so tonight I implore religious leaders around the world to react with restraint and understanding to what I am about to say. Please, let us **not** repeat the bloody violence of history. Let us **not** make the mistakes of our past."

The images on the ceiling dissolved into a drawing of an ancient walled city—a perfectly circular metropolis located on the banks of a river that flowed through a desert.

Langdon recognized it at once as ancient Baghdad, its unusual circular construction fortified by three concentric walls topped by merlons and embrasures.

"In the eighth century," Edmond said, "the city of Baghdad rose to prominence as the greatest center of learning on earth, welcoming all religions, philosophies, and sciences to its universities and libraries. For five hundred years, the outpouring of scientific innovation that flowed from the city was like nothing the world had ever seen, and its influence is still felt today in modern culture."

Overhead, the sky of stars reappeared, this time many of the stars bearing names beside them: **Vega, Betelgeuse, Rigel, Algebar, Deneb, Acrab, Kitalpha.**

"Their names are all derived from Arabic," Edmond said. "To this day, more than two-thirds of the stars in the sky have names from that language because they were discovered by astronomers in the Arab world."

The sky rapidly filled with so many stars with Arabic names that the heavens were nearly blotted out. The names dissolved again, leaving only the expanse of the heavens.

"And, of course, if we want to **count** the stars . . ."

Roman numerals began appearing one by one beside the brightest stars.

I, II, III, IV, V . . .

The numbers stopped abruptly and disappeared.

"We don't use Roman numerals," Edmond said. "We use **Arabic** numerals."

The numbering now began again using the Arabic numbering system.

1, 2, 3, 4, 5 . . .

"You may also recognize **these** Islamic inventions," Edmond said. "And we all still use their Arabic names."

The word ALGEBRA floated across the sky, surrounded by a series of multivariable equations. Next came the word ALGORITHM with a diverse array of formulas. Then AZIMUTH with a diagram depicting angles on the earth's horizon. The flow accelerated . . . NADIR, ZENITH, ALCHEMY, CHEMISTRY, CIPHER, ELIXIR, ALCOHOL, ALKALINE, ZERO . . .

As the familiar Arabic words streamed by, Langdon thought how tragic it was that so many Americans pictured Baghdad simply as one of those many dusty, war-torn Middle Eastern cities in the news, never knowing it was once the very heart of human scientific progress.

"By the end of the eleventh century," Edmond said, "the greatest intellectual exploration and discovery on earth was taking place in and around Baghdad. Then, almost overnight, that changed. A brilliant scholar named Hamid al-Ghazali—now considered one of the most influential Muslims in history— wrote a series of persuasive texts questioning the logic of Plato and Aristotle and declaring mathematics to be 'the philosophy of the devil.' This began a confluence of events that undermined scientific thinking. The study of theology was made compulsory, and eventually the entire Islamic scientific movement collapsed."

The scientific words overhead evaporated, and were replaced by images of Islamic religious texts.

"Revelation replaced investigation. And to this day, the Islamic scientific world is still trying to recover." Edmond paused. "Of course, the Christian scientific world did not fare any better."

Paintings of the astronomers Copernicus, Galileo, and Bruno appeared on the ceiling.

"The Church's systematic murder, imprisonment, and denunciation of some of history's most brilliant scientific minds delayed human progress by at least a century. Fortunately, today, with our better understanding of the benefits of science, the Church has tempered its attacks . . ." Edmond sighed. "Or has it?"

A globe logo with a crucifix and serpent appeared with the text:

Madrid Declaration on Science & Life

"Right here in Spain, the World Federation of the Catholic Medical Associations recently declared war on genetic engineering, proclaiming that 'science lacks soul' and therefore should be restrained by the Church."

The globe logo now transformed into a different circle—a schematic blueprint for a massive particle accelerator.

"And this was Texas's Superconducting Super Collider—slated to be the largest particle collider in the world—with the potential for exploring the very moment of Creation. This machine was, ironically, positioned in the heart of America's Bible Belt."

The image dissolved into a massive ring-shaped cement structure stretching out across the Texas desert. The facility was only half built, covered with dust and dirt, apparently abandoned midway through its construction.

"America's super collider could have enormously advanced humankind's understanding of the universe, but the project was canceled due to cost overruns and political pressure from some startling sources."

A news clip showed a young televangelist waving the bestselling book **The God Particle** and angrily shouting, "We should be looking for God inside our hearts! Not inside of atoms! Spending billions on this absurd experiment is an embarrassment to the state of Texas and an affront to God!"

Edmond's voice returned. "These conflicts I've described—those in which religious superstition has trumped reason—are merely skirmishes in an ongoing war."

The ceiling blazed suddenly with a collage of violent images from modern society—picket lines outside genetic research labs, a priest setting himself on fire outside a Transhumanism conference, evangelicals shaking their fists and holding up the book of Genesis, a Jesus fish eating a Darwin fish, angry religious billboards condemning stem-cell research, gay rights, and abortion, along with equally angry billboards in response.

As Langdon lay in the darkness, he could feel his heart pounding. For a moment, he thought the grass beneath him was trembling, as if a subway were approaching. Then, as the vibrations grew stronger, he realized the earth was **indeed** shaking. Deep, rolling vibrations shuddered up through the grass beneath his back, and the entire dome trembled with a roar.

The roar, Langdon now recognized, was the sound of thundering river rapids, being broadcast through subwoofers beneath the turf. He felt a cold, damp mist swirling across his face and body, as if he were lying in the middle of a raging river.

"Do you hear that sound?" Edmond called over the booming rapids. "That is the inexorable swelling of the River of Scientific Knowledge!"

The water roared even louder now, and the mist felt wet on Langdon's cheeks.

"Since man first discovered fire," Edmond shouted, "this river has been gaining power. Every discovery became a tool with which we made new discoveries, each time adding a drop to this river. Today, we ride the crest of a tsunami, a deluge that rages forward with unstoppable force!"

The room trembled more violently still.

"**Where do we come from!**" Edmond yelled. "**Where are we going!** We have always been **destined** to find the answers! Our methods of inquiry have been evolving exponentially for millennia!"

The mist and wind whipped through the room now, and the thundering of the river reached an almost deafening pitch.

"Consider this!" Edmond declared. "It took early humans over a **million** years to progress from discovering fire to inventing the wheel. Then it took only a few **thousand** years to invent the printing press. Then it took only a couple **hundred** years to build a telescope. In the centuries that followed, in ever-shortening spans, we bounded from the steam engine, to gas-powered automobiles, to the Space Shuttle! And then, it took only two **decades** for us to start modifying our own DNA!

"We now measure scientific progress in **months**," Kirsch shouted, "advancing at a mind-boggling pace. It will not take long before today's fastest supercomputer will look like an abacus; today's most advanced surgical methods will seem barbaric; and today's energy sources will seem as quaint to us as using a candle to light a room!"

Edmond's voice and the roar of pounding water continued in the thundering darkness.

"The early Greeks had to look back **centuries** to study ancient culture, but we need look back only a single **generation** to find those who lived without the technologies we take for granted today. The timeline of human development is compressing; the space that separates 'ancient' and 'modern' is shrinking to nothing at all. And for this reason, I give you my word that the next few years in human development will be shocking, disruptive, and wholly unimaginable!"

Without warning, the thundering of the river stopped.

The sky of stars returned. So did the warm breeze and the crickets.

The guests in the room seemed to exhale in unison.

In the abrupt silence, Edmond's voice returned at a whisper.

"My friends," he said softly. "I know you are here because I promised you a discovery, and I thank you for indulging me in a bit of preamble. Now let us throw off the shackles of our past thinking. It is time for us to share in the thrill of discovery."

With those words, a low creeping fog rolled in from all sides, and the sky overhead began to glow with a predawn light, faintly illuminating the audience below.

Suddenly a spotlight blazed to life and swung dramatically to the back of the hall. Within moments, nearly all the guests were sitting up, craning backward through the fog in anticipation of seeing their host appear in the flesh. After a few seconds, however, the spotlight swung back to the front of the room.

The audience turned with it.

There, at the front of the room, smiling in the blaze of the spotlight, stood Edmond Kirsch. His hands were resting confidently on the sides of a podium that seconds ago had not been there. "Good evening, friends," the great showman said amiably as the fog began to lift.

Within seconds, people were on their feet, giving their host a wild standing ovation. Langdon joined them, unable to hold back his smile.

Leave it to Edmond to appear in a puff of smoke.

So far, tonight's presentation, despite being antagonistic toward religious faith, had been a tour de force—bold and unflinching—like the man himself. Langdon now understood why the world's growing population of freethinkers so idolized Edmond.

If nothing else, he speaks his mind in a way few others would dare.

When Edmond's face appeared on the screen overhead, Langdon noticed he looked far less pale than before, clearly having been professionally made up. Even so, Langdon could tell his friend was exhausted.

The applause continued so loudly that Langdon barely felt the vibration in his breast pocket. Instinctively, he reached in to grab his phone but suddenly realized it was off. Strangely, the vibration was coming from the other device in his pocket—the bone conduction headset—through which Winston now seemed to be talking very loudly.

Lousy timing.

Langdon fished the transceiver from his jacket pocket and fumbled it into place on his head. The instant the node touched his jawbone, Winston's accented voice materialized in Langdon's head.

"—fessor Langdon? Are you there? The phones are disabled. You're my only contact. Professor Langdon?!"

"Yes—Winston? I'm here," Langdon replied over the sound of applause around him.

"Thank goodness," Winston said. "Listen carefully. We may have a serious problem."

CHAPTER 21

As a man who had experienced countless moments of triumph on the world stage, Edmond Kirsch was eternally motivated by achievement, but he seldom felt total contentment. In this instant, however, standing at the podium receiving a wild ovation, Edmond permitted himself the thrilling joy of knowing he was about to change the world.

Sit down, my friends, he willed them. **The best is yet to come.**

As the fog dissipated, Edmond resisted the urge to glance skyward, where he knew a close-up of his own face was being projected across the ceiling and also to millions of people around the world.

This is a global moment, he thought proudly. **It transcends borders, class, and creeds.**

Edmond glanced to his left to give a nod of gratitude to Ambra Vidal, who was watching from the corner and had worked tirelessly with him to mount this spectacle. To his surprise, however, Ambra was not looking at him. Instead, she was staring into the crowd, her expression a mask of concern.

Something's wrong, Ambra thought, watching from the wings.

In the center of the room, a tall, elegantly dressed man was pushing his way through the crowd, waving his arms and heading in Ambra's direction.

That's Robert Langdon, she realized, recognizing the American professor from Kirsch's video.

Langdon was approaching fast, and both of Ambra's Guardia agents immediately stepped away from the wall, positioning themselves to intercept him.

What does he want?! Ambra sensed alarm in Langdon's expression.

She spun toward Edmond at the podium, wondering if he had noticed this commotion as well, but Edmond Kirsch was not looking at the audience. Eerily, he was staring directly at her.

Edmond! Something's wrong!

In that instant, an earsplitting crack echoed inside the dome, and Edmond's head jolted backward. Ambra watched in abject horror as a red crater blossomed in Edmond's forehead. His eyes rolled slightly backward, but his hands held firmly to the podium as his entire body went rigid. He teetered for an instant, his face a mask of confusion, and then, like a falling tree, his body tipped to one side and plummeted toward the floor, his blood-spattered head bouncing hard on the artificial turf as he hit the ground.

Before Ambra could even comprehend what she had witnessed, she felt herself being tackled to the ground by one of the Guardia agents.

Time stood still.

Then . . . pandemonium.

Illuminated by the glowing projection of Edmond's bloody corpse, a tidal wave of guests stampeded toward the back of the hall trying to escape any more gunfire.

As chaos broke out around him, Robert Langdon felt riveted in place, paralyzed by shock. Not far away, his friend lay crumpled on his side, still facing the audience, the bullet hole in his forehead gushing red. Cruelly, Edmond's lifeless face was being illuminated in the stark glare of the spotlight on the television camera, which sat unattended on a tripod, apparently still broadcasting a live feed to the domed ceiling and also to the world.

As if moving through a dream, Langdon felt himself running to the TV camera and wrenching it skyward, pivoting the lens away from Edmond. Then he turned and looked through the tangle of fleeing guests toward the podium and his fallen friend, knowing for certain that Edmond was gone.

My God . . . I tried to alert you, Edmond, but Winston's warning came too late.

Not far from Edmond's body, on the floor, Langdon saw a Guardia agent crouched protectively over Ambra Vidal. Langdon hurried directly toward her, but the agent reacted on instinct—launching himself upward and outward, taking three long strides and driving his body into Langdon's.

The guard's shoulder crashed squarely into Langdon's sternum, expelling every bit of air in Langdon's
lungs and sending a shock wave of pain through his
body as he sailed backward through the air, landing
hard on the artificial turf. Before he could even take
a breath, powerful hands flipped him onto his stomach, twisted his left arm behind his back, and pressed
an iron palm onto the back of his head, leaving Langdon totally immobilized with his left cheek squashed
into the turf.

"You **knew** about this before it happened," the
guard shouted. "How are you involved!"

———

Twenty yards away, Guardia Real agent Rafa Díaz
scrambled through throngs of fleeing guests and tried
to reach the spot on the sidewall where he had seen
the flash of a gunshot.

Ambra Vidal is safe, he assured himself, having seen
his partner pull her to the floor and cover her body
with his own. In addition, Díaz felt certain there was
nothing to be done for the victim. **Edmond Kirsch
was dead before he hit the ground.**

Eerily, Díaz noted, one of the guests appeared to
have had advance warning of the attack, rushing the
podium only an instant before the gunshot.

Whatever the reason, Díaz knew it could wait.

At the moment, he had only one task.

Apprehend the shooter.

As Díaz arrived at the site of the telltale flash, he found a slit in the fabric wall and plunged his hand through the opening, violently tearing the hole all the way down to the floor and clambering out of the dome into a maze of scaffolding.

To his left, the agent caught a glimpse of a figure—a tall man dressed in a white military uniform—sprinting toward the emergency exit at the far side of the enormous space. An instant later, the fleeing figure crashed through the door and disappeared.

Díaz gave pursuit, weaving through the electronics outside the dome and finally bursting through the door into a cement stairwell. He peered over the railing and saw the fugitive two floors below, spiraling downward at breakneck speed. Díaz raced after him, leaping five stairs at a time. Somewhere below, the exit door crashed open loudly and then slammed shut again.

He's exited the building!

When Díaz reached the ground floor, he sprinted to the exit—a pair of double doors with horizontal push bars—and threw all of his weight into them. The doors, rather than flying open like those upstairs, moved only an inch and then jammed to a stop. Díaz's body crashed into the wall of steel, and he landed in a heap, a searing pain erupting in his shoulder.

Shaken, he pulled himself up and tried the doors again.

They opened just far enough to allow him to glimpse the problem.

Strangely, the outer door handles had been bound shut by a loop of wire—a string of beads wrapped around the handles from the outside. Díaz's confusion deepened when he realized the pattern of the beads was quite familiar to him, as it would be to any good Spanish Catholic.

Is that a rosary?

Using all of his force, Díaz heaved his aching body into the doors again, but the string of beads refused to break. He stared again through the narrow opening, baffled both by the presence of a rosary and also by his inability to break it.

"¿Hola?" he shouted through the doors. "¡¿Hay alguien?!"

Silence.

Through the slit in the doors, Díaz could make out a high concrete wall and a deserted service alley. Chances were slim that anyone would be coming by to remove the loop. Seeing no other option, he grabbed his handgun from the holster beneath his blazer. He cocked the weapon and extended the barrel through the doorway slit. He pressed the muzzle into the string of rosary beads.

I'm firing a bullet into a holy rosary? Qué Dios me perdone.

The remaining pieces of the crucifix bobbed up and down before Díaz's eyes.

He pulled the trigger.

The gunshot thundered in the cement landing, and the doors flew open. The rosary shattered, and Díaz lurched forward, staggering out into the empty alley as rosary beads bounced across the pavement all around him.

The assassin in white was gone.

————

A hundred meters away, Admiral Luis Ávila sat in silence in the backseat of the black Renault that now accelerated away from the museum.

The tensile strength of the Vectran fiber on which Ávila had strung the rosary beads had done its job, delaying his pursuers just long enough.

And now I am gone.

As Ávila's car sped northwest along the meandering Nervión River and disappeared among the fast-moving cars on the Avenida Abandoibarra, Admiral Ávila finally permitted himself to exhale.

His mission tonight could not have gone any more smoothly.

In his mind, he began to hear the joyful strains of the Oriamendi hymn—its age-old lyrics once sung in bloody battle right here in Bilbao. **¡Por Dios, por la Patria y el Rey!** Ávila sang in his mind. **For God, for Country, and King!**

The battle cry had long since been forgotten . . . but the war had just begun.

CHAPTER 22

Madrid's Palacio Real is Europe's largest royal palace as well as one of its most stunning architectural fusions of Classical and Baroque styles. Built on the site of a ninth-century Moorish castle, the palace's three-story facade of columns spans the entire five-hundred-foot width of the sprawling Plaza de la Armería on which it sits. The interior is a mind-boggling labyrinth of 3,418 rooms that wind through almost a million and a half square feet of floor space. The salons, bedrooms, and hallways are adorned with a collection of priceless religious art, including masterpieces by Velázquez, Goya, and Rubens.

For generations, the palace had been the private residence of Spanish kings and queens. Now, however, it was used primarily for state functions, with the royal family taking residence in the more casual and secluded Palacio de la Zarzuela outside the city.

In recent months, however, Madrid's formal palace had become the permanent home for Crown Prince Julián—the forty-two-year-old future king of Spain—who had moved into the palace at the behest of his handlers, who wanted Julián to "be more visible to the country" during this somber period prior to his eventual coronation.

Prince Julián's father, the current king, had been bedridden for months with a terminal illness. As the fading king's mental faculties eroded, the palace had begun the slow transfer of power, preparing the prince to ascend to the throne once his father passed. With a shift in leadership now imminent, Spaniards had turned their eyes to Crown Prince Julián, with a single question on their minds:

What kind of ruler will he **turn out to be?**

Prince Julián had always been a discreet and cautious child, having borne the weight of his eventual sovereignty since boyhood. Julián's mother had died from preterm complications while carrying her second child, and the king, to the surprise of many, had chosen never to remarry, leaving Julián the lone successor to the Spanish throne.

An heir with no spare, the UK tabloids coldly called the prince.

Because Julián had matured under the wing of his deeply conservative father, most traditionalist Spaniards believed he would continue their kings' austere tradition of preserving the dignity of the Spanish crown through maintaining established conventions, celebrating ritual, and above all, remaining ever reverential to Spain's rich Catholic history.

For centuries, the legacy of the Catholic kings had served as Spain's moral center. In recent years, though, the country's bedrock of faith seemed to be dissolving, and Spain found herself locked in a violent tug-of-war between the very old and the very new.

A growing number of liberals were now flooding blogs and social media with rumors suggesting that once Julián was finally able to emerge from his father's shadow, he would reveal his true self—a bold, progressive, secular leader finally willing to follow the lead of so many European countries and abolish the monarchy entirely.

Julián's father had always been very active in his role as king, leaving Julián little room to participate in politics. The king openly stated that he believed Julián should enjoy his youth, and not until the prince was married and settled down did it make sense for him to engage in matters of state. And so Julián's first forty years—endlessly chronicled in the Spanish press—had been a life of private schools, horseback riding, ribbon cuttings, fund-raisers, and world travel. Despite having accomplished little of note in his life, Prince Julián was, without a doubt, Spain's most eligible bachelor.

Over the years, the handsome forty-two-year-old prince had publicly dated countless eligible women, and while he had a reputation for being a hopeless romantic, nobody had ever quite stolen his heart. In recent months, however, Julián had been spotted several times with a beautiful woman who, despite looking like a retired fashion model, was in fact the highly respected director of Bilbao's Guggenheim Museum.

The media immediately hailed Ambra Vidal as "a perfect match for a modern king." She was cultured, successful, and most importantly, not a scion of one of Spain's noble families. Ambra Vidal was of the people.

The prince apparently agreed with their assessment, and after only a very short courtship, Julián proposed to her—in a most unexpected and romantic way—and Ambra Vidal accepted.

In the weeks that followed, the press reported daily on Ambra Vidal, noting that she was turning out to be much more than a pretty face. She quickly revealed herself as a fiercely independent woman who, despite being the future queen consort of Spain, flatly refused to permit the Guardia Real to interfere with her daily schedule or let their agents provide her with protection at anything other than a major public event.

When the commander of the Guardia Real discreetly suggested Ambra start wearing clothing that was more conservative and less formfitting, Ambra made a public joke out of it, saying she had been reprimanded by the commander of the "Guardarropía Real"—the Royal Wardrobe.

The liberal magazines splashed her face all over their covers. "Ambra! Spain's Beautiful Future!" When she refused an interview, they hailed her as "independent"; when she granted an interview, they hailed her as "accessible."

Conservative magazines countered by deriding the brash new queen-to-be as a power-hungry opportunist who would be a dangerous influence on the future king. As evidence, they cited her blatant disregard for the prince's reputation.

Their initial concern centered on Ambra's habit of addressing Prince Julián by his first name alone, eschewing the traditional custom of referring to him as **Don** Julián or **su alteza.**

Their second concern, however, seemed far more serious. For the past several weeks, Ambra's work schedule had made her almost entirely unavailable to the prince, and yet she had been sighted repeatedly in Bilbao, having lunch near the museum with an outspoken atheist—American technologist Edmond Kirsch.

Despite Ambra's insistence that the lunches were simply planning meetings with one of the museum's major donors, sources inside the palace suggested that Julián's blood was beginning to boil.

Not that anyone could blame him.

The truth of the matter was that Julián's stunning fiancée—only weeks after their engagement—had been choosing to spend most of her time with another man.

angdon's face remained pressed hard into the turf. The weight of the agent on top of him was crushing.

Strangely, he felt nothing.

Langdon's emotions were scattered and numb—twisting layers of sadness, fear, and outrage. One of the world's most brilliant minds—a dear friend—had just been publicly executed in the most brutal manner. **He was killed only moments before he revealed the greatest discovery of his life.**

Langdon now realized that the tragic loss of human life was accompanied by a second loss—a scientific one.

Now the world may never know what Edmond found.

Langdon flushed with sudden anger, followed by steely determination.

I will do everything possible to find out who is responsible for this. I will honor your legacy, Edmond. I will find a way to share your discovery with the world.

"You **knew**," the guard's voice rasped, close in his ear. "You were heading for the podium like you **expected** something to happen."

"I . . . was . . . warned," Langdon managed, barely able to breathe.

"Warned by **whom**?!"

Langdon could feel his transducer headset twisted and askew on his cheek. "The headset on my face . . . it's an automated docent. Edmond Kirsch's computer warned me. It found an anomaly on the guest list—a retired admiral from the Spanish navy."

The guard's head was now close enough to Langdon's ear that he could hear the man's radio earpiece crackle to life. The voice in the transmission was breathless and urgent, and although Langdon's Spanish was spotty, he heard enough to decipher the bad news.

. . . **el asesino ha huido** . . .

The assassin had escaped.

. . . **salida bloqueada** . . .

An exit had been blocked.

. . . **uniforme militar blanco** . . .

As the words "military uniform" were spoken, the guard on top of Langdon eased off the pressure. "**¿Uniforme naval?**" he asked his partner. "**Blanco . . . ¿Como de almirante?**"

The response was affirmative.

A naval uniform, Langdon realized. **Winston was right.**

The guard released Langdon and got off him. "Roll over."

Langdon twisted painfully onto his back and propped himself up on his elbows. His head was spinning and his chest felt bruised.

"Don't move," the guard said.

Langdon had no intention of moving; the officer standing over him was about two hundred pounds of solid muscle and had already shown he was dead serious about his job.

"¡Inmediatamente!" the guard barked into his radio, continuing with an urgent request for support from local authorities and roadblocks around the museum.

. . . policía local . . . bloqueos de carretera . . .

From his position on the floor, Langdon could see Ambra Vidal, still on the ground near the sidewall. She tried to stand up, but faltered, collapsing on her hands and knees.

Somebody help her!

But the guard was now shouting across the dome, seeming to address nobody in particular. "¡Luces! ¡Y cobertura de móvil!" *I need lights and phone service!*

Langdon reached up and straightened the transducer headset on his face.

"Winston, are you there?"

The guard turned, eyeing Langdon strangely.

"I am here." Winston's voice was flat.

"Winston, Edmond was shot. We need the lights back on right away. We need cellular service restored. Can you control that? Or contact someone who can?"

Seconds later, the lights in the dome rose abruptly, dissolving the magical illusion of a moonlit meadow and illuminating a deserted expanse of artificial turf scattered with abandoned blankets.

The guard seemed startled by Langdon's apparent

power. After a moment, he reached down and pulled Langdon to his feet. The two men faced each other in the stark light.

The agent was tall, the same height as Langdon, with a shaved head and a muscular body that strained at his blue blazer. His face was pale with muted features that set off his sharp eyes, which, at the moment, were focused like lasers on Langdon.

"You were in the video tonight. You're Robert Langdon."

"Yes. Edmond Kirsch was my student and friend."

"I am Agent Fonseca with the Guardia Real," he announced in perfect English. "Tell me how you knew about the navy uniform."

Langdon turned toward Edmond's body, which lay motionless on the grass beside the podium. Ambra Vidal knelt beside the body along with two museum security guards and a staff paramedic, who had already abandoned efforts to revive him. Ambra gently covered the corpse with a blanket.

Clearly, Edmond was gone.

Langdon felt nauseated, unable to pull his eyes from his murdered friend.

"We can't help him," the guard snapped. "Tell me how you knew."

Langdon returned his eyes to the guard, whose tone left no room for misinterpretation. It was an order.

Langdon quickly relayed what Winston had told him—that the docent program had flagged one of the guest's headsets as having been abandoned, and when a human docent found the headset in a trash receptacle, they checked **which** guest had been assigned that headset, alarmed to find that he was a last-minute write-in on the guest list.

"Impossible." The guard's eyes narrowed. "The guest list was locked yesterday. Everyone underwent a background check."

"Not **this** man," Winston's voice announced in Langdon's headset. "I was concerned and ran the guest's name, only to find he was a former Spanish navy admiral, discharged for alcoholism and post-traumatic stress suffered in a terrorist attack in Seville five years ago."

Langdon relayed the information to the guard.

"The bombing of the cathedral?" The guard looked incredulous.

"Furthermore," Winston told Langdon, "I found the officer had no connection whatsoever to Mr. Kirsch, which concerned me, and so I contacted museum security to set off alarms, but without more conclusive information, they argued we should not ruin Edmond's event—especially while it was being live-streamed to the world. Knowing how hard Edmond worked on tonight's program, their logic made sense to me, and so I immediately contacted you, Robert, in hopes you could spot this man so I could discreetly guide a security team to him. I should have taken stronger action. I failed Edmond."

Langdon found it somewhat unnerving that Edmond's machine seemed to experience guilt. He glanced back toward Edmond's covered body and saw Ambra Vidal approaching.

Fonseca ignored her, still focused directly on Langdon. "The computer," he asked, "did it give you a **name** for the naval officer in question?"

Langdon nodded. "His name is Admiral Luis Ávila."

As he spoke the name, Ambra stopped short and stared at Langdon, a look of utter horror on her face.

Fonseca noted her reaction and immediately moved toward her. "Ms. Vidal? You're familiar with the name?"

Ambra seemed unable to reply. She lowered her gaze and stared at the floor as if she had just seen a ghost.

"Ms. Vidal," Fonseca repeated. "Admiral Luis Ávila—do you **know** this name?"

Ambra's shell-shocked expression left little doubt that she did indeed know the killer. After a stunned moment, she blinked twice and her dark eyes began to clear, as if she were emerging from a trance. "No . . . I don't know the name," she whispered, glancing at Langdon and then back at her security guard. "I was just . . . shocked to hear that the killer was an officer of the Spanish navy."

She's lying, Langdon sensed, puzzled as to why she would attempt to disguise her reaction. **I saw it. She recognized that man's name.**

"Who was in charge of the guest list?!" Fonseca demanded, taking another step toward Ambra. "Who added this man's name?"

Ambra's lips were trembling now. "I . . . I have no idea."

The guard's questions were interrupted by a sudden cacophony of cell phones ringing and beeping throughout the dome. Winston had apparently found a way to restore cell service, and one of the phones now ringing was in Fonseca's blazer pocket.

The Guardia agent reached for his phone and, seeing the caller ID, took a deep breath and answered. **"Ambra Vidal está a salvo,"** he announced.

Ambra Vidal is safe. Langdon moved his gaze to the distraught woman. She was already looking at him. When their eyes met, they held each other's stare for a long moment.

Then Langdon heard Winston's voice materialize in his headset.

"Professor," Winston whispered. "Ambra Vidal knows very well how Luis Ávila got onto the guest list. She added his name herself."

Langdon needed a moment to make sense of the information.

Ambra Vidal herself placed the killer on the guest list?

And now she's lying about it?!

Before Langdon could fully process this information, Fonseca was handing his cell phone to Ambra.

The agent said, **"Don Julián quiere hablar con usted."**

Ambra seemed almost to recoil from the phone. "Tell him I'm fine," she replied. "I'll call him in a little while."

The guard's expression was one of utter disbelief. He covered the phone and whispered to Ambra, **"Su alteza Don Julián, el príncipe, ha pedido—"**

"I don't care if he's the prince," she fired back. "If he's going to be my **husband,** he will have to learn to give me space when I need it. I just witnessed a murder, and I need a minute to myself! Tell him I'll call him shortly."

Fonseca stared at the woman, his eyes flashing an emotion that bordered on contempt. Then he turned and walked off to continue his call in private.

For Langdon, the bizarre exchange had solved one small mystery. **Ambra Vidal is engaged to Prince Julián of Spain?** This news explained the celebrity treatment she was receiving and also the presence of the Guardia Real, although it certainly did not explain her refusal to accept her fiancé's call. **The prince must be worried to death if he saw this on television.**

Almost instantly, Langdon was struck by a second, far darker revelation.

Oh my God . . . Ambra Vidal is connected to Madrid's Royal Palace.

The unexpected coincidence sent a chill through him as he recalled Edmond's threatening voice mail from Bishop Valdespino.

CHAPTER 24

Two hundred yards from Madrid's Royal Palace, inside Almudena Cathedral, Bishop Valdespino had momentarily stopped breathing. He still wore his ceremonial robes and was seated at his office laptop, riveted by the images being transmitted from Bilbao.

This will be a massive news story.

From all he could see, the global media were already going wild. The top news outlets were lining up authorities on science and religion to speculate about Kirsch's presentation, while everyone else offered hypotheses as to **who** murdered Edmond Kirsch and why. The media seemed to concur that, by all appearances, someone out there was deadly serious about making sure Kirsch's discovery never saw the light of day.

After a long moment of reflection, Valdespino took out his cell phone and placed a call.

Rabbi Köves answered on the first ring. "Terrible!" The rabbi's voice was nearly a shriek. "I was watching on television! We need to go to the authorities right now and tell them what we know!"

"Rabbi," Valdespino replied, his tone measured. "I

agree this is a horrifying turn of events. But before we take action, we need to think."

"There is nothing to think about!" Köves fired back. "Clearly, someone will stop at nothing to bury Kirsch's discovery, and they are butchers! I am convinced they also killed Syed. They must know who we are and will be coming for **us** next. You and I have a moral obligation to go to the authorities and tell them what Kirsch told us."

"A moral obligation?" Valdespino challenged. "It sounds more like you want to make the information public so nobody has a motive to silence you and me personally."

"Certainly, our safety is a consideration," the rabbi argued, "but we also have a moral obligation to the world. I realize this discovery will call into question some fundamental religious beliefs, but if there is one thing I have learned in my long life, it is that **faith** always survives, even in the face of great hardship. I believe faith will survive **this** too, even if we reveal Kirsch's findings."

"I hear you, my friend," the bishop finally said, maintaining as even a tone as possible. "I can hear the resolution in your voice, and I respect your thinking. I want you to know that I am open to discussion, and even to being swayed in my thinking. And yet, I beseech you, if we are going to unveil this discovery to the world, let us do it **together**. In the light of day. With honor. Not in desperation on the heels of this horrific assassination. Let us plan it, rehearse it, and frame the news properly."

Köves said nothing, but Valdespino could hear the old man breathing.

"Rabbi," the bishop continued, "at the moment, the single most pressing issue is our personal safety. We are dealing with killers, and if you make yourself too visible—for example, by going to the authorities or to a television station—it could end violently. I'm fearful for **you** in particular; I have protection here inside the palace complex, but you . . . you are alone in Budapest! Clearly, Kirsch's discovery is a life-and-death matter. Please let **me** arrange for your protection, Yehuda."

Köves fell silent a moment. "From **Madrid**? How can you possibly—"

"I have the security resources of the royal family at my disposal. Remain inside your home with your doors locked. I will request that two Guardia Real agents collect you and bring you to Madrid, where we can make sure you are safe in the palace complex and where you and I can sit down face-to-face and discuss how best to move forward."

"If I come to Madrid," the rabbi said tentatively, "what if you and I cannot agree on how to proceed?"

"We **will** agree," the bishop assured him. "I know I am old-fashioned, but I am also a realist, like yourself. Together we will find the best course of action. I have faith in **that**."

"And if your faith is misplaced?" Köves pressed.

Valdespino felt his stomach tighten, but he paused a moment, exhaled, and replied as calmly as he could. "Yehuda, if, in the end, you and I cannot find a way to proceed together, then we will part as friends, and we will each do what we feel is best. You have my word on that."

"Thank you," Köves replied. "On your word, I will come to Madrid."

"Good. In the meantime, lock your doors and speak to no one. Pack a bag, and I'll call you with details when I have them." Valdespino paused. "And have faith. I'll see you very soon."

Valdespino hung up, a feeling of dread in his heart; he suspected that continuing to control Köves would require more than a plea for rationality and prudence.

Köves is panicking . . . just like Syed.

Both of them fail to see the bigger picture.

Valdespino closed his laptop, tucked it under his arm, and made his way through the darkened sanctuary. Still wearing his ceremonial robes, he exited the cathedral into the cool night air and headed across the plaza toward the gleaming white facade of the Royal Palace.

Above the main entrance, Valdespino could see the Spanish coat of arms—a crest flanked by the Pillars of Hercules and the ancient motto PLUS ULTRA, meaning "further beyond." Some believed the phrase referred to Spain's centuries-long quest to expand the empire during its golden age. Others believed it reflected the country's long-held belief that a life in heaven existed beyond this one.

Either way, Valdespino sensed the motto was less relevant every day. As he eyed the Spanish flag flying high above the palace, he sighed sadly, his thoughts turning back to his ailing king.

I will miss him when he's gone.

I owe him so much.

For months now, the bishop had made daily visits to his beloved friend, who was bedridden in Palacio de la Zarzuela on the outskirts of the city. A few days ago, the king had summoned Valdespino to his bedside, a look of deep concern in his eyes.

"Antonio," the king had whispered, "I fear my son's engagement was . . . rushed."

Insane is a more accurate description, Valdespino thought.

Two months earlier, when the prince had confided in Valdespino that he intended to propose marriage to Ambra Vidal after knowing her only a very short time, the stupefied bishop had begged Julián to be more prudent. The prince had argued that he was in love and that his father deserved to see his only son married. Moreover, he said, if he and Ambra were to have a family, her age would require that they not wait too long.

Valdespino calmly smiled down at the king. "Yes, I agree. Don Julián's proposal took us all by surprise. But he only wanted to make you happy."

"His duty is to his **country**," the king said forcefully, "not to his father. And while Ms. Vidal is lovely, she is an unknown to us, an outsider. I question her motives in accepting Don Julián's proposal. It was far too hasty, and a woman of honor would have rejected him."

"You are correct," Valdespino replied, although in Ambra's defense, Don Julián had given her little choice.

The king gently reached out and took the bishop's bony hand in his own. "My friend, I don't know where the time has gone. You and I have grown old. I want to thank you. You have counseled me wisely through the years, through the loss of my wife, through the changes in our country, and I have benefited greatly from the strength of your conviction."

"Our friendship is an honor I will treasure forever."

The king smiled weakly. "Antonio, I know you have made sacrifices in order to stay with me. Rome, for one."

Valdespino shrugged. "Becoming a cardinal would have brought me no closer to God. My place has always been here with you."

"Your loyalty has been a blessing."

"And I will never forget the compassion you showed me all those years ago."

The king closed his eyes, gripping the bishop's hand tightly. "Antonio . . . I am concerned. My son will soon find himself at the helm of a massive ship, a ship he is not prepared to navigate. Please guide him. Be his polestar. Place your steady hand atop his on the rudder, especially in rough seas. Above all, when he goes off course, I beg you to help him find his way back . . . back to all that is pure."

"Amen," the bishop whispered. "I give you my word."

Now, in the cool night air, as Valdespino made his

way across the plaza, he raised his eyes to the heavens. **Your Majesty, please know that I am doing all I can to honor your final wishes.**

Valdespino took solace in knowing that the king was far too weak now to watch television. **If he had seen tonight's broadcast out of Bilbao, he would have died on the spot to witness what his beloved country had come to.**

To Valdespino's right, beyond the iron gates, all along Calle de Bailén, media trucks had gathered and were extending their satellite towers.

Vultures, Valdespino thought, the evening air whipping at his robes.

CHAPTER 25

There will be time to mourn, Langdon told himself, fighting back intense emotion. **Now is the time for action.**

Langdon had already asked Winston to search museum security feeds for any information that might be helpful in apprehending the shooter. Then he had quietly added that Winston should search for any connections between Bishop Valdespino and Ávila.

Agent Fonseca was returning now, still on the phone. "**Sí . . . sí**," he was saying. "**Claro. Inmediatemente.**" Fonseca ended the call and turned his attention to Ambra, who stood nearby, looking dazed.

"Ms. Vidal, we're leaving," Fonseca announced, his tone sharp. "Don Julián has demanded that we get you to safety inside the Royal Palace at once."

Ambra's body tensed visibly. "I'm not abandoning Edmond like that!" She motioned to the crumpled corpse beneath the blanket.

"Local authorities will be taking over this matter," Fonseca replied. "And the coroner is on his way. Mr. Kirsch will be handled respectfully and with great care. At the moment, we need to leave. We're afraid you're in danger."

"I am most certainly **not** in danger!" Ambra declared, stepping toward him. "An assassin just had the perfect opportunity to shoot me and did not. Clearly, he was after Edmond!"

"Ms. Vidal!" The veins in Fonseca's neck twitched. "The prince wants you in Madrid. He is worried about your safety."

"No," she fired back. "He's worried about the political fallout."

Fonseca exhaled a long, slow breath and lowered his voice. "Ms. Vidal, what happened tonight has been a terrible blow for Spain. It has also been a terrible blow for the prince. Your hosting tonight's event was an unfortunate decision."

Winston's voice spoke suddenly inside Langdon's head. "Professor? The museum's security team has been analyzing the building's external camera feeds. It appears they've found something."

Langdon listened and then waved a hand at Fonseca, interrupting the agent's reprimand of Ambra. "Sir, the computer said one of the museum's rooftop cameras got a partial photo of the top of the getaway car."

"Oh?" Fonseca looked surprised.

Langdon relayed the information as Winston gave it to him. "A black sedan leaving the service alley . . . license plates not legible from that high angle . . . an unusual sticker on the windshield."

"What sticker?" Fonseca demanded. "We can alert local authorities to look for it."

"The sticker," Winston replied in Langdon's head,

"is not one I recognized, but I compared its shape to all known symbols in the world, and I received a single match."

Langdon was amazed how fast Winston had been able to make all this happen.

"The match I received," Winston said, "was for an ancient alchemical symbol—**amalgamation**."

I beg your pardon? Langdon had expected the logo of a parking garage or a political organization. "The car sticker shows the symbol for . . . amalgamation?"

Fonseca looked on, clearly lost.

"There must be some mistake, Winston," Langdon said. "Why would anyone display the symbol for an alchemical process?"

"I don't know," Winston replied. "This is the only match I got, and I'm showing ninety-nine percent correspondence."

Langdon's eidetic memory quickly conjured the alchemical symbol for amalgamation.

$$\underset{\rule{0.5em}{0.4pt}}{\underset{\rule{0.5em}{0.4pt}}{\underset{\rule{0.5em}{0.4pt}}{\Psi}}}$$

"Winston, describe exactly what you see in the car window."

The computer replied immediately. "The symbol consists of one vertical line crossed by three transverse lines. On top of the vertical line sits an upward-facing arch."

Precisely. Langdon frowned. "The arch on top—does it have capstones?"

"Yes. A short horizontal line sits on top of each arm."

Okay then, it's amalgamation.

Langdon puzzled for a moment. "Winston, can you send us the photo from the security feed?"

"Of course."

"Send it to **my** phone," Fonseca demanded.

Langdon relayed the agent's cell-phone number to Winston, and a moment later, Fonseca's device pinged. They all gathered around the agent and looked at the grainy black-and-white photo. It was an overhead shot of a black sedan in a deserted service alley.

Sure enough, in the lower-left-hand corner of the windshield, Langdon could see a sticker displaying the exact symbol Winston had described.

Amalgamation. How bizarre.

Puzzled, Langdon reached over and used his fingertips to enlarge the photo on Fonseca's screen. Leaning in, he studied the more detailed image.

Immediately Langdon saw the problem. "It's not amalgamation," he announced.

Although the image was very **close** to what Winston had described, it was not exact. And in symbology, the difference between "close" and "exact" could be the difference between a Nazi swastika and a Buddhist symbol of prosperity.

This is why the human mind is sometimes better than a computer.

"It's not **one** sticker," Langdon declared. "It's **two** different stickers overlapping a bit. The sticker on the bottom is a special crucifix called the papal cross. It's very popular right now."

With the election of the most liberal pontiff in Vatican history, thousands of people around the globe were showing their support for the pope's new policies by displaying the triple cross, even in Langdon's hometown of Cambridge, Massachusetts.

"The U-shaped symbol on top," Langdon said, "is a separate sticker entirely."

"I now see you are correct," Winston said. "I'll find the phone number for the company."

Again Langdon was amazed by Winston's speed. **He's already identified the company logo?** "Excellent," Langdon said. "If we call them, they can track the car."

Fonseca looked bewildered. "Track the car! How?"

"This getaway car was **hired**," Langdon said, pointing to the stylized **U** on the windshield. "It's an Uber."

CHAPTER 26

From the look of wide-eyed disbelief on Fonseca's face, Langdon couldn't tell what surprised the agent more: the quick decryption of the windshield sticker, or Admiral Ávila's odd choice of getaway car.

He hired an Uber, Langdon thought, wondering if the move was brilliant or incredibly shortsighted.

Uber's ubiquitous "on-demand driver" service had taken the world by storm over the past few years. Via smartphone, anyone requiring a ride could instantly connect with a growing army of Uber drivers who made extra money by hiring out their own cars as improvised taxis. Only recently legalized in Spain, Uber required its Spanish drivers to display Uber's U logo on their windshields. Apparently, the driver of this Uber getaway car was also a fan of the new pope.

"Agent Fonseca," Langdon said. "Winston says he has taken the liberty of sending the image of the getaway car to local authorities to distribute at roadblocks."

Fonseca's mouth fell open, and Langdon sensed that this highly trained agent was not accustomed to playing catch-up. Fonseca seemed uncertain whether to thank Winston or tell him to mind his own damn business.

"And he is now dialing Uber's emergency number."

"No!" Fonseca commanded. "Give **me** the number. I'll call myself. Uber will be more likely to assist a senior member of the Royal Guard than they will a computer."

Langdon had to admit Fonseca was probably right. Besides, it seemed far better that the Guardia assist in the manhunt than waste their skills transporting Ambra to Madrid.

After getting the number from Winston, Fonseca dialed, and Langdon felt rising confidence that they might catch the assassin in a matter of minutes. Locating vehicles was at the heart of Uber's business; any customer with a smartphone could literally access the precise locations of every Uber driver on earth. All Fonseca would need to do was ask the company to locate the driver who had just picked up a passenger behind the Guggenheim Museum.

"¡**Hostia!**" Fonseca cursed. "**Automatizada.**" He stabbed at a number on his keypad and waited, apparently having reached an automated list of menu options. "Professor, once I get through to Uber and order a trace on the car, I will be handing this matter over to local authorities so Agent Díaz and I can transport you and Ms. Vidal to Madrid."

"Me?" Langdon replied, startled. "No, I can't possibly join you."

"You can and you **will**," Fonseca declared. "As will

your computer toy," he added, pointing to Langdon's headset.

"I'm sorry," Langdon responded, his tone hardening. "There is no way I can accompany you to Madrid."

"That's odd," Fonseca replied. "I thought you were a Harvard professor?"

Langdon gave him a puzzled look. "I am."

"Good," Fonseca snapped. "Then I assume you're smart enough to realize you have no choice."

With that, the agent stalked off, returning to his phone call.

Langdon watched him go. **What the hell?**

"Professor?" Ambra had stepped very close to Langdon and whispered behind him. "I need you to listen to me. It's very important."

Langdon turned, startled to see that Ambra's expression was one of profound fear. Her mute shock seemed to have passed, and her tone was desperate and clear.

"Professor," she said, "Edmond showed you enormous respect by featuring you in his presentation. For this reason, I'm going to trust you. I need to tell you something."

Langdon eyed her, uncertain.

"Edmond's murder was my fault," she whispered, her deep brown eyes welling with tears.

"I beg your pardon?"

Ambra glanced nervously at Fonseca, who was now out of earshot. "The guest list," she said, returning to

Langdon. "The last-minute addition. The name that was added?"

"Yes, Luis Ávila."

"I am the person who added that name," she confessed, her voice cracking. "It was **me**!"

Winston was correct . . . , Langdon thought, stunned.

"**I'm** the reason Edmond was murdered," she said, now on the verge of tears. "I let his killer inside this building."

"Hold on," Langdon said, placing a hand on her trembling shoulder. "Just talk to me. **Why** did you add his name?"

Ambra shot another anxious glance at Fonseca, who was still on the phone twenty yards away. "Professor, I received a last-minute request from someone I trust deeply. He asked me to add Admiral Ávila's name to the guest list as a personal favor. The request came only minutes before the doors opened, and I was busy, so I added the name without thinking. I mean, he was an admiral in the navy! How could I possibly have known?" She looked again at Edmond's body and covered her mouth with a slender hand. "And now . . ."

"Ambra," Langdon whispered. "**Who** was it that asked you to add Ávila's name?"

Ambra swallowed hard. "It was my fiancé . . . the crown prince of Spain. Don Julián."

Langdon stared at her in disbelief, trying to process her words. The director of the Guggenheim had just claimed that the crown prince of Spain had helped orchestrate the assassination of Edmond Kirsch. **That's impossible.**

"I'm sure the palace never expected I would learn the killer's identity," she said. "But now that I know . . . I fear I'm in danger."

Langdon put a hand on her shoulder. "You're perfectly safe here."

"No," she whispered forcefully, "there are things going on here that you don't understand. You and I need to get out. **Now!**"

"We can't run," Langdon countered. "We'll never—"

"Please listen to me," she urged. "I **know** how to help Edmond."

"I'm sorry?" Langdon sensed that she was still in shock. "Edmond can't **be** helped."

"Yes, he can," she insisted, her tone lucid. "But first, we'll need to get inside his home in Barcelona."

"What are you talking about?"

"Please just listen to me carefully. I know what Edmond would want us to do."

For the next fifteen seconds, Ambra Vidal spoke to Langdon in hushed tones. As she talked, Langdon felt his heart rate climbing. **My God,** he thought. **She's right. This changes everything.**

When she was finished, Ambra looked up at him defiantly. "Now do you see why we need to go?"

Langdon nodded without hesitation. "Winston," he said into his headset. "Did you hear what Ambra just told me?"

"I did, Professor."

"Were you already aware of this?"

"No."

Langdon considered his next words very carefully.
"Winston, I don't know if computers can feel loyalty
to their creators, but if you can, this is your moment
of truth. We could really use your help."

CHAPTER 27

As Langdon moved toward the podium, he kept one eye on Fonseca, who was still engrossed in his phone call to Uber. He watched as Ambra drifted casually toward the center of the dome, talking on her phone too—or at least **pretending** to talk—precisely as Langdon had suggested.

Tell Fonseca you decided to call Prince Julián.

As Langdon reached the podium, he reluctantly turned his gaze to the crumpled form on the floor. **Edmond.** Gently, Langdon pulled back the blanket that Ambra had placed over him. Edmond's once bright eyes were now two lifeless slits below a crimson hole in his forehead. Langdon shuddered at the gruesome image, his heart pounding with loss and rage.

For an instant, Langdon could still see the young mop-haired student who had entered his class full of hope and talent—and had gone on to accomplish so much in so brief a time. Horrifically, tonight, someone had murdered this astonishingly gifted human being, almost certainly in an attempt to bury his discovery forever.

And unless I take bold action, Langdon knew, **my student's greatest accomplishment will never see the light of day.**

Positioning himself so that the podium was partially blocking Fonseca's line of sight, Langdon knelt down beside Edmond's body, closed his eyes, folded his hands together, and assumed the reverent posture of prayer.

The irony of praying over an atheist almost caused Langdon to smile. **Edmond, I know that you of all people don't want anyone praying for you. Don't worry, my friend, I'm not actually here to pray.**

As he knelt over Edmond, Langdon fought a rising fear. **I assured you the bishop was harmless. If Valdespino turns out to be involved in this** . . . Langdon pushed it from his mind.

Once he felt certain that Fonseca had spotted him praying, Langdon very discreetly leaned forward and reached inside Edmond's leather jacket, removing his oversized turquoise phone.

He glanced quickly back toward Fonseca, who was still on the phone and now seemed less interested in Langdon than he did in Ambra, who appeared to be engrossed in her own phone call and was wandering farther and farther away from Fonseca.

Langdon returned his eyes to Edmond's phone and took a calming breath.

One more thing to do.

Gently, he reached down and lifted Edmond's right hand. It already felt cold. Bringing the phone to his fingertips, Langdon carefully pressed Edmond's index finger to the fingerprint recognition disk.

The phone clicked and unlocked.

Langdon quickly scrolled to the settings menu and

disabled the password protection feature. **Permanently unlocked.** Then he slipped the phone into his jacket pocket and covered Edmond's body again with the blanket.

———

Sirens wailed in the distance as Ambra stood alone in the center of the deserted auditorium and held her cell phone to her ear, pretending to be absorbed in a conversation, all the while very aware of Fonseca's eyes on her.

Hurry, Robert.

A minute ago, the American professor had leaped into action after Ambra had shared with him a recent conversation she'd had with Edmond Kirsch. Ambra told Langdon that two nights ago, in this very room, she and Edmond had been working late on the final details of the presentation when Edmond had taken a break to have his third spinach smoothie of the night. Ambra had noticed how exhausted he looked.

"I've got to say, Edmond," she had said, "I'm not sure this vegan diet is working for you. You're looking pale, and much too thin."

"Too thin?" He laughed. "Look who's talking."

"I'm not too thin!"

"Borderline." He winked playfully at her indignant expression. "As for my being pale, give me a break. I'm a computer geek who sits all day in the glow of an LCD screen."

"Well, you're addressing the entire world in two

days, and a little color would do you some good. Either get outside tomorrow or invent a computer screen that gives you a tan."

"That's not a bad idea," he said, looking impressed. "You should patent that." He laughed and then returned his attention to the matter at hand. "So you're clear on the order of events for Saturday night?"

Ambra nodded, glancing down at the script. "I welcome people inside the anteroom, and then we all move into this auditorium for your introductory video, after which you **magically** appear at the podium over there." She pointed to the front of the room. "And then, at the podium, you make your announcement."

"Perfect," Edmond said, "with one small addition." He grinned. "When I speak at the podium, it will be more of an **intermission**—a chance for me to welcome my guests in person, let everyone stretch their legs, and prep them a bit more before I begin the second half of the evening—a multimedia presentation that explains my discovery."

"So the announcement itself is prerecorded? Like the intro?"

"Yes, I just finished it a few days ago. We're a visual culture—multimedia presentations are always more gripping than some scientist talking at a podium."

"You're not exactly 'just some scientist,'" Ambra said, "but I agree. I can't wait to see it."

For security purposes, Ambra knew, Edmond's presentation was stored on his own private, trusted, off-site servers. Everything would be live-streamed into the museum projection system from a remote location.

"When we're ready for the second half," she asked, "who will activate the presentation, you or me?"

"I'll do it myself," he said, pulling out his phone. "With **this**." He held up his oversized smartphone with its turquoise Gaudí case. "It's all part of the show. I simply dial into my remote server on an encrypted connection . . ."

Edmond pressed a few buttons and the speaker-phone rang once and connected.

A computerized female voice answered. "GOOD EVE-NING, EDMOND. I AM AWAITING YOUR PASSWORD."

Edmond smiled. "And then, with the whole world watching, I simply type my password into my phone, and my discovery is live-streamed to our theater here and, simultaneously, to the entire world."

"Sounds dramatic," Ambra said, impressed. "Unless, of course, you forget your password."

"That **would** be awkward, yes."

"I trust you've written it down?" she said wryly.

"Blasphemy," Edmond said, laughing. "Computer scientists **never** write down passwords. Not to worry, though. Mine is only forty-seven characters long. I'm sure I won't forget it."

Ambra's eyes widened. "Forty-seven?! Edmond, you can't even remember the four-digit PIN for your museum security card! How are you going to remember **forty-seven** random characters?"

He laughed again at her alarm. "I don't have to;

they're not random." He lowered his voice. "My password is actually my favorite line of poetry."

Ambra felt confused. "You used a line of poetry as a password?"

"Why not? My favorite line of poetry has exactly forty-seven letters."

"Well, it doesn't sound very secure."

"No? You think you can guess my favorite line of poetry?"

"I didn't even know you **like** poetry."

"Exactly. Even if someone found out that my password was a line of poetry, and even if someone guessed the exact line out of millions of possibilities, they would still need to guess the very long phone number I use to dial into my secure server."

"The phone number you just speed-dialed from your phone?"

"Yes, a phone that has its own access PIN and never leaves my breast pocket."

Ambra threw up her hands, smiling playfully. "Okay, you're the boss," she said. "By the way, who's your favorite poet?"

"Nice try," he said, wagging his finger. "You'll have to wait till Saturday. The line of poetry I've chosen is **perfect**." He grinned. "It's about the future—a prophecy—and I'm happy to say it's already coming true."

Now, as her thoughts returned to the present, Ambra glanced over at Edmond's body, and realized with a rush of panic that she was no longer able to see Langdon.

Where is he?!

More alarming, she now spotted the second Guardia officer—Agent Díaz—climbing back into the dome through the slit cut into the fabric wall. Díaz scanned the dome and then began moving directly toward Ambra.

He'll never let me out of here!

Suddenly Langdon was beside her. He placed his hand gently on the small of her back and began guiding her away, the two of them moving briskly toward the far end of the dome—the passageway through which everyone had entered.

"Ms. Vidal!" Díaz shouted. "Where are you two going?!"

"We'll be right back," Langdon called, hastening her across the deserted expanse, moving in a direct line toward the rear of the room and the exit tunnel.

"Mr. Langdon!" It was Agent Fonseca's voice, shouting behind them. "You are forbidden to leave this room!"

Ambra felt Langdon's hand pressing more urgently on her back.

"Winston," Langdon whispered into his headset. "**Now!**"

A moment later, the entire dome went black.

CHAPTER 28

Agent Fonseca and his partner Díaz dashed through the darkened dome, illuminating the way with their cell-phone flashlights and plunging into the tunnel through which Langdon and Ambra had just disappeared.

Halfway up the tunnel, Fonseca found Ambra's phone lying on the carpeted floor. The sight of it stunned him.

Ambra jettisoned her phone?

The Guardia Real, with Ambra's permission, used a very simple tracking application to keep tabs on her location at all times. There could be only one explanation for her leaving her phone behind: she wanted to escape their protection.

The notion made Fonseca extremely nervous, although not nearly as nervous as the prospect of having to inform his boss that the future queen consort of Spain was now missing. The Guardia commander was obsessive and ruthless when it came to protecting the prince's interests. Tonight, the commander had personally tasked Fonseca with the simplest of directives: "Keep Ambra Vidal safe and out of trouble at all times."

I can't keep her safe if I don't know where she is!

The two agents hurried on to the end of the tunnel and arrived at the darkened anteroom, which now looked like a convention of ghosts—a host of pale shell-shocked faces illuminated by their cell-phone screens as they communicated to the outside world, relaying what they had just witnessed.

"Turn on the lights!" several people were shouting.

Fonseca's phone rang, and he answered.

"Agent Fonseca, this is museum security," said a young woman in terse Spanish. "We know you've lost lights up there. It appears to be a computer malfunction. We'll have power back momentarily."

"Are the internal security feeds still up?" Fonseca demanded, knowing the cameras were all equipped with night vision.

"They are, yes."

Fonseca scanned the darkened room. "Ambra Vidal just entered the anteroom outside the main theater. Can you see where she went?"

"One moment, please."

Fonseca waited, heart pounding with frustration. He had just received word that Uber was experiencing difficulties tracking the shooter's getaway car.

Could anything else go wrong tonight?

Fatefully, tonight was his first time on Ambra Vidal's detail. Normally, as a senior officer, Fonseca was assigned only to Prince Julián himself, and yet, this morning, his boss had taken him aside and informed him: "Tonight, Ms. Vidal will be hosting an event against the wishes of Prince Julián. You will accompany her and make sure she is safe."

Fonseca never imagined that the event Ambra was hosting would turn out to be an all-out assault on religion, culminating in a public assassination. He was still trying to digest Ambra's angry refusal to take Prince Julián's concerned call.

It all seemed inconceivable, and yet her bizarre behavior was only escalating. By all appearances, Ambra Vidal was attempting to ditch her security detail so she could run off with an American professor.

If Prince Julián hears about this . . .

"Agent Fonseca?" The security woman's voice returned. "We can see that Ms. Vidal and a male companion exited the anteroom. They moved down the catwalk and have just entered the gallery housing Louise Bourgeois's **Cells** exhibit. Out the door, turn right, second gallery on your right."

"Thank you! Keep tracking them!"

Fonseca and Díaz ran through the anteroom and exited onto the catwalk. Far below, they could see throngs of guests moving quickly across the lobby toward the exits.

To the right, exactly as security had promised, Fonseca saw the opening into a large gallery. The exhibit sign read: CELLS.

The gallery was expansive and housed a collection of strange cage-like enclosures, each containing its own amorphous white sculpture.

"Ms. Vidal!" Fonseca shouted. "Mr. Langdon!"

Receiving no answer, the two agents began searching.

Several rooms behind the Guardia agents, just out-side the domed auditorium, Langdon and Ambra were climbing carefully through a maze of scaffold-ing, making their way silently toward the dimly lit "Exit" sign in the distance.

Their actions of the last minute had been a blur—with Langdon and Winston collaborating on a quick deception.

On Langdon's cue, Winston had killed the lights and plunged the dome into darkness. Langdon had made a mental snapshot of the distance between their position and the tunnel exit, his estimate nearly per-fect. At the mouth of the tunnel, Ambra had hurled her phone into the darkened passageway. Then, rather than entering the passage, they turned around, remaining **inside** the dome, and doubled back along the inner wall, running their hands along the fabric until they found the torn opening through which the Guardia agent had exited in order to pursue Edmond's killer. After climbing through the opening in the fab-ric wall, the two made their way to the outer wall of the room and moved toward a lit sign that marked an emergency exit stairwell.

Langdon recalled with amazement how quickly Winston had arrived at the decision to help them. "If Edmond's announcement can be triggered by a password," Winston had said, "then we must find it and use it at once. My original directive was to assist

Edmond in every way possible to make his announcement tonight a success. Obviously, I have failed him in this, and anything I can do to help rectify that failure I will do."

Langdon was about to thank him, but Winston raced on without taking a breath. The words streamed from Winston at an inhumanly fast pace, like an audiobook playing at accelerated speed.

"If I myself were able to access Edmond's presentation," Winston said, "I would do so immediately, but as you heard, it is stored in a secure server off-site. It appears that all we require to release his discovery to the world is his customized phone and password. I have already searched all published texts for a forty-seven-letter line of poetry, and unfortunately the possibilities number in the hundreds of thousands, if not more, depending on how one breaks the stanzas. Furthermore, because Edmond's interfaces generally lock out users after a few failed password attempts, a brute-force attack will be impossible. This leaves us only one option: we must find his password in another manner. I am in agreement with Ms. Vidal that you must gain access immediately to Edmond's home in Barcelona. It seems logical that if he had a favorite line of poetry, he would possess a **book** containing that poem, and perhaps even have highlighted his favorite line in some manner. Therefore, I calculate a very high probability that Edmond would want you to go to Barcelona, find his password, and use it to release his announcement as planned. In addition, I have now determined that the last-minute phone call that requested Admiral Ávila be added to the guest list did indeed originate in the Royal Palace in Madrid, as Ms. Vidal stated. For this reason, I have decided that we cannot trust the Guardia Real agents, and I will devise a way to divert them and thereby facilitate your escape."

Incredibly, it appeared that Winston had found a way to do just that.

Langdon and Ambra had now reached the emergency exit, where Langdon quietly opened the door, ushered Ambra through, and closed the door behind them.

"Good," Winston's voice said, materializing again in Langdon's head. "You're in the stairwell."

"And the Guardia agents?" Langdon asked.

"Far away," Winston replied. "I am currently on the phone with them, posing as a museum security officer and misdirecting them to a gallery at the far end of the building."

Incredible, Langdon thought, giving Ambra a reassuring nod. "All good."

"Descend the stairs to ground level," Winston said, "and exit the museum. Also, please be advised, once you exit the building, your museum headset will no longer have a connection to me."

Damn. The thought had not occurred to Langdon. "Winston," he said hurriedly, "are you aware that Edmond shared his discovery with a number of religious leaders last week?"

"That seems unlikely," Winston replied, "although his introduction tonight certainly implied that his work has profound religious implications, so perhaps he wanted to discuss his findings with leaders in that field?"

"I think so, yes. One of them, however, was Bishop Valdespino from Madrid."

"Interesting. I see numerous references online stating that he is a very close adviser to the king of Spain."

"Yes, and one more thing," Langdon said. "Were you aware that Edmond received a threatening voice mail from Valdespino after their meeting?"

"I was not. It must have come on a private line."

"Edmond played it for me. Valdespino urged him to cancel his presentation and also warned that the clerics with whom Edmond had consulted were considering a preemptive announcement to undermine him somehow before he could go public." Langdon slowed on the stairs, permitting Ambra to press ahead. He lowered his voice. "Did you find any connection between Valdespino and Admiral Ávila?"

Winston paused a few seconds. "I found no direct connection, but that does not mean one does not exist. It just means it's not documented."

They approached the ground floor.

"Professor, if I may . . . ," Winston said. "Considering the events of this evening, logic would suggest that powerful forces are intent on burying Edmond's discovery. Bearing in mind that his presentation named **you** as the person whose insight helped inspire his breakthrough, Edmond's enemies might consider you a dangerous loose end."

Langdon had never considered the possibility and felt a sudden flash of danger as he reached the ground floor. Ambra was already there, heaving open the metal door.

"When you exit," Winston said, "you will find yourselves in an alley. Move to your left around the building and proceed down to the river. From there I will facilitate your transportation to the location we discussed."

BIO-EC346, Langdon thought, having urged Winston to take them there. **The place where Edmond and I were supposed to meet after the event.** Langdon had finally deciphered the code, realizing that BIO-EC346 was not some secret science club at all. It was something far more mundane. Nonetheless, he hoped it would be the key to their escape from Bilbao.

If we can make it there undetected . . . , he thought, knowing there would soon be roadblocks everywhere. **We need to move quickly.**

As Langdon and Ambra stepped over the threshold into the cool night air, Langdon was startled to see what looked like rosary beads scattered across the ground. He didn't have time to wonder why. Winston was still talking.

"Once you reach the river," his voice commanded, "go to the walkway beneath La Salve Bridge and wait until—"

Langdon's headset blared suddenly with deafening static.

"Winston?" Langdon shouted. "Wait until— **what**?!"

But Winston was gone, and the metal door had just slammed shut behind them.

CHAPTER 29

Miles to the south, on the outskirts of Bilbao, an Uber sedan raced south along Highway AP-68 en route toward Madrid. In the backseat, Admiral Ávila had removed his white jacket and naval cap, enjoying a sense of freedom as he sat back and reflected on his simple escape.

Precisely as the Regent promised.

Almost immediately after entering the Uber vehicle, Ávila had drawn his pistol and pressed it against the head of the trembling driver. At Ávila's command, the driver had tossed his smartphone out the window, effectively severing his vehicle's only connection with the company's headquarters.

Then Ávila had gone through the man's wallet, memorizing his home address and the names of his wife and two children. **Do as I say,** Ávila had told him, **or your family will die.** The man's knuckles had turned white on the steering wheel, and Ávila knew he had a devoted driver for the night.

I am invisible now, Ávila thought as police cars raced by in the opposite direction, sirens wailing.

As the car sped south, Ávila settled in for the long ride, savoring the afterglow of his adrenaline-fueled high. **I have served the cause well,** he thought. He glanced at the tattoo on his palm, realizing that the

protection it provided had been an unnecessary precaution. **At least for now.**

Feeling confident that his terrified Uber driver
would obey orders, Ávila lowered his pistol. As the
car rushed toward Madrid, he gazed once again at
the two stickers on the car's windshield.

What are the chances? he thought.

The first sticker was to be expected—the Uber
logo. The second sticker, however, could only have
been a sign from above.

The papal cross. The symbol was everywhere these
days—Catholics around Europe showing solidarity
with the new pope, praising his sweeping liberaliza-
tion and modernization of the Church.

Ironically, Ávila's realization that his driver was
a devotee of the liberal pope had made pulling a
gun on the man an almost pleasurable experience.
Ávila was appalled at how the lazy masses adored
this new pontiff, who was permitting the followers
of Christ to pick and choose from a buffet table of
God's laws, deciding which rules were palatable to
them and which were not. Almost overnight, inside
the Vatican, questions of birth control, gay marriage,
female priests, and other liberal causes were all on the
table for discussion. Two thousand years of tradition
seemed to be evaporating in the blink of an eye.

**Fortunately, there are still those who fight for the
old ways.**

Ávila heard strains of the Oriamendi hymn playing
in his mind.

And I am honored to serve them.

CHAPTER 30

S pain's oldest and most elite security force—the
Guardia Real—has a fierce tradition that dates
back to medieval times. Guardia agents consider
it their sworn duty before God to ensure the safety
of the royal family, to protect royal property, and to
defend royal honor.

Commander Diego Garza—overseer of the Guardia's nearly two thousand troops—was a stunted and
weedy sixty-year-old with a swarthy complexion, tiny
eyes, and thinning black hair worn slicked back over
a mottled scalp. His rodent-like features and diminu-
tive stature made Garza nearly invisible in a crowd,
which helped camouflage his enormous influence
within the palace walls.

Garza had learned long ago that true power stemmed
not from physical strength but from political leverage. His command of the Guardia Real troops certainly gave him clout, but it was his prescient political
savvy that had established Garza as the palace's go-to
man on a wide array of matters, both personal and
professional.

A reliable curator of secrets, Garza had never once
betrayed a confidence. His reputation for steadfast
discretion, along with an uncanny ability to solve del-

icate problems, had made him indispensable to the king. Now, however, Garza and others in the palace faced an uncertain future as Spain's aging sovereign lived out his final days at the Palacio de la Zarzuela.

For more than four decades, the king had ruled a turbulent country as it established a parliamentary monarchy following thirty-six years of bloody dictatorship under the ultraconservative general Francisco Franco. Since Franco's death in 1975, the king had tried to work hand in hand with the government to cement Spain's democratic process, inching the country ever so slowly back to the left.

For the youth, the changes were too slow.

For the aging traditionalists, the changes were blasphemous.

Many members of Spain's establishment still fiercely defended Franco's conservative doctrine, especially his view of Catholicism as a "state religion" and moral backbone of the nation. A rapidly growing number of Spain's youth, however, stood in stark opposition to this view—brazenly denouncing the hypocrisy of organized religion and lobbying for greater separation of church and state.

Now, with a middle-aged prince poised to ascend to the throne, nobody was certain in which direction the new king would lean. For decades, Prince Julián had done an admirable job of performing his bland ceremonial duties, deferring to his father on matters of politics and never once tipping his hand as to his personal beliefs. While most pundits suspected he would be far more liberal than his father, there was really no way to know for sure.

Tonight, however, that veil would be lifted.

In light of the shocking events in Bilbao, and the king's inability to speak publicly due to his health, the prince would have no choice but to weigh in on the evening's troubling events.

Several high-ranking government officials, including the country's president, had already condemned the murder, shrewdly deferring further comment until the Royal Palace had made a statement—thereby depositing the entire mess in Prince Julián's lap. Garza was not surprised; the involvement of the future queen, Ambra Vidal, made this a political grenade that nobody felt like touching.

Prince Julián will be tested tonight, Garza thought, hurrying up the grand staircase toward the palace's royal apartments. **He is going to need guidance, and with his father incapacitated, that guidance must come from me.**

Garza strode the length of the **residencia** hallway and finally reached the prince's door. He took a deep breath and knocked.

Odd, he thought, getting no answer. **I know he's in there.** According to Agent Fonseca in Bilbao, Prince Julián had just called from the apartment and was trying to reach Ambra Vidal to make sure she was safe, which, thank heavens, she was.

Garza knocked again, feeling rising concern when he again got no answer.

Hastily, he unlocked the door. "Don Julián?" he called as he stepped inside.

The apartment was dark except for the flickering light of the television in the living room. "Hello?"

Garza hurried in and found Prince Julián standing alone in the darkness, a motionless silhouette facing the bay window. He was still impeccably dressed in the tailored suit he had worn to his meetings this evening, having not yet so much as loosened his necktie.

Watching in silence, Garza felt unsettled by his prince's trancelike state. **This crisis appears to have left him stunned.**

Garza cleared his throat, making his presence known.

When the prince finally spoke, he did so without turning from the window. "When I called Ambra," he said, "she refused to speak to me." Julián's tone sounded more perplexed than hurt.

Garza was unsure how to reply. Given the night's events, it seemed incomprehensible that Julián's thoughts were on his relationship with Ambra—an engagement that had been strained right from its poorly conceived beginnings.

"I imagine Ms. Vidal is still in shock," Garza offered quietly. "Agent Fonseca will deliver her to you later this evening. You can speak then. And let me just add how relieved I am, knowing that she is safe."

Prince Julián nodded absently.

"The shooter is being tracked," Garza said, attempting to change the subject. "Fonseca assures me they will have the terrorist in custody soon." He used the word "terrorist" intentionally in hopes of snapping the prince out of his daze.

But the prince only gave another blank nod.

"The president has denounced the assassination," Garza continued, "but the government does hope that **you** will further comment . . . considering Ambra's involvement with the event." Garza paused. "I realize the situation is awkward, given your engagement, but I would suggest you simply say that one of the things you most admire in your fiancée is her independence, and while you know she doesn't share the political views of Edmond Kirsch, you applaud her standing by her commitments as director of the museum. I'd be happy to write something for you, if you like? We should make a statement in time for the morning news cycle."

Julián's gaze never left the window. "I'd like to get Bishop Valdespino's input on any statement we make."

Garza clenched his jaw and swallowed his disapproval. Post-Franco Spain was an **estado aconfesional,** meaning it no longer had a state religion, and the Church was not supposed to have any involvement in political matters. Valdespino's close friendship with the king, however, had always afforded the bishop an unusual amount of influence in the daily affairs of the palace. Unfortunately, Valdespino's hard-line politics and religious zeal left little room for the diplomacy and tact that were required to handle tonight's crisis.

We need nuance and finesse—not dogma and fireworks!

Garza had learned long ago that Valdespino's pious exterior concealed a very simple truth: Bishop Valdespino always served his own needs before those of God. Until recently, it was something Garza could ignore, but now, with the balance of power shifting in the palace, the sight of the bishop sidling up to Julián was a cause for significant concern.

Valdespino is too close to the prince as it is.

Garza knew that Julián had always considered the bishop "family"—more of a trusted uncle than a religious authority. As the king's closest confidant, Valdespino had been tasked with overseeing young Julián's moral development, and he had done so with dedication and fervor—vetting all of Julián's tutors, introducing him to the doctrines of faith, and even advising him on matters of the heart. Now, years later, even when Julián and Valdespino did not see eye to eye, their bond remained blood-deep.

"Don Julián," Garza said in a calm tone, "I feel strongly that tonight's situation is something you and I should handle alone."

"Is it?" declared a man's voice in the darkness behind him.

Garza spun around, stunned to see a robed ghost seated in the shadows.

Valdespino.

"I must say, Commander," Valdespino hissed, "I figured that **you** of all people would realize how much you need me tonight."

"This is a **political** situation," Garza stated firmly, "not a religious one."

Valdespino scoffed. "The fact that you can make such a statement tells me that I have grossly overestimated your political acumen. If you would like my opinion, there is only one appropriate response to this crisis. We must immediately assure the nation that Prince Julián is a deeply religious man, and that Spain's future king is a devout Catholic."

"I agree . . . and we will include a mention of Don Julián's faith in any statement he makes."

"And when Prince Julián appears before the press, he will need me at his side, with my hand on his shoulder—a potent symbol of the strength of his bond with the Church. That single image will do more to reassure the nation than any words you can write."

Garza bristled.

"The world has just witnessed a brutal live assassination on Spanish soil," Valdespino declared. "In times of violence, nothing comforts like the hand of God."

CHAPTER 31

T he Széchenyi Chain Bridge—one of eight bridges in Budapest—spans more than a thousand feet across the Danube. An emblem of the link between East and West, the bridge is considered one of the most beautiful in the world.

What am I doing? wondered Rabbi Köves, peering over the railing into the swirling black waters below. **The bishop advised me to stay at home.**

Köves knew he shouldn't have ventured out, and yet whenever he felt unsettled, something about the bridge had always pulled at him. For years, he'd walked here at night to reflect while he admired the timeless view. To the east, in Pest, the illuminated facade of Gresham Palace stood proudly against the bell towers of Szent István Bazilika. To the west, in Buda, high atop Castle Hill, rose the fortified walls of Buda Castle. And northward, on the banks of the Danube, stretched the elegant spires of the parliament building, the largest in all of Hungary.

Köves suspected, however, that it was not the view that continually brought him to Chain Bridge. It was something else entirely.

The padlocks.

All along the bridge's railings and suspension wires

hung hundreds of padlocks—each bearing a different pair of initials, each locked forever to the bridge.

Tradition was that two lovers would come together on this bridge, inscribe their initials on a padlock, secure the lock to the bridge, and then throw the key into the deep water, where it would be lost forever—a symbol of their eternal connection.

The simplest of promises, Köves thought, touching one of the dangling locks. **My soul is locked to your soul, forever.**

Whenever Köves needed to be reminded that boundless love existed in the world, he would come to see these locks. Tonight felt like one of those nights. As he stared down into the swirling water, he felt as if the world were suddenly moving far too fast for him. **Perhaps I don't belong here anymore.**

What had once been life's quiet moments of solitary reflection—a few minutes alone on a bus, or walking to work, or waiting for an appointment—now felt unbearable, and people impulsively reached for their phones, their earbuds, and their games, unable to fight the addictive pull of technology. The miracles of the past were fading away, whitewashed by a ceaseless hunger for all-that-was-new.

Now, as Yehuda Köves stared down into the water, he felt increasingly weary. His vision seemed to blur, and he began to see eerie, amorphous shapes moving beneath the water's surface. The river suddenly looked like a churning stew of creatures coming to life in the deep.

"**A víz él,**" a voice said behind him. "The water is alive."

The rabbi turned and saw a young boy with curly hair and hopeful eyes. The boy reminded Yehuda of himself in younger years.

"I'm sorry?" the rabbi said.

The boy opened his mouth to speak, but instead of language, an electronic buzzing noise issued from his throat and a blinding white light flashed from his eyes.

Rabbi Köves awoke with a gasp, sitting bolt upright in his chair.

"**Oy gevalt!**"

The phone on his desk was blaring, and the old rabbi spun around, scanning the study of his **házikó** in a panic. Thankfully, he was entirely alone. He could feel his heart pounding.

Such a strange dream, he thought, trying to catch his breath.

The phone was insistent, and Köves knew that at this hour it had to be Bishop Valdespino, calling to provide him with an update on his transportation to Madrid.

"Bishop Valdespino," the rabbi answered, still feeling disoriented. "What is the news?"

"Rabbi Yehuda Köves?" an unfamiliar voice inquired. "You don't know me, and I don't want to frighten you, but I need you to listen to me carefully."

Köves was suddenly wide-awake.

The voice was female but was masked somehow, sounding distorted. The caller spoke in rushed English with a slight Spanish accent. "I'm filtering my voice for privacy. I apologize for that, but in a moment, you will understand why."

"Who is this?!" Köves demanded.

"I am a watchdog—someone who does not appreciate those who try to conceal the truth from the public."

"I . . . don't understand."

"Rabbi Köves, I know you attended a private meeting with Edmond Kirsch, Bishop Valdespino, and Allamah Syed al-Fadl three days ago at the Montserrat monastery."

How does she know this?!

"In addition, I know Edmond Kirsch provided the three of you with extensive information about his recent scientific discovery . . . and that you are now involved in a conspiracy to conceal it."

"What?!"

"If you do not listen to me very carefully, then I predict you will be dead by morning, eliminated by the long arm of Bishop Valdespino." The caller paused. "Just like Edmond Kirsch and your friend Syed al-Fadl."

CHAPTER 32

Bilbao's La Salve Bridge crosses the Nervión River in such close proximity to the Guggenheim Museum that the two structures often have the appearance of being fused into one. Immediately recognizable by its unique central support—a towering, bright red strut shaped like a giant letter H—the bridge takes the name "La Salve" from folkloric tales of sailors returning from sea along this river and saying prayers of gratitude for their safe arrival home.

After exiting the rear of the building, Langdon and Ambra had quickly covered the short distance between the museum and the riverbank and were now waiting, as Winston had requested, on a walkway in the shadows directly beneath the bridge.

Waiting for what? Langdon wondered, uncertain.

As they lingered in the darkness, he could see Ambra's slender frame shivering beneath her sleek evening dress. He removed his tails jacket and placed it around her shoulders, smoothing the fabric down her arms.

Without warning, she suddenly turned and faced him.

For an instant, Langdon feared he had overstepped

a boundary, but Ambra's expression was not one of displeasure, but rather one of gratitude.

"Thank you," she whispered, gazing up at him. "Thank you for helping me."

With her eyes locked on his, Ambra Vidal reached out, took Langdon's hands, and clasped them in her own, as if she were trying to absorb any warmth or comfort he could offer.

Then, just as quickly, she released them. "Sorry," she whispered. "**Conducta impropia**, as my mother would say."

Langdon gave her a reassuring grin. "Extenuating circumstances, as **my** mother would say."

She managed a smile, but it was short-lived. "I feel absolutely ill," she said, glancing away. "Tonight, what happened to Edmond . . ."

"It's appalling . . . dreadful," Langdon said, knowing he was still too much in shock to express his emotions fully.

Ambra was staring at the water. "And to think that my fiancé, Don Julián, is involved . . ."

Langdon could hear the betrayal in her voice and was uncertain how to reply. "I realize how it appears," he said, treading lightly on this delicate ground, "but we really don't know that for sure. It's possible Prince Julián had no advance notice about the killing tonight. The assassin could have been acting alone, or working for someone other than the prince. It makes little sense that the future king of Spain would orchestrate the public assassination of a civilian—especially one traceable directly back to him."

"It's only traceable because **Winston** figured out that Ávila was a late addition to the guest list. Maybe Julián thought nobody would ever figure out who pulled the trigger."

Langdon had to admit she had a point.

"I never should have discussed Edmond's presentation with Julián," Ambra said, turning back to him. "He was urging me not to participate, and so I tried to reassure him that my involvement would be minimal, that it was all nothing but a video screening. I think I even told Julián that Edmond was launching his discovery from a smartphone." She paused. "Which means, if they see that we took Edmond's phone, they'll realize that his discovery can **still** be broadcast. And I really don't know how far Julián will go to interfere."

Langdon studied the beautiful woman a long moment. "You don't trust your fiancé at all, do you?"

Ambra took a deep breath. "The truth is, I don't know him as well as you might assume."

"Then why did you agree to marry him?"

"Quite simply, Julián put me in a position where I had no choice."

Before Langdon could respond, a low rumble began shaking the cement beneath their feet, reverberating through the grotto-like space beneath the bridge. The sound grew louder and louder. It seemed to be coming from up the river, to their right.

Langdon turned and saw a dark shape speeding toward them—a powerboat approaching with no running lights. As it neared the high cement bank, it slowed and began to glide up perfectly beside them.

Langdon stared down at the craft and shook his head. Until this moment, he had been unsure how much faith to place in Edmond's computerized docent, but now, seeing a yellow water taxi approaching the bank, he realized that Winston was the best ally they could possibly have.

The disheveled captain waved them aboard. "Your British man, he call me," the man said. "He say VIP client pay triple for . . . how you say . . . **velocidad y discreción**? I do it—you see? No lights!"

"Yes, thank you," Langdon replied. **Good call, Winston. Speed and discretion.**

The captain reached out and helped Ambra aboard, and as she disappeared into the small covered cabin to get warm, he gave Langdon a wide-eyed smile. "This my VIP? Señorita Ambra Vidal?"

"Velocidad y discreción," Langdon reminded him.

"¡**Sí, sí**! Okay!" The man scurried to the helm and revved the engines. Moments later, the powerboat was skimming westward through the darkness along the Nervión River.

Off the port side of the boat, Langdon could see the Guggenheim's giant black widow, eerily illuminated by the spinning lights of police cars. Overhead, a news chopper streaked across the sky toward the museum.

The first of many, Langdon suspected.

Langdon pulled Edmond's cryptic note card from

his pants pocket. **BIO-EC346.** Edmond had told him to give it to a taxi driver, although Edmond probably never imagined the vehicle would be a water taxi.

"Our British friend . . . ," Langdon yelled to the driver over the sound of the roaring engines. "I assume he told you where we are going?"

"Yes, yes! I warn him by boat I can take you only **almost** there, but he say no problem, you walk three hundred meters, no?"

"That's fine. And how far is it from here?"

The man pointed to a highway that ran along the river on the right. "Road sign say seven kilometers, but in boat, a little more."

Langdon glanced out at the illuminated highway sign.

AEROPUERTO BILBAO (BIO) ✈ 7 KM

He smiled ruefully at the sound of Edmond's voice in his mind. **It's a painfully simple code, Robert.** Edmond was right, and when Langdon had finally figured it out earlier tonight, he had been embarrassed that it had taken him so long.

BIO was indeed a code—although it was no more difficult to decipher than similar codes from around the world: BOS, LAX, JFK.

BIO is the local airport code.

The rest of Edmond's code had fallen into place instantly.

EC346.

Langdon had never seen Edmond's private jet, but

he knew the plane existed, and he had little doubt that the country code for a Spanish jet's tail number would start with the letter **E** for España.

EC346 is a private jet.

Clearly, if a cabdriver had taken him to Bilbao Airport, Langdon could have presented Edmond's card to security and been escorted directly to Edmond's private plane.

I hope Winston reached the pilots to warn them we are coming, Langdon thought, looking back in the direction of the museum, which was growing smaller and smaller in their wake.

Langdon considered going inside the cabin to join Ambra, but the fresh air felt good, and he decided to give her a couple of minutes alone to gather herself.

I could use a moment too, he thought, moving toward the bow.

At the front of the boat, with the wind whipping through his hair, Langdon untied his bow tie and pocketed it. Then he released the top button of his wingtip collar and breathed as deeply as he could, letting the night air fill his lungs.

Edmond, he thought. **What have you done?**

ommander Diego Garza was fuming as he
paced the darkness of Prince Julián's apartment and endured the bishop's self-righteous
lecture.

You are trespassing where you do not belong,
Garza wanted to shout at Valdespino. **This is not
your domain!**

Once again, Bishop Valdespino had inserted himself
into palace politics. Having materialized like a spec-
ter in the darkness of Julián's apartment, Valdespino
was adorned in full ecclesiastical vestments and was
now giving an impassioned sermon to Julián about
the importance of Spain's traditions, the devoted reli-
giosity of past kings and queens, and the comforting
influence of the Church in times of crisis.

This is not the moment, Garza seethed.

Tonight, Prince Julián would need to deliver a delicate public relations performance, and the last thing
Garza needed was to have him distracted by Valdespino's attempts to impose a religious agenda.

The buzz of Garza's phone conveniently interrupted
the bishop's monologue.

"**Sí, dime,**" Garza answered loudly, positioning

himself between the prince and the bishop. "¿Qué tal va?"

"Sir, it's Agent Fonseca in Bilbao," the caller said in rapid-fire Spanish. "I'm afraid we've been unable to capture the shooter. The car company we thought could track him has lost contact. The shooter seems to have anticipated our actions."

Garza swallowed his anger and exhaled calmly, trying to ensure that his voice would reveal nothing about his true state of mind. "I understand," he replied evenly. "At the moment, your only concern is Ms. Vidal. The prince is waiting to see her, and I've assured him that you'll have her here shortly."

There was a long silence on the line. Too long.

"Commander?" Fonseca asked, sounding tentative. "I'm sorry, sir, but I have bad news on that front. It appears that Ms. Vidal and the American professor have left the building"—he paused—"without us."

Garza almost dropped his phone. "I'm sorry, can you . . . repeat that?"

"Yes, sir. Ms. Vidal and Robert Langdon have fled the building. Ms. Vidal intentionally abandoned her phone so we would be unable to track her. We have no idea where they've gone."

Garza realized his jaw had fallen slack, and the prince was now staring at him with apparent concern. Valdespino was also leaning in to hear, his eyebrows arched with unmistakable interest.

"Ah—that's excellent news!" Garza blurted suddenly, nodding with conviction. "Good work. We'll

see you all here later this evening. Let's just confirm transport protocols and security. One moment,
please."

Garza covered the phone and smiled at the prince.
"All is well. I'll just step into the other room to sort
out the details so that you gentlemen can have some
privacy."

Garza was reluctant to leave the prince alone with
Valdespino, but this was not a call he could take in
front of either of them, so he walked to one of the
guest bedrooms, stepped inside, and closed the door.

"**¿Qué diablos ha pasado?**" he seethed into the
phone. **What the hell happened?**

Fonseca relayed a story that sounded like utter fantasy.

"The lights went out?" Garza demanded. "A **computer** posed as a security officer and gave you bad
intel? How am I supposed to respond to that?"

"I realize it is hard to imagine, sir, but that is precisely what happened. What we are struggling to
understand is why the computer had a sudden change
of heart."

"Change of heart?! It's a goddamned computer!"

"What I mean is that the computer had previously
been helpful—identifying the shooter by name,
attempting to thwart the assassination, and also discovering that the getaway vehicle was an Uber car.
Then, very suddenly, it seemed to be working **against**
us. All we can figure is that Robert Langdon must
have said something to it, because after its conversation with him, everything changed."

Now I'm battling a computer? Garza decided he was getting too old for this modern world. "I'm sure I don't need to tell you, Agent Fonseca, how embarrassing this would be for the prince both personally and politically if it were known that his fiancée had fled with the American, and that the prince's Guardia Real had been tricked by a computer."

"We are acutely aware of that."

"Do you have any idea what would inspire the two of them to run away? It seems entirely unwarranted and reckless."

"Professor Langdon was quite resistant when I told him he would be joining us in Madrid this evening. He made it clear he did not want to come."

And so he fled a murder scene? Garza sensed something else was going on, but he could not imagine what. "Listen to me carefully. It is absolutely critical that you locate Ambra Vidal and bring her back to the palace before any of this information leaks out."

"I understand, sir, but Díaz and I are the only two agents on the scene. We can't possibly search all of Bilbao alone. We'll need to alert the local authorities, gain access to traffic cams, air support, every possible—"

"Absolutely not!" Garza replied. "We can't afford the embarrassment. Do your job. Find them on your own, and return Ms. Vidal to our custody as quickly as possible."

"Yes, sir."

Garza hung up, incredulous.

As he stepped out of the bedroom, a pale young

woman hurried up the hallway toward him. She was wearing her usual techie Coke-bottle glasses and beige pantsuit, and was anxiously clutching a computer tablet.

God save me, Garza thought. **Not now.**

Mónica Martín was the palace's newest and youngest-ever "public relations coordinator"—a post that included the duties of media liaison, PR strategist, and communications director—which Martín seemed to carry out in a permanent state of high alert.

At only twenty-six years of age, Martín held a communications degree from Madrid's Complutense University, had done two years of postgrad work at one of the top computer schools in the world—Tsinghua University in Beijing—and then had landed a high-powered PR job at Grupo Planeta followed by a top "communications" post at Spanish television network Antena 3.

Last year, in a desperate attempt to connect via digital media with the young people of Spain, and to keep up with the mushrooming influence of Twitter, Facebook, blogs, and online media, the palace had fired a seasoned PR professional with decades of print and media experience and replaced him with this tech-savvy millennial.

Martín owes everything to Prince Julián, Garza knew.

The young woman's appointment to the palace staff had been one of Prince Julián's few contributions to palace operations—a rare instance when he flexed his muscle with his father. Martín was considered one of the best in the business, but Garza found her paranoia and nervous energy utterly exhausting.

"Conspiracy theories," Martín announced to him, waving her tablet as she arrived. "They're exploding all over."

Garza stared at his PR coordinator in disbelief. **Do I look like I care?** He had more important things to worry about tonight than the conspiratorial rumor mill. "Would you mind telling me what you are doing strolling through the royal residence!"

"The control room just pinged your GPS." She pointed to the phone on Garza's belt.

Garza closed his eyes and exhaled, swallowing his irritation. In addition to a new PR coordinator, the palace had recently implemented a new "division of electronic security," which supported Garza's team with GPS services, digital surveillance, profiling, and preemptive data mining. Every day, Garza's staff was more diverse and youthful.

Our control room looks like a college campus computer center.

Apparently, the newly implemented technology used to track Guardia agents was also tracking Garza himself. It felt unnerving to think that a bunch of kids in the basement knew his whereabouts at every instant.

"I came to you personally," Martín said, holding out her tablet, "because I knew you'd want to see this."

Garza snatched the device from her and eyed the

screen, seeing a stock photo and bio of the silver-bearded Spaniard who had been identified as the Bilbao shooter—royal navy admiral Luis Ávila.

"There's a lot of damaging chatter," said Martín, "and much is being made of Ávila's being a former employee of the royal family."

"Ávila worked for the **navy**!" Garza spluttered.

"Yes, but technically, the king is the commander of the armed forces—"

"Stop right there," Garza ordered, shoving the tablet back at her. "Suggesting the king is somehow complicit in a terrorist act is an absurd stretch made by conspiracy nuts, and is wholly irrelevant to our situation tonight. Let's just count our blessings and get back to work. After all, this lunatic could have killed the queen consort but chose instead to kill an American atheist. All in all, not a bad outcome!"

The young woman didn't flinch. "There's something else, sir, which relates to the royal family. I didn't want you to be blindsided."

As Martín spoke, her fingers flew across the tablet, navigating to another site. "This is a photo that has been online for a few days, but nobody noticed it. Now, with everything about Edmond Kirsch going viral, this photo is starting to appear in the news." She handed Garza the tablet.

Garza eyed a headline: "Is This the Last Photo Taken of Futurist Edmond Kirsch?"

A blurry photograph showed Kirsch dressed in a dark suit, standing on a rocky bluff beside a perilous cliff.

"The photo was taken three days ago," Martín said, "while Kirsch was visiting the Abbey of Montserrat. A worker on-site recognized Kirsch and snapped a photo. After Kirsch's murder tonight, the worker re-posted the photo as one of the last ever taken of the man."

"And this relates to us, how?" Garza asked point-edly.

"Scroll down to the next photo."

Garza scrolled down. On seeing the second image, he had to reach out and steady himself on the wall. "This . . . this can't be true."

In this wider-frame version of the same shot, Edmond Kirsch could be seen standing beside a tall man wearing a traditional Catholic purple cassock. The man was Bishop Valdespino.

"It's true, sir," Martín said. "Valdespino met with Kirsch a few days ago."

"But . . ." Garza hesitated, momentarily speech-less. "But why wouldn't the bishop have mentioned this? Especially considering all that has happened tonight!"

Martín gave a suspicious nod. "That's why I chose to speak to you first."

Valdespino met with Kirsch! Garza could not quite wrap his mind around it. **And the bishop declined to mention it?** The news was alarming, and Garza felt eager to warn the prince.

"Unfortunately," the young woman said, "there's a lot more." She began manipulating her tablet again.

"Commander?" Valdespino's voice called suddenly

from the living room. "What is the news on Ms. Vidal's transport?"

Mónica Martín's head snapped up, eyes wide. "Is that the bishop?" she whispered. "Valdespino is **here** in the residence?"

"Yes. Counseling the prince."

"Commander!" Valdespino called again. "Are you there?"

"Believe me," Martín whispered, her tone panicked, "there is more information that you **must** have right away—before you say another word to the bishop or the prince. Trust me when I tell you that tonight's crisis impacts us far more deeply than you can imagine."

Garza studied his PR coordinator a moment and made his decision. "Downstairs in the library. I'll meet you there in sixty seconds."

Martín nodded and slipped away.

Alone now, Garza took a deep breath and forced his features to relax, hoping to erase all traces of his growing anger and confusion. Calmly, he strolled back into the living room.

"All is well with Ms. Vidal," Garza announced with a smile as he entered. "She'll be here later. I'm headed down to the security office to confirm her transportation personally." Garza gave Julián a confident nod and then turned to Bishop Valdespino. "I'll be back shortly. Don't go away."

With that, he turned and strode out.

As Garza exited the apartment, Bishop Valdespino stared after him, frowning.

"Is something wrong?" the prince asked, eyeing the bishop closely.

"Yes," Valdespino replied, turning back to Julián. "I've been taking confessions for fifty years. I know a lie when I hear one."

CHAPTER 34

🌐 ConspiracyNet.com

BREAKING NEWS

ONLINE COMMUNITY ERUPTS WITH QUESTIONS

In the wake of Edmond Kirsch's assassination, the futurist's massive online following has erupted in a firestorm of speculation over two urgent issues.

WHAT WAS KIRSCH'S DISCOVERY?
WHO KILLED HIM, AND WHY?

Regarding Kirsch's discovery, theories have already flooded the Internet and span a wide range of topics—from Darwin, to extraterrestrials, to Creationism, and beyond.

No motive has yet been confirmed for this killing, but theories include religious zealotry, corporate espionage, and jealousy.

ConspiracyNet has been promised exclusive information about the killer, and we will share it with you the moment it arrives.

CHAPTER 35

Ambra Vidal stood alone in the cabin of the water taxi, clutching Robert Langdon's jacket around her. Minutes ago, when Langdon asked why she had agreed to marry a man she barely knew, Ambra had replied truthfully.

I was given no choice.

Her engagement to Julián was a misfortune she could not bear to relive tonight, not with everything else that had happened.

I was trapped.

I'm still trapped.

Now, as Ambra looked at her own reflection in the dirty window, she felt an overwhelming sense of loneliness engulf her. Ambra Vidal was not one to indulge in self-pity, but at the moment her heart felt brittle and adrift. **I'm engaged to a man who is involved somehow in a brutal murder.**

The prince had sealed Edmond's fate with a single phone call only an hour before the event. Ambra had been frantically preparing for the arrival of the guests when a young staff member had rushed in, excitedly waving a slip of paper.

"¡Señora Vidal! ¡Mensaje para usted!"

The girl was giddy and explained in breathless Spanish that an important call had just come in to the museum's front desk.

"Our caller ID," she squeaked, "said Royal Palace of Madrid, and so of course I answered! And it was someone calling from the office of Prince Julián!"

"They called the front desk?" Ambra asked. "They have my cell number."

"The prince's assistant said he tried your mobile," the staffer explained, "but they couldn't get through."

Ambra checked her phone. **Odd. No missed call.** Then she realized that some technicians had just been testing the museum's cellular jamming system, and Julián's assistant must have called while her phone was disabled.

"It seems the prince got a call today from a very important friend in Bilbao who wants to attend tonight's event." The girl handed Ambra the slip of paper. "He hoped you would be able to add one name to tonight's guest list?"

Ambra eyed the message.

Almirante Luis Ávila (ret.)
Armada Española

A retired officer from the Spanish navy?

"They left a number and said you can call back directly if you want to discuss it, but that Julián was about to go into a meeting, so you probably won't reach him. But the caller insisted that the prince **does** hope this request is not an imposition."

An imposition? Ambra smoldered. **Considering what you've already put me through?**

"I'll take care of it," Ambra said. "Thank you."

The young staffer danced away as if she'd just relayed the word of God Himself. Ambra glared at the prince's request, irritated that he would think it appropriate to exert his influence with her in this way, especially after lobbying so hard against her participation in tonight's event.

Once again, you leave me no choice, she thought.

If she ignored this request, the result would be an uncomfortable confrontation with a prominent naval officer at the front door. Tonight's event was meticulously choreographed and would attract unparalleled media coverage. **The last thing I need is an embarrassing tussle with one of Julián's high-powered friends.**

Admiral Ávila had not been vetted or placed on the "cleared" list, but Ambra suspected that demanding a security check was both unnecessary and potentially insulting. After all, the man was a distinguished naval officer with enough power to pick up the phone, call the Royal Palace, and ask the future king for a favor.

And so, facing a tight schedule, Ambra made the only decision she could make. She wrote Admiral Ávila's name on the guest list at the front door, and also added it to the docenting database so a headset could be initialized for this new guest.

Then she went back to work.

And now Edmond is dead, Ambra reflected, returning to the present moment in the darkness of the water taxi. As she tried to rid her mind of the painful memories, a strange thought occurred to her.

I never spoke directly to Julián . . . the entire message was relayed through third parties.

The notion brought with it a small ray of hope.

Is it possible that Robert is right? And that maybe Julián is innocent?

She considered it a moment longer and then hurried outside.

She found the American professor standing alone on the bow, hands on the railing as he stared out into the night. Ambra joined him there, startled to see that the boat had left the main branch of the Nervión River and was now skimming northward along a small tributary that seemed less of a river than a perilous channel with high muddy banks. The shallow water and tight quarters made Ambra nervous, but their boat captain seemed unfazed, racing along the narrow gorge at top speed, his headlight blazing the way.

She quickly told Langdon about the call from Prince Julián's office. "All I really know is that the museum's front desk got a call that originated in the Royal Palace of Madrid. Technically, that call could have been from **anyone** there claiming to be Julián's assistant."

Langdon nodded. "That may be why the person chose to **relay** the request to you rather than talk to you directly. Any idea who might be involved?" Considering Edmond's history with Valdespino, Langdon was inclined to look toward the bishop himself.

"It could be anybody," Ambra said. "It's a delicate time in the palace right now. With Julián taking center stage, a lot of the old advisers are scrambling to find favor and gain Julián's ear. The country is changing, and I think a lot of the old guard are desperate to retain power."

"Well, whoever is involved," Langdon said, "let's hope they don't figure out we're trying to locate Edmond's password and release his discovery."

As he spoke the words, Langdon felt the stark simplicity of their challenge.

He also sensed its blunt peril.

Edmond was murdered to keep this information from being released.

For an instant, Langdon wondered if his safest option might be simply to fly directly home from the airport and let someone else handle all this.

Safe, yes, he thought, **but an option . . . no.**

Langdon felt a profound sense of duty toward his old student, along with moral outrage that a scientific breakthrough could be so brutally censored. He also felt a deep intellectual curiosity to learn exactly what Edmond had discovered.

And finally, Langdon knew, **there is Ambra Vidal.**

The woman was clearly in crisis, and when she had looked into his eyes and pleaded for help, Langdon had sensed in her a deep well of personal conviction and self-reliance . . . yet he had also seen heavy clouds of fear and regret. **There are secrets there,** he sensed, **dark and confining. She is reaching out for help.**

Ambra raised her eyes suddenly, as if sensing Langdon's thoughts. "You look cold," she said. "You need your jacket back."

He smiled softly. "I'm fine."

"Are you thinking you should leave Spain as soon as we get to the airport?"

Langdon laughed. "Actually, that did cross my mind."

"Please don't." She reached out to the railing and placed her soft hand on top of his. "I'm not sure what we're facing tonight. You were close to Edmond, and he told me more than once how much he valued your friendship and trusted your opinion. I'm scared, Robert, and I really don't think I can face this alone."

Ambra's flashes of unguarded candor were startling to Langdon, and yet also utterly captivating. "Okay," he said, nodding. "You and I owe it to Edmond and, frankly, to the scientific community, to find that password and make his work public."

Ambra smiled softly. "Thank you."

Langdon glanced behind the boat. "I imagine your Guardia agents have realized by now that we've left the museum."

"No doubt. But Winston was quite impressive, wasn't he?"

"Mind-boggling," Langdon replied, only now starting to grasp the quantum leap Edmond had made in the development of AI. Whatever Edmond's "proprietary breakthrough technologies" had been, clearly he had been poised to usher in a brave new world of human–computer interaction.

Tonight, Winston had proven himself a faithful servant to his creator as well as an invaluable ally to Langdon and Ambra. In a matter of minutes, Winston had identified a threat on the guest list, attempted to thwart Edmond's assassination, identified the get-away car, and facilitated Langdon and Ambra's escape from the museum.

"Let's hope Winston phoned ahead to alert Edmond's pilots," Langdon said.

"I'm sure he did," Ambra said. "But you're right. I should call Winston to double-check."

"Hold on," Langdon said, surprised. "You can **call** Winston? When we left the museum and went out of range, I thought . . ."

Ambra laughed and shook her head. "Robert, Winston is not **physically** located inside the Guggenheim; he is located in a secret computer facility somewhere and accessed remotely. Do you really think Edmond would build a resource like Winston and not be able to communicate with him at all times, anywhere in the world? Edmond talked to Winston all the time—at home, traveling, out for walks—the two of them could connect at any moment with a simple phone call. I've seen Edmond chat for hours with Winston. Edmond used him like a personal assistant—to call for dinner reservations, to coordinate with his pilots, to do anything that needed doing, really. In fact, when we were mounting the museum show, I talked to Winston quite often myself by phone."

Ambra reached inside the pocket of Langdon's tails jacket and pulled out Edmond's turquoise-covered phone, flicking it on. Langdon had powered it down in the museum to save its battery.

"You should turn on your phone too," she said, "so we **both** have access to Winston."

"You're not worried about being tracked if we turn these on?"

Ambra shook her head. "The authorities haven't had time to get the necessary court order, so I think it's worth the risk—especially if Winston can update us on the Guardia's progress and the situation at the airport."

Uneasy, Langdon turned on his phone and watched it come to life. As the home screen materialized, he squinted into the light and felt a twinge of vulnerability, as if he had just become instantly locatable to every satellite in space.

You've seen too many spy movies, he told himself.

All at once, Langdon's phone began pinging and vibrating as a backlog of messages from this evening began pouring in. To his astonishment, Langdon had received more than two hundred texts and e-mails since turning off his phone.

As he scanned the in-box, he saw the messages were all from friends and colleagues. The earlier e-mails had congratulatory header lines—**Great lecture! I can't believe you're there!**—but then, very suddenly, the tone of the headers turned anxious and deeply concerned, including a message from his book editor, Jonas Faukman: MY GOD—ROBERT, ARE YOU OKAY??!! Langdon had never seen his scholarly editor employ all caps or double punctuation.

Until now, Langdon had been feeling wonderfully invisible in the darkness of Bilbao's waterways, as if the museum were a fading dream.

It's all over the world, he realized. **News of Kirsch's mysterious discovery and brutal murder . . . along with my name and face.**

"Winston has been trying to reach us," Ambra said, staring into the glow of Kirsch's cell phone. "Edmond has received fifty-three missed calls in the last half hour, all from the same number, all exactly thirty seconds apart." She chuckled. "Tireless persistence is among Winston's many virtues."

Just then, Edmond's phone began ringing.

Langdon smiled at Ambra. "I wonder who it is."

She held out the phone to him. "Answer it."

Langdon took the phone and pressed the speaker button. "Hello?"

"Professor Langdon," chimed Winston's voice with its familiar British accent. "I'm glad we're back in contact. I've been trying to reach you."

"Yes, we can see that," Langdon replied, impressed that the computer sounded so utterly calm and unruffled after fifty-three consecutive failed calls.

"There have been some developments," Winston said. "There is a possibility that the airport authorities will be alerted to your names before you arrive. Once again, I will suggest you follow my directions very carefully."

"We're in your hands, Winston," Langdon said. "Tell us what to do."

"First thing, Professor," Winston said, "if you have not yet jettisoned your cell phone, you need to do so immediately."

"Really?" Langdon gripped his phone more tightly. "Don't the authorities need a court order before any-one—"

"On an American cop show perhaps, but you are dealing with Spain's Guardia Real and the Royal Palace. They will do what is necessary."

Langdon eyed his phone, feeling strangely reluctant to part with it. **My whole life is in there.**

"What about Edmond's phone?" Ambra asked, sounding alarmed.

"Untraceable," Winston replied. "Edmond was always concerned about hacking and corporate espionage. He personally wrote an IMEI/IMSI veiling program that varies his phone's C2 values to outsmart any GSM interceptors."

Of course he did, Langdon thought. **For the genius who created Winston, outsmarting a local phone company would be a cakewalk.**

Langdon frowned at his own apparently inferior phone. Just then Ambra reached over and gently pried it from his hands. Without a word, she held it over the railing and let go. Langdon watched the phone plummet down and splash into the dark waters of the Nervión River. As it disappeared beneath the surface, he felt a pang of loss, staring back after it as the boat raced on.

"Robert," Ambra whispered, "just remember the wise words of Disney's Princess Elsa."

Langdon turned. "I'm sorry?"

Ambra smiled softly. "Let it go."

CHAPTER 36

S u misión todavía no ha terminado," declared
the voice on Ávila's phone. **Your mission is not
yet complete.**

Ávila sat up at attention in the backseat of the Uber
as he listened to his employer's news.

"We've had an unexpected complication," his contact said in rapid Spanish. "We need you to redirect
to Barcelona. Right away."

Barcelona? Ávila had been told he would be traveling to Madrid for further service.

"We have reason to believe," the voice continued,
"that two associates of Mr. Kirsch are traveling to
Barcelona tonight in hopes of finding a way to trigger
Mr. Kirsch's presentation remotely."

Ávila stiffened. "Is that **possible?**"

"We're not sure yet, but if they succeed, obviously it
will undo all of your hard work. I need a man on the
ground in Barcelona right away. **Discreetly.** Get there
as fast as you can, and call me."

With that, the connection was terminated.

The bad news felt strangely welcome to Ávila. **I am
still needed.** Barcelona was farther than Madrid but
still only a few hours at top speed on a superhigh-
way in the middle of the night. Without wasting a

moment, Ávila raised his gun and pressed it against the Uber driver's head. The man's hands tensed visibly on the wheel.

"**Llévame a Barcelona,**" Ávila commanded.

The driver took the next exit, toward Vitoria-Gasteiz, eventually accelerating onto the A-1 highway, heading east. The only other vehicles on the road at this hour were thundering tractor trailers, all racing to complete their runs to Pamplona, to Huesca, to Lleida, and finally to one of the largest port cities on the Mediterranean Sea—Barcelona.

Ávila could scarcely believe the strange sequence of events that had brought him to this moment. **From the depths of my deepest despair, I have risen to the moment of my most glorious service.**

For a dark instant, Ávila was back in that bottomless pit, crawling across the smoke-filled altar at the Cathedral of Seville, searching the bloodstained rubble for his wife and child, only to realize they were gone forever.

For weeks after the attack, Ávila did not leave his home. He lay trembling on his couch, consumed by an endless waking nightmare of fiery demons that dragged him into a dark abyss, shrouding him in blackness, rage, and suffocating guilt.

"The abyss is **purgatory,**" a nun whispered beside him, one of the hundreds of grief counselors trained by the Church to assist survivors. "Your soul is trapped in a dark limbo. Absolution is the only escape. You must find a way to **forgive** the people who did this, or your rage will consume you whole." She made the sign of the cross. "Forgiveness is your only salvation."

Forgiveness? Ávila tried to speak, but demons clenched his throat. At the moment, revenge felt like the only salvation. **But revenge against whom?** Responsibility for the bombing had never been claimed.

"I realize acts of religious terrorism seem unforgivable," the nun continued. "And yet, it may be helpful to remember that our own faith waged a centuries-long Inquisition in the name of our God. We killed innocent women and children in the name of our beliefs. For this, we have had to ask forgiveness from the world, and from ourselves. And through time, we have healed."

Then she read to him from the Bible: " 'Do not resist an evil person. Whoever slaps you on your right cheek, turn the other to him. Love your enemies, do good to those who hate you, bless those who curse you, pray for those who mistreat you.' "

That night, alone and in pain, Ávila stared into the mirror. The man looking back at him was a stranger. The nun's words had done nothing to ease his pain.

Forgiveness? Turn my other cheek!

I have witnessed evil for which there is no absolution!

In a growing rage, Ávila drove his fist into the mirror, shattering the glass, and collapsing in sobs of anguish on his bathroom floor.

As a career naval officer, Ávila had always been a man in control—a champion of discipline, honor, and the chain of command—but that man was gone. Within weeks, Ávila had fallen into a haze, anesthetizing himself with a potent blend of alcohol and prescription drugs. Soon his yearning for the numbing effects of chemicals occupied every waking hour, diminishing him to a hostile recluse.

Within months, the Spanish navy had quietly forced him to retire. A once powerful battleship now stuck in dry dock, Ávila knew he would never sail again. The navy to which he had given his life had left him with only a modest stipend on which he could barely live.

I'm fifty-eight years old, he realized. **And I have nothing.**

He spent his days sitting alone in his living room, watching TV, drinking vodka, and waiting for any ray of light to appear. **La hora más oscura es justo antes del amanecer,** he would tell himself over and over. But the old navy aphorism proved false over and over. **The darkest hour is not just before the dawn,** he sensed. **The dawn is never coming.**

On his fifty-ninth birthday, a rainy Thursday morning, staring at an empty bottle of vodka and an eviction warning, Ávila mustered the courage to go to his closet, take down his navy service pistol, load it, and put the barrel to his temple.

"**Perdóname,**" he whispered, and closed his eyes. Then he squeezed the trigger. The explosion was far quieter than he imagined. More of a click than a gunshot.

Cruelly, the gun had failed to fire. Years in a dusty

closet without being cleaned had apparently taken a toll on the admiral's cheap ceremonial pistol. It seemed even this simple act of cowardice was beyond Ávila's abilities.

Enraged, he hurled the gun at the wall. This time, an explosion rocked the room. Ávila felt a searing heat rip through his calf, and his drunken fog lifted in a flash of blinding pain. He fell to the floor screaming and clutching his bleeding leg.

Panicked neighbors pounded on his door, sirens wailed, and Ávila soon found himself at Seville's Hospital Provincial de San Lázaro attempting to explain how he had tried to kill himself by shooting himself in the leg.

The next morning, as he lay in the recovery room, broken and humiliated, Admiral Luis Ávila received a visitor.

"You're a lousy shot," the young man said in Spanish. "No wonder they forced you to retire."

Before Ávila could reply, the man threw open the window shades and let the sunlight pour in. Ávila shielded his eyes, now able to see that the kid was muscle-bound and had a buzz cut. He wore a T-shirt with the face of Jesus on it.

"My name's Marco," he said, his accent Andaluz. "I'm your trainer for rehab. I asked to be assigned to you because you and I have something in common."

"Military?" Ávila said, noting his brash demeanor.

"Nope." The kid locked eyes with Ávila. "I was there that Sunday morning. In the cathedral. The terrorist attack."

Ávila stared in disbelief. "You were **there**?"

The kid reached down and pulled up one leg of his sweats, revealing a prosthetic limb. "I realize you've been through hell, but I was playing semipro **fútbol,** so don't expect too much sympathy from me. I'm more of a God-helps-those-who-help-themselves kind of guy."

Before Ávila knew what had happened, Marco heaved him into a wheelchair, rolled him down the hall to a small gym, and propped him up between a pair of parallel bars.

"This will hurt," the kid said, "but try to get to the other end. Just do it once. Then you can have breakfast."

The pain was excruciating, but Ávila was not about to complain to someone with only one leg, so using his arms to bear most of his weight, he shuffled all the way to the end of the bars.

"Nice," Marco said. "Now do it again."

"But you said—"

"Yeah, I lied. Do it again."

Ávila eyed the kid, stunned. The admiral had not taken an order in years, and strangely, he found something refreshing about it. It made him feel young—the way he had felt as a raw recruit years ago. Ávila turned around and began shuffling back the other way.

"So tell me," Marco said. "Do you still go to mass at the Seville cathedral?"

"Never."

"Fear?"

Ávila shook his head. "Rage."

Marco laughed. "Yeah, let me guess. The nuns told you to **forgive** the attackers?"

Ávila stopped short on the bars. "Exactly!"

"Me too. I tried. Impossible. The nuns gave us terrible advice." He laughed.

Ávila eyed the young man's Jesus shirt. "But it looks like you're still . . ."

"Oh yeah, I'm **definitely** still a Christian. More devout than ever. I was fortunate to find my mission—helping victims of God's enemies."

"A noble cause," Ávila said enviously, feeling his own life was purposeless without his family or the navy.

"A great man helped bring me back to God," Marco continued. "That man, by the way, was the pope. I've met him personally many times."

"I'm sorry . . . the pope?"

"Yes."

"As in . . . the leader of the Catholic Church?"

"Yes. If you like, I could probably arrange an audience for you."

Ávila stared at the kid as if he'd lost his mind. "**You** can get me an audience with the pope?"

Marco looked hurt. "I realize you're a big naval officer and can't imagine that a crippled physical trainer from Seville has access to the vicar of Christ, but I'm telling you the truth. I can arrange a meeting with him if you like. He could probably help you find your way back, just the way he helped me."

Ávila leaned on the parallel bars, uncertain how to reply. He idolized the then pope—a staunch conservative leader who preached strict traditionalism and orthodoxy. Unfortunately, the man was under fire from all sides of the modernizing globe, and there were rumblings that he would soon choose to retire in the face of growing liberal pressure. "I'd be honored to meet him, of course, but—"

"Good," Marco interjected. "I'll try to set it up for tomorrow."

Ávila never imagined that the following day he would find himself sitting deep within a secure sanctuary, face-to-face with a powerful leader who would teach him the most empowering religious lesson of his life.

The roads to salvation are many.

Forgiveness is not the only path.

ocated on the ground floor of the Madrid palace, the royal library is a spectacularly ornate suite of chambers containing thousands of priceless tomes, including Queen Isabella's illuminated **Book of Hours,** the personal Bibles of several kings, and an iron-bound codex from the era of Alfonso XI.

Garza entered in a rush, not wanting to leave the prince alone upstairs in the clutches of Valdespino for too long. He was still trying to make sense of the news that Valdespino had met with Kirsch only days ago and had decided to keep the meeting a secret. **Even in light of Kirsch's presentation and murder tonight?**

Garza moved across the vast darkness of the library toward PR coordinator Mónica Martín, who was waiting in the shadows holding her glowing tablet.

"I realize you're busy, sir," Martín said, "but we have a highly time-sensitive situation. I came upstairs to find you because our security center received a disturbing e-mail from ConspiracyNet.com."

"From **whom**?"

"ConspiracyNet is a popular conspiracy-theory site. The journalism is shoddy, and it's written at a child's level, but they have **millions** of followers. If you ask me, they hawk fake news, but the site is quite well respected among conspiracy theorists."

In Garza's mind, the terms "well respected" and "conspiracy theory" seemed mutually exclusive.

"They've been scooping the Kirsch situation all night," Martín continued. "I don't know where they're getting their information, but the site has become a hub for news bloggers and conspiracy theorists. Even the networks are turning to them for breaking news."

"Come to the point," Garza pressed.

"ConspiracyNet has new information that relates to the palace," Martín said, pushing her glasses up on her face. "They're going public with it in ten minutes and wanted to give us a chance to comment beforehand."

Garza stared at the young woman in disbelief. "The Royal Palace doesn't comment on sensationalist gossip!"

"At least look at it, sir." Martín held out her tablet.

Garza snatched the screen and found himself looking at a second photo of navy admiral Luis Ávila. The photo was uncentered, as if taken by accident, and showed Ávila in full dress whites striding in front of a painting. It looked as if it had been taken by a museumgoer who was attempting to photograph a piece of artwork and had inadvertently captured Ávila as he blindly stepped into the shot.

"I know what Ávila looks like," Garza snapped, eager to get back to the prince and Valdespino. "Why are you showing this to me?"

"Swipe to the next photo."

Garza swiped. The next screen showed an enlargement of the photo—this one focused on the admiral's right hand as it swung out in front of him. Garza immediately saw a marking on Ávila's palm. It appeared to be a tattoo.

Garza stared at the image for a long moment. The symbol was one he knew well, as did many Spaniards, especially the older generations.

The symbol of Franco.

Emblazoned in many places in Spain during the middle of the twentieth century, the symbol was synonymous with the ultraconservative dictatorship of General Francisco Franco, whose brutal regime advocated nationalism, authoritarianism, militarism, antiliberalism, and National Catholicism.

This ancient symbol, Garza knew, consisted of six letters, which, when put together, spelled a single word in Latin—a word that perfectly defined Franco's self-image.

Victor.

Ruthless, violent, and uncompromising, Francisco Franco had risen to power with the military support of Nazi Germany and Mussolini's Italy. He killed thousands of his opponents before seizing total control of the country in 1939 and proclaiming himself **El Caudillo**—the Spanish equivalent of the Führer. During the Civil War and well into the first years of dictatorship, those who dared oppose him disappeared into concentration camps, where an estimated three hundred thousand were executed.

Depicting himself as the defender of "Catholic Spain" and the enemy of godless communism, Franco had embraced a starkly male-centric mentality, officially excluding women from many positions of power in society, giving them barely any rights to professorships, judgeships, bank accounts, or even the right to flee an abusive husband. He annulled all marriages that had not been performed according to Catholic doctrine, and, among other restrictions, he outlawed divorce, contraception, abortion, and homosexuality.

Fortunately, everything had now changed.

Even so, Garza was stunned by how quickly the nation had forgotten one of the darkest periods in its history.

Spain's **pacto de olvido**—a nationwide political agreement to "forget" everything that had happened under Franco's vicious rule—meant that schoolchildren in Spain had been taught very little about the dictator. A poll in Spain had revealed that teenagers were far more likely to recognize the actor James Franco than they were dictator Francisco Franco.

The older generations, however, would never forget. This VICTOR symbol—like the Nazi swastika—could still conjure fear in the hearts of those old enough to remember those brutal years. To this day, wary souls warned that the highest reaches of Spanish government and the Catholic Church still harbored a secret faction of Francoist supporters—a hidden fraternity of traditionalists sworn to return Spain to its far-right convictions of the past century.

Garza had to admit that there were plenty of old-timers who looked at the chaos and spiritual apathy of contemporary Spain and felt that the country could be saved only by a stronger state religion, a more authoritarian government, and the imposition of clearer moral guidelines.

Look at our youth! they would shout. **They are all adrift!**

In recent months, with the Spanish throne soon to be occupied by the younger Prince Julián, there was a rising fear among traditionalists that the Royal Palace itself would soon become another voice for progressive change in the country. Fueling their concern was the prince's recent engagement to Ambra Vidal—who was not only Basque but outspokenly agnostic—and who, as Spain's queen, would no doubt have the prince's ear on matters of church and state.

Dangerous days, Garza knew. **A contentious cusp between past and future.**

In addition to a deepening religious rift, Spain faced a political crossroads as well. Would the country retain its monarch? Or would the royal crown be forever abolished as it had been in Austria, Hungary, and so many other European countries? Only time would tell. In the streets, older traditionalists waved Spanish flags, while young progressives proudly wore their antimonarchic colors of purple, yellow, and red—the colors of the old Republican banner.

Julián will be inheriting a powder keg.

"When I first saw the Franco tattoo," Martín said, drawing Garza's attention back to the tablet, "I thought it might have been digitally added to the photo as a ploy—you know, to stir the pot. Conspiracy sites all compete for traffic, and a Francoist connection will get a massive response, especially considering the anti-Christian nature of Kirsch's presentation tonight."

Garza knew she was right. **Conspiracy theorists will go crazy over this.**

Martín motioned to the tablet. "Read the commentary they intend to run."

With a feeling of dread, Garza glanced at the lengthy text that accompanied the photo.

🌐 ConspiracyNet.com

EDMOND KIRSCH UPDATE

Despite initial suspicions that Edmond Kirsch's murder was the work of religious zealots, the discovery of this ultraconservative Francoist symbol suggests the assassination may have **political** motivations as well. Suspicions that conservative players in the highest reaches of Spanish government, perhaps even within the Royal Palace itself, are now battling for control in the power vacuum left by the king's absence and imminent death . . .

"Disgraceful," Garza snapped, having read enough. "All this speculation from a tattoo? It means nothing. With the exception of Ambra Vidal's presence at the shooting, this situation has absolutely nothing to do with the politics of the Royal Palace. No comment."

"Sir," Martín pressed. "If you would please read the rest of the commentary, you'll see that they are trying to link Bishop Valdespino directly to Admiral Ávila. They're suggesting that the bishop may be a secret Francoist who has been whispering in the king's ear for years, keeping him from making sweeping changes to the country." She paused. "This allegation is gaining a lot of traction online."

Once again, Garza found himself at a total loss for words. He no longer recognized the world in which he lived.

Fake news now carries as much weight as real news.

Garza eyed Martín and did his best to speak calmly. "Mónica, this is all a fiction created by blog-writing fantasists for their own amusement. I can assure you that Valdespino is not a Francoist. He has served the king faithfully for decades, and there is no way he is involved with a Francoist assassin. The palace has no comment on any of it. Am I clear?" Garza turned toward the door, eager to get back to the prince and Valdespino.

"Sir, wait!" Martín reached out and grabbed his arm.

Garza halted, staring down in shock at his young employee's hand.

Martín immediately pulled back. "I'm sorry, sir, but ConspiracyNet also sent us a recording of a telephone conversation that just took place in Budapest." She blinked nervously behind her thick glasses. "You're not going to like this either."

CHAPTER 38

My boss was assassinated.

Captain Josh Siegel could feel his hands trembling on the stick as he taxied Edmond Kirsch's Gulfstream G550 toward the main runway at Bilbao Airport.

I'm in no condition to fly, he thought, knowing his copilot was as rattled as he was.

Siegel had piloted private jets for Edmond Kirsch for many years, and Edmond's horrifying murder tonight had come as a devastating shock. An hour ago, Siegel and his copilot had been sitting in the airport lounge watching the live feed from the Guggenheim Museum.

"Typical Edmond drama," Siegel had joked, impressed by his boss's ability to draw a huge crowd. As he watched Kirsch's program, he found himself, along with the other viewers in the lounge, leaning forward, his curiosity spiking, until, in a flash, the evening went horribly wrong.

In the aftermath, Siegel and his copilot sat in a daze, watching the television coverage and wondering what they should do next.

Siegel's phone rang ten minutes later; the caller was Edmond's personal assistant, Winston. Siegel had never met him, and although the Brit seemed a bit of an odd duck, Siegel had become quite accustomed to coordinating flights with him.

"If you have not seen the television," Winston said, "you should turn it on."

"We saw it," Siegel said. "We're both devastated."

"We need you to return the plane to Barcelona," Winston said, his tone eerily businesslike considering what had just transpired. "Prepare yourselves for takeoff, and I'll be back in touch shortly. Please do **not** take off until we speak."

Siegel had no idea if Winston's instructions would have aligned with Edmond's wishes, but at the moment, he was thankful for any kind of guidance.

On orders from Winston, Siegel and his copilot had filed their flight manifest to Barcelona with **zero** passengers—a "deadhead" flight, as it was regrettably known in the business—and then had pushed back out of the hangar and begun their preflight checklist.

Thirty minutes passed before Winston called back. "Are you prepped for takeoff?"

"We are."

"Good. I assume you'll be using the usual east-bound runway?"

"That's right." Siegel at times found Winston painfully thorough and unnervingly well informed.

"Please contact the tower and request clearance to take off. Taxi out to the far end of the airfield, but do **not** pull onto the runway."

"I should stop on the access road?"

"Yes, just for a minute. Please alert me when you get there."

Siegel and his copilot looked at each other in surprise. Winston's request made no sense at all.

The tower might have something to say about that.

Nonetheless, Siegel had guided the jet along various ramps and roads toward the runway head at the western edge of the airport. He was now taxiing along the final hundred meters of the access road, where the pavement turned ninety degrees to the right and merged into the eastbound runway head.

"Winston?" Siegel said, gazing out at the high chain-link security fence that surrounded the perimeter of the airport property. "We've reached the end of the access ramp."

"Please hold there," Winston said. "I'll be back in touch."

I can't hold here! Siegel thought, wondering what the hell Winston was doing. Fortunately, the Gulfstream's rearview camera showed no planes behind his, so at least Siegel was not blocking traffic. The only lights were those of the control tower—a faint glow at the other end of the runway, nearly two miles away.

Sixty seconds passed.

"This is air traffic control," a voice crackled in his headset. "EC346, you are cleared for takeoff on runway number one. I repeat, you are cleared."

Siegel wanted nothing more than to take off, but he

was still waiting for word from Edmond's assistant. "Thank you, control," he said. "We need to hold here just another minute. We've got a warning light that we're checking."

"Roger that. Please advise when ready."

ere?" The water taxi's captain looked confused. "You want stop **here**? Airport is more far. I take you there."

"Thanks, we'll get out here," Langdon said, following Winston's advice.

The captain shrugged and brought the boat to a stop beside a small bridge marked PUERTO BIDEA. The riverbank here was covered with high grass and looked more or less accessible. Ambra was already clambering out of the boat and making her way up the incline.

"How much do we owe you?" Langdon asked the captain.

"No pay," the man said. "Your British man, he pay me before. Credit card. Triple money."

Winston paid already. Langdon was still not quite used to working with Kirsch's computerized assistant. **It's like having Siri on steroids.**

Winston's abilities, Langdon realized, should come as no surprise considering daily accounts of artificial intelligence performing all kinds of complex tasks, including writing novels—one such book nearly winning a Japanese literary prize.

Langdon thanked the captain and jumped out of

the boat onto the bank. Before heading up the hill, he turned back to the bewildered driver, raised his index finger to his lips, and said, "**Discreción, por favor.**"

"**Sí, sí,**" the captain assured him, covering his eyes. "**¡No he visto nada!**"

With that, Langdon hurried up the slope, crossed a train track, and joined Ambra on the edge of a sleepy village road lined with quaint shops.

"According to the map," Winston's voice chimed on Edmond's speakerphone, "you should be at the intersection of Puerto Bidea and the Río Asua waterway. You should see a small roundabout in the town center?"

"I see it," Ambra replied.

"Good. Just off the roundabout, you will find a small road called Beike Bidea. Follow it away from the village center."

Two minutes later, Langdon and Ambra had left the village and were hurrying along a deserted country road where stone farmhouses sat on acres of grassy pastureland. As they moved deeper into countryside, Langdon sensed that something was wrong. To their right, in the distance, above the crest of a small hill, the sky was aglow with a hazy dome of light pollution.

"If those are the terminal lights," Langdon said, "we are **very** far away."

"The terminal is three kilometers from your position," Winston said.

Ambra and Langdon exchanged startled looks.

Winston had told them the walk would take only eight minutes.

"According to Google's satellite images," Winston went on, "there should be a large field to your right. Does it look traversable?"

Langdon glanced over at the hayfield to their right, which sloped gently upward in the direction of the terminal lights.

"We can certainly climb it," Langdon said, "but three kilometers will take—"

"Just climb the hill, Professor, and follow my directions precisely." Winston's tone was polite and as emotionless as ever, and yet Langdon realized he had just been admonished.

"Nice job," Ambra whispered, looking amused as she started up the hill. "That's the closest thing to irritation I've ever heard from Winston."

———

"EC346, this is air traffic control," blared the voice in Siegel's headset. "You must either clear the ramp and take off or return to the hangar for repairs. What is your status?"

"Still working on it," Siegel lied, glancing at his rearview camera. No planes—only the faint lights of the distant tower. "I just need another minute."

"Roger that. Keep us apprised."

The copilot tapped Siegel on the shoulder and pointed out through the windshield.

Siegel followed his partner's gaze but saw only the

high fence in front of the plane. Suddenly, on the other side of the mesh of the barrier, he saw a ghostly vision. **What in the world?**

In the darkened field beyond the fence, two spectral silhouettes were materializing out of the blackness, coming over the crest of a hill and moving directly toward the jet. As the figures drew closer, Siegel saw the distinctive diagonal black sash on a white dress that he had seen earlier on television.

Is that Ambra Vidal?

Ambra had flown on occasion with Kirsch, and Siegel always felt his heart flutter a bit when the striking Spanish beauty was aboard. He could not begin to fathom what in the world she was doing in a pasture outside Bilbao Airport.

The tall man accompanying Ambra was also wearing formal black-and-white attire, and Siegel recalled that he too had been part of the evening's program.

The American professor Robert Langdon.

Winston's voice returned suddenly. "Mr. Siegel, you should now see two individuals on the other side of the fence, and you will no doubt recognize both of them." Siegel found the Brit's manner spookily composed. "Please know that there are circumstances tonight that I cannot fully explain, but I am going to ask you to comply with my wishes on behalf of Mr. Kirsch. All you need to know right now is the following." Winston paused for the briefest of moments. "The same people who murdered Edmond Kirsch are now trying to kill Ambra Vidal and Robert Langdon. To keep them safe, we require your assistance."

"But . . . of course," Siegel stammered, trying to process the information.

"Ms. Vidal and Professor Langdon need to board your aircraft right now."

"Out here?!" Siegel demanded.

"I am aware of the technicality posed by a revised passenger manifest, but—"

"Are you aware of the technicality posed by a ten-foot-high security fence surrounding the airport?!"

"I am indeed," Winston said very calmly. "And, Mr. Siegel, while I realize that you and I have worked together only a few months, I need you to trust me. What I am about to suggest to you is precisely what Edmond would want you to do in this situation."

Siegel listened in disbelief as Winston outlined his plan.

"What you're suggesting is impossible!" Siegel argued.

"On the contrary," Winston said, "it is quite feasible. The thrust of each engine is over fifteen thousand pounds, and your nose cone is designed to endure seven-hundred-mile—"

"I'm not worried about the **physics** of it," Siegel snapped. "I'm worried about the **legality**—and about having my pilot's license revoked!"

"I can appreciate that, Mr. Siegel," Winston responded evenly. "But the future queen consort of Spain is in grave danger right now. Your actions here will help save her life. Believe me, when the truth comes out, you will not be receiving a reprimand, you will be receiving a royal medal from the king."

———

Standing in deep grass, Langdon and Ambra gazed up at the high security fence illuminated in the jet's headlights.

At Winston's urging, they stepped back from the fence just as the jet engines revved and the plane began rolling forward. Rather than following the curve of the access ramp, however, the jet continued straight toward them, crossing the painted safety lines and rolling out onto the asphalt skirt. It slowed to a crawl, inching closer and closer to the fence.

Langdon could now see that the jet's nose cone was aligned perfectly with one of the fence's heavy steel support posts. As the massive nose cone connected with the vertical post, the jet engines revved ever so slightly.

Langdon expected more of a fight, but apparently two Rolls-Royce engines and a forty-ton jet were more than this fence post could take. With a metallic groan, the post tipped toward them, pulling with it a huge mound of asphalt attached to its base like the root ball of a toppled tree.

Langdon ran over and grabbed the fallen fence, pulling it down low enough that he and Ambra could make their way across it. By the time they staggered onto the tarmac, the jet's gangway stairs had been deployed and a uniformed pilot was waving them aboard.

Ambra eyed Langdon with a tight smile. "Still doubting Winston?"

Langdon no longer had any words.

As they hurried up the staircase and into the plush interior cabin, Langdon heard the second pilot in the cockpit talking to the tower.

"Yes, control, I read you," the pilot was saying, "but your ground radar must be miscalibrated. We did **not** leave the access ramp. I repeat, we are still squarely on the access ramp. Our warning light is now off, and we're ready for takeoff."

The copilot slammed the door as the pilot engaged the Gulfstream's reverse thrust, inching the plane backward, away from the sagging fence. Then the jet began its wide turn back onto the runway.

In the seat opposite Ambra, Robert Langdon closed his eyes for a moment and exhaled. The engines roared outside, and he felt the pressure of acceleration as the jet thundered down the runway.

Seconds later, the plane was shooting skyward and banking hard to the southeast, plunging through the night toward Barcelona.

CHAPTER 40

Rabbi Yehuda Köves rushed from his study, crossed the garden, and slipped out the front door of his home, descending the steps to the sidewalk.

I am no longer safe at home, the rabbi told himself, his heart pounding relentlessly. **I must get to the synagogue.**

The Dohány Street Synagogue was not only Köves's lifelong sanctuary, it was a veritable fortress. The shrine's barricades, barbed fences, and twenty-four-hour guards served as a sharp reminder of Budapest's long history of anti-Semitism. Tonight, Köves felt grateful to hold the keys to such a citadel.

The synagogue was fifteen minutes away from his house—a peaceful stroll Köves took every day—and yet tonight, as he started out along Kossuth Lajos Street, he felt only fear. Lowering his head, Köves warily scanned the shadows before him as he began his journey.

Almost immediately he saw something that put him on edge.

A dark figure sat hunched on a bench across the street—a powerfully built man wearing blue jeans and a baseball cap—poking casually at his smartphone, his bearded face illuminated by the glow of the device.

He is not from this neighborhood, Köves knew, increasing his pace.

The man in the baseball cap glanced up, watched the rabbi a moment, and then returned to his phone. Köves pressed on. After one block, he glanced nervously behind him. To his dismay, the man in the baseball cap was no longer on the bench. He had crossed the street and was walking along the sidewalk behind Köves.

He's following me! The old rabbi's feet moved faster, and his breath grew short. He wondered if leaving his home had been a terrible mistake.

Valdespino urged me to stay inside! Whom have I decided to trust?

Köves had planned to wait for Valdespino's men to come and escort him to Madrid, but the phone call had changed everything. The dark seeds of doubt were sprouting quickly.

The woman on the phone had warned him: **The bishop is sending men not to transport you, but rather to remove you—just like he removed Syed al-Fadl**. Then she had presented evidence so persuasive that Köves had panicked and fled.

Now, as he hurried along the sidewalk, Köves feared he might not reach the safety of his synagogue after all. The man in the baseball cap was still behind him, tailing Köves at about fifty meters.

A deafening screech tore through the night air, and Köves jumped. The sound, he realized with relief, was a city bus braking at a bus stop just down the block. Köves felt as if it had been sent by God Himself as he rushed toward the vehicle and scrambled aboard. The bus was packed with raucous college students, and two of them politely made room for Köves in front.

"**Köszönöm**," the rabbi wheezed, breathless. **Thank you.**

Before the bus could pull away, however, the man in the jeans and baseball cap sprinted up behind the bus and narrowly managed to climb aboard.

Köves went rigid, but the man walked past him without a glance and took a seat in the back. In the reflection of the windshield, the rabbi could see that the man had returned to his smartphone, apparently engrossed in some sort of video game.

Don't be paranoid, Yehuda, he chided himself. **He has no interest in you.**

When the bus arrived at the Dohány Street stop, Köves gazed longingly at the spires of the synagogue only a few blocks away, and yet he could not bring himself to leave the safety of the crowded bus.

If I get out, and the man follows me . . .

Köves remained in his seat, deciding he was probably safer in a crowd. **I can just ride the bus for a while and catch my breath,** he thought, although he now wished he had used the toilet before fleeing his home so abruptly.

It was only moments later, as the bus pulled away from Dohány Street, that Rabbi Köves realized the terrible flaw in his plan.

It's Saturday night, and the passengers are all kids.
Köves now realized that everyone on this bus would almost certainly get off in the exact same place—one stop away, in the heart of Budapest's Jewish quarter.

After World War II, this neighborhood had been left in ruins, but the decaying structures were now the hub of one of Europe's most vibrant bar scenes—the famous "ruin bars"—trendy nightclubs housed in dilapidated buildings. On weekends, throngs of students and tourists gathered here to party in the bombed-out skeletons of graffiti-covered warehouses and old mansions, now retooled with the latest sound systems, colorful lighting, and eclectic art.

Sure enough, when the bus screeched to its next stop, all of the students piled out together. The man in the cap remained seated in the back, still engrossed in his phone. Instinct told Köves to get out as fast as he could, and so he clambered to his feet, hurried down the aisle, and descended into the crowd of students on the street.

The bus revved up to pull away, but then suddenly halted, its door hissing open to release one final passenger—the man in the baseball cap. Köves felt his pulse skyrocket once again, and yet the man did not glance even once at Köves. Instead, he turned his back to the crowd and walked briskly in the other direction, placing a phone call as he went.

Stop imagining things, Köves told himself, trying to breathe calmly.

The bus departed and the pack of students immediately began moving down the street toward the bars.

For safety, Rabbi Köves would stay with them as long as possible, eventually making a sharp left and walking back toward the synagogue.

It's only a few blocks, he told himself, ignoring the heaviness of his legs and the increasing pressure in his bladder.

The ruin bars were packed, their boisterous clientele spilling out into the streets. All around Köves, the sounds of electronic music throbbed, and the tang of beer permeated the air, mixing with the sweet fumes of Sopianae cigarettes and Kürtőskalács chimney cakes.

As he neared the corner, Köves still had the eerie sense he was being watched. He slowed down and stole one more glance behind him. Thankfully, the man in the jeans and baseball cap was nowhere to be seen.

———

In a darkened entryway, the crouched silhouette remained motionless for ten long seconds before carefully peering out of the shadows toward the corner.

Nice try, old man, he thought, knowing he had ducked out of sight just in time.

The man double-checked the syringe in his pocket. Then he stepped from the shadows, adjusted his baseball cap, and hurried after his mark.

uardia commander Diego Garza sprinted back up toward the residential apartments, still clutching Mónica Martín's computer tablet.

The tablet contained a recording of a phone call—a conversation between a Hungarian rabbi named Yehuda Köves and some kind of online whistle-blower—and the shocking contents of the recording had left Commander Garza precious few options.

Whether or not Valdespino was actually behind the murderous conspiracy alleged by this whistle-blower, Garza knew that when the recording went public, Valdespino's reputation would be forever destroyed.

I must warn the prince and insulate him from the fallout.

Valdespino must be removed from the palace before this story breaks.

In politics, perception was everything—and the information mongers, justly or not, were about to throw Valdespino under the bus. Clearly, the crown prince could not be seen anywhere near the bishop tonight.

PR coordinator Mónica Martín had strongly advised Garza to have the prince make a statement immediately, or risk looking complicit.

She's right, Garza knew. **We have to get Julián on television. Now.**

Garza reached the top of the stairs and moved breathlessly along the corridor toward Julián's apartment, glancing down at the tablet in his hand.

In addition to the image of the Francoist tattoo and the recording of the rabbi's phone call, the impending ConspiracyNet data-dump was apparently going to include a third and final revelation—something that Martín warned would be the most inflammatory of all.

A data constellation, she had called it—describing what amounted to a collection of seemingly random and disparate data points or factoids that conspiracy theorists were encouraged to analyze and connect in meaningful ways to create possible "constellations."

They're no better than Zodiac nuts! he fumed. **Fabricating animal shapes out of the random arrangements of stars!**

Unfortunately, the ConspiracyNet data points that were displayed on the tablet in Garza's hand appeared to have been especially formulated to coalesce into a single constellation, and from the palace's viewpoint, it was not a pretty one.

🌐 ConspiracyNet.com

The Kirsch Assassination

What We Know So Far

• Edmond Kirsch shared his scientific discovery with three religious leaders—Bishop Antonio Valdespino, Allamah Syed al-Fadl, and Rabbi Yehuda Köves.

• Kirsch and al-Fadl are both dead, and Rabbi Yehuda Köves is no longer answering his home phone and appears to have gone missing.

• Bishop Valdespino is alive and well, and was last seen walking across the plaza toward the Royal Palace.

• Kirsch's assassin—identified as navy admiral Luis Ávila—has body markings that tie him to a faction of ultraconservative Francoists. (Is Bishop Valdespino—a known conservative—a Francoist as well?)

• And finally, according to sources inside the Guggenheim, the event's guest list was locked, and yet assassin Luis Ávila was added at the last minute per the request of someone inside the Royal Palace. (The individual on-site who fulfilled that request was future queen consort Ambra Vidal.)

> ConspiracyNet would like to acknowledge the substantial ongoing contributions of civilian watchdog monte@iglesia.org on this story.

¿Monte@iglesia.org?

Garza had already decided the e-mail address had to be a fake.

Iglesia.org was a prominent evangelical Catholic website in Spain, an online community of priests, laypeople, and students who were devoted to the teachings of Jesus. The informant seemed to have spoofed the domain so that the allegations would appear to come from iglesia.org.

Clever, Garza thought, knowing that Bishop Valdespino was deeply admired by the devout Catholics behind the site. Garza wondered if this online "contributor" was the same informant who had called the rabbi.

As he reached the apartment door, Garza wondered how he would break the news to the prince. The day had started quite normally, and suddenly it seemed as if the palace was engaged in a war with ghosts. **A faceless informant named Monte? An array of data points?** Making matters even worse, Garza still had no news on the status of Ambra Vidal and Robert Langdon.

God help us if the press learns of Ambra's defiant actions tonight.

The commander entered without knocking. "Prince Julián?" he called, hurrying toward the living room. "I need to speak to you alone for a moment."

Garza reached the living room and stopped short.

The room was empty.

"Don Julián?" he called, wheeling back toward the kitchen. "Bishop Valdespino?"

Garza searched the entire apartment, but the prince and Valdespino were gone.

He immediately called the prince's cell phone and was startled to hear a telephone ringing. The sound was faint but audible, somewhere in the apartment. Garza called the prince again, and listened for the muffled ringing, this time tracking the sound to a small painting on the wall, which he knew concealed the apartment's wall safe.

Julián locked his phone in the safe?

It was beyond belief to Garza that the prince would abandon his phone on a night when communication was so critical.

And where did they go?

Garza now tried Valdespino's cell number, hoping the bishop would answer. To his utter astonishment, a second muffled ringtone sounded inside the vault.

Valdespino abandoned his phone as well?

With rising panic, a wild-eyed Garza dashed out of the apartment. For the next several minutes, he ran down hallways shouting, searching both upstairs and downstairs.

They can't have evaporated into thin air!

When Garza finally stopped running, he found himself standing breathless at the base of Sabatini's elegant grand staircase. He lowered his head in defeat. The tablet in his hands was asleep now, but in the blackened screen, he could see the reflection of the ceiling fresco directly overhead.

The irony felt cruel. The fresco was Giaquinto's grand masterpiece—**Religion Protected by Spain.**

CHAPTER 42

As the Gulfstream G550 jet climbed to cruising altitude, Robert Langdon stared blankly out the oval window and tried to gather his thoughts. The past two hours had been a whirlwind of emotions—from the thrill of watching Edmond's presentation begin to unfold to the gut-wrenching horror of seeing his grisly murder. And the mystery of Edmond's presentation seemed only to deepen the more Langdon considered it.

What secret had Edmond unveiled?

Where do we come from? Where are we going?

Edmond's words in the spiral sculpture earlier tonight replayed in Langdon's mind: **Robert, the discovery I've made . . . it very clearly answers both of these questions.**

Edmond had claimed to have solved two of life's greatest mysteries, and yet, Langdon wondered, how could Edmond's news have been so dangerously disruptive that someone would have **murdered** him to keep it silent?

All Langdon knew for sure was that Edmond was referring to human origin and human destiny.

What shocking origin did Edmond uncover?

What mysterious destiny?

Edmond had appeared optimistic and upbeat about the future, so it seemed unlikely that his prediction was something apocalyptic. **Then what could Edmond possibly have predicted that would concern the clerics so deeply?**

"Robert?" Ambra materialized next to him with a hot cup of coffee. "You said black?"

"Perfect, yes, thank you." Langdon gratefully accepted the mug, hoping some caffeine might help unknot his tangled thoughts.

Ambra took a seat opposite him and poured herself a glass of red wine from an elegantly embossed bottle. "Edmond carries a stash of Château Montrose aboard. Seems a pity to waste it."

Langdon had tasted Montrose only once, in an ancient secret wine cellar beneath Trinity College Dublin, while he was there researching the illuminated manuscript known as **The Book of Kells**.

Ambra cradled her wine goblet in two hands, and as she brought it to her lips, she gazed up at Langdon over the rim. Once again, he found himself strangely disarmed by the woman's natural elegance.

"I've been thinking," she said. "You mentioned earlier that Edmond was in Boston and asked you about various Creation stories?"

"Yes, about a year ago. He was interested in the different ways that major religions answered the question 'Where do we come from?'"

"So, maybe that's a good place for us to start?" she said. "Maybe we can unravel what he was working on?"

"I'm all for starting at the beginning," Langdon replied, "but I'm not sure what there is to unravel. There are only **two** schools of thought on where we came from—the religious notion that God created humans fully formed, and the Darwinian model in which we crawled out of the primordial ooze and eventually evolved into humans."

"So what if Edmond discovered a **third** possibility?" Ambra asked, her brown eyes flashing. "What if that's part of his discovery? What if he has proven that the human species came neither from Adam and Eve **nor** from Darwinian evolution?"

Langdon had to admit that such a discovery—an alternative story of human origin—would be earth-shattering, but he simply could not imagine what it might be. "Darwin's theory of evolution is extremely well established," he said, "because it is based on sci-entifically **observable** fact, and clearly illustrates how organisms evolve and adapt to their environments over time. The theory of evolution is universally ac-cepted by the sharpest minds in science."

"Is it?" Ambra said. "I've seen books that argue Darwin was entirely wrong."

"What she says is true," Winston chimed in from the phone, which was recharging on the table between them. "More than fifty titles were published over the past two decades alone."

Langdon had forgotten Winston was still with them.

"Some of these books were bestsellers," Winston added. "**What Darwin Got Wrong . . . Defeating**

Darwinism . . . Darwin's Black Box . . . Darwin on Trial . . . The Dark Side of Charles Dar—"

"Yes," Langdon interrupted, fully aware of the substantial collection of books claiming to disprove Darwin. "I actually read two of them a while back."

"And?" Ambra pressed.

Langdon smiled politely. "Well, I can't speak for all of them, but the two I read argued from a fundamentally Christian viewpoint. One went so far as to suggest that the earth's fossil record was placed there by God 'in order to test our faith.'"

Ambra frowned. "Okay, so they didn't sway your thinking."

"No, but they made me curious, and so I asked a Harvard biology professor for his opinion of the books." Langdon smiled. "The professor, by the way, happened to be the late Stephen J. Gould."

"Why do I know that name?" Ambra asked.

"Stephen J. Gould," Winston said at once. "Renowned evolutionary biologist and paleontologist. His theory of 'punctuated equilibrium' explained some of the gaps in the fossil record and helped support Darwin's model of evolution."

"Gould just chuckled," Langdon said, "and told me that most of the anti-Darwin books were published by the likes of the Institute for Creation Research—an organization that, according to its own informational materials, views the Bible as an infallible literal account of historical and scientific fact."

"Meaning," Winston said, "they believe that Burning Bushes can speak, that Noah fit every living species onto a single boat, and that people turn into pillars of salt. Not the firmest of footings for a scientific research company."

"True," Langdon said, "and yet there are some non-religious books that attempt to discredit Darwin from a historical standpoint—accusing him of **stealing** his theory from the French naturalist Jean-Baptiste Lamarck, who first proposed that organisms transformed themselves in response to their environment."

"That line of thought is irrelevant, Professor," Winston said. "Whether or not Darwin was guilty of plagiarism has no bearing on the veracity of his evolutionary theory."

"I can't argue with that," Ambra said. "And so, Robert, I assume if you asked Professor Gould, 'Where do we come from?' he would reply, without a doubt, that we evolved from apes."

Langdon nodded. "I'm paraphrasing here, but Gould essentially assured me that there was no question whatsoever among real scientists that evolution is happening. Empirically, we can **observe** the process. The better questions, he believed, were: **Why** is evolution happening? And **how** did it all start?"

"Did he offer any answers?" Ambra said.

"None that I could understand, but he did illustrate his point with a thought experiment. It's called the Infinite Hallway." Langdon paused, taking another sip of coffee.

"Yes, a helpful illustration," Winston chimed in before Langdon could speak. "It goes like this: imagine yourself walking down a long hallway—a corridor so long that it's impossible to see where you came from or where you're going."

Langdon nodded, impressed by the breadth of Winston's knowledge.

"Then, behind you in the distance," Winston continued, "you hear the sound of a bouncing ball. Sure enough, when you turn, you see a ball bouncing toward you. It is bouncing closer and closer, until it finally bounces past you, and just keeps going, bouncing into the distance and out of sight."

"Correct," Langdon said. "The question is not: **Is** the ball bouncing? Because clearly, the ball **is** bouncing. We can observe it. The question is: **Why** is it bouncing? How did it **start** bouncing? Did someone kick it? Is it a special ball that simply enjoys bouncing? Are the laws of physics in this hallway such that the ball has no choice but to bounce forever?"

"Gould's point being," Winston concluded, "that just as with evolution, we cannot see far enough into the past to know how the process began."

"Exactly," Langdon said. "All we can do is observe that it is **happening**."

"This was similar, of course," Winston said, "to the challenge of understanding the Big Bang. Cosmologists have devised elegant formulas to describe the expanding universe for any given Time—'T'—in the past or future. However, when they try to look back to the **instant** when the Big Bang occurred—where T equals zero—the mathematics all goes mad, describing what seems to be a mystical speck of infinite heat and infinite density."

Langdon and Ambra looked at each other, impressed.

"Correct again," Langdon said. "And because the human mind is not equipped to handle 'infinity' very well, most scientists now discuss the universe only in terms of moments **after** the Big Bang—where T is greater than zero—which ensures that the **mathematical** does not turn **mystical**."

One of Langdon's Harvard colleagues—a solemn physics professor—had become so fed up with philosophy majors attending his Origins of the Universe seminar that he finally posted a sign on his classroom door.

> In my classroom, T > 0.
> For all inquiries where T = 0,
> please visit the Religion Department.

"How about Panspermia?" Winston asked. "The notion that life on earth was seeded from another planet by a meteor or cosmic dust? Panspermia is considered a scientifically valid possibility to explain the existence of life on earth."

"Even if it's true," Langdon offered, "it doesn't answer how life **first** began in the universe. We're just kicking the can down the road, ignoring the origin of the bouncing ball and postponing the big question: Where does life come from?"

Winston fell silent.

Ambra sipped her wine, looking amused by their interplay.

As the Gulfstream G550 reached altitude and leveled off, Langdon found himself imagining what it would mean to the world if Edmond truly had found the answer to the age-old question: Where do we come from?

And yet, according to Edmond, that answer was only **part** of the secret.

Whatever the truth might be, Edmond had protected the details of his discovery with a formidable password—a single, forty-seven-letter line of poetry. If all went according to plan, Langdon and Ambra would soon uncover it inside Edmond's home in Barcelona.

CHAPTER 43

N early a decade after its inception, the "dark web" remains a mystery to the vast majority of online users. Inaccessible via traditional search engines, this sinister shadowland of the World Wide Web provides anonymous access to a mind-boggling menu of illegal goods and services.

From its humble beginning hosting Silk Road—the first online black market to sell illegal drugs—the dark web blossomed into a massive network of illicit sites dealing in weapons, child pornography, political secrets, and even professionals for hire, including prostitutes, hackers, spies, terrorists, and assassins.

Every week, the dark web hosted literally millions of transactions, and tonight, outside the ruin bars of Budapest, one of those transactions was about to be completed.

The man in the baseball cap and blue jeans moved stealthily along Kazinczy Street, staying in the shadows as he tracked his prey. Missions like this one had become his bread and butter over the past few years and were always negotiated through a handful of popular networks—Unfriendly Solution, Hitman Network, and BesaMafia.

Assassination for hire was a billion-dollar industry and growing daily, due primarily to the dark web's guarantee of anonymous negotiations and untraceable payment via Bitcoin. Most hits involved insurance fraud, bad business partnerships, or turbulent marriages, but the rationale was never the concern of the person carrying out the job.

No questions, the killer mused. **That is the unspoken rule that makes my business work.**

Tonight's job was one he had accepted several days ago. His anonymous employer had offered him 150,000 euros for staking out the home of an old rabbi and remaining "on call" in case action needed to be taken. Action, in this case, meant breaking into the man's home and injecting him with potassium chloride, resulting in immediate death from an apparent heart attack.

Tonight, unexpectedly, the rabbi had left his home in the middle of the night and taken a city bus to a seedy neighborhood. The assassin had tailed him and then used the encrypted overlay program on his smartphone to inform his employer of the development.

Target has exited home. Traveled to bar district. Possibly meeting someone?

His employer's response was almost immediate.

Execute.

Now, among the ruin bars and dark alleyways, what had begun as a stakeout had become a deadly game of cat and mouse.

———

Rabbi Yehuda Köves was sweating and out of breath as he made his way along Kazinczy Street. His lungs burned, and he felt as if his aging bladder were about to burst.

All I need is a toilet and some rest, he thought, pausing among a crowd congregating outside Bar Szimpla—one of Budapest's largest and most famous ruin bars. The patrons here were such a diverse mix of ages and professions that nobody gave the old rabbi a second look.

I'll stop just for a moment, he decided, moving toward the bar.

Once a spectacular stone mansion with elegant balconies and tall windows, the Bar Szimpla was now a dilapidated shell covered with graffiti. As Köves moved through the wide portico of this once grand city residence, he passed through a doorway inscribed with an encoded message: Egg-esh-Ay-ged-reh!

It took him a moment to realize that it was nothing but the phonetic spelling of the Hungarian word **egészségedre**—meaning "cheers!"

Entering, Köves stared in disbelief at the bar's cavernous interior. The derelict mansion was built around a sprawling courtyard dotted with some of the strangest objects the rabbi had ever seen—a couch made from a bathtub, mannequins riding bicycles suspended in the air, and a gutted East German Trabant sedan, which now served as makeshift seating for patrons.

The courtyard was enclosed by high walls adorned with a patchwork of spray-painted graffiti, Soviet-era posters, classical sculptures, and hanging plants that spilled over interior balconies packed with patrons who all swayed to the thumping music. The air smelled of cigarettes and beer. Young couples kissed passionately in plain sight while others discreetly smoked from small pipes and drank shots of **pálinka,** a popular fruit brandy bottled in Hungary.

Köves always found it ironic that humans, despite being God's most sublime creation, were still just animals at the core, their behavior driven to a great extent by a quest for creature comforts. **We comfort our physical bodies in hopes our souls will follow.** Köves spent much of his time counseling those who overindulged in the animal temptations of the body—primarily food and sex—and with the rise of Internet addiction and cheap designer drugs, his job had grown more challenging every day.

The only creature comfort Köves needed at the moment was a restroom, and so he was dismayed to find a line ten people deep. Unable to wait, he gingerly climbed the stairs, where he was told he would find numerous other restrooms. On the second floor of the mansion, the rabbi moved through a labyrinth of adjoining sitting rooms and bedrooms, each with its own little bar or seating area. He asked one of the bartenders about a bathroom, and the man pointed to a hallway a good distance away, apparently accessible along a balcony walkway that overlooked the courtyard.

Köves quickly made his way to the balcony, placing a steadying hand on the railing as he moved along it. As he walked, he peered absently into the bustling courtyard below, where a sea of young people gyrated in rhythm to the deep pulse of the music.

Then Köves saw it.

He stopped short, his blood turning cold.

There, in the middle of the crowd, the man in the baseball cap and jeans was staring directly up at him. For one brief instant, the two men locked eyes. Then, with the speed of a panther, the man in the cap sprang into action, pushing his way past patrons and sprinting up the staircase.

——————

The assassin bounded up the stairs, scrutinizing every face he passed. Bar Szimpla was quite familiar to him, and he quickly made his way to the balcony where his target had been standing.

The rabbi was gone.

I did not pass you, the killer thought, **which means you moved deeper into the building.**

Raising his gaze to a darkened corridor ahead, the assassin smiled, suspecting he knew precisely where his mark would try to hide.

The corridor was cramped and smelled of urine. At the far end was a warped wooden door.

The killer padded loudly down the corridor and banged on the door.

Silence.

He knocked again.

A deep voice inside grunted that the room was occupied.

"Bocsásson meg!" the killer apologized in a chirpy voice, and made a show of loudly moving away. Then he silently turned around and came back to the door, pressing his ear to the wood. Inside, he could hear the rabbi whispering desperately in Hungarian.

"Someone is trying to kill me! He was outside my house! Now he has trapped me inside Bar Szimpla in Budapest! Please! Send help!"

Apparently, his target had dialed 112—Budapest's equivalent of 911. Response times were notoriously slow, but nonetheless, the killer had heard enough.

Glancing behind him to make sure he was alone, he leveled his muscular shoulder toward the door, leaned back, and synchronized his attack with the thunderous beat of the music.

The old butterfly latch exploded on the first try. The door flew open. The killer stepped inside, closed the door behind him, and faced his prey.

The man cowering in the corner looked as confused as he did terrified.

The killer took the rabbi's phone, ended the call, and tossed the phone into the toilet.

"Wh-who sent you?!" the rabbi stammered.

"The beauty of my situation," the man replied, "is that I have no way to know."

The old man was wheezing now, sweating profusely. He suddenly began to gasp, his eyes bulging out as he reached up and seized his own chest with both hands.

Really? the killer thought, smiling. **He's having a heart attack?**

On the bathroom floor, the old man writhed and choked, his eyes pleading for compassion as his face turned red and he clawed at his chest. Finally, he pitched face-first onto the grimy tile, where he lay trembling and shuddering as his bladder emptied itself into his pants, a trickle of urine now running across the floor.

Finally, the rabbi was still.

The killer crouched down and listened for breathing. Not a sound.

Then he stood up, smirking. "You made my job far easier than I anticipated."

With that, the killer strode toward the door.

———

Rabbi Köves's lungs strained for air.

He had just given the performance of a lifetime.

Teetering near unconsciousness, he lay motionless and listened as his attacker's footsteps retreated across the bathroom floor. The door creaked open and then clicked closed.

Silence.

Köves forced himself to wait another couple of seconds to ensure that his attacker had walked down the hall out of earshot. Then, unable to wait another instant, Köves exhaled and began pulling in deep life-giving breaths. Even the stale air of the bathroom tasted heaven-sent.

Slowly, he opened his eyes, his vision hazy from lack of oxygen. As Köves raised his throbbing head, his vision began to clear. To his bewilderment, he saw a dark figure standing just inside the closed door.

The man in the baseball cap was smiling down at him.

Köves froze. **He never left the room.**

The killer took two long strides to the rabbi, and with a viselike grip, he grabbed the rabbi's neck and shoved his face back into the tile floor.

"You could stop your breathing," snarled the killer, "but you couldn't stop your heart." He laughed. "Not to worry, I can help you with that."

An instant later, a searing point of heat tore into the side of Köves's neck. A molten fire seemed to flow down his throat and up over his skull. This time, when his heart seized, he knew it was for real.

After dedicating much of his life to the mysteries of **Shamayim**—the dwelling place of God and the righteous dead—Rabbi Yehuda Köves knew that all the answers were just a heartbeat away.

CHAPTER 44

Alone in the spacious restroom of the G550 jet, Ambra Vidal stood at the sink and let warm water run gently over her hands as she stared into the mirror, barely recognizing herself in the reflection.

What have I done?

She took another sip of wine, longing for her old life of only a few months ago—anonymous, single, engrossed in her museum work—but all of that was gone now. It had evaporated the moment Julián proposed.

No, she chided herself. **It evaporated the moment you said yes.**

The horror of tonight's assassination had settled in her gut, and now her logical mind was fearfully weighing the implications.

I invited Edmond's assassin to the museum.

I was tricked by someone in the palace.

And now I know too much.

There was no proof that Prince Julián was behind the bloody killing, nor that he was even **aware** of the assassination plan. Even so, Ambra had seen enough of the palace's inner workings to suspect that none of this could have happened without the prince's knowledge, if not his blessing.

I told Julián too much.

In recent weeks, Ambra had felt the growing need to justify every second she spent away from her jealous fiancé, and so she had privately shared with Julián much of what she knew about Edmond's upcoming presentation. Ambra now feared her openness might have been reckless.

Ambra turned off the water and dried her hands, reaching for her wine goblet and draining the last few drops. In the mirror before her she saw a stranger—a once confident professional who was now filled with regret and shame.

The mistakes I've made in a few short months . . .

As her mind reeled back in time, she wondered what she could possibly have done differently. Four months ago, on a rainy night in Madrid, Ambra was attending a fund-raiser at the Reina Sofía Museum of Modern Art . . .

Most of the guests had migrated to room 206.06 to view the museum's most famous work—**El Guernica**—a sprawling twenty-five-foot-long Picasso that evoked the horrific bombing of a small Basque town during the Spanish Civil War. Ambra, however, found the painting too painful to view—a vivid reminder of the brutal oppression endured under Spain's fascistic dictator General Francisco Franco between 1939 and 1975.

Instead, she had chosen to slip alone into a quiet

gallery to enjoy the work of one of her favorite Spanish artists, Maruja Mallo, a female Surrealist from Galicia whose success in the 1930s had helped shatter the glass ceiling for female artists in Spain.

Ambra was standing alone admiring **La Verbena**—a political satire filled with complex symbols—when a deep voice spoke behind her.

"**Es casi tan guapa como tú,**" the man declared. **It's almost as beautiful as you are.**

Seriously? Ambra stared straight ahead and resisted the urge to roll her eyes. At events like these, the museum sometimes felt more like an awkward pickup bar than a cultural center.

"**¿Qué crees que significa?**" the voice behind her pressed. **What do you think it means?**

"I have no idea," she lied, hoping that speaking English might make the man move on. "I just like it."

"I like it too," the man replied in almost accentless English. "Mallo was ahead of her time. Sadly, for the untrained eye, this painting's superficial beauty can camouflage the deeper substance within." He paused. "I imagine a woman like **you** must face that problem all the time."

Ambra groaned. **Do lines like this really work on women?** Affixing a polite smile to her face, she spun around to dispatch the man. "Sir, that's very kind of you to say, but—"

Ambra Vidal froze midsentence.

The man facing her was someone she had seen on television and in magazines for her entire life.

"Oh," Ambra stammered. "You're . . ."

"Presumptuous?" the handsome man ventured. "Clumsily bold? I'm sorry, I live a sheltered life, and I'm not very good at this sort of thing." He smiled and extended a polite hand. "My name is Julián."

"I think I know your name," Ambra told him, blushing as she shook hands with Prince Julián, the future king of Spain. He was far taller than she had imagined, with soft eyes and a confident smile. "I didn't know you were going to be here tonight," she continued, quickly regaining her composure. "I imagined you as more of a Prado man—you know, Goya, Velázquez . . . the classics."

"You mean conservative and old-fashioned?" He laughed warmly. "I think you have me confused with my father. Mallo and Miró have always been favorites of mine."

Ambra and the prince talked for several minutes, and she was impressed by his knowledge of art. Then again, the man grew up in Madrid's Royal Palace, which possessed one of Spain's finest collections; he'd probably had an original El Greco hanging in his nursery.

"I realize this will seem forward," the prince said, presenting her with a gold-embossed business card, "but I would love for you to join me at a dinner party tomorrow night. My direct number is on the card. Just let me know."

"Dinner?" Ambra joked. "You don't even know my name."

"Ambra Vidal," he replied matter-of-factly. "You're thirty-nine years old. You hold a degree in art history from the Universidad de Salamanca. You're the director of our Guggenheim Museum in Bilbao. You recently spoke out on the controversy surrounding Luis Quiles, whose artwork, I agree, graphically mirrors the horrors of modern life and may not be appropriate for young children, but I'm not sure I agree with you that his work resembles that of Banksy. You've never been married. You have no children. And you look fantastic in black."

Ambra's jaw dropped. "My goodness. Does this approach really work?"

"I have no idea," he said with a smile. "I guess we'll find out."

As if on cue, two Guardia Real agents materialized and ushered the prince off to mingle with some VIPs.

Ambra clutched the business card in her hand and felt something she had not felt in years. Butterflies. **Did a prince just ask me for a date?**

Ambra had been a gangly teenager, and the boys who asked her out had always felt themselves to be on an equal footing with her. Later in life, though, when her beauty had blossomed, Ambra suddenly found men to be intimidated in her presence, fumbling and self-conscious and entirely too deferential. Tonight, however, a powerful man had boldly strode up to her and taken total control. It made her feel feminine. And young.

The very next night, a driver collected Ambra at her hotel and took her to the Royal Palace, where she found herself seated next to the prince in the company of two dozen other guests, many of whom she recognized from the society pages or politics. The prince introduced her as his "lovely new friend" and deftly launched a conversation about art in which Ambra could participate fully. She had the sensation that she was being auditioned somehow, but strangely, she didn't really mind. She felt flattered.

At the evening's end, Julián took her aside and whispered, "I hope you had fun. I'd love to see you again." He smiled. "How about Thursday night?"

"Thank you," Ambra replied, "but I'm afraid I'm flying back to Bilbao in the morning."

"Then I'll fly up as well," he said. "Have you been to the restaurant Etxanobe?"

Ambra had to laugh. Etxanobe was one of Bilbao's most coveted dining experiences. A favorite of art aficionados from around the world, the restaurant boasted an avant-garde decor and colorful cuisine that made diners feel as if they were seated in a landscape painted by Marc Chagall.

"That would be lovely," she heard herself say.

At Etxanobe, over stylishy presented plates of sumac-seared tuna and truffled asparagus, Julián opened up about the political challenges he faced as he attempted to emerge from the shadow of his ailing father, and also about the personal pressure he felt to continue the royal line. Ambra recognized in him the innocence of a cloistered little boy but also saw the makings of a leader with a fervent passion for his country. She found it an alluring combination.

That night, when Julián's security guards whisked him back to his private plane, Ambra knew she was smitten.

You barely know him, she reminded herself. **Take it slow.**

The next several months seemed to pass in an instant as Ambra and Julián saw each other constantly—dinners at the palace, picnics on the grounds of his country estate, even a movie matinee. Their rapport was unforced, and Ambra couldn't remember ever being happier. Julián was endearingly old-fashioned, often holding her hand or stealing a polite kiss, but never crossing the conventional boundaries, and Ambra appreciated his fine manners.

One sunny morning, three weeks ago, Ambra was in Madrid, where she was scheduled to appear in a segment of a morning TV show about the Guggenheim's upcoming exhibits. RTVE's **Telediario** was watched by millions live around the country, and Ambra was a little apprehensive about doing live television, but she knew the spot would provide superb national coverage for the museum.

The night before the show, she and Julián met for a deliciously casual dinner at Trattoria Malatesta and then slipped quietly through El Parque del Retiro. Watching the families out strolling and the scores of children laughing and running about, Ambra felt totally at peace, lost in the moment.

"Do you like children?" Julián asked.

"I adore them," she replied honestly. "In fact, sometimes I feel like children are the only thing missing in my life."

Julián smiled broadly. "I know the feeling."

In that instant, the way he looked at her felt different somehow, and Ambra suddenly realized **why** Julián was asking the question. A surge of fear gripped her, and a voice in her head screamed out, **Tell him! TELL HIM NOW!**

She tried to speak, but she couldn't make a sound.

"Are you okay?" he asked, looking concerned.

Ambra smiled. "It's the **Telediario** show. I'm just a little nervous."

"Exhale. You'll be great."

Julián flashed her a broad smile and then leaned forward and gave her a quick soft kiss on the lips.

The next morning, at seven thirty, Ambra found herself on a television soundstage, engaged in a surprisingly comfortable on-air chat with the three charming **Telediario** hosts. She was so caught up in her enthusiasm for the Guggenheim that she barely noticed the television cameras and the live studio audience, or remembered that five million people were watching at home.

"**Gracias, Ambra, y muy interesante**," said the female host as the segment concluded. "**Un gran placer conocerte.**"

Ambra nodded her thanks and waited for the interview to end.

Strangely, the female host gave her a coy smile and continued the segment by turning to address the home audience directly. "This morning," she began in Spanish, "a very special guest has made a surprise visit to the **Telediario** studio, and we'd like to bring him out."

All three hosts stood up, clapping as a tall, elegant

man strode onto the set. When the audience saw him, they jumped to their feet, cheering wildly.

Ambra stood too, staring in shock.

Julián?

Prince Julián waved to the crowd and politely shook the hands of the three hosts. Then he walked over and stood beside Ambra, placing an arm around her.

"My father has always been a romantic," he said, speaking Spanish and looking directly into the camera to address the viewers. "When my mother died, he never stopped loving her. I inherited his romanticism, and I believe when a man finds love, he knows in an instant." He looked at Ambra and smiled warmly. "And so . . ." Julián stepped back and faced her.

When Ambra realized what was about to happen, she felt paralyzed with disbelief. **NO! Julián! What are you doing?**

Without warning, the crown prince of Spain was suddenly kneeling down before her. "Ambra Vidal, I am asking you not as a prince, but simply as a man in love." He looked up at her with misty eyes, and the cameras wheeled around to get a close-up of his face. "I love you. Will you marry me?"

The audience and the show's hosts all gasped in joy, and Ambra could feel millions of eyes around the country focusing intently on her. Blood rushed to her face, and the lights felt suddenly scalding hot on her skin. Her heart began to pound wildly as she stared down at Julián, a thousand thoughts racing through her head.

How could you put me in this position?! We've

only recently met! There are things I haven't told you about myself . . . things that could change everything!

Ambra had no idea how long she had stood in silent panic, but finally one of the hosts gave an awkward laugh and said, "I believe Ms. Vidal is in a trance! Ms. Vidal? A handsome prince is kneeling before you and professing his love before the entire world!"

Ambra searched her mind for some graceful way out. All she heard was silence, and she knew she was trapped. There was only one way this public moment could end. "I'm hesitating because I can't believe this fairy tale has a happy ending." She relaxed her shoulders and smiled warmly down at Julián. "Of course I will marry you, Prince Julián."

The studio erupted in wild applause.

Julián stood up and took Ambra in his arms. As they embraced, she realized that they had never shared a long hug before this moment.

Ten minutes later, the two were sitting in the back of his limousine.

"I can see I startled you," Julián said. "I'm sorry. I was trying to be romantic. I have strong feelings for you, and—"

"Julián," Ambra interrupted forcefully, "I have strong feelings for you too, but you put me in an impossible position back there! I never imagined you would propose so quickly! You and I barely know each other. There are so many things I need to tell you—important things about my past."

"Nothing in your past matters."

"This might matter. **A lot.**"

He smiled and shook his head. "I love you. It won't matter. Try me."

Ambra studied the man before her. **Okay, then.** This was most certainly not how she had wanted this conversation to go, but he had given her no choice. "Well, here it is, Julián. When I was a little girl, I had a terrible infection that almost killed me."

"Okay."

As Ambra spoke, she felt a deep emptiness welling up inside her. "And the result was that my life's dream of having children . . . well, it can only be a dream."

"I don't understand."

"Julián," she said flatly. "I **can't** have children. My childhood health problems left me infertile. I've always wanted children, but I am unable to have any of my own. I'm sorry. I know how important that is to you, but you've just proposed to a woman who cannot give you an heir."

Julián went white.

Ambra locked eyes with him, willing him to speak. **Julián, this is the moment when you hold me close and tell me everything's okay. This is the moment you tell me it doesn't matter, and that you love me anyway.**

And then it happened.

Julián shifted away from her ever so slightly.

In that instant, Ambra knew it was over.

CHAPTER 45

The Guardia's division of electronic security is located in a windowless warren of rooms on the subterranean level of the Royal Palace. Intentionally isolated from the palace's vast Guardia barracks and armory, the division's headquarters consists of a dozen computer cubicles, one telephone switchboard, and a wall of security monitors. The eight-person staff—all under the age of thirty-five—is responsible for providing secure communication networks for the staff of the Royal Palace and the Guardia Real, as well as handling electronic surveillance support for the physical palace itself.

Tonight, as always, the basement suite of rooms was stuffy, reeking of microwaved noodles and popcorn. The fluorescent lights hummed loudly.

This is where I asked them to put my office, Martín thought.

Although "public relations coordinator" was technically not a Guardia post, Martín's job required access to powerful computers and a tech-savvy staff; thus, the division of electronic security had seemed a far more logical home for her than an underequipped office upstairs.

Tonight, Martín thought, **I will need every bit of technology available.**

For the past few months, her primary focus had been to help the palace stay on message during the gradual transfer of power to Prince Julián. It had not been easy. The transition between leaders had provided an opportunity for protesters to speak out against the monarchy.

According to the Spanish constitution, the monarchy stood as "a symbol of Spain's enduring unity and permanence." But Martín knew there had been nothing **unified** about Spain for some time now. In 1931, the Second Republic had marked the end of the monarchy, and then the putsch of General Franco in 1936 had plunged the country into civil war.

Today, although the reinstated monarchy was considered a liberal democracy, many liberals continued to denounce the king as an outdated vestige of an oppressive religio-military past, as well as a daily reminder that Spain still had a way to go before it could fully join the modern world.

Mónica Martín's messaging this month had included the usual portrayals of the king as a beloved symbol who held no real power. Of course, it was a tough sell when the sovereign was commander in chief of the armed forces as well as head of state.

Head of state, Martín mused, **in a country where separation between church and state has always been controversial.** The ailing king's close relationship with Bishop Valdespino had been a thorn in the side of secularists and liberals for many years.

And then there is Prince Julián, she thought.

Martín knew she owed her job to the prince, but he certainly had been making that job more difficult recently. A few weeks ago, the prince had made the worst PR blunder Martín had ever witnessed.

On national television, Prince Julián had gotten down on his knees and made a ludicrous proposal to Ambra Vidal. The excruciating moment could not have been any more awkward unless Ambra had declined to marry him, which, fortunately, she had the good sense not to do.

Unfortunately, in the aftermath, Ambra Vidal had revealed herself to be more of a handful than Julián had anticipated, and the fallout from her extracurricular behavior this month had become one of Martín's primary PR concerns.

Tonight, however, Ambra's indiscretions seemed all but forgotten. The tidal wave of media activity generated by the events in Bilbao had swelled to an unprecedented magnitude. In the past hour, a viral proliferation of conspiracy theories had taken the world by storm, including several new hypotheses involving Bishop Valdespino.

The most significant development concerned the Guggenheim assassin, who had been given access to Kirsch's event "on orders of someone inside the Royal Palace." This damning bit of news had unleashed a deluge of conspiracy theories accusing the bedridden king and Bishop Valdespino of conspiring to murder Edmond Kirsch—a virtual demigod in the digital world, and a beloved American hero who had chosen to live in Spain.

This is going to destroy Valdespino, Martín thought.

"Everyone, listen up!" Garza now shouted as he strode into the control room. "Prince Julián and Bishop Valdespino are together somewhere on the premises! Check all security feeds and find them. Now!"

The commander stalked into Martín's office and quietly updated her on the situation with the prince and the bishop.

"Gone?" she said, incredulous. "And they left their phones in the prince's **safe**?"

Garza shrugged. "Apparently so we can't track them."

"Well, we'd **better** find them," Martín declared. "Prince Julián needs to make a statement right now, and he needs to distance himself from Valdespino as much as possible." She relayed all the latest developments.

Now it was Garza's turn to look incredulous. "It's all hearsay. There's no way Valdespino could be behind an assassination."

"Maybe not, but the killing seems to be tied to the Catholic Church. Someone just found a direct connection between the shooter and a highly placed church official. Have a look." Martín pulled up the latest ConspiracyNet update, which was once again credited to the whistle-blower called monte@iglesia.org. "This went live a few minutes ago."

Garza crouched down and began reading the update. "The **pope**!" he protested. "Ávila has a personal connection with—"

"Keep reading."

When Garza finished, he stepped back from the screen and blinked his eyes repeatedly, as if trying to wake himself from a bad dream.

At that moment, a male voice called from the control room. "Commander Garza? I've located them!"

Garza and Martín hurried over to the cubicle of Agent Suresh Bhalla, an Indian-born surveillance specialist who pointed to the security feed on his monitor, on which two forms were visible—one in flowing bishop's robes and the other in a formal suit. They appeared to be walking on a wooded path.

"East garden," Suresh said. "Two minutes ago."

"They've **exited** the building?!" Garza demanded.

"Hold on, sir." Suresh fast-forwarded the footage, managing to follow the bishop and the prince on various cameras located at intervals across the palace complex as the two men left the garden and moved through an enclosed courtyard.

"Where are they going?!"

Martín had a good idea where they were going, and she noted that Valdespino had taken a shrewd circuitous route that kept them out of sight of the media trucks on the main plaza.

As she anticipated, Valdespino and Julián arrived at the southern service entrance of Almudena Cathedral, where the bishop unlocked the door and ushered Prince Julián inside. The door swung shut, and the two men were gone.

Garza stared mutely at the screen, clearly struggling to make sense of what he had just seen. "Keep me posted," he finally said, and motioned Martín aside.

Once they were out of earshot, Garza whispered, "I have no idea how Bishop Valdespino persuaded Prince Julián to follow him out of the palace, or to leave his phone behind, but clearly the prince has no idea about these accusations against Valdespino, or he would know to distance himself."

"I agree," Martín said. "And I'd hate to speculate as to what the bishop's endgame might be, but . . ." She stopped.

"But what?" Garza demanded.

Martín sighed. "It appears Valdespino may have just taken an extremely valuable hostage."

———

Some 250 miles to the north, inside the atrium of the Guggenheim Museum, Agent Fonseca's phone began buzzing. It was the sixth time in twenty minutes. When he glanced down at the caller ID, he felt his body snap to attention.

"¿Sí?" he answered, his heart pounding.

The voice on the line spoke in Spanish, slowly and deliberately. "Agent Fonseca, as you are well aware, Spain's future queen consort has made some terrible missteps this evening, associating herself with the wrong people and causing significant embarrassment to the Royal Palace. In order that no further damage be done, it is crucial that you get her back to the palace as quickly as possible."

"I'm afraid Ms. Vidal's location is unknown at the moment."

"Forty minutes ago, Edmond Kirsch's jet took off from Bilbao Airport—headed for Barcelona," the voice asserted. "I believe Ms. Vidal was on that plane."

"How would you know that?" Fonseca blurted, and then instantly regretted his impertinent tone.

"If you were doing your job," the voice replied sharply, "**you** would know too. I want you and your partner to pursue her at once. A military transport is fueling at Bilbao Airport for you right now."

"If Ms. Vidal is on that jet," Fonseca said, "she is probably traveling with the American professor Robert Langdon."

"Yes," the caller said angrily. "I have no idea how this man persuaded Ms. Vidal to abandon her security and run off with him, but Mr. Langdon is clearly a liability. Your mission is to find Ms. Vidal and bring her back, by force if necessary."

"And if Langdon interferes?"

There was a heavy silence. "Do your best to limit collateral damage," the caller replied, "but this crisis is severe enough that Professor Langdon would be an acceptable casualty."

CHAPTER 46

🌐 ConspiracyNet.com

BREAKING NEWS

KIRSCH COVERAGE GOES MAINSTREAM!

Edmond Kirsch's scientific announcement tonight began as an online presentation that attracted a staggering three million online viewers. In the wake of his assassination, however, the Kirsch story is now being covered on mainstream networks live around the world, with current viewership estimated at over eighty million.

CHAPTER 47

s Kirsch's Gulfstream G550 began its descent into Barcelona, Robert Langdon drained his second mug of coffee and gazed down at the remains of the impromptu late-night snack that he and Ambra had just shared from Edmond's galley—nuts, rice cakes, and assorted "vegan bars" that all tasted the same to him.

Across the table, Ambra had just finished her second glass of red wine and was looking much more relaxed.

"Thanks for listening," she said, sounding sheepish. "Obviously, I haven't been able to talk about Julián with anyone."

Langdon gave her an understanding nod, having just heard the story of Julián's awkward proposal to her on television. **She didn't have a choice**, Langdon agreed, knowing full well that Ambra could not risk shaming the future king of Spain on national television.

"Obviously, if I'd known he was going to propose so quickly," Ambra said, "I would have told him I can't have children. But it all happened without warning." She shook her head and looked sadly out the window.

"I thought I liked him. I don't know, maybe it was just the thrill of—"

"A tall, dark, handsome prince?" Langdon ventured with a lopsided grin.

Ambra laughed quietly and turned back to him. "He did have **that** going for him. I don't know, he seemed like a good man. Sheltered maybe, but a romantic—not the kind of man who would ever be involved in killing Edmond."

Langdon suspected she was right. The prince had little to gain from Edmond's death, and there was no solid evidence to suggest that the prince was involved in any way—only a phone call from someone inside the palace asking to add Admiral Ávila to the guest list. At this point, Bishop Valdespino seemed to be the most obvious suspect, having been privy to Edmond's announcement early enough to formulate a plan to stop it, and also knowing better than anyone just how destructive it might be to the authority of the world's religions.

"Obviously, I can't marry Julián," Ambra said quietly. "I keep thinking he'll break off the engagement now that he knows I can't have children. His bloodline has held the crown for most of the last four centuries. Something tells me that a museum administrator from Bilbao will not be the reason the lineage ends."

The speaker overhead crackled, and the pilots announced that it was time to prepare for their landing in Barcelona.

Jarred from her ruminations about the prince,

Ambra stood and began tidying up the cabin—rinsing their glasses in the galley and disposing of the uneaten food.

"Professor," Winston chimed from Edmond's phone on the table, "I thought you should be aware that there is new information now going viral online—strong evidence suggesting a secret link between Bishop Valdespino and the assassin Admiral Ávila."

Langdon was alarmed by the news.

"Unfortunately, there is more," Winston added. "As you know, Kirsch's secret meeting with Bishop Valdespino included two other religious leaders—a prominent rabbi and a well-loved imam. Last night, the imam was found dead in the desert near Dubai. And, in the last few minutes, there is troubling news coming out of Budapest: it seems the rabbi has been found dead of an apparent heart attack."

Langdon was stunned.

"Bloggers," Winston said, "are already questioning the coincidental timing of their deaths."

Langdon nodded in mute disbelief. One way or the other, Bishop Antonio Valdespino was now the **only** living person on earth who knew what Kirsch had discovered.

———

When the Gulfstream G550 touched down onto the lone runway at Sabadell Airport in the foothills of Barcelona, Ambra was relieved to see no signs of waiting paparazzi or press.

According to Edmond, in order to avoid dealing with starstruck fans at Barcelona's El-Prat Airport, he chose to keep his plane at this small jetport.

That was not the real reason, Ambra knew.

In reality, Edmond loved attention, and admitted to keeping his plane at Sabadell only to have an excuse to drive the winding roads to his home in his favorite sports car—a Tesla Model X P90D that Elon Musk had allegedly hand-delivered to him as a gift. Supposedly, Edmond had once challenged his jet pilots to a one-mile drag race on the runway—Gulfstream vs. Tesla—but his pilots had done the math and declined.

I'll miss Edmond, Ambra thought ruefully. Yes, he was self-indulgent and brash, but his brilliant imagination deserved so much more from life than what happened to him tonight. **I just hope we can honor him by unveiling his discovery.**

When the plane arrived inside Edmond's single-plane hangar and powered down, Ambra could see that everything here was quiet. Apparently, she and Professor Langdon were still flying under the radar.

As she led the way down the jet's staircase, Ambra breathed deeply, trying to clear her head. The second glass of wine had taken hold, and she regretted drinking it. Stepping down onto the cement floor of the hangar, she faltered slightly and felt Langdon's strong hand on her shoulder, steadying her.

"Thanks," she whispered, smiling back at the professor, whose two cups of coffee had left him looking wide-awake and wired.

"We should get out of sight as quickly as possible,"

Langdon said, eyeing the sleek black SUV parked in the corner. "I assume that's the vehicle you told me about?"

She nodded. "Edmond's secret love."

"Odd license plate."

Ambra eyed the car's vanity plate and chuckled.

E-WAVE

"Well," she explained, "Edmond told me that Google and NASA recently acquired a ground-breaking supercomputer called D-Wave—one of the world's first 'quantum' computers. He tried to explain it to me, but it was pretty complicated—something about superpositions and quantum mechanics and creating an entirely new breed of machine. Anyhow, Edmond said he wanted to build something that would blow D-Wave out of the water. He planned to call his new computer E-Wave."

"E for Edmond," Langdon mused.

And E is one step beyond D, Ambra thought, recalling Edmond's story about the famous computer in **2001: A Space Odyssey,** which, according to urban legend, had been named HAL because each letter occurred alphabetically one letter ahead of IBM.

"And the car key?" Langdon asked. "You said you know where he hides it."

"He doesn't use a key." Ambra held up Edmond's phone. "He showed me this when we came here last month." She touched the phone screen, launched the Tesla app, and selected the summon command.

Instantly, in the corner of the hangar, the SUV's headlights blazed to life, and the Tesla—without the slightest sound—slid smoothly up beside them and stopped.

Langdon cocked his head, looking unnerved by the prospect of a car that drove itself.

"Don't worry," Ambra assured him. "I'll let **you** drive to Edmond's apartment."

Langdon nodded his agreement and began circling around to the driver's side. As he passed the front of the car, he paused, staring down at the license plate and laughing out loud.

Ambra knew exactly what had amused him— Edmond's license-plate frame: AND THE GEEK SHALL INHERIT THE EARTH.

"Only Edmond," Langdon said as he climbed in behind the wheel. "Subtlety was never his forte."

"He loved this car," Ambra said, getting in next to Langdon. "Fully electric and faster than a Ferrari."

Langdon shrugged, eyeing the high-tech dashboard. "I'm not really a car guy."

Ambra smiled. "You **will** be."

CHAPTER 48

As Ávila's Uber raced eastward through the darkness, the admiral wondered how many times during his years as a naval officer he had made port in Barcelona.

His previous life seemed a world away now, having ended in a fiery flash in Seville. Fate was a cruel and unpredictable mistress, and yet there seemed an eerie equilibrium about her now. The same fate that had torn out his soul in the Cathedral of Seville had now granted him a second life—a fresh start born within the sanctuary walls of a very different cathedral.

Ironically, the person who had taken him there was a simple physical therapist named Marco.

"A meeting with the pope?" Ávila had asked his trainer months ago, when Marco first proposed the idea. "Tomorrow? In Rome?"

"Tomorrow in **Spain,**" Marco had replied. "The pope is here."

Ávila eyed him as if he were crazy. "The media have said nothing about His Holiness being in Spain."

"A little trust, Admiral," Marco replied with a laugh. "Unless you've got somewhere else to be tomorrow?"

Ávila glanced down at his injured leg.

"We'll leave at nine," Marco prompted. "I promise our little trip will be far less painful than rehab."

The next morning, Ávila got dressed in a navy uniform that Marco had retrieved from Ávila's home, grabbed a pair of crutches, and hobbled out to Marco's car—an old Fiat. Marco drove out of the hospital lot and headed south on Avenida de la Raza, eventually leaving the city and getting on Highway N-IV heading south.

"Where are we going?" Ávila asked, suddenly uneasy.

"Relax," Marco said, smiling. "Just trust me. It'll only take half an hour."

Ávila knew there was nothing but parched pastureland on the N-IV for at least another 150 kilometers. He was beginning to think he had made a terrible mistake. Half an hour into the journey, they approached the eerie ghost town of El Torbiscal—a once prosperous farming village whose population had recently dwindled to zero. **Where in the world is he taking me?!** Marco drove on for several minutes, then exited the highway and turned north.

"Can you see it?" Marco asked, pointing into the distance across a fallow field.

Ávila saw nothing. Either the young trainer was hallucinating or Ávila's eyes were getting old.

"Isn't it amazing?" Marco declared.

Ávila squinted into the sun, and finally saw a dark form rising out of the landscape. As they drew closer, his eyes widened in disbelief.

Is that . . . a cathedral?

The scale of the building looked like something he might expect to see in Madrid or Paris. Ávila had lived in Seville his entire life but had never known of a cathedral out here in the middle of nowhere. The closer they drove, the more impressive the complex appeared, its massive cement walls providing a level of security that Ávila had seen only in Vatican City.

Marco left the main highway and drove along a short access road toward the cathedral, approaching a towering iron gate that blocked their way. As they came to a stop, Marco pulled a laminated card from the glove box and placed it on the dashboard.

A security guard approached, eyed the card, and then peered into the vehicle, smiling broadly when he saw Marco. "**Bienvenidos,**" the guard said. "**¿Qué tal, Marco?**"

The two men shook hands, and Marco introduced Admiral Ávila.

"**Ha venido a conocer al papa,**" Marco told the guard. **He's come to meet the pope.**

The guard nodded, admiring the medals on Ávila's uniform, and waved them on. As the huge gate swung open, Ávila felt like he was entering a medieval castle.

The soaring Gothic cathedral that appeared before them had eight towering spires, each with a triple-tiered bell tower. A trio of massive cupolas made up the body of the structure, the exterior of which was composed of dark brown and white stone, giving it an unusually modern feel.

Ávila lowered his gaze to the access road, which forked into three parallel roadways, each lined with a phalanx of tall palm trees. To his surprise, the entire area was jammed with parked vehicles—hundreds of them—luxury sedans, dilapidated buses, mud-covered mopeds . . . everything imaginable.

Marco bypassed them all, driving straight to the church's front courtyard, where a security guard saw them, checked his watch, and waved them into an empty parking spot that had clearly been reserved for them.

"We're a little late," Marco said. "We should hurry inside."

Ávila was about to reply, but the words were lodged in his throat.

He had just seen the sign in front of the church:

Iglesia Católica Palmariana

My God! Ávila felt himself recoil. **I've heard of this church!**

He turned to Marco, trying to control his pounding heart. "This is **your** church, Marco?" Ávila tried not to sound alarmed. "You're a . . . **Palmarian?**"

Marco smiled. "You say the word like it's some kind of disease. I'm just a devout Catholic who believes that Rome has gone astray."

Ávila raised his eyes again to the church. Marco's strange claim about knowing the pope suddenly made sense. **The pope** is **here in Spain.**

A few years ago, the television network Canal Sur had aired a documentary titled **La Iglesia Oscura,** whose purpose was to unveil some of the secrets of the Palmarian Church. Ávila had been stunned to learn of the strange church's existence, not to mention its growing congregation and influence.

According to lore, the Palmarian Church had been founded after some local residents claimed to have witnessed a series of mystical visions in a field nearby. Allegedly, the Virgin Mary had appeared to them and warned that the Catholic Church was rife with the "heresy of modernism" and that the true faith needed to be protected.

The Virgin Mary had urged the Palmarians to establish an alternative church and denounce the current pope in Rome as a false pope. This conviction that the Vatican's pope was **not** the valid pontiff was known as **sedevacantism**—a belief that St. Peter's "seat" was literally "vacant."

Furthermore, the Palmarians claimed to have evidence that the "true" pope was in fact their own founder—a man named Clemente Domínguez y Gómez, who took the name Pope Gregory XVII. Under Pope Gregory—the "antipope," in the view of mainstream Catholics—the Palmarian Church grew steadily. In 2005, when Pope Gregory died while presiding over an Easter mass, his supporters hailed the timing of his death as a miraculous sign from above, confirming that this man was in fact connected directly to God.

Now, as Ávila gazed up at the massive church, he couldn't help but view the building as sinister.

Whoever the current antipope might be, I have no interest in meeting him.

In addition to criticism over their bold claims about the papacy, the Palmarian Church endured allegations of brainwashing, cultlike intimidation, and even responsibility for several mysterious deaths, including that of church member Bridget Crosbie, who, according to her family's attorneys, had been "unable to escape" one of the Palmarian churches in Ireland.

Ávila didn't want to be rude to his new friend, but this was not at all what he had expected from today's trip. "Marco," he said with an apologetic sigh, "I'm sorry, but I don't think I can do this."

"I had a feeling you were going to say that," Marco replied, seemingly unfazed. "And I admit, I had the same reaction when I first came here. I too had heard all the gossip and dark rumors, but I can assure you, it's nothing more than a smear campaign led by the Vatican."

Can you blame them? Ávila wondered. **Your church declared them illegitimate!**

"Rome needed a reason to excommunicate us, so they made up lies. For years, the Vatican has been spreading disinformation about the Palmarians."

Ávila assessed the magnificent cathedral in the middle of nowhere. Something about it felt strange to him. "I'm confused," he said. "If you have no ties to the Vatican, where does all your money come from?"

Marco smiled. "You would be amazed at the number of secret followers the Palmarians have within the Catholic clergy. There are many conservative Catholic parishes here in Spain that do not approve of the liberal changes emanating from Rome, and they are quietly funneling money to churches like ours, where traditional values are upheld."

The answer was unexpected, but it rang true for Ávila. He too had sensed a growing schism within the Catholic Church—a rift between those who believed the Church needed to modernize or die and those who believed the Church's true purpose was to remain steadfast in the face of an evolving world.

"The current pope is a remarkable man," Marco said. "I told him your story, and he said he would be honored to welcome a decorated military officer to our church, and meet with you personally after the service today. Like his predecessors, he had a military background before finding God, and he understands what you're going through. I really think his viewpoint might help you find peace."

Marco opened his door to get out of the car, but Ávila could not move. He just sat in place, staring up at the massive structure, feeling guilty for harboring a blind prejudice against these people. To be fair, he knew nothing of the Palmarian Church except the rumors, and it was not as if the Vatican were without scandal. Moreover, Ávila's own church had not helped him at all after the attack. **Forgive your enemies**, the nun had told him. **Turn the other cheek.**

"Luis, listen to me," Marco whispered. "I realize I tricked you a bit into coming here, but it was with good intentions . . . I wanted you to meet this man. His ideas have changed my life dramatically. After I lost my leg, I was in the place where you are now. I wanted to die. I was sinking into darkness, and this man's words gave me a purpose. Just come and hear him preach."

Ávila hesitated. "I'm happy for you, Marco. But I think I'll be fine on my own."

"Fine?" The young man laughed. "A week ago, you put a gun to your head and pulled the trigger! You are **not** fine, my friend."

He's right, Ávila knew, **and one week from now, when my therapy is done, I will be back home, alone and adrift again.**

"What are you afraid of?" Marco pressed. "You're a naval officer. A grown man who commanded a ship! Are you afraid the pope is going to brainwash you in ten minutes and take you hostage?"

I'm not sure what I'm afraid of, Ávila thought, staring down at his injured leg, feeling strangely small and impotent. For most of his life, he had been the one in charge, the one giving orders. He was uncertain about the prospect of taking orders from someone else.

"Never mind," Marco finally said, refastening his seat belt. "I'm sorry. I can see you're uncomfortable. I didn't mean to pressure you." He reached down to start the car.

Ávila felt like a fool. Marco was practically a child, one-third Ávila's age, missing a leg, trying to help out a fellow invalid, and Ávila had thanked him by being ungrateful, skeptical, and condescending.

"No," Ávila said. "Forgive me, Marco. I'd be honored to listen to the man preach."

CHAPTER **49**

The windshield on Edmond's Tesla Model X was expansive, morphing seamlessly into the car's roof somewhere behind Langdon's head, giving him the disorienting sense he was floating inside a glass bubble.

Guiding the car along the wooded highway north of Barcelona, Langdon was surprised to find himself driving well in excess of the roadway's generous 120 kph speed limit. The vehicle's silent electric engine and linear acceleration seemed to make every speed feel nearly identical.

In the seat beside him, Ambra was busy browsing the Internet on the car's massive dashboard computer display, relaying to Langdon the news that was now breaking worldwide. An ever-deepening web of intrigue was emerging, including rumors that Bishop Valdespino had been wiring funds to the antipope of the Palmarian Church—who allegedly had military ties with conservative Carlists and appeared to be responsible not only for Edmond's death, but also for the deaths of Syed al-Fadl and Rabbi Yehuda Köves.

As Ambra read aloud, it became clear that media outlets everywhere were now asking the same question: What could Edmond Kirsch possibly have dis-

covered that was so threatening that a prominent
bishop and a conservative Catholic sect would **murder** him in an effort to silence his announcement?

"The viewership numbers are incredible," Ambra
said, glancing up from the screen. "Public interest in
this story is unprecedented . . . it seems like the entire
world is transfixed."

In that instant, Langdon realized that perhaps
there was a macabre silver lining to Edmond's horrific
murder. With all the media attention, Kirsch's global
audience had grown far larger than he could ever
have imagined. Right now, even in death, Edmond
held the world's ear.

The realization made Langdon even more committed to achieving his goal—to find Edmond's forty-
seven-letter password and launch his presentation to
the world.

"There's no statement yet from Julián," Ambra said,
sounding puzzled. "Not a single word from the Royal
Palace. It makes no sense. I've had personal experience with their PR coordinator, Mónica Martín, and
she's all about transparency and sharing information
before the press can twist it. I'm sure she's urging
Julián to make a statement."

Langdon suspected she was right. Considering the
media was accusing the palace's primary religious
adviser of conspiracy—possibly even murder—it
seemed logical that Julián should make a statement
of some sort, even if only to say that the palace was
investigating the accusations.

"Especially," Langdon added, "if you consider that

the country's future queen consort was standing right beside Edmond when he was shot. It could have been **you**, Ambra. The prince should at least say he's relieved that you're safe."

"I'm not sure he is," she said matter-of-factly, turning off the browser and leaning back in her seat.

Langdon glanced over. "Well, for whatever it's worth, **I'm** glad you're safe. I'm not sure I could have handled tonight all alone."

"Alone?" an accented voice demanded through the car's speakers. "How quickly we forget!"

Langdon laughed at Winston's indignant outburst. "Winston, did Edmond really program you to be defensive and insecure?"

"No," Winston said. "He programmed me to observe, learn, and mimic human behavior. My tone was more an attempt at humor—which Edmond encouraged me to develop. Humor cannot be programmed . . . it must be learned."

"Well, you're learning well."

"Am I?" Winston entreated. "Perhaps you could say that again?"

Langdon laughed out loud. "As I said, you're learning well."

Ambra had now returned the dashboard display to its default page—a navigation program consisting of a satellite photo on which a tiny "avatar" of their car was visible. Langdon could see that they had wound through the Collserola Mountains and were now merging onto Highway B-20 toward Barcelona. To the south of their location, on the satellite photo,

Langdon spotted something unusual that drew his attention—a large forested area in the middle of the urban sprawl. The green expanse was elongated and amorphous, like a giant amoeba.

"Is that Parc Güell?" he asked.

Ambra glanced at the screen and nodded. "Good eye."

"Edmond stopped there frequently," Winston added, "on his way home from the airport."

Langdon was not surprised. Parc Güell was one of the best-known masterpieces of Antoni Gaudí—the same architect and artist whose work Edmond displayed on his phone case. **Gaudí was a lot like Edmond,** Langdon thought. **A groundbreaking visionary for whom the normal rules did not apply.**

A devout student of nature, Antoni Gaudí had taken his architectural inspiration from organic forms, using "God's natural world" to help him design fluid biomorphic structures that often appeared to have grown out of the ground themselves. **There are no straight lines in nature,** Gaudí was once quoted as saying, and indeed, there were very few straight lines in his work either.

Often described as the progenitor of "living architecture" and "biological design," Gaudí invented never-before-seen techniques of carpentry, ironwork, glasswork, and ceramics in order to "sheathe" his buildings in dazzling, colorful skins.

Even now, nearly a century after Gaudí's death, tourists from around the world traveled to Barcelona to get a glimpse of his inimitable modernist style. His

works included parks, public buildings, private mansions, and, of course, his magnum opus—Sagrada
Família—the massive Catholic basilica whose sky-
scraping "sea sponge spires" dominated Barcelona's
skyline, and which critics hailed as being "unlike
anything in the entire history of art."

Langdon had always marveled at Gaudí's audacious vision for Sagrada Família—a basilica so colossal that it remained under construction today, nearly
140 years after its groundbreaking.

Tonight, as Langdon eyed the car's satellite image
of Gaudí's famous Parc Güell, he recalled his first
visit to the park as a college student—a stroll through
a fantasyland of twisting treelike columns supporting elevated walkways, nebulous misshapen benches,
grottoes with fountains resembling dragons and fish,
and an undulating white wall so distinctively fluid
that it looked like the whipping flagellum of a giant
single-celled creature.

"Edmond loved everything Gaudí," Winston continued, "in particular his concept of nature as organic
art."

Langdon's mind touched again on Edmond's discovery. **Nature. Organics. The Creation.** He flashed
on Gaudí's famous Barcelona **Panots**—hexagonal
paving tiles commissioned for the sidewalks of the
city. Each tile bore an identical swirling design of
seemingly meaningless squiggles, and yet when they
were all arranged and rotated as intended, a startling
pattern emerged—an underwater seascape that gave
the impression of plankton, microbes, and undersea

flora—**La Sopa Primordial**, as the locals often called the design.

Gaudí's primordial soup, Langdon thought, again startled by how perfectly the city of Barcelona dovetailed with Edmond's curiosity about the beginnings of life. The prevailing scientific theory was that life had begun in the earth's primordial soup—those early oceans where volcanoes spewed rich chemicals, which swirled around one another, constantly bombarded by lightning bolts from endless storms . . . until suddenly, like some kind of microscopic golem, the first single-celled creature sprang to life.

"Ambra," Langdon said, "you're a museum curator—you must have discussed art frequently with Edmond. Did he ever tell you **specifically** what it was about Gaudí that spoke to him?"

"Only what Winston mentioned," she replied. "His architecture feels as if it were created by nature herself. Gaudí's grottoes seem carved by the wind and rain, his supporting pillars seem to have grown out of the earth, and his tile work resembles primitive sea life." She shrugged. "Whatever the reason, Edmond admired Gaudí enough to move to Spain."

Langdon glanced over at her, surprised. He knew Edmond owned houses in several countries around the world, but in recent years, he'd chosen to settle in Spain. "You're saying Edmond moved here because of the art of Gaudí?"

"I believe he did," Ambra said. "I once asked him, 'Why Spain?' and he told me he had the rare opportunity to rent a unique property here—a property unlike anything else in the world. I assume he meant his apartment," she said.

"Where's his apartment?"

"Robert, Edmond lived in Casa Milà."

Langdon did a double take. "**The** Casa Milà?"

"The one and only," she replied with a nod. "Last year, he rented the entire top floor as his penthouse apartment."

Langdon needed a moment to process the news. Casa Milà was one of Gaudí's most famous buildings—a dazzlingly original "house" whose tiered facade and undulating stone balconies resembled an excavated mountain, sparking its now popular nickname "La Pedrera"—meaning "the stone quarry."

"Isn't the top floor a Gaudí museum?" Langdon asked, recalling one of his visits to the building in the past.

"Yes," Winston offered. "But Edmond made a donation to UNESCO, which protects the house as a World Heritage Site, and they agreed to temporarily close it down and let him live there for two years. After all, there's no shortage of Gaudí art in Barcelona."

Edmond lived inside a Gaudí exhibit at Casa Milà? Langdon puzzled. **And he moved in for only two years?**

Winston chimed in. "Edmond even helped Casa Milà create a new educational video about its architecture. It's worth seeing."

"The video is actually quite impressive," Ambra agreed, leaning forward and touching the browser screen. A keyboard appeared, and she typed: **Lape drera.com**. "You should watch this."

"I'm kind of driving," Langdon replied.

Ambra reached over to the steering column and gave two quick pulls on a small lever. Langdon could feel the steering wheel suddenly stiffen in his hands and immediately noticed that the car appeared to be guiding itself, remaining perfectly centered in its lane.

"Autopilot," she said.

The effect was quite unsettling, and Langdon could not help but leave his hands hovering over the wheel and his foot over the brake.

"Relax." Ambra reached over and placed a comforting hand on his shoulder. "It's far safer than a human driver."

Reluctantly, Langdon lowered his hands to his lap.

"There you go." She smiled. "Now you can watch this Casa Milà video."

The video began with a dramatic low shot of pounding surf, as if taken from a helicopter flying only a few feet above the open ocean. Rising in the distance was an island—a stone mountain with sheer cliffs that climbed hundreds of feet above the crashing waves.

Text materialized over the mountain.

La Pedrera wasn't created by Gaudí.

For the next thirty seconds, Langdon watched as the surf began carving the mountain into the distinctive organic-looking exterior of Casa Milà. Next

the ocean rushed inside, creating hollows and cavernous rooms, in which waterfalls carved staircases
and vines grew, twisting into iron banisters as mosses
grew beneath them, carpeting the floors.

Finally, the camera pulled back out to sea and
revealed the famous image of Casa Milà—"the
quarry"—carved into a massive mountain.

—La Pedrera—
a masterpiece of nature

Langdon had to admit, Edmond had a knack for
drama. Seeing this computer-generated video made
him eager to revisit the famous building.

Returning his eyes to the road, Langdon reached
down and disengaged the autopilot, taking back control. "Let's just hope Edmond's apartment contains
what we're looking for. We need to find that password."

CHAPTER 50

Commander Diego Garza led his four armed Guardia agents directly across the center of Plaza de la Armería, keeping his eyes straight ahead and ignoring the clamoring media outside the fence, all of whom were aiming television cameras at him through the bars and shouting for a comment.

At least they'll see that someone is taking action.

When he and his team arrived at the cathedral, the main entrance was locked—not surprising at this hour—and Garza began pounding on the door with the handle of his sidearm.

No answer.

He kept pounding.

Finally, the locks turned and the door swung open. Garza found himself face-to-face with a cleaning woman, who looked understandably alarmed by the small army outside the door.

"Where is Bishop Valdespino?" Garza demanded.

"I . . . I don't know," the woman replied.

"I know the bishop is here," Garza declared. "And he is with Prince Julián. You haven't seen them?"

She shook her head. "I just arrived. I clean on Saturday nights after—"

Garza pushed past her, directing his men to spread out through the darkened cathedral.

"Lock the door," Garza told the cleaning woman. "And stay out of the way."

With that, he cocked his weapon and headed directly for Valdespino's office.

———

Across the plaza, in the palace's basement control room, Mónica Martín was standing at the water-cooler and taking a pull on a long-overdue cigarette. Thanks to the liberal "politically correct" movement sweeping Spain, smoking in palace offices had been banned, but with the deluge of alleged crimes being pinned on the palace tonight, Martín figured a bit of secondhand smoke was a tolerable infraction.

All five news stations on the bank of muted televisions lined up before her continued their live coverage of the assassination of Edmond Kirsch, flagrantly replaying the footage of his brutal murder over and over. Of course, each retransmission was preceded by the usual warning.

CAUTION: The following clip contains graphic images that may not be appropriate for all viewers.

Shameless, she thought, knowing these warnings were not sensitive network precautions but rather clever teasers to ensure that nobody changed the channel.

Martín took another pull on her cigarette, scanning the various networks, most of which were milking the growing conspiracy theories with "Breaking News" headlines and ticker-tape crawls.

Futurist killed by Church?
Scientific discovery lost forever?
Assassin hired by royal family?

You're supposed to report the news, she grumbled. **Not spread vicious rumors in the form of questions.**

Martín had always believed in the importance of responsible journalism as a cornerstone of freedom and democracy, and so she was routinely disappointed by journalists who incited controversy by broadcasting ideas that were patently absurd—all the while avoiding legal repercussions by simply turning every ludicrous statement into a leading question.

Even respected science channels were doing it, asking their viewers: "Is It Possible That This Temple in Peru Was Built by Ancient Aliens?"

No! Martín wanted to shout at the television. **It's not freaking possible! Stop asking moronic questions!**

On one of the television screens, she could see that CNN seemed to be doing its best to be respectful.

Remembering Edmond Kirsch
Prophet. Visionary. Creator.

Martín picked up the remote and turned up the volume.

". . . a man who loved art, technology, and innovation," said the news anchor sadly. "A man whose almost mystical ability to predict the future made him a household name. According to his colleagues, every single prediction made by Edmond Kirsch in the field of computer science has become a reality."

"That's right, David," interjected his female cohost. "I just wish we could say the same for his **personal** predictions."

They now played archival footage of a robust, tanned Edmond Kirsch giving a press conference on the sidewalk outside 30 Rockefeller Center in New York City. "Today I am thirty years old," Edmond said, "and my life expectancy is only sixty-eight. However, with future advances in medicine, longevity technology, and telomere regeneration, I predict I will live to see my hundred-and-tenth birthday. In fact, I am so confident of this fact that I just reserved the Rainbow Room for my hundred-and-tenth-birthday party." Kirsch smiled and gazed up to the top of the building. "I just now paid my entire bill—**eighty** years in advance—including provisions for inflation."

The female anchor returned, sighing somberly. "As the old adage goes: 'Men plan, and God laughs.'"

"So true," the male host chimed. "And on top of the intrigue surrounding Kirsch's death, there is also an explosion of speculation over the nature of his discovery." He stared earnestly at the camera. "Where do we come from? Where are we going? Two fascinating questions."

"And to answer these questions," the female host

added excitedly, "we are joined by two very accomplished women—an Episcopal minister from Ver-
mont and an evolutionary biologist from UCLA.
We'll be back after the break with their thoughts."

Martín already knew their thoughts—**polar oppo-
sites, or they would not be on your show.** No doubt
the minister would say something like: "We come
from God and we're going to God," and the biologist would respond, "We evolved from apes and we're
going extinct."

**They will prove nothing except that we viewers
will watch anything if it's sufficiently hyped.**

"Mónica!" Suresh shouted nearby.

Martín turned to see the director of electronic security rounding the corner, practically at a jog.

"What is it?" she asked.

"Bishop Valdespino just called me," he said breathlessly.

She muted the TV. "The bishop called . . . **you**?
Did he tell you what the hell he's doing?!"

Suresh shook his head. "I didn't ask, and he didn't
offer. He was calling to see if I could check something on our phone servers."

"I don't understand."

"You know how ConspiracyNet is now reporting that someone inside this palace placed a call to
the Guggenheim shortly before tonight's event—a
request for Ambra Vidal to add Ávila's name to the
guest list?"

"Yes. And I asked you to look into it."

"Well, Valdespino seconded your request. He called

to ask if I would log into the palace's switchboard and find the record of that call to see if I could figure out **where** in the palace it had originated, in hopes of getting a better idea of who here might have placed it."

Martín felt confused, having imagined that Valdespino himself was the most likely suspect.

"According to the Guggenheim," Suresh continued, "their front desk received a call from Madrid Royal Palace's primary number tonight, shortly before the event. It's in their phone logs. But here's the problem. I looked into our switchboard logs to check our outbound calls with the same time stamp." He shook his head. "Nothing. Not a single call. Someone **deleted** the record of the palace's call to the Guggenheim."

Martín studied her colleague a long moment. "Who has **access** to do that?"

"That's exactly what Valdespino asked me. And so I told him the truth. I told him that I, as head of electronic security, could have deleted the record, but that I had not done so. And that the only other person with clearance and access to those records is Commander Garza."

Martín stared. "You think **Garza** tampered with our phone records?"

"It makes sense," Suresh said. "Garza's job, after all, is to protect the palace, and now, if there's any investigation, as far as the palace is concerned, that call never happened. Technically speaking, we have plausible deniability. Deleting the record goes a long way to taking the palace off the hook."

"Off the hook?" Martín demanded. "There's no

doubt that that call was made! Ambra put Ávila on the guest list! And the Guggenheim front desk will verify—"

"True, but now it's the word of a young front-desk person at a museum against the entire Royal Palace. As far as our records are concerned, that call simply didn't occur."

Suresh's cut-and-dried assessment seemed overly optimistic to Martín. "And you told Valdespino all of this?"

"It's just the truth. I told him that whether or not Garza actually **placed** the call, Garza appears to have deleted it in an effort to protect the palace." Suresh paused. "But after I hung up with the bishop, I realized something else."

"That being?"

"Technically, there's a **third** person with access to the server." Suresh glanced nervously around the room and moved closer. "Prince Julián's log-in codes give him full access to all systems."

Martín stared. "That's ridiculous."

"I know it sounds crazy," he said, "but the prince was in the palace, alone in his apartment, at the time that call was made. He could easily have placed it and then logged onto the server and deleted it. The software is simple to use and the prince is a lot more tech-savvy than people think."

"Suresh," Martín snapped, "do you really think Prince Julián—the future king of Spain—**personally** sent an assassin into the Guggenheim Museum to kill Edmond Kirsch?"

"I don't know," he said. "All I'm saying is that it's possible."

"Why would Prince Julián do such a thing?!"

"You, of all people, shouldn't have to ask. Remember all the bad press you had to deal with about Ambra and Edmond Kirsch spending time together? The story about how he flew her to his apartment in Barcelona?"

"They were working! It was business!"

"Politics is all appearances," Suresh said. "You taught me that. And you and I know the prince's marriage proposal has not worked out for him publicly the way he imagined."

Suresh's phone pinged and he read the incoming message, his face clouding with disbelief.

"What is it?" Martín demanded.

Without a word, Suresh turned and ran back toward the security center.

"Suresh!" Martín stubbed out her cigarette and ran after him, joining him at one of his team's security workstations, where his tech was playing a grainy surveillance tape.

"What are we looking at?" Martín demanded.

"Rear exit of the cathedral," the techie said. "Five minutes ago."

Martín and Suresh leaned in and watched the video feed as a young acolyte exited the rear of the cathedral, hurried along the relatively quiet Calle Mayor, unlocked an old beat-up Opel sedan, and climbed in.

Okay, Martín thought, **he's going home after mass. So what?**

On-screen, the Opel pulled out, drove a short distance, and then pulled up unusually close to the cathedral's rear gate—the same gate through which the acolyte had just exited. Almost instantly, two dark figures slipped out through the gate, crouching low, and jumped into the backseat of the acolyte's car. The two passengers were—without a doubt—Bishop Valdespino and Prince Julián.

Moments later, the Opel sped off, disappearing around the corner and out of frame.

CHAPTER 51

S tanding like a rough-hewn mountain on the corner of Carrer de Provença and Passeig de Gràcia, the 1906 Gaudí masterpiece known as Casa Milà is half apartment building and half timeless work of art.

Conceived by Gaudí as a perpetual curve, the nine-story structure is immediately recognizable by its billowing limestone facade. Its swerving balconies and uneven geometry give the building an organic aura, as if millennia of buffeting winds had carved out hollows and bends like those in a desert canyon.

Although Gaudí's shocking modernist design was shunned at first by the neighborhood, Casa Milà was universally lauded by art critics and quickly became one of Barcelona's brightest architectural jewels. For three decades, Pere Milà, the businessman who commissioned the building, had resided with his wife in the sprawling main apartment while renting out the building's twenty remaining flats. To this day, Casa Milà—at Passeig de Gràcia 92—is considered one of the most exclusive and coveted addresses in all of Spain.

As Robert Langdon navigated Kirsch's Tesla through sparse traffic on the elegant tree-lined avenue, he sensed they were getting close. Passeig de Gràcia was Barcelona's version of the Champs-Élysées in Paris—the widest and grandest of avenues, impeccably landscaped and lined with designer boutiques.

Chanel . . . Gucci . . . Cartier . . . Longchamp . . .

Finally, Langdon saw it, two hundred meters away.

Softly lit from below, Casa Milà's pale, pitted limestone and oblong balconies set it instantly apart from its rectilinear neighbors—as if a beautiful piece of ocean coral had washed into shore and come to rest on a beach made of cinder blocks.

"I was afraid of this," Ambra said, pointing urgently down the elegant avenue. "Look."

Langdon lowered his gaze to the wide sidewalk in front of Casa Milà. It looked like there were a half-dozen media trucks parked in front, and a host of reporters were giving live updates using Kirsch's residence as a backdrop. Several security agents were positioned to keep the crowds away from the entrance. Edmond's death, it seemed, had transformed anything Kirsch-related into a news story.

Langdon scanned Passeig de Gràcia for a place to pull over, but he saw nothing, and traffic was moving steadily.

"Get down," he urged Ambra, realizing he had no choice now but to drive directly past the corner where all the press were assembled.

Ambra slid down in her seat, crouching on the floor, entirely out of view. Langdon turned his head away as they drove past the crowded corner.

"It looks like they're surrounding the main entrance," he said. "We'll never get in."

"Take a right," Winston interjected with a note of cheerful confidence. "I imagined this might happen."

———

Blogger Héctor Marcano gazed up mournfully at the top floor of Casa Milà, still trying to accept that Edmond Kirsch was truly gone.

For three years, Héctor had been reporting on technology for Barcinno.com—a popular collaborative platform for Barcelona's entrepreneurs and cutting-edge start-ups. Having the great Edmond Kirsch living here in Barcelona had felt almost like working at the feet of Zeus himself.

Héctor had first met Kirsch more than a year ago when the legendary futurist graciously agreed to speak at Barcinno's flagship monthly event—FuckUp Night—a seminar in which a wildly successful entrepreneur spoke openly about his or her biggest failures. Kirsch sheepishly admitted to the crowd that he had spent more than $400 million over six months chasing his dream of building what he called E-Wave—a quantum computer with processing speeds so fast they would facilitate unprecedented advances across all the sciences, especially in complex systems modeling.

"I'm afraid," Edmond had admitted, "so far, my quantum leap in quantum computing is a quantum dud."

Tonight, when Héctor heard that Kirsch planned to announce an earth-shattering discovery, he was thrilled at the thought that it might be related to E-Wave. **Did he discover the key to making it work?** But after Kirsch's philosophical preamble, Héctor realized his discovery was something else entirely.

I wonder if we'll ever know what he found, Héctor thought, his heart so heavy that he had come to Kirsch's home not to blog, but to pay reverent homage.

"E-Wave!" someone shouted nearby. "E-Wave!"

All around Héctor, the assembled crowd began pointing and aiming their cameras at a sleek black Tesla that was now easing slowly onto the plaza and inching toward the crowd with its halogen headlights glaring.

Héctor stared at the familiar vehicle in astonishment. Kirsch's Tesla Model X with its E-Wave license plate was as famous in Barcelona as the pope-mobile was in Rome. Kirsch would often make a show of double-parking on Carrer de Provença outside the DANiEL ViOR jewelry shop, getting out to sign autographs and then thrilling the crowd by letting his car's self-park feature drive the empty vehicle on a preprogrammed route up the street and across the wide sidewalk—its sensors detecting any pedestrians or obstacles—until it reached the garage gate, which it would then open, and slowly wind down the spiral ramp into the private garage beneath Casa Milà.

While self-park was a standard feature on all Teslas—easily opening garage doors, driving straight in, and turning themselves off—Edmond had proudly hacked his Tesla's system to enable the more complex route.

All part of the show.

Tonight, the spectacle was considerably stranger. Kirsch was deceased, and yet his **car** had just appeared, moving slowly up Carrer de Provença, continuing across the sidewalk, aligning itself with the elegant garage door, and inching forward as people cleared the way.

Reporters and cameramen rushed to the vehicle, squinting through the heavily tinted windows and shouting in surprise.

"It's empty! Nobody is driving! Where did it come from?!"

The Casa Milà security guards had apparently witnessed this trick before, and they held people back from the Tesla and away from the garage door as it opened.

For Héctor, the sight of Edmond's empty car creeping toward its garage conjured images of a bereft dog returning home after losing its master.

Like a ghost, the Tesla made its way silently through the garage door, and the crowd broke into emotional applause to see Edmond's beloved car, as it had done so many times before, begin its descent down the spiral ramp into Barcelona's very first subterranean parking facility.

"I didn't know you were so claustrophobic," Ambra whispered, lying beside Langdon on the floor of the Tesla. They were crammed into the small area between the second and third row of seats, hidden beneath a black vinyl car cover that Ambra had taken from the cargo area, invisible through the tinted windows.

"I'll survive," Langdon managed shakily, more nervous about the self-driving car than his phobia. He could feel the vehicle winding down a steep spiral ramp and feared it would crash at any moment.

Two minutes earlier, while they were double-parked on Carrer de Provença, outside the DANiEL ViOR jewelry shop, Winston had given them crystal-clear directions.

Ambra and Langdon, without exiting the car, had climbed back to the Model X's third row of seats, and then with the press of a single button on the phone, Ambra had activated the car's customized self-park feature.

In the darkness, Langdon had felt the car driving itself slowly down the street. And with Ambra's body pressed against his in the tight space, he could not help but recall his first teenage experience in the backseat of a car with a pretty girl. **I was more nervous back then,** he thought, which seemed ironic considering he was now lying in a driverless car spooning the future queen of Spain.

Langdon felt the car straighten out at the bottom of the ramp, make a few slow turns, and then slide to a full stop.

"You have arrived," Winston said.

Immediately Ambra pulled back the tarp and carefully sat up, peering out the window. "Clear," she said, clambering out.

Langdon got out after her, relieved to be standing in the open air of the garage.

"Elevators are in the main foyer," Ambra said, motioning up the winding driveway ramp.

Langdon's gaze, however, was suddenly transfixed by a wholly unexpected sight. Here, in this underground parking garage, on the cement wall directly in front of Edmond's parking space, hung an elegantly framed painting of a seaside landscape.

"Ambra?" Langdon said. "Edmond decorated his parking spot with a **painting**?"

She nodded. "I asked him the same question. He told me it was his way of being welcomed home every night by a radiant beauty."

Langdon chuckled. **Bachelors.**

"The artist is someone Edmond revered greatly," Winston said, his voice now transferring automatically to Kirsch's cell phone in Ambra's hand. "Do you recognize him?"

Langdon did not. The painting seemed to be nothing more than an accomplished watercolor seascape—nothing like Edmond's usual avant-garde taste.

"It's Churchill," Ambra said. "Edmond quoted him all the time."

Churchill. Langdon needed a moment to realize she was referring to none other than Winston Churchill himself, the celebrated British statesman who, in addition to being a military hero, historian, orator, and Nobel Prize—winning author, was an artist of remarkable talent. Langdon now recalled Edmond quoting the British prime minister once in response to a comment someone made about religious people hating him: **You have enemies? Good. That means you've stood up for something!**

"It was the diversity of Churchill's talents that most impressed Edmond," Winston said. "Humans rarely display proficiency across such a broad spectrum of activities."

"And that's why Edmond named you 'Winston'?"

"It is," the computer replied. "High praise from Edmond."

Glad I asked, Langdon thought, having imagined Winston's name was an allusion to Watson—the IBM computer that had dominated the **Jeopardy!** television game show a decade ago. No doubt Watson was probably now considered a primitive, single-celled bacterium on the evolutionary scale of synthetic intelligence.

"Okay, then," Langdon said, motioning to the elevators. "Let's head upstairs and try to find what we came for."

———

At that precise moment, inside Madrid's Almudena Cathedral, Commander Diego Garza was clutching his phone and listening in disbelief as the palace's PR coordinator, Mónica Martín, gave him an update.

Valdespino and Prince Julián left the safety of the compound?

Garza could not begin to imagine what they were thinking.

They're driving around Madrid in an acolyte's car? That's madness!

"We can contact the transportation authorities," Martín said. "Suresh believes they can use traffic cams to help track—"

"No!" Garza declared. "Alerting **anyone** to the fact that the prince is outside the palace without security is far too dangerous! His safety is our primary concern."

"Understood, sir," Martín said, sounding suddenly uneasy. "There's something else you should know. It's about a missing phone record."

"Hold on," Garza said, distracted by the arrival of his four Guardia agents, who, to his mystification, strode over and encircled him. Before Garza could react, his agents had skillfully relieved him of his sidearm and phone.

"Commander Garza," his lead agent said, stone-faced. "I have direct orders to place you under arrest."

asa Milà is built in the shape of an infinity sign—an endless curve that doubles back over itself and forms two undulating chasms that penetrate the building. Each of these open-air light wells is nearly a hundred feet deep, crumpled like a partially collapsed tube, and from the air they resembled two massive sinkholes in the roof of the building.

From where Langdon stood at the base of the narrower light well, the effect looking skyward was decidedly unsettling—like being lodged in the throat of a giant beast.

Beneath Langdon's feet, the stone floor was sloped and uneven. A helix staircase spiraled up the interior of the shaft, its railing forged of wrought iron latticework that mimicked the uneven chambers of a sea sponge. A small jungle of twisting vines and swooping palms spilled over the banisters as if about to overgrow the entire space.

Living architecture, Langdon mused, marveling at Gaudí's ability to imbue his work with an almost biological quality.

Langdon's eyes climbed higher again, up the sides of the "gorge," scaling the curved walls, where a quilt of brown and green tiles intermingled with muted frescoes depicting plants and flowers that seemed to be growing up toward the oblong patch of night sky at the top of the open shaft.

"Elevators are this way," Ambra whispered, leading him around the edge of the courtyard. "Edmond's apartment is all the way up."

As they boarded the uncomfortably small elevator, Langdon pictured the building's top-floor garret, which he had visited once to see the small Gaudí exhibit housed there. As he recalled, the Casa Milà attic was a dark, sinuous series of rooms with very few windows.

"Edmond could live **anywhere**," Langdon said as the elevator began to climb. "I still can't believe he leased an **attic**."

"It's a strange apartment," Ambra agreed. "But as you know, Edmond was eccentric."

When the elevator reached the top floor, they disembarked into an elegant hallway and climbed an additional set of winding stairs to a private landing at the very top of the building.

"This is it," Ambra said, motioning to a sleek metal door that had no knob or keyhole. The futuristic portal looked entirely out of place in this building and clearly had been added by Edmond.

"You said you know where he hides his key?" Langdon asked.

Ambra held up Edmond's phone. "The same place where he seems to hide everything."

She pressed the phone against the metal door, which

beeped three times, and Langdon heard a series of dead bolts sliding open. Ambra pocketed the phone and pushed the door open.

"After you," she said with a flourish.

Langdon stepped over the threshold into a dimly lit foyer whose walls and ceiling were pale brick. The floor was stone, and the air tasted thin.

As he moved through the entryway into the open space beyond, he found himself face-to-face with a massive painting, which hung on the rear wall, impeccably illuminated by museum-quality pin lights.

When Langdon saw the work, he stopped dead in his tracks. "My God, is that . . . the **original**?"

Ambra smiled. "Yes, I was going to mention it on the plane, but I thought I'd surprise you."

Speechless, Langdon moved toward the masterpiece. It was about twelve feet long and more than four feet tall—far larger than he recalled from seeing it previously in the Boston Museum of Fine Arts. **I heard this was sold to an anonymous collector, but I had no idea it was Edmond!**

"When I first saw it in the apartment," Ambra said, "I could not believe that Edmond had a taste for this style of art. But now that I know what he was working on this year, the painting seems eerily appropriate."

Langdon nodded, incredulous.

This celebrated masterpiece was one of the signature works by French Postimpressionist Paul Gauguin—a groundbreaking painter who epitomized the Symbolist movement of the late 1800s and helped pave the way for modern art.

As Langdon moved toward the painting, he was immediately struck by how similar Gauguin's palette was to that of the Casa Milà entryway—a blend of organic greens, browns, and blues—also depicting a very naturalistic scene.

Despite the intriguing collection of people and animals that appeared in Gauguin's painting, Langdon's gaze moved immediately to the upper-left-hand corner—to a bright yellow patch, on which was inscribed the title of this work.

Langdon read the words in disbelief: **D'où Venons Nous / Que Sommes Nous / Où Allons Nous.**

Where do we come from? What are we? Where are we going?

Langdon wondered if being confronted by these questions every day as he returned to his home had somehow helped inspire Edmond.

Ambra joined Langdon in front of the painting. "Edmond said he wanted to be motivated by these questions whenever he entered his home."

Hard to miss, Langdon thought.

Seeing how prominently Edmond had displayed the masterpiece, Langdon wondered if perhaps the painting itself might hold some clue as to what Edmond had discovered. At first glance, the painting's subject seemed far too primitive to hint at an advanced scientific discovery. Its broad uneven brushstrokes depicted a Tahitian jungle inhabited by an assortment of native Tahitians and animals.

Langdon knew the painting well, and as he recalled, Gauguin intended this work to be "read" from right to left—in the reverse direction from that of standard French text. And so Langdon's eye quickly traced the familiar figures in reverse direction.

On the far right, a newborn baby slept on a boulder, representing life's beginning. **Where do we come from?**

In the middle, an assortment of people of different ages carried out the daily activities of life. **What are we?**

And on the left, a decrepit old woman sat alone, deep in thought, seeming to ponder her own mortality. **Where are we going?**

Langdon was surprised that he hadn't thought of this painting immediately when Edmond first described the focus of his discovery. **What is our origin? What is our destiny?**

Langdon eyed the other elements of the painting— dogs, cats, and birds, which seemed to be doing nothing in particular; a primitive goddess statue in the background; a mountain, twisting roots, and trees. And, of course, Gauguin's famous "strange white bird," which sat beside the elderly woman and, according to the artist, represented "the futility of words."

Futile or not, Langdon thought, **words are what we came here for. Preferably forty-seven characters' worth.**

For an instant, he wondered if the painting's unusual title might relate directly to the forty-seven-letter password they were seeking, but a quick count in both French and English did not add up.

"Okay, we're looking for a line of poetry," Langdon said hopefully.

"Edmond's library is this way," Ambra told him. She pointed to her left, down a wide corridor, which Langdon could see was appointed with elegant home furnishings that were interspersed with assorted Gaudí artifacts and displays.

Edmond lives in a museum? Langdon still couldn't quite wrap his mind around it. The Casa Milà loft was not exactly the homiest place he had ever seen. Constructed entirely of stone and brick, it was essentially a continuous ribbed tunnel—a loop of 270 parabolic arches of varying heights, each about a yard apart. There were very few windows, and the atmosphere tasted dry and sterile, clearly heavily processed to protect the Gaudí artifacts.

"I'll join you in a moment," Langdon said. "First, I'm going to find Edmond's restroom."

Ambra glanced awkwardly back toward the entrance. "Edmond always asked me to use the lobby downstairs . . . he was mysteriously protective of this apartment's private bathroom."

"It's a bachelor pad—his bathroom is probably a mess, and he was embarrassed."

Ambra smiled. "Well, I think it's that way." She pointed in the opposite direction from the library, down a very dark tunnel.

"Thanks. I'll be right back."

Ambra headed off toward Edmond's office, and Langdon went in the opposite direction, making his way down the narrow corridor—a dramatic tunnel of brick archways that reminded him of an underground grotto or medieval catacomb. Eerily, as he moved along the stone tunnel, banks of soft motion-sensitive lights illuminated at the base of each parabolic arch, lighting his way.

Langdon passed an elegant reading area, a small exercise area, and even a pantry, all interspersed with various display tables of Gaudí drawings, architectural sketches, and 3-D models of his projects.

When he passed an illuminated display table of **biological** artifacts, however, Langdon stopped short, surprised by the contents—a fossil of a prehistoric fish, an elegant nautilus shell, and a sinuous skeleton of a snake. For a passing moment, Langdon imagined Edmond must have mounted this scientific display himself—perhaps relating to his studies of the origins of life. Then Langdon saw the annotation on the case and realized that these artifacts had belonged to Gaudí and echoed various architectural features of this home: the fish scales were the tiled patterns on the walls, the nautilus was the curling ramp into the garage, and the snake skeleton with its hundreds of closely spaced ribs was this very hallway.

Accompanying the display were the architect's humble words:

> Nothing is invented, for it's written in nature
>   first.
> Originality consists of returning to the origin.
>   —ANTONI GAUDÍ

Langdon turned his eyes down the winding, vault-ribbed corridor and once again felt like he was standing inside a living creature.

A perfect home for Edmond, he decided. **Art inspired by science.**

As Langdon followed the first bend in the serpentine tunnel, the space widened, and the motion-activated lights illuminated. His gaze was drawn immediately to a huge glass display case in the center of the hall.

A catenary model, he thought, having always marveled at these ingenious Gaudí prototypes. "Catenary" was an architectural term that referred to the curve that was formed by a cord hanging loosely between two fixed points—like a hammock or the velvet rope suspended between two stanchions in a theater.

In the catenary model before Langdon, dozens of chains had been suspended loosely from the top of the case—resulting in long lengths that swooped down and then back up to form limply hanging U-shapes. Because gravitational tension was the inverse of gravitational compression, Gaudí could study the precise shape assumed by a chain when naturally hanging under its own weight, and he could mimic that shape to solve the architectural challenges of gravitational compression.

But it requires a magic mirror, Langdon mused, moving toward the case. As anticipated, the floor of the case was a mirror, and as he peered down into the reflection, he saw a magical effect. The entire model flipped upside down—and the hanging loops became soaring spires.

In this case, Langdon realized, he was seeing an inverted aerial view of Gaudí's towering Basílica de la Sagrada Família, whose gently sloping spires quite possibly had been designed using this very model.

Pressing on down the hall, Langdon found himself in an elegant sleeping space with an antique four-poster bed, a cherrywood armoire, and an inlaid chest of drawers. The walls were decorated with Gaudí design sketches, which Langdon realized were simply more of the museum's exhibit.

The only piece of art in the room that seemed to have been added was a large calligraphied quote hanging over Edmond's bed. Langdon read the first three words and immediately recognized the source.

> God is dead. God remains dead. And we have
> killed him. How shall we comfort ourselves,
> the murderers of all murderers?
>
> —NIETZSCHE

"God is dead" were the three most famous words written by Friedrich Nietzsche, the renowned nineteenth-century German philosopher and atheist. Nietzsche was notorious for his scathing critiques of religion, but also for his reflections on science—especially Darwinian evolution—which he believed had transported humankind to the brink of nihilism, an awareness that life had no meaning, no higher purpose, and offered no direct evidence of the existence of God.

Seeing the quote over the bed, Langdon wondered if perhaps Edmond, for all his antireligious bluster, might have been struggling with his own role in attempting to rid the world of God.

The Nietzsche quote, as Langdon recalled, concluded with the words: **"Is not the greatness of this deed too great for us? Must we ourselves not become gods simply to appear worthy of it?"**

This bold idea—that man must **become** God in order to kill God—was at the core of Nietzsche's thinking, and perhaps, Langdon realized, partially explained the God complexes suffered by so many pioneering technology geniuses like Edmond. **Those who erase God . . . must be gods.**

As Langdon pondered the notion, he was struck by a second realization.

Nietzsche was not just a philosopher—he was also a poet!

Langdon himself owned Nietzsche's **The Peacock and the Buffalo,** a compilation of 275 poems and aphorisms that offered thoughts on God, death, and the human mind.

Langdon quickly counted the characters in the framed quote. They were not a match, and yet a surge of hope swelled within him. **Could Nietzsche be the poet of the line we're seeking? If so, will we find a book of Nietzsche's poetry in Edmond's office?** Either way, Langdon would ask Winston to access an online compilation of Nietzsche's poems and search them all for a line containing forty-seven characters.

Eager to get back to Ambra and share his thoughts, Langdon hurried through the bedroom into the restroom that was visible beyond.

As he entered, the lights inside came on to reveal an elegantly decorated bathroom containing a pedestal sink, a freestanding shower unit, and a toilet.

Langdon's eyes were drawn immediately to a low antique table cluttered with toiletries and personal items. When he saw the items on the table, he inhaled sharply, taking a step back.

Oh God. Edmond . . . no.

The table before him looked like a back-alley drug lab—used syringes, pill bottles, loose capsules, and even a rag spotted with blood.

Langdon's heart sank.

Edmond was taking drugs?

Langdon knew that chemical addiction had become painfully commonplace these days, even among the rich and famous. Heroin was cheaper than beer now, and people were popping opioid painkillers like they were ibuprofen.

Addiction would certainly explain his recent weight loss, Langdon thought, wondering if maybe Edmond had been pretending to have "gone vegan" only in an attempt to cover for his thinness and sunken eyes.

Langdon walked to the table and picked up one of the bottles, reading the prescription label, fully expecting to find one of the common opioids like OxyContin or Percocet.

Instead he saw: **Docetaxel.**

Puzzled, he checked another bottle: **Gemcitabine.**
What are these? he wondered, checking a third bottle: **Fluorouracil.**

Langdon froze. He had heard of Fluorouracil through a colleague at Harvard, and he felt a sudden wave of dread. An instant later, he spied a pamphlet lying among the bottles. The title was "Does Veganism Slow Pancreatic Cancer?"

Langdon's jaw dropped as the truth hit him.

Edmond wasn't a drug addict.

He was secretly fighting a deadly cancer.

CHAPTER 53

Ambra Vidal stood in the soft light of the attic apartment and ran her eyes across the rows of books lining the walls of Edmond's library.

His collection is larger than I remembered.

Edmond had transformed a wide section of curved hallway into a stunning library by building shelves between the vertical supports of Gaudí's vaults. His library was unexpectedly large and well stocked, especially considering Edmond had allegedly planned to be here for only two years.

It looks like he moved in for good.

Eyeing the crowded shelves, Ambra realized that locating Edmond's favorite line of poetry would be far more time-consuming than anticipated. As she continued walking along the shelves, scanning the spines of the books, she saw nothing but scientific tomes on cosmology, consciousness, and artificial intelligence:

THE BIG PICTURE
FORCES OF NATURE
ORIGINS OF CONSCIOUSNESS
THE BIOLOGY OF BELIEF
INTELLIGENT ALGORITHMS
OUR FINAL INVENTION

She reached the end of one section and stepped around an architectural rib into the next section of shelves. Here she found a wide array of scientific topics—thermodynamics, primordial chemistry, psychology.

No poetry.

Noting that Winston had been quiet for some time now, Ambra pulled out Kirsch's cell phone. "Winston? Are we still connected?"

"I am here," his accented voice chimed.

"Did Edmond actually **read** all of these books in his library?"

"I believe so, yes," Winston replied. "He was a voracious consumer of text and called this library his 'trophy room of knowledge.'"

"And is there, by any chance, a **poetry** section in here?"

"The only titles of which I'm specifically aware are the nonfiction volumes that I was asked to read in e-book format so Edmond and I could discuss their contents—an exercise, I suspect, that was more for **my** education than for his. Unfortunately, I do not have this entire collection cataloged, so the only way you will be able to find what you are looking for will be by an actual physical search."

"I understand."

"While you search, there is one thing, I think, that may interest you—breaking news from Madrid regarding your fiancé, Prince Julián."

"What's happening?" Ambra demanded, halting abruptly. Her emotions still churned over Julián's possible involvement in Kirsch's assassination. **There's no proof,** she reminded herself. **Nothing confirms that Julián helped put Ávila's name on the guest list.**

"It was just reported," Winston said, "that a raucous demonstration is forming outside the Royal Palace. Evidence continues to suggest that Edmond's assassination was secretly arranged by Bishop Valdespino, probably with the help of someone inside the palace, perhaps even the prince. Fans of Kirsch are now picketing. Have a look."

Edmond's smartphone began streaming footage of angry protesters at the palace gates. One carried a sign in English that read: PONTIUS PILATE KILLED YOUR PROPHET—YOU KILLED OURS!

Others were carrying spray-painted bedsheets emblazoned with a single-word battle cry—¡APOSTASÍA!—accompanied by a logo that was now being stenciled with increasing frequency on the sidewalks of Madrid.

Apostasy had become a popular rallying cry for Spain's liberal youth. **Renounce the Church!**

"Has Julián made a statement yet?" Ambra asked.

"That's one of the problems," Winston replied. "Not a word from Julián, nor the bishop, nor anyone at all in the palace. The continued silence has made everyone suspicious. Conspiracy theories are rampant, and the national press has now begun questioning where **you** are, and why **you** have not commented publicly on this crisis either?"

"Me?!" Ambra was horrified at the thought.

"You **witnessed** the murder. You are the future queen consort and the love of Prince Julián's life. The public wants to hear you say that you are certain Julián is not involved."

Ambra's gut told her that Julián could not possibly have known about Edmond's murder; when she thought back to their courtship, she recalled a tender and sincere man—admittedly naive and impulsively romantic—but certainly no murderer.

"Similar questions are surfacing now about Professor Langdon," Winston said. "Media outlets have begun asking why the professor has disappeared without comment, especially after featuring so prominently in Edmond's presentation. Several conspiracy blogs are suggesting that his disappearance may actually be related to his involvement in Kirsch's murder."

"But that's crazy!"

"The topic is gaining traction. The theory stems from Langdon's past search for the Holy Grail and the bloodline of Christ. Apparently, the Salic descendants of Christ have historical ties to the Carlist movement, and the assassin's tattoo—"

"Stop," Ambra interrupted. "This is absurd."

"And yet others are speculating that Langdon has disappeared because he himself has become a **target** tonight. Everyone has become an armchair detective.

Much of the world is collaborating at this moment to figure out what mysteries Edmond uncovered . . . and who wanted to silence him."

Ambra's attention was drawn by the sound of Langdon's footsteps approaching briskly up the winding corridor. She turned just as he appeared around the corner.

"Ambra?" he called, his voice taut. "Were you aware that Edmond was seriously ill?"

"Ill?" she said, startled. "No."

Langdon told her what he had found in Edmond's private bathroom.

Ambra was thunderstruck.

Pancreatic cancer? That's the reason Edmond was so pale and thin?

Incredibly, Edmond had never said a word about being ill. Ambra now understood his maniacal work ethic over the past few months. **Edmond knew he was running out of time.**

"Winston," she demanded. "Did you know about Edmond's illness?"

"Yes," Winston replied without hesitation. "It was something he kept very private. He learned of his disease twenty-two months ago and immediately changed his diet and began working with increased intensity. He also relocated to this attic space, where he would breathe museum-quality air and be protected from UV radiation; he needed to live in darkness as much as possible because his medications made him photosensitive. Edmond managed to outlive his doctors' projections by a considerable margin. Recently, though, he had started to fail. Based on empirical evidence I gathered from worldwide databases on pancreatic cancer, I analyzed Edmond's deterioration and calculated that he had nine days to live."

Nine days, Ambra thought, overcome with guilt for teasing Edmond about his vegan diet and about working too hard. **The man was sick; he was racing tirelessly to create his final moment of glory before his time ran out.** This sad realization only further fueled Ambra's determination to locate this poem and complete what Edmond had started.

"I haven't found any poetry books yet," she said to Langdon. "So far, it's all science."

"I think the poet we're looking for might be Friedrich Nietzsche," Langdon said, telling her about the framed quote over Edmond's bed. "That particular quote doesn't have forty-seven letters, but it certainly implies Edmond was a fan of Nietzsche."

"Winston," Ambra said. "Can you search Nietzsche's collected works of poetry and isolate any lines that have exactly forty-seven letters?"

"Certainly," Winston replied. "German originals or English translations?"

Ambra paused, uncertain.

"Start with English," Langdon prompted. "Edmond planned to input the line of poetry on his phone, and his keypad would have no easy way to input any of German's umlauted letters or **Eszetts.**"

Ambra nodded. **Smart.**

"I have your results," Winston announced almost immediately. "I have found nearly three hundred translated poems, resulting in one hundred and ninety-two lines of precisely forty-seven letters."

Langdon sighed. "That many?"

"Winston," Ambra pressed. "Edmond described his favorite line as a **prophecy** . . . a prediction about the future . . . one that was already coming true. Do you see anything that fits that description?"

"I'm sorry," Winston replied. "I see nothing here that suggests a prophecy. Linguistically speaking, the lines in question are all extracted from longer stanzas and appear to be partial thoughts. Shall I display them for you?"

"There are too many," Langdon said. "We need to find a physical book and hope that Edmond marked his favorite line in some way."

"Then I suggest you hurry," Winston said. "It appears your presence here may no longer be a secret."

"Why do you say that?" Langdon demanded.

"Local news is reporting that a military plane has just landed at Barcelona's El Prat Airport and that two Guardia Real agents have deplaned."

———

On the outskirts of Madrid, Bishop Valdespino was feeling grateful to have escaped the palace before the walls had closed in on him. Wedged beside Prince Julián in the backseat of his acolyte's tiny Opel sedan, Valdespino hoped that desperate measures now being enacted behind the scenes would help him regain control of a night careening wildly off course.

"La Casita del Príncipe," Valdespino had ordered the acolyte as the young man drove them away from the palace.

The cottage of the prince was situated in a secluded rural area forty minutes outside Madrid. More mansion than cottage, the **casita** had served as the private residence for the heir to the Spanish throne since the middle of the 1700s—a secluded spot where boys could be boys before settling into the serious business of running a country. Valdespino had assured Julián that retiring to his cottage would be far safer than remaining in the palace tonight.

Except I am not taking Julián to the cottage, the bishop knew, glancing over at the prince, who was gazing out the car window, apparently deep in thought.

Valdespino wondered if the prince was truly as naive as he appeared, or if, like his father, Julián had mastered the skill of showing the world only that side of himself that he wanted to be seen.

CHAPTER 54

The handcuffs on Garza's wrists felt unnecessarily tight.

These guys are serious, he thought, still utterly bewildered by the actions of his own Guardia agents.

"What the hell is going on?!" Garza demanded again as his men marched him out of the cathedral and into the night air of the plaza.

Still no reply.

As the entourage moved across the wide expanse toward the palace, Garza realized there was an array of TV cameras and protesters outside the front gate.

"At least take me around back," he said to his lead man. "Don't make this a public spectacle."

The soldiers ignored his plea and pressed on, forcing Garza to march directly across the plaza. Within seconds, voices outside the gate started shouting, and the blazing glare of spotlights swung toward him. Blinded and fuming, Garza forced himself to assume a calm expression and hold his head high as the Guardia marched him within a few yards of the gate, directly past the yelling cameramen and reporters.

A cacophony of voices began hurling questions at Garza.

"Why are you being arrested?"

"What did you do, Commander?"

"Were you involved in the assassination of Edmond Kirsch?"

Garza fully expected his agents to continue past the crowd without even a glance, but to his shock, the agents stopped abruptly, holding him still in front of the cameras. From the direction of the palace, a familiar pantsuited figure was striding briskly across the plaza toward them.

It was Mónica Martín.

Garza had no doubt that she would be stunned to see his predicament.

Strangely, though, when Martín arrived she eyed him not with surprise, but with contempt. The guards forcibly turned Garza to face the reporters.

Mónica Martín held up her hand to quiet the crowd and then drew a small sheet of paper from her pocket. Adjusting her thick glasses, she read a statement directly into the television cameras.

"The Royal Palace," she announced, "is hereby arresting Commander Diego Garza for his role in the murder of Edmond Kirsch, as well as his attempts to implicate Bishop Valdespino in that crime."

Before Garza could even process the preposterous accusation, the guards were muscling him off toward the palace. As he departed, he could hear Mónica Martín continuing her statement.

"Regarding our future queen, Ambra Vidal," she declared, "and the American professor Robert Langdon, I'm afraid I have some deeply disturbing news."

———

Downstairs in the palace, director of electronic
security Suresh Bhalla stood in front of the television, riveted by the live broadcast of Mónica Martín's
impromptu press conference in the plaza.

She does not look happy.

Only five minutes ago, Martín had received a personal phone call, which she had taken in her office,
speaking in hushed tones and taking careful notes.
Sixty seconds later, she had emerged, looking as
shaken as Suresh had ever seen her. With no explanation, Martín carried her notes directly out to the
plaza and addressed the media.

Whether or not her claims were accurate, one thing
was certain—the person who had ordered this statement had just placed Robert Langdon in very serious
danger.

Who gave those orders to Mónica? Suresh wondered.

As he tried to make sense of the PR coordinator's
bizarre behavior, his computer pinged with an incoming message. Suresh went over and eyed the screen,
stunned to see who had written him.

monte@iglesia.org

The informant, thought Suresh.

It was the same person who had been feeding
information to ConspiracyNet all night. And now,

for some reason, that person was contacting Suresh directly.

Warily, Suresh sat down and opened the e-mail. It read:

i hacked valdespino's texts.

he has dangerous secrets.

the palace should access his sms records.

now.

Alarmed, Suresh read the message again. Then he deleted it.

For a long moment, he sat in silence, pondering his options.

Then, coming to a decision, he quickly generated a master key card to the royal apartments and slipped upstairs unseen.

CHAPTER 55

With increasing urgency, Langdon ran his eyes along the collection of books lining Edmond's hallway.

Poetry . . . there's got to be some poetry here somewhere.

The Guardia's unexpected arrival in Barcelona had started a dangerous ticking clock, and yet Langdon felt confident that time would not run out. After all, once he and Ambra had located Edmond's favorite line of poetry, they would need only seconds to enter it into Edmond's phone and play the presentation for the world. **As Edmond intended.**

Langdon glanced over at Ambra, who was on the opposite side of the hall, farther down, continuing her search of the left-hand side as Langdon combed the right. "Do you see anything over there?"

Ambra shook her head. "So far only science and philosophy. No poetry. No Nietzsche."

"Keep looking," Langdon told her, returning to his search. Currently, he was scanning a section of thick tomes on history:

PRIVILEGE, PERSECUTION AND PROPHECY: THE
CATHOLIC CHURCH IN SPAIN

BY THE SWORD AND THE CROSS: THE HISTORICAL EVOLUTION OF THE CATHOLIC WORLD MONARCHY

The titles reminded him of a dark tale Edmond had shared years ago after Langdon had commented that Edmond, for an American atheist, seemed to have an unusual obsession with Spain and Catholicism. "My mother was a native Spaniard," Edmond had replied flatly. "And a guilt-ridden Catholic."

As Edmond shared the tragic tale of his childhood and his mother, Langdon could only listen with great surprise. Edmond's mother, Paloma Calvo, the computer scientist explained, had been the daughter of simple laborers in Cádiz, Spain. At nineteen, she fell in love with a university teacher from Chicago, Michael Kirsch, who was on sabbatical in Spain, and had become pregnant. Having witnessed the shunning of other unwed mothers in her strict Catholic community, Paloma saw no option but to accept the man's halfhearted offer to marry her and move to Chicago. Shortly after her son, Edmond, was born, Paloma's husband was struck by a car and killed while biking home from class.

Castigo divino, her own father called it. **Divine punishment.**

Paloma's parents refused to let their daughter return home to Cádiz and bring shame to their household. Instead, they warned that Paloma's dire circumstances were a clear sign of God's anger, and that the kingdom of heaven would never accept her unless she dedicated herself body and soul to Christ for the rest of her life.

After giving birth to Edmond, Paloma worked as a maid in a motel and tried to raise him as best as she could. At night, in their meager apartment, she read Scripture and prayed for forgiveness, but her destitution only deepened, and with it, her certainty that God was not yet satisfied with her penance.

Disgraced and fearful, Paloma became convinced after five years that the most profound act of maternal love she could show her child would be to give him a new life, one shielded from God's punishment of Paloma's sins. And so she placed five-year-old Edmond in an orphanage and returned to Spain, where she entered a convent. Edmond had never seen her again.

When he was ten, Edmond learned that his mother had died in the convent during a self-imposed religious fast. Overcome with physical pain, she had hanged herself.

"It's not a pleasant story," Edmond told Langdon. "As a high school student, I learned these details— and as you can imagine, my mother's unwavering zealotry has a lot to do with my abhorrence of religion. I call it—'Newton's Third Law of Child Rearing: For every lunacy, there is an equal and opposite lunacy.'"

After hearing the story, Langdon understood why Edmond had been so full of anger and bitterness when they met during Edmond's freshman year at

Harvard. Langdon also marveled that Edmond had never once complained about the rigors of his childhood. Instead, he had declared himself **fortunate** for the early hardship because it had served as a potent motivation for Edmond to achieve his two childhood goals—first, to get out of poverty, and second, to help expose the hypocrisy of the faith he believed destroyed his mother.

Success on both counts, Langdon thought sadly, continuing to peruse the apartment's library.

As he began scanning a new section of bookshelves, he spotted many titles he recognized, most of them relevant to Edmond's lifelong concerns for the dangers of religion:

THE GOD DELUSION
GOD IS NOT GREAT
THE PORTABLE ATHEIST
LETTER TO A CHRISTIAN NATION
THE END OF FAITH
THE GOD VIRUS: HOW RELIGION INFECTS OUR
   LIVES AND CULTURE

Over the last decade, books advocating rationality over blind faith had sprung up on nonfiction bestseller lists. Langdon had to admit that the cultural shift away from religion had become increasingly visible—even on the Harvard campus. Recently, the **Washington Post** had run an article on "godlessness at Harvard," reporting that for the first time in the

school's 380-year history, the freshman class consisted of more agnostics and atheists than Protestants
and Catholics combined.

Similarly, across the Western world, antireligious
organizations were sprouting up, pushing back
against what they considered the dangers of religious
dogma—American Atheists, the Freedom from Religion Foundation, Americanhumanist.org, the Atheist Alliance International.

Langdon had never given these groups much
thought until Edmond had told him about the
Brights—a global organization that, despite its often
misunderstood name, endorsed a naturalistic world-
view with no supernatural or mystical elements. The
Brights' membership included powerhouse intellec-
tuals like Richard Dawkins, Margaret Downey, and
Daniel Dennett. Apparently, the growing army of
atheists was now packing some very big guns.

Langdon had spotted books by both Dawkins and
Dennett only minutes ago while skimming the section of the library devoted to evolution.

The Dawkins classic **The Blind Watchmaker** forcefully challenged the teleological notion that human
beings—much like complex watches—could exist
only if they had a "designer." Similarly, one of Dennett's books, **Darwin's Dangerous Idea**, argued that
natural selection **alone** was sufficient to explain the
evolution of life, and that complex biological designs
could exist without help from a divine designer.

God is not needed for life, Langdon mused, flashing
on Edmond's presentation. The question "Where do

we come from?" suddenly rang a bit more forcefully in Langdon's mind. **Could that be part of Edmond's discovery?** he wondered. **The idea that life exists on its own—without a Creator?**

This notion, of course, stood in direct opposition to every major Creation story, which made Langdon increasingly curious to know if he might be on the right track. Then again, the idea seemed entirely unprovable.

"Robert?" Ambra called behind him.

Langdon turned to see that Ambra had completed searching her side of the library and was shaking her head. "Nothing over here," she said. "All nonfiction. I'll help you look on your side."

"Same here so far," Langdon said.

As Ambra crossed to Langdon's side of the library, Winston's voice crackled on the speakerphone.

"Ms. Vidal?"

Ambra raised Edmond's phone. "Yes?"

"Both you and Professor Langdon need to see something right away," Winston said. "The palace has just made a public statement."

Langdon moved quickly toward Ambra, standing close by her side, watching as the tiny screen in her hand began streaming a video.

He recognized the plaza in front of Madrid's Royal Palace, where a uniformed man in handcuffs was being marched roughly into the frame by four Guardia Real agents. The agents turned their prisoner toward the camera, as if to disgrace him before the eyes of the world.

"Garza?!" Ambra exclaimed, sounding stunned. "The head of the Guardia Real is under arrest?!"

The camera turned now to show a woman in thick glasses who pulled a piece of paper out of a pocket of her pantsuit and prepared to read a statement.

"That's Mónica Martín," Ambra said. "Public relations coordinator. What is going **on**?"

The woman began reading, enunciating every word clearly and distinctly. "The Royal Palace is hereby arresting Commander Diego Garza for his role in the murder of Edmond Kirsch, as well as his attempts to implicate Bishop Valdespino in that crime."

Langdon could feel Ambra stagger slightly beside him as Mónica Martín continued reading.

"Regarding our future queen, Ambra Vidal," the PR coordinator said in an ominous tone, "and the American professor Robert Langdon, I'm afraid I have some deeply disturbing news."

Langdon and Ambra exchanged a startled glance.

"The palace has just received confirmation from Ms. Vidal's security detail," Martín continued, "that Ms. Vidal was taken from the Guggenheim Museum against her will tonight by Robert Langdon. Our Guardia Real are now on full alert, coordinating with local authorities in Barcelona, where it is believed that Robert Langdon is holding Ms. Vidal hostage."

Langdon was speechless.

"As this is now formally classified as a hostage situation, the public is urged to assist the authorities by reporting any and all information relating to the whereabouts of Ms. Vidal or Mr. Langdon. The palace has no further comment at this time."

Reporters started screaming questions at Martín, who abruptly turned and marched off toward the palace.

"This is . . . madness," Ambra stammered. "My agents **saw** me leave the museum willingly!"

Langdon stared at the phone, trying to make sense of what he had just witnessed. Despite the torrent of questions now swirling in his mind, he was entirely lucid about one key point.

I am in serious danger.

CHAPTER 56

Robert, I'm so sorry." Ambra Vidal's dark eyes were wild with fear and guilt. "I have no idea who is behind this false story, but they've just put you at enormous risk." The future queen of Spain reached for Edmond's phone. "I'm going to call Mónica Martín right now."

"Do **not** call Ms. Martín," Winston's voice chimed from the phone. "That is precisely what the palace wants. It's a ploy. They're trying to flush you out, trick you into making contact and revealing your location. Think logically. Your two Guardia agents **know** you were not kidnapped, and yet they've agreed to help spread this lie and fly to Barcelona to hunt you? Clearly, the entire palace is involved in this. And with the commander of the Royal Guard under arrest, these orders must be coming from higher up."

Ambra drew a short breath. "Meaning . . . Julián?"

"An inescapable conclusion," Winston said. "The prince is the only one in the palace who has the authority to arrest Commander Garza."

Ambra closed her eyes for a long moment, and Langdon sensed a wave of melancholy washing over her, as if this seemingly incontrovertible proof of Julián's involvement had just erased her last remaining hope that perhaps her fiancé was an innocent bystander in all of this.

"This is about Edmond's discovery," Langdon declared. "Someone in the palace knows we are trying to show Edmond's video to the world, and they're desperate to stop us."

"Perhaps they thought their work was finished when they silenced Edmond," Winston added. "They didn't realize that there were loose ends."

An uncomfortable silence hung between them.

"Ambra," Langdon said quietly, "I obviously don't know your fiancé, but I strongly suspect Bishop Valdespino has Julián's ear in this matter. Remember, Edmond and Valdespino were at odds before the museum event even started."

She nodded, looking uncertain. "Either way, you're in danger."

Suddenly they became aware of the faint sound of sirens wailing in the distance.

Langdon felt his pulse quicken. "We need to find this poem **now**," he declared, resuming his search of the bookshelves. "Launching Edmond's presentation is the key to our safety. If we go public, then whoever is trying to silence us will realize they're too late."

"True," Winston said, "but the local authorities will still be hunting for you as a kidnapper. You won't be safe unless you beat the palace at their own game."

"How?" Ambra demanded.

Winston continued without hesitation. "The palace used the media against you, but that's a knife that cuts both ways."

Langdon and Ambra listened as Winston quickly
outlined a very simple plan, one that Langdon had
to admit would instantly create confusion and chaos
among their assailants.

"I'll do it," Ambra readily agreed.

"Are you sure?" Langdon asked her warily. "There
will be no going back for you."

"Robert," she said, "I'm the one who got you into
this, and now you're in danger. The palace had the
gall to use the media as a weapon against you, and
now I'm going to turn it around on them."

"Fittingly so," Winston added. "Those who live by
the sword will die by the sword."

Langdon did a double take. **Did Edmond's computer really just paraphrase Aeschylus?** He wondered if it might not be more appropriate to quote
Nietzsche: **"Whoever fights monsters should see to
it that in the process he does not become a monster."**

Before Langdon could protest any further, Ambra
was moving down the hall, Edmond's phone in hand.
"Find that password, Robert!" she called over her
shoulder. "I'll be right back."

Langdon watched her disappear into a narrow turret whose staircase spiraled up to Casa Milà's notoriously precarious rooftop deck.

"Be careful!" he called after her.

Alone now in Edmond's apartment, Langdon
peered down the winding snake-rib hallway and tried
to make sense of what he had seen here—cases of
unusual artifacts, a framed quote proclaiming that

God was dead, and a priceless Gauguin that posed
the same questions Edmond had asked of the world
earlier tonight. **Where do we come from? Where are
we going?**

He had found nothing yet that hinted at Edmond's
possible **answers** to these questions. So far, Langdon's search of the library had yielded only one volume that seemed potentially relevant—**Unexplained
Art**—a book of photographs of mysterious man-made
structures, including Stonehenge, the Easter Island
heads, and Nazca's sprawling "desert drawings"—
geoglyphs drawn on such a massive scale that they
were discernible only from the air.

Not much help, he decided, and resumed his search
of the shelves.

Outside, the sirens grew louder.

CHAPTER 57

I am not a monster," Ávila declared, exhaling as he relieved himself in a grungy urinal in a deserted rest stop on Highway N-240.

At his side, the Uber driver was trembling, apparently too nervous to urinate. "You threatened . . . my family."

"And if you behave," Ávila replied, "I assure you that no harm will come to them. Just take me to Barcelona, drop me off, and we will part as friends. I will return your wallet, forget your home address, and you need never think of me again."

The driver stared straight ahead, his lips quivering.

"You are a man of the faith," Ávila said. "I saw the papal cross on your windshield. And no matter what you think of me, you can find peace in knowing that you are doing the work of God tonight." Ávila finished at the urinal. "The Lord works in mysterious ways."

Ávila stepped back and checked the ceramic pistol tucked into his belt. It was loaded with his lone remaining bullet. He wondered if he'd need to use it tonight.

He walked to the sink and ran water into his palms, seeing the tattoo that the Regent had directed him to place there in case he was caught. **An unnecessary precaution,** Ávila suspected, now feeling like an untraceable spirit moving through the night.

He raised his eyes to the filthy mirror, startled by his appearance. The last time Ávila had seen himself, he was wearing full dress whites with a starched collar and a naval cap. Now, having stripped off the top of his uniform, he looked more like a trucker—wearing only his V-neck T-shirt and a baseball cap borrowed from his driver.

Ironically, the disheveled man in the mirror reminded Ávila of his appearance during his days of drunken self-loathing following the explosion that killed his family.

I was in a bottomless pit.

The turning point, he knew, had been the day when his physical therapist, Marco, had tricked him into driving out into the countryside to meet the "pope."

Ávila would never forget approaching the eerie spires of the Palmarian church, passing through their towering security gates, and entering the cathedral partway through the morning mass, where throngs of worshippers were kneeling in prayer.

The sanctuary was lit only by natural light from high stained-glass windows, and the air smelled heavily of incense. When Ávila saw the gilded altars and burnished wood pews, he realized that the rumors of the Palmarians' massive wealth were true. This church was as beautiful as any cathedral Ávila had ever seen, and yet he knew that **this** Catholic church was unlike any other.

The Palmarians are the sworn enemy of the Vatican.

Standing with Marco at the rear of the cathedral, Ávila gazed out over the congregation and wondered how this sect could have thrived after blatantly flaunting its opposition to Rome. Apparently, the Palmarians' denunciation of the Vatican's growing liberalism had struck a chord with believers who craved a more conservative interpretation of the faith.

Hobbling up the aisle on his crutches, Ávila felt like a miserable cripple making a pilgrimage to Lourdes in hopes of a miracle cure. An usher greeted Marco and led the two men to seats that had been cordoned off in the very front row. Nearby parishioners glanced over with curiosity to see who was getting this special treatment. Ávila wished Marco had not convinced him to wear his decorated naval uniform.

I thought I was meeting the pope.

Ávila sat down and raised his eyes to the main altar, where a young parishioner in a suit was doing a reading from a Bible. Ávila recognized the passage—the Gospel of Mark.

" 'If you hold anything against anyone,' " the reader declared, " '**forgive** them, so that your Father in heaven may forgive you your sins.' "

More forgiveness? Ávila thought, scowling. He felt like he'd heard this passage a thousand times from the grief counselors and nuns in the months after the terrorist attack.

The reading ended, and the swelling chords of a pipe organ resounded in the sanctuary. The congregants rose in unison, and Ávila reluctantly clambered to his feet, wincing in pain. A hidden door behind the altar opened and a figure appeared, sending a ripple of excitement through the crowd.

The man looked to be in his fifties—upright and regal with a graceful stature and a compelling gaze. He wore a white cassock, a golden tippet, an embroidered sash, and a bejeweled papal **pretiosa** miter. He advanced with his arms outstretched to the congregation, seeming to hover as he moved toward the center of the altar.

"There he is," Marco whispered excitedly. "Pope Innocent the Fourteenth."

He calls himself Pope Innocent XIV? The Palmarians, Ávila knew, recognized the legitimacy of every pope up to Paul VI, who died in 1978.

"We're just in time," Marco said. "He's about to deliver his homily."

The pope moved toward the center of the raised altar, bypassing the formal pulpit and stepping down so that he stood at the same level as his parishioners. He adjusted his lavalier microphone, held out his hands, and smiled warmly.

"Good morning," he intoned in a whisper.

The congregation boomed in response. **"Good morning!"**

The pope continued moving away from the altar, closer to his congregation. "We have just heard a reading from the Gospel of Mark," he began, "a passage I chose personally because this morning I would like to talk about **forgiveness**."

The pope drifted over to Ávila and stopped in the aisle beside him, only inches away. He never once looked down. Ávila glanced uneasily at Marco, who gave him an excited nod.

"We all struggle with forgiveness," the pope said to the congregation. "And that is because there are times when the trespasses against us seem to be **unforgivable**. When someone kills innocent people in an act of pure hatred, should we do as some churches will teach us, and turn the other cheek?" The room fell deathly silent, and the pope lowered his voice even further. "When an anti-Christian extremist sets off a bomb during morning mass in the Cathedral of Seville, and that bomb kills innocent mothers and children, how can we be expected to **forgive**? Bombing is an act of **war**. A war not just against Catholics. A war not just against Christians. But a war against goodness . . . against **God** Himself!"

Ávila closed his eyes, trying to repress the horrific memories of that morning, and all the rage and misery still churning in his heart. As his anger swelled, Ávila suddenly felt the pope's gentle hand on his shoulder. Ávila opened his eyes, but the pope never looked down at him. Even so, the man's touch felt steady and reassuring.

"Let us not forget our own **Terror Rojo**," the pope continued, his hand never leaving Ávila's shoulder. "During our civil war, enemies of God burned Spain's churches and monasteries, murdering more than six thousand priests and torturing hundreds of nuns, forcing the sisters to swallow their rosary beads before violating them and throwing them down mineshafts to their deaths." He paused and let his words sink in. "**That** kind of hatred does not disappear over time; instead, it festers, growing stronger, waiting to rise up again like a cancer. My friends, I warn you, evil will swallow us whole if we do not fight force with force. We will never conquer evil if our battle cry is 'forgiveness.'"

He is correct, Ávila thought, having witnessed firsthand in the military that being "soft" on misconduct was the best way to guarantee increasing misconduct.

"I believe," the pope continued, "that in some cases forgiveness can be **dangerous**. When we **forgive** evil in the world, we are giving evil permission to grow and spread. When we respond to an act of war with an act of mercy, we are encouraging our enemies to commit further acts of violence. There comes a time when we must do as Jesus did and forcefully throw over the money tables, shouting: 'This will not stand!'"

I agree! Ávila wanted to shout as the congregation nodded its approval.

"But do we take action?" the pope asked. "Does the Catholic Church in Rome make a stand like Jesus did? No, it doesn't. Today we face the darkest evils in the world with nothing more than our ability to forgive, to love, and to be compassionate. And so we allow—no, we **encourage**—the evil to grow. In response to repeated crimes against us, we delicately voice our concerns in politically correct language, reminding each other that an evil person is evil only

because of his difficult childhood, or his impover-
ished life, or his having suffered crimes against his
own loved ones—and so his hatred is not his own
fault. I say, **enough**! Evil is evil! We have **all** struggled
in life!"

The congregation broke into spontaneous applause,
something Ávila had never witnessed during a Catholic service.

"I chose to speak about forgiveness today," the pope
continued, his hand still on Ávila's shoulder, "because
we have a special guest in our midst. I would like
to thank Admiral Luis Ávila for blessing us with his
presence. He is a revered and decorated member of
Spain's military, and he has faced unthinkable evil.
Like all of us, he has struggled with forgiveness."

Before Ávila could protest, the pope was recounting
in vivid detail the struggles of Ávila's life—the loss of
his family in a terrorist attack, his descent into alcoholism, and finally his failed suicide attempt. Ávila's
initial reaction was anger with Marco for betraying
a trust, and yet now, hearing his own story told in
this way, he felt strangely empowered. It was a public
admission that he had hit rock bottom, and somehow, perhaps miraculously, he had survived.

"I would suggest to all of you," the pope said, "that
God intervened in Admiral Ávila's life, and saved
him . . . for a higher purpose."

With that, the Palmarian pope Innocent XIV
turned and gazed down at Ávila for the first time.
The man's deep-set eyes seemed to penetrate Ávila's

soul, and he felt electrified with a kind of strength he had not felt in years.

"Admiral Ávila," the pope declared, "I believe that the tragic loss you have endured is beyond forgiveness. I believe your ongoing rage—your **righteous** desire for vengeance—cannot be quelled by turning the other cheek. Nor **should** it be! Your pain will be the catalyst for your own salvation. We are here to support you! To love you! To stand by your side and help transform your anger into a potent force for goodness in the world! Praise be to God!"

"**Praise be to God!**" the congregation echoed.

"Admiral Ávila," the pope continued, staring even more intently into his eyes. "What is the motto of the Spanish Armada?"

"**Pro Deo et patria,**" Ávila replied immediately.

"Yes, **Pro Deo et patria.** For God and country. We are all honored to be in the presence today of a decorated naval officer who has served his **country** so well." The pope paused, leaning forward. "But . . . what about God?"

Ávila gazed up into the man's piercing eyes and felt suddenly off balance.

"Your life is not over, Admiral," the pope whispered. "Your work is not done. **This** is why God saved you. Your sworn mission is only half complete. You have served country, yes . . . but you have not yet served **God!**"

Ávila felt like he had been struck by a bullet.

"Peace be with you!" the pope proclaimed.

"**And also with you!**" the congregation responded.

Ávila suddenly found himself swallowed up by a sea of well-wishers in an outpouring of support unlike anything he'd ever experienced. He searched the parishioners' eyes for any trace of the cultlike fanaticism he had feared, but all he saw was optimism, goodwill, and a sincere passion for doing God's work . . . exactly what Ávila realized he had been lacking.

From that day on, with the help of Marco and his new group of friends, Ávila began his long climb out of the bottomless pit of despair. He returned to his rigorous exercise routine, ate nutritious foods, and, most important, rediscovered his faith.

After several months, when his physical therapy was complete, Marco presented Avila with a leather-bound Bible in which he had flagged a dozen or so passages.

Ávila flipped to a few of them at random.

ROMANS 13:4
**For he is a servant of God—
the avenger who carries out
God's wrath on wrongdoers.**

PSALM 94:1
**O Lord, the God of vengeance,
let your glorious justice shine forth!**

2 TIMOTHY 2:3
**Share in suffering,
as a good soldier of Christ Jesus.**

"Remember," Marco had told him with a smile. "When evil rears its head in the world, God works through each of us in a different way, to exert His will on earth. Forgiveness is not the only path to salvation."

CHAPTER 58

🌐 ConspiracyNet.com

BREAKING NEWS

WHOEVER YOU ARE—TELL US MORE!

Tonight, the self-proclaimed civilian watchdog monte@iglesia.org has submitted a staggering amount of inside information to ConspiracyNet.com.

Thank you!

Because the data "Monte" has shared thus far have exhibited such a high level of reliability and inside access, we feel confident in making this very humble request:

MONTE—WHOEVER YOU ARE—IF YOU HAVE ANY INFORMATION AT ALL ABOUT THE CONTENT OF KIRSCH'S ABORTED PRESENTATION—PLEASE SHARE IT!!

#WHEREDOWECOMEFROM

#WHEREAREWEGOING

Thank you.

—All of us here at ConspiracyNet

As Robert Langdon searched the final few sections of Edmond's library, he felt his hopes fading. Outside, the two-tone police sirens had grown louder and louder before abruptly stopping directly in front of Casa Milà. Through the apartment's tiny portal windows, Langdon could see the flash of spinning police lights.

We're trapped in here, he realized. **We need that forty-seven-letter password, or there will be no way out.**

Unfortunately, Langdon had yet to see a single book of poems.

The shelves in the final section were deeper than the rest and appeared to hold Edmond's collection of large-format art books. As Langdon hurried along the wall, scanning the titles, he saw books that reflected Edmond's passion for the hippest and newest in contemporary art.

SERRA . . . KOONS . . . HIRST . . . BRU-GUERA . . . BASQUIAT . . . BANKSY . . . ABRAMOVIĆ . . .

The collection stopped abruptly at a series of smaller volumes, and Langdon paused in hopes of finding a book on poetry.

Nothing.

The books here were commentaries and critiques of abstract art, and Langdon spotted a few titles that Edmond had sent for him to peruse.

WHAT ARE YOU LOOKING AT?
WHY YOUR FIVE-YEAR-OLD COULD NOT HAVE
   DONE THAT
HOW TO SURVIVE MODERN ART

I'm still trying to survive it, Langdon thought, quickly moving on. He stepped around another rib and started sifting through the next section.

Modern art books, he mused. Even at a glance, Langdon could see that this group was dedicated to an earlier period. **At least we're moving back in time . . . toward art I understand.**

Langdon's eyes moved quickly along the book spines, taking in biographies and catalogues raisonnés of the Impressionists, Cubists, and Surrealists who had stunned the world between 1870 and 1960 by entirely redefining art.

VAN GOGH . . . SEURAT . . . PICASSO . . . MUNCH . . . MATISSE . . . MAGRITTE . . . KLIMT . . . KANDINSKY . . . JOHNS . . . HOCKNEY . . . GAUGUIN . . . DUCHAMP . . . DEGAS . . . CHAGALL . . . CÉZANNE . . . CASSATT . . . BRAQUE . . . ARP . . . ALBERS . . .

This section terminated at one last architectural rib, and Langdon moved past it, finding himself in the final section of the library. The volumes here appeared to be dedicated to the group of artists that Edmond, in Langdon's presence, liked to call "the school of boring dead white guys"—essentially, anything predating the modernist movement of the mid-nineteenth century.

Unlike Edmond, it was here that Langdon felt most at home, surrounded by the Old Masters.

VERMEER . . . VELÁZQUEZ . . . TITIAN . . . TINTORETTO . . . RUBENS . . . REMBRANDT . . . RAPHAEL . . . POUSSIN . . . MICHELANGELO . . . LIPPI . . . GOYA . . . GIOTTO . . . GHIRLANDAIO . . . EL GRECO . . . DÜRER . . . DA VINCI . . . COROT . . . CARAVAGGIO . . . BOTTICELLI . . . BOSCH . . .

The last few feet of the final shelf were dominated by a large glass cabinet, sealed with a heavy lock. Langdon peered through the glass and saw an ancient-looking leather box inside—a protective casing for a massive antique book. The text on the outside of the box was barely legible, but Langdon could see enough to decrypt the title of the volume inside.

My God, he thought, now realizing why this book had been locked away from the hands of visitors. **It's probably worth a fortune.**

Langdon knew there were precious few early editions of this legendary artist's work in existence.

I'm not surprised Edmond invested in this, he thought, recalling that Edmond had once referred to this British artist as "the only premodern with any imagination." Langdon disagreed, but he could certainly understand Edmond's special affection for this artist. **They are both cut from the same cloth.**

Langdon crouched down and peered through the glass at the box's gilded engraving: **The Complete Works of William Blake.**

William Blake, Langdon mused. **The Edmond Kirsch of the eighteen hundreds.**

Blake had been an idiosyncratic genius—a prolific luminary whose painting style was so progressive that some believed he had magically glimpsed the future in his dreams. His symbol-infused religious illustrations depicted angels, demons, Satan, God, mythical creatures, biblical themes, and a pantheon of deities from his own spiritual hallucinations.

And just like Kirsch, Blake loved to challenge Christianity.

The thought caused Langdon to stand up abruptly.

William Blake.

He drew a startled breath.

Finding Blake among so many other visual artists had caused Langdon to forget one crucial fact about the mystical genius.

Blake was not only an artist and illustrator . . .

Blake was a prolific poet.

For an instant, Langdon felt his heart begin to race. Much of Blake's poetry espoused revolutionary ideas that meshed perfectly with Edmond's views. In fact, some of Blake's most widely known aphorisms—those in "satanic" works like **The Marriage of Heaven and**

Hell—could almost have been written by Edmond himself.

ALL RELIGIONS ARE ONE
THERE IS NO NATURAL RELIGION

Langdon now recalled Edmond's description of his favorite line of poetry. **He told Ambra it was a "prophecy."** Langdon knew of no poet in history who could be considered more of a prophet than William Blake, who, in the 1790s, had penned two dark and ominous poems:

AMERICA A PROPHECY
EUROPE A PROPHECY

Langdon owned both works—elegant reproductions of Blake's handwritten poems and accompanying illustrations.

Langdon peered at the large leather box inside the cabinet.

The original editions of Blake's "prophecies" would have been published as large-format illuminated texts!

With a surge of hope, Langdon crouched down in front of the cabinet, sensing the leather box might very well contain what he and Ambra had come here to find—a poem that contained a prophetic forty-seven-character line. The only question now was whether Edmond had somehow **marked** his favorite passage.

Langdon reached out and pulled the cabinet handle.

Locked.

He glanced toward the spiral staircase, wondering whether he should simply dash upstairs and ask Winston to run a search on all of William Blake's poetry. The sound of sirens had been replaced by the distant thrum of helicopter blades and voices yelling in the stairwell outside Edmond's door.

They're here.

Langdon eyed the cabinet and noted the faint greenish tint of modern museum-grade UV glass.

He whipped off his jacket, held it over the glass, turned his body, and without hesitation, rammed his elbow into the pane. With a muffled crunch, the cabinet door shattered. Carefully, Langdon reached through the jagged shards, unlocking the door. Then he swung the door open and gently lifted out the leather box.

Even before Langdon set the box on the floor, he could tell that something was wrong. **It's not heavy enough.** Blake's complete works seemed to weigh almost nothing.

Langdon set down the box and carefully raised the lid.

Just as he feared . . . empty.

He exhaled, staring into the vacant container. **Where the hell is Edmond's book?!**

He was about to close the box when Langdon noticed something unexpected taped to the inside of the lid—an elegantly embossed ivory note card.

Langdon read the text on the card.

Then, in utter disbelief, he read it again.

Seconds later, he was racing up the spiral staircase toward the roof.

———

At that instant, on the second floor of Madrid's Royal Palace, director of electronic security Suresh Bhalla was moving quietly through Prince Julián's private apartment. After locating the digital wall safe, he entered the master override code that was kept for emergencies.

The safe popped open.

Inside, Suresh saw two phones—a secure palace-issued smartphone that belonged to Prince Julián and an iPhone that, he deduced, in all likelihood was the property of Bishop Valdespino.

He grabbed the iPhone.

Am I really doing this?

Again he pictured the message from monte@iglesia .org.

i hacked valdespino's texts.
he has dangerous secrets.
the palace should access his sms records.
now.

Suresh wondered what secrets the bishop's texts could possibly reveal . . . and why the informant had decided to give the Royal Palace a heads-up.

Perhaps the informant is trying to protect the palace from collateral damage?

All Suresh knew was that if there was information that was of danger to the royal family, it was his job to access it.

He had already considered obtaining an emergency subpoena, but the PR risks and the delay made it impractical. Fortunately, Suresh had far more discreet and expedient methods at his disposal.

Holding Valdespino's phone, he pressed the home button and the screen lit up.

Locked with a password.

No problem.

"Hey, Siri," Suresh said, holding the phone to his mouth. "What time is it?"

Still in locked mode, the phone displayed a clock. On this clock screen, Suresh ran through a series of simple commands—creating a new time zone for the clock, asking to share the time zone via SMS, adding a photo, and then, rather than trying to send the text, hitting the home button.

Click.

The phone unlocked.

This simple hack compliments of YouTube, Suresh thought, amused that iPhone users believed their password offered them any privacy at all.

Now, with full access to Valdespino's phone, Suresh opened the iMessage app, fully anticipating that he would have to restore Valdespino's deleted texts by tricking the iCloud backup into rebuilding the catalog.

Sure enough, he found the bishop's text history entirely empty.

Except for one message, he realized, seeing a lone

inbound text that had arrived a couple of hours ago from a blocked number.

Suresh clicked open the text and read the three-line message. For a moment, he thought he was hallucinating.

This can't be true!

Suresh read the message again. The text was absolute proof of Valdespino's involvement in acts of unthinkable treachery and deceit.

Not to mention arrogance, Suresh thought, stunned that the old cleric would feel so invulnerable as to communicate a message like this electronically.

If this text goes public . . .

Suresh shuddered at the possibility and immediately ran downstairs to find Mónica Martín.

CHAPTER 60

As the EC145 helicopter streaked in low over the city, Agent Díaz stared down at the sprawl of lights beneath him. Despite the late hour, he could see the flicker of televisions and computers in the majority of apartment windows, painting the city with a faint blue haze.

The whole world is watching.

It made him nervous. He could feel this night spiraling wildly out of control, and he feared this growing crisis was headed for a disturbing conclusion.

In front of him, Agent Fonseca shouted and pointed into the distance directly ahead. Díaz nodded, spotting their target at once.

Hard to miss.

Even from a distance, the pulsating cluster of spinning blue police lights was unmistakable.

God help us.

Just as Díaz had feared, Casa Milà was overrun by local police cars. The Barcelona authorities had responded to an anonymous tip on the heels of Mónica Martín's press announcement from the Royal Palace.

Robert Langdon has kidnapped the future queen of Spain.

The palace needs the public's help in finding them.

A blatant lie, Díaz knew. With my own eyes I saw them leave the Guggenheim together.

While Martín's ploy had been effective, it had set in motion an incredibly dangerous game. Creating a public manhunt by involving local authorities was perilous—not just for Robert Langdon, but for the future queen, who now had a very good chance of being caught in the cross fire of a bunch of amateur local cops. If the palace's goal was to keep the future queen safe, this was definitely not the way to do it.

Commander Garza would never have permitted this situation to escalate so far.

Garza's arrest remained a mystery to Díaz, who had no doubt that the charges against his commander were just as fictitious as those against Langdon.

Nonetheless, Fonseca had taken the call and received his orders.

Orders from above Garza's head.

As the helicopter neared Casa Milà, Agent Díaz surveyed the scene below and realized there would be no safe place to land. The broad avenue and corner plaza in front of the building were packed with media trucks, police cars, and crowds of onlookers.

Díaz looked down at the building's famous rooftop—an undulating figure eight of sloping pathways and staircases that wound above the building and provided visitors with breathtaking views of the Barcelona skyline . . . as well as views down into the building's two gaping light wells, each of which dropped nine stories to interior courtyards.

No landing there.

In addition to the heaving hills and valleys of the terrain, the roof deck was protected by towering Gaudí chimneys that resembled futuristic chess pieces—helmeted sentinels that allegedly had so impressed filmmaker George Lucas that he'd used them as models for his menacing storm troopers in **Star Wars.**

Díaz glanced away to scan the neighboring buildings for possible landing sites, but his gaze suddenly stopped on an unexpected vision atop Casa Milà.

A small figure stood among the huge statues.

Poised at a railing near the edge of the roof, the person was dressed in white, starkly illuminated by the upward-facing media lights in the plaza below. For an instant, the vision reminded Díaz of seeing the pope on his balcony over St. Peter's Square, addressing his followers.

But this was not the pope.

This was a beautiful woman in a very familiar white dress.

———

Ambra Vidal could see nothing through the glare of the media lights, but she could hear a helicopter closing in and knew time was running out. Desperately, she leaned out over the railing and attempted to shout to the swarm of media people below.

Her words vanished into the deafening roar of helicopter rotors.

Winston had predicted that the television crews on the street would direct their cameras upward the instant Ambra was spotted on the edge of the roof. Indeed, that was exactly what had happened, and yet Ambra knew Winston's plan had failed.

They can't hear a word I'm saying!

The rooftop of Casa Milà stood too high over the blaring traffic and chaos below. And now the thrum of the helicopter threatened to drown out everything entirely.

"I have **not** been kidnapped!" Ambra yelled once again, mustering as much volume as she could. "The statement from the Royal Palace about Robert Langdon was inaccurate! I am **not** a hostage!"

You are the future queen of Spain, Winston had reminded her moments earlier. **If you call off this manhunt, the authorities will stop dead in their tracks. Your statement will create utter confusion. Nobody will know which orders to follow.**

Ambra knew Winston was right, but her words had been lost in the rotor wash above the boisterous crowd.

Suddenly the sky erupted in a thunderous howl. Ambra recoiled back from the railing as the helicopter swooped closer and halted abruptly, hovering directly in front of her. The fuselage doors were wide open, and two familiar faces stared intently out at her—Agents Fonseca and Díaz.

To Ambra's horror, Agent Fonseca raised some kind

of device, which he aimed directly at her head. For a moment, the strangest of thoughts raced through her mind. **Julián wants me dead. I am a barren woman. I cannot give him an heir. Killing me is his only escape from this engagement.**

Ambra staggered back, away from the threatening-looking device, clutching Edmond's cell phone in one hand and reaching out for balance with the other. But as she placed her foot behind her, the ground seemed to disappear. For an instant, she felt only empty space where she had expected solid cement. Her body twisted as she tried to regain her balance, but she felt herself pitching sidelong down a short flight of stairs.

Her left elbow smashed into the cement, and the rest of her crashed down an instant later. Even so, Ambra Vidal felt no pain. Her entire focus shifted to the object that had flown out of her hand—Edmond's oversized turquoise cell phone.

My God, no!

She watched with dread as the phone skittered across the cement, bouncing down the stairs toward the edge of the nine-story drop to the building's inner courtyard. She lunged for the phone, but it disappeared under the protective fencing, tumbling into the abyss.

Our connection to Winston . . . !

Ambra scrambled after it, arriving at the fence just in time to see Edmond's phone tumbling end over end toward the lobby's elegant stone floor, where, with a sharp crack, it exploded in a shower of shimmering glass and metal.

In an instant, Winston was gone.

Bounding up the steps, Langdon burst out of the stairwell turret onto the Casa Milà roof deck. He found himself in the middle of a deafening maelstrom. A helicopter was hovering very low beside the building, and Ambra was nowhere to be seen.

Dazed, Langdon scanned the area. **Where is she?** He had forgotten how bizarre this rooftop was—lopsided parapets . . . steep staircases . . . cement soldiers . . . bottomless pits.

"Ambra!"

When he spotted her, he felt a surge of dread. Ambra Vidal was lying crumpled on the cement at the edge of the light well.

As Langdon raced up and over a rise toward her, the sharp zing of a bullet whipped past his head and exploded in the cement behind him.

Jesus! Langdon dropped to his knees and scrambled toward lower ground as two more bullets sailed over his head. For a moment, he thought the shots were coming from the helicopter, but as he clambered toward Ambra, he saw a swarm of police flooding out of another turret on the far side of the rooftop with their guns drawn.

They want to kill me, he realized. **They think I**

kidnapped the future queen! Her rooftop announcement apparently had gone unheard.

As Langdon looked toward Ambra, now only ten yards away, he realized to his horror that her arm was bleeding. **My God, she's been shot!** Another bullet sailed over his head as Ambra began clawing at the railing that encircled the drop-off to the inner courtyard. She struggled to pull herself up.

"Stay down!" Langdon shouted, scrambling to Ambra and crouching protectively over her body. He looked up at the towering, helmeted storm-trooper figures that dotted the rooftop's perimeter like silent guardians.

There was a deafening roar overhead, and buffeting winds whipped around them as the helicopter dropped down and hovered over the enormous shaft beside them, cutting off the police's line of sight.

"¡Dejen de disparar!" boomed an amplified voice from the chopper. "¡Enfunden las armas!" **Stop shooting! Holster your weapons!**

Directly in front of Langdon and Ambra, Agent Díaz was crouched in the open bay door with one foot balanced on the skid and one hand outstretched toward them.

"Get in!" he shouted.

Langdon felt Ambra recoil beneath him.

"NOW!" Díaz screamed over the deafening rotors. The agent pointed to the light well's safety railing, urging them to climb onto it, grab his hand, and make the short leap over the abyss into the hovering aircraft.

Langdon hesitated an instant too long.

Díaz grabbed the bullhorn from Fonseca and aimed it directly at Langdon's face. "PROFESSOR, GET IN THE HELICOPTER NOW!" The agent's voice boomed like thunder. "THE LOCAL POLICE HAVE ORDERS TO SHOOT YOU! WE KNOW YOU DID **NOT** KIDNAP MS. VIDAL! I NEED YOU BOTH ON BOARD IMMEDIATELY— BEFORE SOMEONE GETS KILLED!"

CHAPTER 61

I n the howling wind, Ambra felt Langdon's arms lifting her up and guiding her toward Agent Díaz's outstretched hand in the hovering chopper.

She was too dazed to protest.

"She's bleeding!" Langdon shouted as he clambered into the aircraft after her.

Suddenly the helicopter was lifting skyward, away from the undulating rooftop, leaving behind a small army of confused policemen, all staring upward.

Fonseca heaved the fuselage door shut and then moved up front toward the pilot. Díaz slid in beside Ambra to examine her arm.

"It's only a scrape," she said blankly.

"I'll find a first-aid kit." Díaz headed to the rear of the cabin.

Langdon was seated opposite Ambra, facing backward. Now that the two of them were suddenly alone, he caught her eye and gave her a relieved smile. "I'm so glad you're okay."

Ambra replied with a weak nod, but before she could thank him, Langdon was leaning forward in his seat, whispering to her in an excited tone.

"I think I found our mysterious poet," he exclaimed, his eyes filled with hope. "**William Blake**. Not only is there a copy of Blake's complete works in Edmond's library . . . but many of Blake's poems are **prophecies!**" Langdon held out his hand. "Let me have Edmond's phone—I'll ask Winston to search Blake's work for any forty-seven-letter lines of poetry!"

Ambra looked at Langdon's waiting palm and felt overcome with guilt. She reached out and took his hand in hers. "Robert," she said with a remorseful sigh, "Edmond's phone is gone. It fell off the edge of the building."

Langdon stared back at her, and Ambra saw the blood drain from his face. **I'm so sorry, Robert.** She could see him struggling to process the news and figure out where the loss of Winston now left them.

In the cockpit, Fonseca was yelling into his phone. "Confirmed! We have both of them safely aboard. Prepare the transport plane for Madrid. I will contact the palace and alert—"

"Don't bother!" Ambra shouted to the agent. "I am not going to the palace!"

Fonseca covered his phone, turned in his seat, and looked back at her. "You most certainly **are**! My orders tonight were to keep you safe. You should never have left my custody. You're lucky I was able to get here to rescue you."

"**Rescue?!**" Ambra demanded. "If that was a **rescue,** it was only necessary because the palace told ridiculous lies about Professor Langdon kidnapping me—which **you** know is not true! Is Prince Julián really so desperate that he's willing to risk the life of an innocent man? Not to mention **my** life?"

Fonseca stared her down and turned back around in his seat.

Just then, Díaz returned with the first-aid kit.

"Ms. Vidal," he said, taking a seat beside her. "Please understand that our chain of command has been disrupted tonight due to the arrest of Commander Garza. Nonetheless, I want you to know that Prince Julián had **nothing** to do with the media statement that came out of the palace. In fact, we cannot even confirm that the prince knows what's happening right now. We have been unable to reach him for over an hour."

What? Ambra stared at him. "Where is he?"

"His current whereabouts are unknown," Díaz said, "but his communication with us earlier this evening was crystal clear. The prince wants you **safe**."

"If that's true," Langdon declared, abruptly returning from his thoughts, "then taking Ms. Vidal to the palace is a deadly mistake."

Fonseca spun around. "What did you say?!"

"I don't know who is giving you orders now, sir," Langdon said, "but if the prince **truly** wants to keep his fiancée safe, then I suggest you listen to me very carefully." He paused, his tone intensifying. "Edmond Kirsch was murdered to keep his discovery from going public. And whoever silenced him will stop at nothing to make sure that job is finished."

"It's finished already," Fonseca scoffed. "Edmond is dead."

"But his discovery is not," Langdon replied. "Edmond's presentation is very much alive and can **still** be released to the world."

"Which is why you came to his apartment," Díaz ventured. "Because you believe you can launch it."

"Precisely," Langdon replied. "And **that** has made us targets. I don't know who manufactured the media statement claiming Ambra was kidnapped, but it was clearly someone desperate to stop us. So if you are part of **that** group—the people trying to bury Edmond's discovery forever—then you should simply toss Ms. Vidal and myself out of this helicopter right now while you still can."

Ambra stared at Langdon, wondering if he'd lost his mind.

"**However,**" Langdon continued, "if your sworn duty as a Guardia Real agent is to protect the royal family, including the future queen of Spain, then you need to realize there is no more dangerous place for Ms. Vidal right now than a palace that just issued a public statement that almost got her killed." Langdon reached into his pocket and extracted an elegantly embossed linen note card. "I suggest you take her to the address at the bottom of this card."

Fonseca took the card and studied it, his brow furrowing. "That's ridiculous."

"There is a security fence around the entire property," Langdon said. "Your pilot can touch down, drop the four of us off, and then fly away before anyone realizes we're even there. I know the person in charge. We can hide there, off the grid, until we sort this all out. You can accompany us."

"I'd feel safer in a military hangar at the airport."

"Do you really want to trust a military team that is probably taking orders from the same people who just nearly got Ms. Vidal killed?"

Fonseca's stony expression never wavered.

Ambra's thoughts were racing wildly now, and she wondered what was written on the card. **Where does Langdon want to go?** His sudden intensity seemed to imply there was more at stake than simply keeping her safe. She heard a renewed optimism in his voice and sensed he had not yet given up hope that they could somehow still launch Edmond's presentation.

Langdon retrieved the linen card from Fonseca and handed it to Ambra. "I found this in Edmond's library."

Ambra studied the card, immediately recognizing what it was.

Known as "loan logs" or "title cards," these elegantly embossed placeholders were given by museum curators to donors in exchange for a piece of artwork on temporary loan. Traditionally, two identical cards were printed—one placed on display in the museum to thank the donor, and one held by the donor as collateral for the piece he had loaned.

Edmond loaned out his book of Blake's poetry?

According to the card, Edmond's book had traveled no more than a few kilometers away from his Barcelona apartment.

THE COMPLETE WORKS OF
WILLIAM BLAKE

From the private collection of
EDMOND KIRSCH

On loan to
LA BASÍLICA DE LA
SAGRADA FAMÍLIA

Carrer de Mallorca, 401
08013 Barcelona, Spain

"I don't understand," Ambra said. "Why would an outspoken atheist lend a book to a **church**?"

"Not just any church," Langdon countered. "Gaudí's most enigmatic architectural masterpiece . . ." He pointed out the window, into the distance behind them. "And soon to be the tallest church in Europe."

Ambra turned her head, peering back across the city to the north. In the distance—surrounded by cranes, scaffolding, and construction lights—the unfinished towers of Sagrada Família shone brightly, a cluster of perforated spires that resembled giant sea sponges climbing off the ocean floor toward the light.

For more than a century, Gaudí's controversial Basílica de la Sagrada Família had been under construction, relying solely on private donations from the faithful. Criticized by traditionalists for its eerie organic shape and use of "biomimetic design," the church was hailed by modernists for its structural fluidity and use of "hyperboloid" forms to reflect the natural world.

"I'll admit it's unusual," Ambra said, turning back to Langdon, "but it's **still** a Catholic church. And you know Edmond."

———

I do know Edmond, Langdon thought. **Enough to know he believes Sagrada Família hides a secret purpose and symbolism that go far beyond Christianity.**

Since the bizarre church's groundbreaking in 1882, conspiracy theories had swirled about its mysteriously encoded doors, cosmically inspired helicoid columns, symbol-laden facades, magic-square mathematical carvings, and ghostly "skeletal" construction that clearly resembled twisting bones and connective tissue.

Langdon was aware of the theories, of course, and yet never gave them much credence. A few years back, however, Langdon was surprised when Edmond confessed that he was one of a growing number of Gaudí fans who quietly believed that Sagrada Família was secretly conceived as something other than a Christian church, perhaps even as a mystical shrine to science and nature.

Langdon found the notion highly unlikely, and he reminded Edmond that Gaudí was a devout Catholic whom the Vatican had held in such high esteem that they christened him "God's architect," and even considered him for beatification. Sagrada Família's unusual design, Langdon assured Kirsch, was nothing more than an example of Gaudí's unique modernist approach to Christian symbolism.

Edmond's reply was a coy smile, as if he were secretly holding some mysterious piece of the puzzle that he was not ready to share.

Another Kirsch secret, Langdon now thought. **Like his hidden battle with cancer.**

"Even if Edmond did loan his book to Sagrada Família," Ambra continued, "and even if we find it, we will never be able to locate the correct line by reading it page by page. And I really doubt Edmond used a highlighter on a priceless manuscript."

"Ambra?" Langdon replied with a calm smile. "Look at the **back** of the card."

She glanced down at the card, flipped it over, and read the text on the back.

Then, with a look of disbelief, Ambra read it again.

When her eyes snapped back up to Langdon's, they were filled with hope.

"As I was saying," Langdon said with a smile, "I think we should go there."

Ambra's excited expression faded as quickly as it came. "There is still a problem. Even if we find his password—"

"I know—we lost Edmond's phone, meaning we have no way to access Winston and communicate with him."

"Exactly."

"I believe I can solve that problem."

Ambra eyed him skeptically. "I'm sorry?"

"All we need is to locate Winston **himself**—the actual computer that Edmond built. If we no longer have access to Winston remotely, we'll just have to take the password to Winston **in person**."

Ambra stared at him as if he were mad.

Langdon continued. "You told me Edmond built Winston in a secret facility."

"Yes, but that facility could be **anywhere** in the world!"

"It's not. It's here in Barcelona. It **has** to be. Barcelona is the city where Edmond lived and worked. And building this synthetic intelligence machine was one of his most recent projects, so it only makes sense that Edmond would have built Winston **here**."

"Robert, even if you're right, you're looking for a needle in a haystack. Barcelona is an **enormous** city. It would be impossible—"

"I can find Winston," Langdon said. "I'm sure of it." He smiled and motioned to the sprawl of city lights beneath them. "This will sound crazy, but seeing this aerial view of Barcelona just now helped me realize something . . ."

His voice trailed off as he looked out the window.

"Would you care to elaborate?" Ambra asked expectantly.

"I should have seen it earlier," he said. "There's something about Winston—an intriguing puzzle—that has been bothering me all night. I think I finally figured it out."

Langdon shot a cautious glance at the Guardia agents and then lowered his voice, leaning toward Ambra. "Will you just trust me on this?" he asked quietly. "I believe I can find Winston. The problem is that finding Winston will do us no good without Edmond's password. Right now, you and I need to focus on finding that line of poetry. Sagrada Família is our best chance of doing that."

Ambra studied Langdon a long moment. Then, with a bewildered nod, she looked toward the front seat and called, "Agent Fonseca! Please have the pilot turn around and take us to Sagrada Família right away!"

Fonseca spun in his seat, glaring at her. "Ms. Vidal, as I told you, I have my orders—"

"Agent Fonseca," interrupted the future queen of Spain, leaning forward and locking eyes with him. "Take us to Sagrada Família, right now, or **my** first order of business when we return will be to have you fired."

CHAPTER 62

🌐 ConspiracyNet.com

BREAKING NEWS

ASSASSIN CULT CONNECTION!

Thanks to yet another tip from monte@iglesia.org, we have just learned that Edmond Kirsch's killer is a member of an ultraconservative, secretive Christian sect known as the **Palmarian Church**!

Luís Ávila has been recruiting online for the Palmarians for more than a year now, and his membership in this controversial religio-military organization also explains the "victor" tattoo on his palm.

This Francoist symbol is in regular use by the Palmarian Church, which, according to Spain's national newspaper, **El Pais,** has its own "pope" and has canonized several ruthless leaders—including Francisco Franco and Adolf Hitler—as saints!

Don't believe us? Look it up.

It all began with a mystical vision.

In 1975, an insurance broker named Clemente Domínguez y Gómez claimed to have had a vision in which he was crowned pope by Jesus Christ Himself. Clemente took the papal name Gregory XVII, breaking from the Vatican and appointing his own cardinals. Although rejected by Rome, this new antipope amassed thousands of followers and vast wealth enabling him to construct a fortresslike church, expand his ministry internationally, and consecrate hundreds of Palmarian bishops worldwide.

The schismatic Palmarian Church still functions today out of its world headquarters—a secure, walled compound called the Mount of Christ the King in El Palmar de Troya, Spain. The Palmarians are not recognized by the Vatican in Rome, and yet continue to attract an ultraconservative Catholic following.

More news on this sect soon, as well as an update on Bishop Antonio Valdespino, who also seems to be implicated in tonight's conspiracy.

CHAPTER 63

Okay, I'm impressed, Langdon thought.

With a few strong words, Ambra had just forced the crew of the EC145 helicopter to make a wide-banking turn and redirect toward the Basílica of the Sagrada Família.

As the aircraft leveled out and began skimming back across the city, Ambra turned to Agent Díaz and demanded the use of his cell phone, which the Guardia agent reluctantly handed over. Ambra promptly launched his browser and began scanning news headlines.

"Damn," she whispered, shaking her head with frustration. "I tried to tell the media you **did not** kidnap me. Nobody could hear me."

"Maybe they need more time to post?" Langdon offered. **This happened less than ten minutes ago.**

"They've had enough time," she replied. "I'm seeing video clips of our helicopter speeding away from Casa Milà."

Already? Langdon sometimes felt that the world had begun to spin too quickly on its axis. He could still recall when "breaking news" was printed on paper and delivered to his doorstep the following morning.

"By the way," Ambra said with a trace of humor, "it appears you and I are one of the world's top-trending news stories."

"I knew I shouldn't have kidnapped you," he replied wryly.

"Not funny. At least we're not the **number one** story." She handed him the phone. "Have a look at this."

Langdon eyed the screen and saw the Yahoo! homepage with its top ten "Trending Now" stories. He looked to the top at the most popular story:

1 "Where Do We Come From?" / Edmond Kirsch

Clearly, Edmond's presentation had inspired people around the globe to research and discuss the topic. **Edmond would be so pleased,** Langdon thought, but when he clicked the link and saw the first ten headlines, he realized he was wrong. The top ten theories for "where do we come from" were all stories about Creationism and extraterrestrials.

Edmond would be horrified.

One of Langdon's former student's most infamous rants had occurred at a public forum called Science & Spirituality, where Edmond had become so exasperated by audience questions that he finally threw up his hands and stalked off the stage, shouting: "How is it that intelligent human beings cannot discuss their origins without invoking the name of God and fucking aliens!"

Langdon kept scanning down the phone screen until he found a seemingly innocuous **CNN Live** link titled "What Did Kirsch Discover?"

He launched the link and held the phone so Ambra could see it as well. As the video began to play he turned up the volume, and he and Ambra leaned together so they could hear the video over the roar of the helicopter's rotors.

A CNN anchor appeared. Langdon had seen her broadcasts many times over the years. "We are joined now by NASA astrobiologist Dr. Griffin Bennett," she said, "who has some ideas regarding Edmond Kirsch's mysterious breaking discovery. Welcome, Dr. Bennett."

The guest—a bearded man in wire-rimmed glasses—gave a somber nod. "Thank you. First off, let me say that I knew Edmond personally. I have enormous respect for his intelligence, his creativity, and his commitment to progress and innovation. His assassination has been a terrible blow to the scientific community, and I hope this cowardly murder will serve to fortify the intellectual community to stand united against the dangers of zealotry, superstitious thinking, and those who resort to violence, not facts, to further their beliefs. I sincerely hope the rumors are true that there are people working hard tonight to find a way to bring Edmond's discovery to the public."

Langdon shot Ambra a glance. "I think he means us."

She nodded.

"There are many people who are hoping for that as well, Dr. Bennett," the anchor said. "And can you shed any light on what **you** think the content of Edmond Kirsch's discovery might be?"

"As a space scientist," Dr. Bennett continued, "I feel I should preface my words tonight with a blanket statement . . . one that I believe Edmond Kirsch would appreciate." The man turned and looked directly into the camera. "When it comes to the notion of extraterrestrial life," he began, "there exists a blinding array of bad science, conspiracy theory, and outright fantasy. For the record, let me say this: Crop circles are a hoax. Alien autopsy videos are trick photography. No cow has ever been mutilated by an alien. The Roswell saucer was a government weather balloon called Project Mogul. The Great Pyramids were built by Egyptians **without** alien technology. And most importantly, every extraterrestrial abduction story ever reported is a flat-out lie."

"How can you be sure, Doctor?" the anchor asked.

"Simple logic," the scientist said, looking annoyed as he turned back to the anchor. "Any life-form advanced enough to travel light-years through interstellar space would have nothing to learn by probing the rectums of farmers in Kansas. Nor would these life-forms need to morph into reptiles and infiltrate governments in order to take over earth. Any life-form with the technology to **travel** to earth would require no subterfuge or subtlety to dominate us instantaneously."

"Well, that's alarming!" the anchor commented

with an awkward laugh. "And how does this relate to your thoughts on Mr. Kirsch's discovery?"

The man sighed heavily. "It is my strong opinion that Edmond Kirsch was going to announce that he had found definitive **proof** that life on earth originated in **space**."

Langdon was immediately skeptical, knowing how Kirsch felt about the topic of extraterrestrial life on earth.

"Fascinating, what makes you say that?" the anchor pressed.

"Life from space is the only rational answer. We already have incontrovertible proof that matter can be exchanged between planets. We have fragments of Mars and Venus along with hundreds of samples from unidentified sources, which would support the idea that life arrived via space rocks in the form of microbes, and eventually evolved into life on earth."

The host nodded intently. "But hasn't this theory—microbes arriving from space—been around for decades, with no proof? How do you think a tech genius like Edmond Kirsch could **prove** a theory like this, which seems more in the realm of astrobiology than computer science."

"Well, there's solid logic to it," Dr. Bennett replied. "Top astronomers have warned for decades that humankind's only hope for long-term survival will be to leave this planet. The earth is already halfway through its life cycle, and eventually the sun will expand into a red giant and consume us. That is, if we survive the more imminent threats of a giant asteroid collision or a massive gamma-ray burst. For these reasons, we are already designing outposts on Mars so we can eventually move into deep space in search of a new host planet. Needless to say, this is a massive undertaking, and if we could find a simpler way to ensure our survival, we would implement it immediately."

Dr. Bennett paused. "And perhaps there **is** a simpler way. What if we could somehow package the human genome in tiny capsules and send millions of them into space in hopes one might take root, seeding human life on a distant planet? This technology does not yet exist, but we are discussing it as a viable option for human survival. And if **we** are considering 'seeding life,' then it follows that a more advanced life-form might have considered it as well."

Langdon now suspected where Dr. Bennett was going with his theory.

"With this in mind," he continued, "I believe Edmond Kirsch may have discovered some kind of alien signature—be it physical, chemical, digital, I don't know—**proving** that life on earth was seeded from space. I should mention that Edmond and I had quite a debate about this several years ago. He never liked the space-microbe theory because he believed, as many do, that genetic material could never survive the deadly radiation and temperatures that would be encountered in the long journey to earth. Personally, I believe that it would be perfectly feasible to seal these 'seeds of life' in radiation-proof, protective pods and shoot them into space with the intent of populating the cosmos in a kind of technology-assisted panspermia."

"Okay," the host said, looking unsettled, "but if someone discovered proof that humans came from a seedpod sent from space, then that means we're not alone in the universe." She paused. "But also, far more incredibly . . ."

"Yes?" Dr. Bennett smiled for the first time.

"It means whoever **sent** the pods would have to be . . . like us . . . **human**!"

"Yes, **my** first conclusion as well." The scientist paused. "Then Edmond set me straight. He pointed out the fallacy in that thinking."

This caught the host off guard. "So Edmond's belief was that whoever sent these 'seeds' was **not** human? How could that be, if the seeds were, so to speak, 'recipes' for human propagation?"

"Humans are half-baked," the scientist replied, "to use Edmond's exact words."

"I'm sorry?"

"Edmond said that if this seedpod theory were true, then the recipe that was sent to earth is probably only half-baked at the moment—not yet finished—meaning humans are not the 'final product' but instead just a transitional species evolving toward something else . . . something alien."

The CNN anchor looked bewildered.

"Any advanced life-form, Edmond argued, would not send a recipe for **humans** any more than they would send a recipe for **chimpanzees**." The scientist chuckled. "In fact, Edmond accused me of being a closet Christian—joking that only a religious mind could believe that mankind is the center of the universe. Or that aliens would airmail fully formed 'Adam and Eve' DNA into the cosmos."

"Well, Doctor," the host said, clearly uncomfortable with the direction the interview was taking. "It's certainly been enlightening speaking with you. Thank you for your time."

The segment ended, and Ambra immediately turned to Langdon. "Robert, if Edmond discovered proof that humans are a half-evolved alien species, then it raises an even bigger issue—what exactly are we evolving **into**?"

"Yes," Langdon said. "And I believe Edmond phrased that issue in a slightly different way—as a question: **Where are we going?**"

Ambra looked startled to have come full circle. "Edmond's second question from tonight's presentation."

"Precisely. Where do we come from? Where are we going? Apparently, the NASA scientist we've just watched thinks Edmond looked to the heavens and found answers to both questions."

"What do **you** think, Robert? Is this what Edmond discovered?"

Langdon could feel his brow furrow with doubt as he weighed the possibilities. The scientist's theory, while exciting, seemed far too general and otherworldly for the acute thinking of Edmond Kirsch. **Edmond liked things simple, clean, and technical. He was a computer scientist.** More importantly,

Langdon could not imagine **how** Edmond would prove such a theory. **Unearth an ancient seedpod? Detect an alien transmission?** Both discoveries would have been instantaneous breakthroughs, but Edmond's discovery had taken time.

Edmond said he had been working on it for months.

"Obviously, I don't know," Langdon told Ambra, "but my gut tells me Edmond's discovery has nothing to do with extraterrestrial life. I really believe he discovered something else entirely."

Ambra looked surprised, and then intrigued. "I guess there's only one way to find out." She motioned out the window.

In front of them shone the glimmering spires of Sagrada Família.

CHAPTER 64

Bishop Valdespino stole another quick glance at Julián, who was still staring blankly out the window of the Opel sedan as it sped along Highway M-505.

What is he thinking? Valdespino wondered.

The prince had been silent for nearly thirty minutes, barely moving except for the occasional reflexive reach into his pocket for his phone, only to realize that he had locked it in his wall safe.

I need to keep him in the dark, Valdespino thought, **just a bit longer.**

In the front seat, the acolyte from the cathedral was still driving in the direction of Casita del Príncipe, although Valdespino soon would need to inform him that the prince's retreat was not their destination at all.

Julián turned suddenly from the window, tapping the acolyte on the shoulder. "Please turn on the radio," he said. "I'd like to hear the news."

Before the young man could comply, Valdespino leaned forward and placed a firm hand on the boy's shoulder. "Let's just sit quietly, shall we?"

Julián turned to the bishop, clearly displeased at having been overridden.

"I'm sorry," Valdespino said at once, sensing a growing distrust in the prince's eyes. "It's late. All that
chatter. I prefer silent reflection."

"I've been doing some reflecting," Julián said, his
voice sharp, "and I'd like to know what's going on in
my country. We've entirely isolated ourselves tonight,
and I'm starting to wonder if it was a good idea."

"It **is** a good idea," Valdespino assured him, "and I
appreciate the trust you've shown me." He removed
his hand from the acolyte's shoulder and motioned to
the radio. "Please turn on the news. Perhaps Radio
María España?" Valdespino hoped the worldwide
Catholic station would be gentler and more tactful
than most media outlets had been about tonight's
troubling developments.

When the newscaster's voice came over the cheap
car speakers, he was discussing Edmond Kirsch's
presentation and assassination. **Every station in the
world is talking about this tonight.** Valdespino just
hoped his own name would not come up as part of
the broadcast.

Fortunately, the topic at the moment appeared to
be the dangers of the antireligious message preached
by Kirsch, especially the threat posed by his influence
on the youth of Spain. As an example, the station
began rebroadcasting a lecture Kirsch had delivered
recently at the University of Barcelona.

"Many of us are afraid to call ourselves atheists,"
Kirsch said calmly to the assembled students. "And
yet atheism is not a philosophy, nor is atheism a view

of the world. Atheism is simply an admission of the obvious."

Several students clapped in agreement.

"The term 'atheist,'" Kirsch continued, "should not even **exist**. No one ever needs to identify himself as a 'nonastrologer' or a 'nonalchemist.' We do not have words for people who doubt that Elvis is still alive, or for people who doubt that aliens traverse the galaxy only to molest cattle. Atheism is nothing more than the noises reasonable people make in the presence of unjustified religious beliefs."

A growing number of students clapped their approval.

"That definition is not mine, by the way," Kirsch told them. "Those words belong to neuroscientist Sam Harris. And if you have not already done so, you must read his book **Letter to a Christian Nation**."

Valdespino frowned, recalling the stir caused by Harris's book, **Carta a una Nación Cristiana**, which, while written for Americans, had reverberated across Spain.

"By a show of hands," Kirsch continued, "how many of you believe in any of the following ancient gods: Apollo? Zeus? Vulcan?" He paused, and then laughed. "Not a single one of you? Okay, so it appears we are all atheists with respect to **those** gods." He paused. "I simply choose to go one god further."

The crowd clapped louder still.

"My friends, I am not saying I know for a fact that there is no God. All I am saying is that if there **is** a divine force behind the universe, it is laughing hysterically at the religions we've created in an attempt to define it."

Everyone laughed.

Valdespino was now pleased that the prince had asked to listen to the radio. **Julián needs to hear this.** Kirsch's devilishly seductive charm was proof that the enemies of Christ were no longer sitting idly by, but rather were actively trying to pull souls away from God.

"I'm an American," Kirsch continued, "and I feel profoundly fortunate to have been born in one of the most technologically advanced and intellectually progressive countries on earth. And so I found it deeply disturbing when a recent poll revealed that **one half** of my countrymen believe quite literally that Adam and Eve existed—that an all-powerful God created two fully formed human beings who single-handedly populated the entire planet, generating all the diverse races, with none of the inherent problems of inbreeding."

More laughter.

"In Kentucky," he continued, "church pastor Peter LaRuffa publicly declared: 'If somewhere within the Bible, I found a passage that said 'two plus two is five,' I would believe it and accept it as true.'"

Still more laughter.

"I agree, it's easy to laugh, but I assure you, these beliefs are far more terrifying than they are funny. Many of the people who espouse them are bright, educated professionals—doctors, lawyers, teachers, and in some cases, people who aspire to the highest offices in the land. I once heard U.S. congressman Paul Broun say, 'Evolution and the Big Bang are lies straight from the pit of hell. I believe the earth is about nine thousand years old, and it was created in six days as we know them.'" Kirsch paused. "Even more troubling, Congressman Broun sits on the **House Science, Space, and Technology Committee,** and when questioned about the existence of a fossil record spanning millions of years, his response was 'Fossils were placed there by God to test our faith.'"

Kirsch's voice grew suddenly quiet and somber. "To permit ignorance is to empower it. To do nothing as our leaders proclaim absurdities is a crime of complacency. As is letting our schools and churches teach outright untruths to our children. The time for action has come. Not until we purge our species of superstitious thinking can we embrace all that our minds have to offer." He paused and a hush fell over the crowd. "I love humankind. I believe our minds and our species have limitless potential. I believe we are on the brink of an enlightened new era, a world where religion finally departs . . . and science reigns."

The crowd erupted with wild applause.

"For heaven's sake," Valdespino snapped, shaking his head in disgust. "Turn it off."

The acolyte obeyed, and the three men drove on in silence.

———

Thirty miles away, Mónica Martín was standing opposite a breathless Suresh Bhalla, who had just dashed in and handed her a cell phone.

"Long story," Suresh gasped, "but you need to read this text that Bishop Valdespino received."

"Hold on." Martín almost dropped the device. "This is the **bishop's** phone?! How the hell did you—"

"Don't ask. Just read."

Alarmed, Martín directed her eyes to the phone and began reading the text on its screen. Within seconds, she felt herself blanch. "My God, Bishop Valdespino is . . ."

"Dangerous," Suresh said.

"But . . . this is impossible! Who is this person who texted the bishop?!"

"Shielded number," Suresh said. "I'm working on identifying it."

"And why wouldn't Valdespino **delete** this message?"

"No idea," Suresh said flatly. "Careless? Arrogant? I'll try to undelete any other texts, and also see if I can identify who Valdespino is texting with, but I wanted to give you this news on Valdespino right away; you'll have to make a statement on it."

"No, I won't!" Martín said, still reeling. "The palace is not going public with this information!"

"No, but someone else will very soon." Suresh quickly explained that the motive for searching Valdespino's phone had been a direct e-mail tip from monte@iglesia.org—the informant who was feeding news to ConspiracyNet—and if this person acted true to form, the bishop's text would not remain private for long.

Martín closed her eyes, trying to picture the world's reaction to incontrovertible proof that a Catholic bishop with very close ties to the king of Spain was directly involved in tonight's treachery and murder.

"Suresh," Martín whispered, slowly opening her eyes. "I need you to figure out who this 'Monte' informant is. Can you do that for me?"

"I can try." He did not sound hopeful.

"Thanks." Martín handed the bishop's phone back to him and hurried to the door. "And send me a screenshot of that text!"

"Where are you going?" Suresh called.

Mónica Martín did not answer.

CHAPTER 65

Lᴀ Sagrada Família—the Basílica of the Holy Family—occupies an entire city block in central Barcelona. Despite its massive footprint, the church seems to hover almost weightlessly above the earth, a delicate cluster of airy spires that ascend effortlessly into the Spanish sky.

Intricate and porous, the towers have varying heights, giving the shrine the air of a whimsical sand castle erected by mischievous giants. Once completed, the tallest of the eighteen pinnacles will climb a dizzying and unprecedented 560 feet—higher than the Washington Monument—making Sagrada Família the tallest church in the world, eclipsing the Vatican's own St. Peter's Basilica by more than a hundred feet.

The body of the church is sheltered by three massive facades. To the east, the colorful Nativity facade climbs like a hanging garden, sprouting polychrome plants, animals, fruits, and people. In stark contrast, the Passion facade to the west is an austere skeleton of harsh stone, hewn to resemble sinews and bone. To the south, the Glory facade twists upward in a chaotic clutter of demons, idols, sins, and vices, eventually giving way to loftier symbols of ascension, virtue, and paradise.

Completing the perimeter are countless smaller facades, buttresses, and towers, most of them sheathed in a mud-like material, giving the effect that the lower half of the building is either melting or has been extruded from the earth. According to one prominent critic, Sagrada Família's lower half resembles "a rotting tree trunk from which had sprouted a family of intricate mushroom spires."

In addition to adorning his church with traditional religious iconography, Gaudí included countless startling features that reflected his reverence for nature—turtles supporting columns, trees sprouting from facades, and even giant stone snails and frogs scaling the outside of the building.

Despite its outlandish exterior, the true surprise of Sagrada Família is glimpsed only after stepping through its doorways. Once inside the main sanctuary, visitors invariably stand slack-jawed as their eyes climb the slanting and twisting tree-trunk columns up two hundred feet to a series of hovering vaults, where psychedelic collages of geometric shapes hover like a crystalline canopy in the tree branches. The creation of a "columned forest," Gaudí claimed, was to encourage the mind to return to thoughts of the earliest spiritual seekers, for whom the forest had served as God's cathedral.

Not surprisingly, Gaudí's colossal Art Nouveau opus is both passionately adored and cynically scorned. Hailed by some as "sensual, spiritual, and organic," it is derided by others as "vulgar, pretentious, and profane." Author James Michener described it as "one of the strangest-looking serious buildings in the world," and **Architectural Review** called it "Gaudí's sacred monster."

If its aesthetics are strange, its finances are even stranger. Funded entirely by private donations, Sagrada Família receives no financial support whatsoever from the Vatican or the world Catholic leadership. Despite periods of near bankruptcy and work stoppages, the church exhibits an almost Darwinian will to survive, having tenaciously endured the death of its architect, a violent civil war, terrorist attacks by Catalan anarchists, and even the drilling of a subway tunnel nearby that threatened to destabilize the very ground on which it sits.

In the face of incredible adversity, Sagrada Família still stands, and continues to grow.

Over the past decade, the church's fortunes have improved considerably, its coffers supplemented by ticket sales to more than four million visitors a year who pay handsomely to tour the partially completed structure. Now, having announced a target completion date of 2026—the centenary of Gaudí's death—Sagrada Família seems to be infused with a fresh vigor, its spires climbing heavenward with a renewed urgency and hope.

Father Joaquim Beña—Sagrada Família's oldest priest and presiding clergyman—was a jovial eighty-year-old with round glasses on a round face that was always smiling atop his tiny robe-draped body. Beña's dream was to live long enough to see the completion of this glorious shrine.

Tonight, however, inside his clerical office, Father Beña was not smiling. He had stayed late on church business, but had ended up riveted to his computer, entirely caught up in the disturbing drama unfolding in Bilbao.

Edmond Kirsch was assassinated.

Over the last three months, Beña had forged a delicate and unlikely friendship with Kirsch. The outspoken atheist had stunned Beña by approaching him personally with an offer to make a huge donation to the church. The amount was unprecedented and would have an enormous positive impact.

Kirsch's offer makes no sense, Beña had thought, suspecting a catch. **Is it a publicity stunt? Perhaps he wants influence over the construction?**

In return for his donation, the renowned futurist had made only one request.

Beña had listened, uncertain. **That's all he wants?**

"This is a personal matter for me," Kirsch had said. "And I'm hoping you'll be willing to honor my request."

Beña was a trusting man, and yet in that moment he sensed he was dancing with the devil. Beña found himself searching Kirsch's eyes for some ulterior motive. And then he saw it. Behind Kirsch's carefree charm there burned a weary desperation, his sunken eyes and thin body reminding Beña of his days in seminary working as a hospice counselor.

Edmond Kirsch is ill.

Beña wondered if the man was dying, and if this donation might be a sudden attempt to make amends with the God whom he had always scorned.

The most self-righteous in life become the most fearful in death.

Beña thought about the earliest Christian evangelist—Saint John—who had dedicated his life to encouraging nonbelievers to experience the glory of Jesus Christ. It seemed that if a nonbeliever like Kirsch wanted to participate in the creation of a shrine to Jesus, then denying him that connection would be both unchristian and cruel.

In addition, there was the matter of Beña's professional obligation to help raise funds for the church, and he could not imagine informing his colleagues that Kirsch's giant gift had been rejected because of the man's history of outspoken atheism.

In the end, Beña accepted Kirsch's terms, and the men had shaken hands warmly.

That was three months ago.

Tonight, Beña had watched Kirsch's presentation at the Guggenheim, first feeling troubled by its antireligious tone, then intrigued by Kirsch's references to a mysterious discovery, and ultimately horrified to see Edmond Kirsch gunned down. In the aftermath, Beña had been unable to leave his computer, riveted by what was quickly becoming a dizzying kaleidoscope of competing conspiracy theories.

Feeling overwhelmed, Beña now sat quietly in the cavernous sanctuary, alone in Gaudí's "forest" of pillars. The mystical woods, however, did little to calm his racing mind.

What did Kirsch discover? Who wanted him dead?

Father Beña closed his eyes and tried to clear his thoughts, but the questions kept recurring.

Where do we come from? Where are we going?

"We come from God!" Beña declared aloud. "And we go to God!"

As he spoke, he felt the words resonate in his chest with such force that the entire sanctuary seemed to vibrate. Suddenly a bright shaft of light pierced the stained-glass window above the Passion facade and streamed down into the basilica.

Awestruck, Father Beña stood up and staggered toward the window, the entire church now thundering as the beam of celestial light descended along the colored glass. When he burst out of the church's main doors, Beña found himself assaulted by a deafening windstorm. Above him to the left, a massive helicopter was descending out of the sky, its searchlight strafing the front of the church.

Beña watched in disbelief as the aircraft touched down inside the perimeter of the construction fences on the northwestern corner of the compound and powered down.

As the wind and noise subsided, Father Beña stood in the main doorway of Sagrada Família and watched as four figures descended from the craft and hurried toward him. The two in front were instantly recognizable from tonight's broadcast—one was the future queen of Spain, and the other was Professor Robert Langdon. They were tailed by two strapping men in monogrammed blazers.

From the look of things, Langdon had not kid-

napped Ambra Vidal after all. As the American professor approached, Ms. Vidal appeared to be by his
side entirely by her own choice.

"Father!" the woman called with a friendly wave.
"Please forgive our noisy intrusion into this sacred
space. We need to speak to you right away. It's very
important."

Beña opened his mouth to reply but could only nod
mutely as the unlikely group arrived before him.

"Our apologies, Father," said Robert Langdon with
a disarming smile. "I know this must all seem very
strange. Do you know who we are?"

"Of course," he managed, "but I thought . . ."

"Bad information," Ambra said. "Everything is fine,
I assure you."

Just then, two security guards stationed outside the
perimeter fence raced in through the security turnstiles,
understandably alarmed by the helicopter's arrival. The
guards spotted Beña and dashed toward him.

Instantly, the two men in monogrammed blazers
spun and faced them, extending their palms in the
universal symbol for "halt."

The guards stopped dead in their tracks, startled,
looking to Beña for guidance.

"¡Tot està bé!" Beña shouted in Catalan. "Tornin
al seu lloc." All is well! Return to your post.

The guards squinted up at the unlikely assembly,
looking uncertain.

"Són els meus convidats," Beña declared, firmly
now. They are my guests. "Confio en la seva discre-
ció." I will rely on your discretion.

The bewildered guards retreated through the security turnstile to resume their patrol of the perimeter.

"Thank you," Ambra said. "I appreciate that."

"I am Father Joaquim Beña," he said. "Please tell me what this is about."

Robert Langdon stepped forward and shook Beña's hand. "Father Beña, we are looking for a rare book owned by the scientist Edmond Kirsch." Langdon produced an elegant note card and handed it to him. "This card claims the book is on loan to this church."

Though somewhat dazed by the group's dramatic arrival, Beña recognized the ivory card at once. An exact copy of this card accompanied the book that Kirsch had given him a few weeks ago.

The Complete Works of William Blake.

The stipulation of Edmond's large donation to Sagrada Família had been that Blake's book be placed on display in the basilica crypt.

A strange request, but a small price to pay.

Kirsch's one additional request—outlined on the **back** of the linen card—was that the book always remain propped open to page 163.

CHAPTER 66

F ive miles to the northwest of Sagrada Família, Admiral Ávila gazed through the windshield of the Uber at the broad expanse of city lights, which glittered against the blackness of the Balearic Sea beyond.

Barcelona at last, the old naval officer thought, pulling out his phone and calling the Regent, as promised.

The Regent answered on the first ring. "Admiral Ávila. Where are you?"

"Minutes outside the city."

"Your arrival is well timed. I have just received troubling news."

"Tell me."

"You have successfully severed the head of the snake. However, just as we feared, the long tail is still writhing dangerously."

"How can I be of service?" Ávila asked.

When the Regent shared his desires, Ávila was surprised. He had not imagined that the night would entail any more loss of life, but he was not about to question the Regent. **I am no more than a foot soldier,** he reminded himself.

"This mission will be dangerous," the Regent said.

"If you are caught, show the authorities the symbol on your palm. You will be freed shortly. We have influence everywhere."

"I don't intend to be caught," Ávila said, glancing at his tattoo.

"Good," the Regent said in an eerily lifeless tone. "If all goes according to plan, soon they will both be dead, and all of this will be over."

The connection was broken.

In the sudden silence, Ávila raised his eyes to the brightest point on the horizon—a hideous cluster of deformed spires ablaze with construction lights.

Sagrada Família, he thought, repulsed by the whimsical silhouette. **A shrine to all that is wrong with our faith.**

Barcelona's celebrated church, Ávila believed, was a monument to weakness and moral collapse—a surrender to liberal Catholicism, brazenly twisting and distorting thousands of years of faith into a warped hybrid of nature worship, pseudoscience, and Gnostic heresy.

There are giant lizards crawling up a church of Christ!

The collapse of tradition in the world terrified Ávila, but he felt buoyed by the appearance of a new group of world leaders who apparently shared his fears and were doing whatever it took to restore tradition. Ávila's own devotion to the Palmarian Church, and especially to Pope Innocent XIV, had given him a new reason to live, helping him see his own tragedy through an entirely new lens.

My wife and child were casualties of war, Ávila thought, **a war waged by the forces of evil against God, against tradition. Forgiveness is not the only road to salvation.**

Five nights ago, Ávila had been asleep in his modest apartment when he was awoken by the loud ping of an arriving text message on his cell phone. "It's midnight," he grumbled, hazily squinting at the screen to find out who had contacted him at this hour.

Número oculto

Ávila rubbed his eyes and read the incoming message.

Compruebe su saldo bancario

Check my bank balance?
Ávila frowned, now suspecting some kind of telemarketing scam. Annoyed, he got out of bed and walked to the kitchen to get a drink of water. As he stood at the sink, he glanced over at his laptop, knowing he would probably not get back to sleep until he took a look.

He logged onto his bank's website, fully anticipating seeing his usual, pitifully small balance—the remains of his military pension. However, when his account information appeared, he leaped to his feet so suddenly that he knocked over a chair.

But that's impossible!

He closed his eyes and then looked again. Then he refreshed the screen.

The number remained.

He fumbled with the mouse, scrolling to his account activity, and was stunned to see that an anonymous deposit of a hundred thousand euros had been wired into his account an hour earlier. The source was numbered and untraceable.

Who would do this?!

The sharp buzzing of his cell phone made Ávila's heart beat faster. He grabbed his phone and looked at his caller ID.

Número oculto

Ávila stared at the phone and then seized it. "¿Sí?"

A soft voice spoke to him in pure Castilian Spanish. "Good evening, Admiral. I trust you have seen the gift we sent you?"

"I . . . have," he stammered. "Who are you?"

"You may call me the Regent," the voice replied. "I represent your brethren, the members of the church that you have faithfully attended for the past two years. Your skills and loyalty have not gone unnoticed, Admiral. We would now like to give you the opportunity to serve a higher purpose. His Holiness has proposed for you a series of missions . . . tasks sent to you by God."

Ávila was now fully awake, his palms sweating.

"The money we gave you is an advance on your

first mission," the voice continued. "If you choose to carry out the mission, consider it an opportunity to prove yourself worthy of taking a place within our highest ranks." He paused. "There exists a powerful hierarchy in our church that is invisible to the world. We believe **you** would be an asset at the top of our organization."

Although excited by the prospect of advancement, Ávila felt wary. "What is the mission? And what if I choose **not** to carry it out?"

"You will not be judged in any way, and you may keep the money in return for your secrecy. Does that sound reasonable?"

"It sounds quite generous."

"We like you. We want to help you. And out of fairness to you, I want to warn you that the pope's mission is a difficult one." He paused. "It may involve violence."

Ávila's body went rigid. **Violence?**

"Admiral, the forces of evil are growing stronger every day. God is at war, and wars entail **casualties**."

Ávila flashed on the horror of the bomb that had killed his family. Shivering, he banished the dark memories. "I'm sorry, I don't know if I can accept a violent mission—"

"The pope handpicked **you**, Admiral," the Regent whispered. "The man you will target in this mission . . . is the man who murdered your family."

CHAPTER 67

Located on the ground floor of Madrid's Royal Palace, the armory is an elegantly vaulted chamber whose high crimson walls are adorned with magnificent tapestries depicting famous battles in Spain's history. Encircling the room is a priceless collection of more than a hundred suits of handcrafted armor, including the battle garb and "tools" of many past kings. Seven life-size horse mannequins stand in the center of the room, posed in full battle gear.

This is where they decide to keep me prisoner? Garza wondered, looking out at the implements of war that surrounded him. Admittedly, the armory was one of the most secure rooms in the palace, but Garza suspected his captors had chosen this elegant holding cell in hopes of intimidating him. **This is the very room in which I was hired.**

Nearly two decades ago, Garza had been ushered into this imposing chamber, where he had been interviewed, cross-examined, and interrogated before finally being offered the job of head of the Royal Guard.

Now Garza's own agents had arrested him. **I'm being charged with plotting an assassination? And**

for framing the bishop? The logic behind the allegations was so twisted that Garza couldn't begin to untangle it.

When it came to the Royal Guard, Garza was the highest-ranking official in the palace, meaning the order to arrest him could have come from only one man . . . Prince Julián himself.

Valdespino poisoned the prince's mind against me, Garza realized. The bishop had always been a political survivor, and tonight he was apparently desperate enough to attempt this audacious media stunt—a bold ploy to clear his own reputation by smearing Garza's. **And now they've locked me in the armory so I can't speak for myself.**

If Julián and Valdespino had joined forces, Garza knew he was lost, entirely outmaneuvered. At this point, the only person on earth with power enough to help Garza was an old man who was living out his final days in a hospital bed in his private residence at Palacio de la Zarzuela.

The king of Spain.

Then again, Garza realized, **the king will never help me if doing so means crossing Bishop Valdespino or his own son.**

He could hear the crowds outside chanting louder now, and it sounded like things might take a violent turn. When Garza realized what they were chanting, he couldn't believe his ears.

"Where does Spain come from?!" they shouted. **"Where is Spain going?!"**

The protesters, it appeared, had seized upon Kirsch's

two provocative questions as an opportunity to rant about the political future of Spain's monarchy.

Where do we come from? Where are we going?

Condemning the oppression of the past, Spain's younger generation was constantly calling for faster change—urging their country to "join the civilized world" as a full democracy and to abolish its monarchy. France, Germany, Russia, Austria, Poland, and more than fifty other countries had abandoned their crowns in the last century. Even in England there was a push for a referendum on ending the monarchy after the current queen died.

Tonight, unfortunately, Madrid's Royal Palace was in a state of disarray, so it was not surprising to hear this age-old battle cry being raised again.

Just what Prince Julián needs, Garza thought, **as he prepares for ascension to the throne.**

The door at the far end of the armory suddenly clicked open and one of Garza's Guardia agents peered in.

Garza shouted to him, "I want an attorney!"

"And I want a statement for the press," the familiar voice of Mónica Martín shouted back as the palace's PR coordinator manuevered around the guard and marched into the room. "Commander Garza, why did you collude with the killers of Edmond Kirsch?"

Garza stared at her in disbelief. **Has everyone gone mad?**

"We know you framed Bishop Valdespino!" Martín declared, striding toward him. "And the palace wants to publish your confession right now!"

The commander had no reply.

Halfway across the room, Martín spun around abruptly, glaring back at the young guard in the doorway. "I said a **private** confession!"

The guard looked uncertain as he stepped back and closed the door.

Martín wheeled back toward Garza and stormed the rest of the way across the floor. "I want a confession now!" she bellowed, her voice echoing off the vaulted ceiling as she arrived directly in front of him.

"Well, you won't get one from me," Garza replied evenly. "I have nothing to do with this. Your allegations are completely untrue."

Martín glanced nervously over her shoulder. Then she stepped closer, whispering in Garza's ear. "I know . . . I need you to listen to me very carefully."

CHAPTER 68

Trending ↑ 2747%

🌐 ConspiracyNet.com

BREAKING NEWS

OF ANTIPOPES . . . BLEEDING PALMS . . . AND EYES SEWN SHUT . . .

Strange tales from within the Palmarian Church.

Posts from online Christian newsgroups have now confirmed that Admiral Luis Ávila is an active member of the Palmarian Church, and has been one for several years.

Serving as a "celebrity" advocate for the Church, navy admiral Luis Ávila has repeatedly credited the Palmarian pope with "saving his life" following a deep depression over the loss of his family in an anti-Christian terrorist attack.

Because it is the policy of ConspiracyNet never to support or condemn religious institutions, we have posted dozens of outside links to the Palmarian Church here.

We inform. You decide.

Please note, many of the online claims regarding the Palmarians are quite shocking, and so we are now asking for help from you—our users—to sort fact from fiction.

The following "facts" were sent to us by star informant monte@iglesia.org, whose perfect track record tonight suggests that these facts are true, and yet before we report them as such, we are hoping some of our users can offer additional hard evidence either to support or refute them.

"FACTS"

• Palmarian pope Clemente lost both eyeballs in a car accident in 1976 and continued to preach for a decade with his eyes sewn shut.

• Pope Clemente had active stigmata on both palms that regularly bled when he had visions.

• Several Palmarian popes were officers of the Spanish military with strong Carlist ideals.

• Palmarian Church members are forbidden from speaking to their own families, and several members have died on the compound from malnutrition or abuse.

• Palmarians are banned from (1) reading books authored by non-Palmarians, (2) attending family weddings or funerals unless their families are Palmarians, (3) attending pools, beaches, boxing matches, dance halls, or any location displaying a Christmas tree or image of Santa Claus.

- Palmarians believe the Antichrist was born in the year 2000.

- Palmarian recruitment houses exist in the USA, Canada, Germany, Austria, and Ireland.

CHAPTER 69

As Langdon and Ambra followed Father Beña toward the colossal bronze doors of Sagrada Família, Langdon found himself marveling, as he always did, over the utterly bizarre details of this church's main entrance.

It's a wall of codes, he mused, eyeing the raised typography that dominated the monolithic slabs of burnished metal. Protruding from the surface were more than eight thousand three-dimensional letters embossed in bronze. The letters ran in horizontal lines, creating a massive field of text with virtually no separation between the words. Although Langdon knew the text was a description of Christ's Passion written in Catalan, its appearance was closer to that of an NSA encryption key.

No wonder this place inspires conspiracy theories.

Langdon's gaze moved upward, climbing the looming Passion facade, where a haunting collection of gaunt, angular sculptures by the artist Josep Maria Subirachs stared down, dominated by a horribly emaciated Jesus dangling from a crucifix that had been canted steeply forward, giving the frightening effect that it was about to topple down onto the arriving guests.

To Langdon's left, another grim sculpture depicted Judas betraying Jesus with a kiss. This effigy, rather strangely, was flanked by a carved grid of numbers—a mathematical "magic square." Edmond had once told Langdon that this square's "magic constant" of thirty-three was in fact a hidden tribute to the Freemasons' pagan reverence for the Great Architect of the Universe—an all-encompassing deity whose secrets were allegedly revealed to those who reached the brotherhood's thirty-third degree.

"A fun story," Langdon had replied with a laugh, "but Jesus being age thirty-three at the time of the Passion is a more likely explanation."

As they neared the entrance, Langdon winced to see the church's most gruesome embellishment—a colossal statue of Jesus, scourged and bound to a pillar with ropes. He quickly shifted his gaze to the inscription above the doors—two Greek letters—alpha and omega.

"Beginning and end," Ambra whispered, also eyeing the letters. "Very Edmond."

Langdon nodded, catching her meaning. **Where do we come from? Where are we going?**

Father Beña opened a small portal in the wall of bronze letters, and the entire group entered, including the two Guardia agents. Beña closed the door behind them.

Silence.

Shadows.

There in the southeast end of the transept, Father Beña shared with them a startling story. He recounted how Kirsch had come to him and offered to make a huge donation to Sagrada Família in return for the church agreeing to display his copy of Blake's illuminated manuscripts in the crypt near Gaudí's tomb.

In the very heart of this church, Langdon thought, his curiosity piqued.

"Did Edmond say **why** he wanted you to do this?" Ambra asked.

Beña nodded. "He told me that his lifelong passion for Gaudí's art had come from his late mother, who had also been a great admirer of the work of William Blake. Mr. Kirsch said he wanted to place the Blake volume near Gaudí's tomb as a tribute to his late mother. It seemed to me there was no harm."

Edmond never mentioned his mother liking Gaudí, Langdon thought, puzzled. Moreover, Paloma Kirsch had died in a convent, and it seemed unlikely that a Spanish nun would admire a heterodox British poet. The entire story seemed like a stretch.

"Also," Beña continued, "I sensed Mr. Kirsch might have been in the throes of a spiritual crisis . . . and perhaps had some health issues as well."

"The notation on the back of this title card," Langdon interjected, holding it up, "says that the Blake book must be displayed in a particular way—lying open to page one hundred and sixty-three?"

"Yes, that's correct."

Langdon felt his pulse quicken. "Can you tell me **which** poem is on that page?"

Beña shook his head. "There **is** no poem on that page."

"I'm sorry?!"

"The book is Blake's **complete** works—his artwork and writings. Page one sixty-three is an illustration."

Langdon shot an uneasy glance at Ambra. **We need a forty-seven-letter line of poetry—not an illustration!**

"Father," Ambra said to Beña. "Would it be possible for us to see it right away?"

The priest wavered an instant, but apparently thought better of refusing the future queen. "The crypt is this way," he said, leading them down the transept toward the center of the church. The two Guardia agents followed behind.

"I must admit," Beña said, "I was hesitant to accept money from so outspoken an atheist, but his request to display his mother's favorite Blake illustration seemed harmless to me—especially considering it was an image of God."

Langdon thought he had misheard. "Did you say Edmond asked you to display an image of **God**?"

Beña nodded. "I sensed he was ill and that perhaps this was his way of trying to make amends for a life of opposition to the divine." He paused, shaking his head. "Although, after seeing his presentation tonight, I must admit, I don't know what to think."

Langdon tried to imagine which of Blake's countless illustrations of God Edmond might have wanted displayed.

As they all moved into the main sanctuary, Langdon felt as if he were seeing this space for the very first time. Despite having visited Sagrada Família many times in various stages of its construction, he had always come during the day, when the Spanish sun poured through the stained glass, creating dazzling bursts of color and drawing the eye upward, ever upward, into a seemingly weightless canopy of vaults.

At night, this is a heavier world.

The basilica's sun-dappled forest of trees was gone, transformed into a midnight jungle of shadows and darkness—a gloomy stand of striated columns stretching skyward into an ominous void.

"Watch your step," the priest said. "We save money where we can."

Lighting these massive European churches, Langdon knew, cost a small fortune, and yet the sparse utility lighting here barely illuminated the way. **One of the challenges of a sixty-thousand-square-foot floor plan.**

As they reached the central nave and turned left, Langdon gazed at the elevated ceremonial platform ahead. The altar was an ultramodern minimalistic table framed by two glistening clusters of organ pipes. Fifteen feet above the altar hung the church's extraordinary baldachin—a suspended cloth ceiling or "canopy of state"—a symbol of reverence inspired by the ceremonial canopies once held up on poles to provide shade for kings.

Most baldachins were now solid architectural features, but Sagrada Família had opted for cloth, in this case an umbrella-shaped canopy that seemed to hover magically in the air above the altar. Beneath the cloth, suspended by wires like a paratrooper, was the figure of Jesus on the cross.

Parachuting Jesus, Langdon had heard it called. Seeing it again, he was not surprised it had become one of the church's most controversial details.

As Beña guided them into increasing darkness, Langdon was having trouble seeing anything at all. Díaz pulled out a penlight and lit the tile floor beneath everyone's feet. Pressing on toward the crypt entrance, Langdon now perceived above him the pale silhouette of a towering cylinder that climbed hundreds of feet up the interior wall of the church.

The infamous Sagrada spiral, he realized, having never dared ascend it.

Sagrada Família's dizzying shaft of circling stairs had appeared on **National Geographic**'s list of "The 20 Deadliest Staircases in the World," earning a spot as number three, just behind the precarious steps up the Angkor Wat Temple in Cambodia and the mossy cliffside stones of the Devil's Cauldron waterfall in Ecuador.

Langdon eyed the first few steps of the staircase, which corkscrewed upward and disappeared into blackness.

"The crypt entrance is just ahead," Beña said, motioning past the stairs toward a darkened void to the left of the altar. As they pressed onward, Langdon spotted a faint golden glow that seemed to emanate from a hole in the floor.

The crypt.

The group arrived at the mouth of an elegant, gently curving staircase.

"Gentlemen," Ambra said to her guards. "Both of you stay here. We'll be back up shortly."

Fonseca looked displeased but said nothing.

Then Ambra, Father Beña, and Langdon began their descent toward the light.

————

Agent Díaz felt grateful for the moment of peace as he watched the three figures disappear down the winding staircase. The growing tension between Ambra Vidal and Agent Fonseca was becoming worrisome.

Guardia agents are not accustomed to threats of dismissal from those they protect—only from Commander Garza.

Díaz still felt baffled by Garza's arrest. Strangely, Fonseca had declined to share with him precisely who had issued the arrest order or initiated the false kidnapping story.

"The situation is complex," Fonseca had said. "And for your own protection, it's better you don't know."

So who was issuing orders? Díaz wondered. **Was it the prince?** It seemed doubtful that Julián would risk Ambra's safety by spreading a bogus kidnapping story. **Was it Valdespino?** Díaz wasn't sure if the bishop had that kind of leverage.

"I'll be back shortly," Fonseca grunted, and headed off, saying he needed to find a restroom. As Fonseca slipped into the darkness, Díaz saw him take out his phone, place a call, and commence a quiet conversation.

Díaz waited alone in the abyss of the sanctuary, feeling less and less comfortable with Fonseca's secretive behavior.

CHAPTER 70

The staircase to the crypt spiraled down three stories into the earth, bending in a wide and graceful arc, before depositing Langdon, Ambra, and Father Beña in the subterranean chamber.

One of Europe's largest crypts, Langdon thought, admiring the vast, circular space. Exactly as he recalled, Sagrada Família's underground mausoleum had a soaring rotunda and housed pews for hundreds of worshippers. Golden oil lanterns placed at intervals around the circumference of the room illuminated an inlaid mosaic floor of twisting vines, roots, branches, leaves, and other imagery from nature.

A crypt was literally a "hidden" space, and Langdon found it nearly inconceivable that Gaudí had successfully concealed a room this large beneath the church. This was nothing like Gaudí's playful "leaning crypt" in Colònia Güell; this space was an austere neo-Gothic chamber with leafed columns, pointed arches, and embellished vaults. The air was deathly still and smelled faintly of incense.

At the foot of the stairs, a deep recess stretched to the left. Its pale sandstone floor supported an unassuming gray slab, laid horizontally, surrounded by lanterns.

The man himself, Langdon realized, reading the inscription.

ANTONIUS GAUDÍ

As Langdon scanned Gaudí's place of rest, he again felt the sharp loss of Edmond. He raised his eyes to the statue of the Virgin Mary above the tomb, whose plinth bore an unfamiliar symbol.

What in the world?

Langdon eyed the strange icon.

Rarely did Langdon see a symbol he could not identify. In this case, the symbol was the Greek letter lambda—which, in his experience, did not occur in Christian symbolism. The lambda was a scientific symbol, common in the fields of evolution, particle physics, and cosmology. Stranger still, sprouting upward out of the top of this particular lambda was a Christian cross.

Religion supported by science? Langdon had never seen anything quite like it.

"Puzzled by the symbol?" Beña inquired, arriving beside Langdon. "You're not alone. Many ask about it. It's nothing more than a uniquely modernist interpretation of a cross on a mountaintop."

Langdon inched forward, now seeing three faint gilded stars accompanying the symbol.

Three stars in that position, Langdon thought, recognizing it at once. **The cross atop Mount Carmel.** "It's a **Carmelite** cross."

"Correct. Gaudí's body lies beneath the Blessed Virgin Mary of Mount Carmel."

"Was Gaudí a Carmelite?" Langdon found it hard to imagine the modernist architect adhering to the twelfth-century brotherhood's strict interpretation of Catholicism.

"Most certainly not," Beña replied with a laugh. "But his **caregivers** were. A group of Carmelite nuns lived with Gaudí and tended to him during his final years. They believed he would appreciate being watched over in death as well, and they made the generous gift of this chapel."

"Thoughtful," Langdon said, chiding himself for misinterpreting such an innocent symbol. Apparently, all the conspiracy theories circulating tonight had caused even Langdon to start conjuring phantoms out of thin air.

"Is that Edmond's book?" Ambra declared suddenly.

Both men turned to see her motioning into the shadows to the right of Gaudí's tomb.

"Yes," Beña replied. "I'm sorry the light is so poor."

Ambra hurried toward a display case, and Langdon followed, seeing that the book had been relegated to a dark region of the crypt, shaded by a massive pillar to the right of Gaudí's tomb.

"We normally display informational pamphlets there," Beña said, "but I moved them elsewhere to make room for Mr. Kirsch's book. Nobody seems to have noticed."

Langdon quickly joined Ambra at a hutch-like case that had a slanted glass top. Inside, propped open to page 163, barely visible in the dim light, sat a massive bound edition of **The Complete Works of William Blake.**

As Beña had informed them, the page in question was not a poem at all, but rather a Blake illustration. Langdon had wondered which of Blake's images of God to expect, but it most certainly was not **this** one.

The Ancient of Days, Langdon thought, squinting through the darkness at Blake's famous 1794 water-color etching.

Langdon was surprised that Father Beña had called this "an image of God." Admittedly, the illustration **appeared** to depict the archetypal Christian God—a bearded, wizened old man with white hair, perched in the clouds and reaching down from the heavens—and yet a bit of research on Beña's part would have revealed something quite different. The figure was not, in fact, the Christian God but rather a deity called Urizen—a god conjured from Blake's own visionary imagination—depicted here measuring the heavens with a huge geometer's compass, paying homage to the scientific laws of the universe.

The piece was so futuristic in style that, centuries

later, the renowned physicist and atheist Stephen Hawking had selected it as the jacket art for his book **God Created the Integers.** In addition, Blake's timeless demiurge watched over New York City's Rockefeller Center, where the ancient geometer gazed down from an Art Deco sculpture titled **Wisdom, Light, and Sound.**

Langdon eyed the Blake book, again wondering why Edmond had gone to such lengths to have it displayed here. **Was it pure vindictiveness? A slap in the face to the Christian Church?**

Edmond's war against religion never wanes, Langdon thought, glancing at Blake's Urizen. Wealth had given Edmond the ability to do whatever he pleased in life, even if it meant displaying blasphemous art in the heart of a Christian church.

Anger and spite, Langdon thought. **Maybe it's just that simple.** Edmond, whether fairly or not, had always blamed his mother's death on organized religion.

"Of course, I'm fully aware," Beña said, "that this painting is not the **Christian** God."

Langdon turned to the old priest in surprise. "Oh?"

"Yes, Edmond was quite up front about it, although he didn't need to be—I'm familiar with Blake's ideas."

"And yet you have no problem displaying the book?"

"Professor," the priest whispered, smiling softly. "This is Sagrada Família. Within these walls, Gaudí blended God, science, and nature. The theme of this painting is nothing new to us." His eyes twinkled cryptically. "Not all of our clergy are as progressive as I am, but as you know, for all of us, Christianity remains a work in progress." He smiled gently, nodding back to the book. "I'm just glad Mr. Kirsch agreed not to display his title card with the book. Considering his reputation, I'm not sure how I would have explained that, especially after his presentation tonight." Beña paused, his face somber. "Do I sense, however, that this image is not what you had hoped to find?"

"You're right. We're looking for a line of Blake's poetry."

" 'Tyger Tyger, burning bright'?" Beña offered. " 'In the forests of the night'?"

Langdon smiled, impressed that Beña knew the first line of Blake's most famous poem—a six-stanza religious query that asked if the same God who had designed the fearsome tiger had also designed the docile lamb.

"Father Beña?" Ambra asked, crouching down and peering intently through the glass. "Do you happen to have a phone or a flashlight with you?"

"No, I'm sorry. Shall I borrow a lantern from Antoni's tomb?"

"Would you, please?" Ambra asked. "That would be helpful."

Beña hurried off.

The instant he left, she whispered urgently to Langdon, "Robert! Edmond didn't choose page one sixty-three because of the painting!"

"What do you mean?" **There's nothing else on page 163.**

"It's a clever decoy."

"You've lost me," Langdon said, eyeing the painting.

"Edmond chose page one sixty-three because it's impossible to display that page without **simultaneously** displaying the page next to it—page one sixty-two!"

Langdon shifted his gaze to the left, examining the folio preceding **The Ancient of Days.** In the dim light, he could not make out much on the page, except that it appeared to consist entirely of tiny handwritten text.

Beña returned with a lantern and handed it to Ambra, who held it up over the book. As the soft glow spread out across the open tome, Langdon drew a startled breath.

The facing page was indeed text—handwritten, as were all of Blake's original manuscripts—its margins embellished with drawings, frames, and various figures. Most significantly, however, the text on the page appeared to be designed in elegant stanzas of poetry.

———

Directly overhead in the main sanctuary, Agent Díaz paced in the darkness, wondering where his partner was.

Fonseca should have returned by now.

When the phone in his pocket began vibrating, he thought it was probably Fonseca calling him, but when he checked the caller ID, Díaz saw a name he had never expected to see.

Mónica Martín

He could not imagine what the PR coordinator wanted, but whatever it was, she should be calling Fonseca directly. **He is lead agent on this team.**

"Hello," he answered. "This is Díaz."

"Agent Díaz, this is Mónica Martín. I have someone here who needs to speak to you."

A moment later, a strong familiar voice came on the line. "Agent Díaz, this is Commander Garza. Please assure me that Ms. Vidal is safe."

"Yes, Commander," Díaz blurted, feeling himself bolt to attention at the sound of Garza's voice. "Ms. Vidal is perfectly safe. Agent Fonseca and I are currently with her and safely situated inside—"

"Not on an open phone line," Garza interrupted forcefully. "If she is in a safe location, keep her there. Don't move. I'm relieved to hear your voice. We tried to phone Agent Fonseca, but there was no answer. Is he with you?"

"Yes, sir. He stepped away to make a call but should return—"

"I don't have time to wait. I'm being detained at the moment, and Ms. Martín has loaned me her phone. Listen to me very carefully. The kidnapping story, as you were no doubt aware, was wholly false. It put Ms. Vidal at great risk."

You have no idea, Díaz thought, recalling the chaotic scene on the roof of Casa Milà.

"Equally untrue is the report that I framed Bishop Valdespino."

"I had imagined as much, sir, but—"

"Ms. Martín and I are trying to figure out how best to manage this situation, but until we do, you need to keep the future queen out of the public eye. Is that clear?"

"Of course, sir. But **who** issued the order?"

"I cannot tell you that over the phone. Just do as I ask, and keep Ambra Vidal away from the media and away from danger. Ms. Martín will keep you apprised of further developments."

Garza hung up, and Díaz stood alone in the darkness, trying to make sense of the call.

As he reached inside his blazer to slide the phone back into his pocket, he heard a rustle of fabric behind him. As he turned, two pale hands emerged from the blackness and clamped down hard on Díaz's head. With blinding speed, the hands wrenched hard to one side.

Díaz felt his neck snap and a searing heat erupt inside his skull.

Then, all went black.

CHAPTER 71

🌐 ConspiracyNet.com

NEW HOPE FOR KIRSCH BOMBSHELL DISCOVERY!

Madrid palace PR coordinator Mónica Martín made an official statement earlier claiming that Spain's queen-to-be Ambra Vidal was kidnapped and is being held captive by American professor Robert Langdon. The palace urged local authorities to get involved and find the queen.

Civilian watchdog monte@iglesia.org has just sent us the following statement:

PALACE'S KIDNAPPING ALLEGATION 100% BOGUS—A PLOY TO USE LOCAL POLICE TO STOP LANGDON FROM ACHIEVING HIS GOAL IN BAR-CELONA (LANGDON/VIDAL BELIEVE THEY CAN STILL FIND WAY TO TRIG-GER WORLDWIDE RELEASE OF KIRSCH DISCOVERY). IF THEY SUCCEED, KIRSCH PRESENTATION COULD GO LIVE AT ANY MOMENT. STAY TUNED.

Incredible! And you heard it here first—Langdon and Vidal are on the run because they want to finish what

Edmond Kirsch started! The palace appears desperate to stop them. (Valdespino again? And where is the prince in all of this?)

More news as we have it, but stay tuned because Kirsch's secrets might still be revealed tonight!

CHAPTER 72

Prince Julián gazed out of the acolyte's Opel sedan at the passing countryside and tried to make sense of the bishop's strange behavior.

Valdespino is hiding something.

It had been over an hour since the bishop had covertly ushered Julián out of the palace—a highly irregular action—assuring him it was for his own safety.

He asked me not to question . . . only to trust.

The bishop had always been like an uncle to him, and a trusted confidant of Julián's father. But Valdespino's proposal of hiding out in the prince's summerhouse had sounded dubious to Julián from the start. **Something is off. I'm being isolated—no phone, no security, no news, and nobody knows where I am.**

Now, as the car bumped over the railroad tracks near Casita del Príncipe, Julián gazed down the wooded road before them. A hundred yards ahead on the left loomed the mouth of the long, tree-lined driveway that led to the remote cottage retreat.

As Julián pictured the deserted residence, he felt a sudden instinct for caution. He leaned forward and placed a firm hand on the shoulder of the acolyte behind the wheel. "Pull over here, please."

Valdespino turned, surprised. "We're almost—"

"I want to know what's going on!" the prince barked, his voice loud inside the small car.

"Don Julián, tonight has been tumultuous, but you must—"

"I must **trust** you?" Julián demanded.

"Yes."

Julián squeezed the shoulder of the young driver and pointed to a grassy shoulder on the deserted country road. "Pull over," he ordered sharply.

"Keep going," Valdespino countered. "Don Julián, I'll explain—"

"**Stop the car!**" the prince bellowed.

The acolyte swerved onto the shoulder, skidding to a stop on the grass.

"Give us some privacy, please," Julián ordered, his heart beating fast.

The acolyte did not need to be told twice. He leaped out of the idling car and hurried off into the darkness, leaving Valdespino and Julián alone in the backseat.

In the pale moonlight, Valdespino looked suddenly frightened.

"You **should** be scared," Julián said in a voice so authoritative that it startled even himself. Valdespino pulled back, looking stunned by the threatening tone—one that Julián had never before used with the bishop.

"I am the future king of Spain," Julián said. "Tonight you've removed my security detail, denied me access to my phone and my staff, prohibited me from hearing any news, and refused to let me contact my fiancée."

"I truly apologize—" Valdespino began.

"You'll have to do better than that," Julián interrupted, glaring at the bishop, who looked strangely small to him now.

Valdespino drew a slow breath and turned to face Julián in the darkness. "I was contacted earlier tonight, Don Julián, and told to—"

"Contacted by whom?"

The bishop hesitated. "By your father. He is deeply upset."

He is? Julián had visited his father only two days ago at Palacio de la Zarzuela and found him in excellent spirits, despite his deteriorating health. "Why is he upset?"

"Unfortunately, he saw the broadcast by Edmond Kirsch."

Julián felt his jaw tighten. His ailing father slept almost twenty-four hours a day and should never have been awake at that hour. Furthermore, the king had always forbidden televisions and computers in palace bedrooms, which he insisted were sanctuaries reserved for sleeping and reading—and the king's nurses would have known enough to prevent him from trying to get out of bed to watch an atheist's publicity stunt.

"It was my fault," Valdespino said. "I gave him a computer tablet a few weeks ago so he wouldn't feel so isolated from the world. He was learning to text and e-mail. He ended up seeing Kirsch's event on his tablet."

Julián felt ill to think of his father, possibly in the final weeks of his life, watching a divisive anti-Catholic broadcast that had erupted in bloody violence. The king should have been reflecting on the many extraordinary things he had accomplished for his country.

"As you can imagine," Valdespino went on, regaining his composure, "his concerns were many, but he was particularly upset by the tenor of Kirsch's remarks and your fiancée's willingness to host the event. The king felt the involvement of the future queen reflected very poorly on you . . . and on the palace."

"Ambra is her own woman. My father knows that."

"Be that as it may, when he called, he was as lucid and angry as I've heard him in years. He ordered me to bring you to him at once."

"Then why are we **here**?" Julián demanded, motioning ahead to the driveway of the casita. "He's at Zarzuela."

"Not anymore," Valdespino said quietly. "He ordered his aides and nurses to dress him, put him in a wheelchair, and take him to another location so he could spend his final days surrounded by his country's history."

As the bishop spoke those words, Julián realized the truth.

La Casita was never our destination.

Tremulous, Julián turned away from the bishop,

gazing **past** the casita's driveway, down the country road that stretched out before them. In the distance, through the trees, he could just make out the illuminated spires of a colossal building.

El Escorial.

Less than a mile away, standing like a fortress at the base of Mount Abantos, was one of the largest religious structures in the world—Spain's fabled El Escorial. With more than eight acres of floor space, the complex housed a monastery, a basilica, a royal palace, a museum, a library, and a series of the most frightening death chambers Julián had ever seen.

The Royal Crypt.

Julián's father had brought him to the crypt when Julián was only eight years old, guiding the boy through the Panteón de Infantes, a warren of burial chambers that overflowed with the tombs of royal children.

Julián would never forget seeing the crypt's horrifying "birthday cake" tomb—a massive round sepulchre that resembled a white layer cake and contained the remains of sixty royal children, all of whom had been placed in "drawers" and slid into the sides of the "cake" for all eternity.

Julián's horror at the sight of this grisly tomb had been eclipsed minutes later when his father took him to see his mother's final resting place. Julián had expected to see a marble tomb fit for a queen, but instead, his mother's body lay in a startlingly plain leaden box in a bare stone room at the end of a long hallway. The king explained to Julián that his mother was currently buried in a **pudridero**—a "decaying chamber"—where royal corpses were entombed for thirty years until nothing but dust remained of their flesh, at which time they were relocated to their permanent sepulchres. Julián remembered needing all of his strength to fight back tears and the urge to be sick.

Next, his father took him to the top of a steep staircase that seemed to descend forever into the subterranean darkness. Here, the walls and stairs were no longer white marble, but rather a majestic amber color. On every third step, votive candles cast flickering light on the tawny stone.

Young Julián reached up and grasped the ancient rope railing, descending with his father, one stair at a time . . . deep into the darkness. At the bottom of the stairs, the king opened an ornate door and stepped aside, motioning for young Julián to enter.

The Pantheon of Kings, his father told him.

Even at eight, Julián had heard of this room—a place of legends.

Trembling, the boy stepped over the threshold and found himself in a resplendent ocher chamber. Shaped like an octagon, the room smelled of incense and seemed to waver in and out of focus in the uneven light of the candles that burned in the overhead chandelier. Julián moved to the center of the room, turning slowly in place, feeling cold and small in the solemn space.

All eight walls contained deep niches where identical black coffins were stacked from floor to ceiling, each with a golden nameplate. The names on the coffins were from the pages of Julián's history books—King Ferdinand . . . Queen Isabella . . . King Charles V, Holy Roman emperor.

In the silence, Julián could feel the weight of his father's loving hand on his shoulder, and the gravity of the moment struck him. **One day my father will be buried in this very room.**

Without a word, father and son climbed out of the earth, away from death, and back into the light. Once they were outside in the blazing Spanish sun, the king crouched down and looked eight-year-old Julián in the eye.

"**Memento mori,**" the monarch whispered. "Remember death. Even for those who wield great power, life is brief. There is only one way to triumph over death, and that is by making our lives masterpieces. We must seize every opportunity to show kindness and to love fully. I see in your eyes that you have your mother's generous soul. Your conscience will be your guide. When life is dark, let your heart show you the way."

Decades later, Julián needed no reminders that he had done precious little to make his life a masterpiece. In fact, he had barely managed to escape the king's shadow and establish himself as his own man.

I've disappointed my father in every way.

For years, Julián had followed his father's advice and let his heart show the way; but it was a tortuous road when his heart longed for a Spain so utterly contrary to that of his father. Julián's dreams for his beloved country were so bold that they could never be uttered until his father's death, and even then, Julián had no idea how his actions would be received, not only by the royal palace, but by the entire nation. All Julián could do was wait, keep an open heart, and respect tradition.

And then, three months ago, everything had changed.

I met Ambra Vidal.

The vivacious, strong-minded beauty had turned Julián's world upside down. Within days of their first meeting, Julián finally understood the words of his father. **Let your heart show you the way . . . and seize every opportunity to love fully!** The elation of falling in love was like nothing Julián had ever experienced, and he sensed he might finally be taking his very first steps toward making his life a masterpiece.

Now, however, as the prince stared blankly down the road ahead, he was overcome by a foreboding sense of loneliness and isolation. His father was dying; the woman he loved was not speaking to him; and he had just admonished his trusted mentor, Bishop Valdespino.

"Prince Julián," the bishop urged gently. "We should go. Your father is frail, and he is eager to speak to you."

Julián turned slowly to his father's lifelong friend. "How much time do you think he has?" he whispered.

Valdespino's voice trembled as if he were on the verge of tears. "He asked me not to worry you, but

I sense the end is coming faster than anyone anticipated. He wants to say good-bye."

"Why didn't you tell me where we were going?"
Julián asked. "Why all the lies and secrecy?"

"I'm sorry, I had no choice. Your father gave me
explicit orders. He ordered me to insulate you from
the outside world and from the news until he had a
chance to speak to you personally."

"Insulate me from . . . **what** news?"

"I think it will be best if you let your father explain."

Julián studied the bishop a long moment. "Before
I see him, there is something I need to know. Is he
lucid? Is he rational?"

Valdespino gave him an uncertain look. "Why do
you ask?"

"Because," Julián replied, "his demands tonight
seem strange and impulsive."

Valdespino nodded sadly. "Impulsive or not, your
father is still the king. I love him, and I do as he commands. We all do."

CHAPTER 73

Standing side by side at the display case, Robert Langdon and Ambra Vidal peered down at the William Blake manuscript, illuminated by the soft glow of the oil lamp. Father Beña had wandered off to straighten up a few pews, politely giving them some privacy.

Langdon was having trouble reading the tiny letters in the poem's handwritten text, but the larger header at the top of the page was perfectly legible.

The Four Zoas

Seeing the words, Langdon instantly felt a ray of hope. **The Four Zoas** was the title of one of Blake's best-known prophetic poems—a massive work that was divided into nine "nights," or chapters. The poem's themes, as Langdon recalled from his college reading, centered on the demise of conventional religion and the eventual dominance of science.

Langdon scanned down the stanzas of text, seeing the handwritten lines come to an end halfway down the page at an elegantly sketched **"finis divisionem"**—the graphic equivalent of "The End."

This is the last page of the poem, he realized. **The finale of one of Blake's prophetic masterpieces!**

Langdon leaned in and squinted at the tiny handwriting, but he couldn't quite read the text in the dim lantern light.

Ambra was already crouched down, her face an inch from the glass. She quietly skimmed the poem, pausing to read one of the lines out loud. " **'And Man walks forth from midst of the fires, the evil is all consum'd.'** " She turned to Langdon. "The evil is all consumed?"

Langdon considered it, nodding vaguely. "I believe Blake is referring to the eradication of corrupt religion. A religionless future was one of his recurring prophecies."

Ambra looked hopeful. "Edmond said his favorite line of poetry was a prophecy that he hoped would come **true.**"

"Well," Langdon said, "a future without religion is certainly something Edmond wanted. How many letters in that line?"

Ambra began counting but shook her head. "Over fifty."

She returned to skimming the poem, pausing a moment later. "How about this one? **'The Expanding eyes of Man behold the depths of wondrous worlds.'**"

"Possible," Langdon said, pondering its meaning. **Human intellect will continue to grow and evolve over time, enabling us to see more deeply into the truth.**

"Too many letters again," Ambra said. "I'll keep going."

As she continued down the page, Langdon began pacing pensively behind her. The lines she'd already read echoed in his mind and conjured a distant memory of his reading Blake in a Princeton "Brit lit" class.

Images began forming, as sometimes happened with Langdon's eidetic memory. These images conjured new images, in endless succession. Suddenly, standing in the crypt, Langdon flashed on his professor, who, upon the class's completion of **The Four Zoas,** stood before them and asked the age-old questions: **Which would you choose? A world without religion? Or a world without science?** Then the professor had added: **Clearly, William Blake had a preference, and nowhere is his hope for the future better summarized than in the final line of this epic poem.**

Langdon drew a startled breath and spun toward Ambra, who was still poring over Blake's text.

"Ambra—skip down to the end of the poem!" he said, now recalling the poem's final line.

Ambra looked to the end of the poem. After focusing a moment, she turned back to him with an expression of wide-eyed disbelief.

Langdon joined her at the book, peering down at the text. Now that he knew the line, he was able to make out the faint handwritten letters:

The dark religions are departed &
sweet science reigns.

"'The dark religions are departed,'" Ambra read aloud. "'And sweet science reigns.'"

The line was not only a prophecy that Edmond would endorse, it was essentially a synopsis of his presentation earlier tonight.

Religions will fade . . . and science will rule.

Ambra began carefully counting the letters in the line, but Langdon knew it was unnecessary. **This is it. No doubt.** His mind had already turned to accessing Winston and launching Edmond's presentation. Langdon's plan for how to make that happen was something he would need to explain to Ambra in private.

He turned to Father Beña, who was just returning. "Father?" he asked. "We're almost done here. Would you mind going upstairs and telling the Guardia agents to summon the helicopter? We'll need to leave at once."

"Of course," Beña said, and headed up the stairs. "I hope you found what you came for. I'll see you upstairs in a moment."

As the priest disappeared up the stairs, Ambra turned away from the book with a look of sudden alarm.

"Robert," she said. "This line is too short. I counted it twice. It's only forty-six letters. We need forty-seven."

"What?" Langdon walked over to her, squinting at the text and carefully counting each handwritten letter. **"The dark religions are departed & sweet science reigns."** Sure enough, he arrived at forty-six. Baffled, he studied the line again. "Edmond definitely said forty-seven, not forty-six?"

"Absolutely."

Langdon reread the line. **But this must be it,** he thought. **What am I missing?**

Carefully, he scanned every letter in the final line of Blake's poem. He was almost to the end when he saw it.

. . . & sweet science reigns.

"The **ampersand**," Langdon blurted. "The symbol Blake used instead of writing out the word 'and.'"

Ambra eyed him strangely and then shook her head. "Robert, if we substitute the word 'and' . . . then the line has forty-**eight** letters. Too many."

Not true. Langdon smiled. **It's a code within a code.**

Langdon marveled at Edmond's cunning little twist. The paranoid genius had used a simple typographic trick to ensure that even if someone discovered **which** line of poetry was his favorite, they would still not be able to type it correctly.

The ampersand code, Langdon thought. **Edmond remembered it.**

The origin of the ampersand was always one of the first things Langdon taught his symbology classes. The symbol "&" was a **logogram**—literally a picture representing a word. While many people assumed the symbol derived from the English word "and," it actually derived from the Latin word **et**. The ampersand's unusual design "&" was a typographical fusion of the letters **E** and **T**—the ligature still visible today in computer fonts like Trebuchet, whose ampersand "**&**" clearly echoed its Latin origin.

Langdon would never forget that the week after he had taught Edmond's class about the ampersand, the young genius had shown up wearing a T-shirt printed with the message—**Ampersand phone home!**—a playful allusion to the Spielberg movie about an extraterrestrial named "ET" who was trying to find his way home.

Now, standing over Blake's poem, Langdon was able to picture Edmond's forty-seven-letter password perfectly in his mind.

thedarkreligionsaredepartedetsweetsciencereigns

Quintessential Edmond, Langdon thought, quickly sharing with Ambra the clever trick Edmond had used to add a level of security to his password.

As the truth dawned on her, Ambra began smiling as broadly as Langdon had seen her smile since they met. "Well," she said, "I guess if we ever had any doubts that Edmond Kirsch was a geek . . ."

The two of them laughed together, taking the moment to exhale in the solitude of the crypt.

"You found the password," she said, sounding grateful. "And I feel sorrier than ever that I lost Edmond's phone. If we still had it, we could trigger Edmond's presentation right now."

"Not your fault," he said reassuringly. "And, as I told you, I know how to find Winston."

At least I think I do, he mused, hoping he was right.

As Langdon pictured the aerial view of Barcelona, and the unusual puzzle that lay ahead, the silence of the crypt was shattered by a jarring sound echoing down the stairwell.

Upstairs, Father Beña was screaming and calling their names.

CHAPTER 74

H urry! Ms. Vidal . . . Professor Langdon . . . come up here quickly!"

Langdon and Ambra bounded up the crypt stairs as Father Beña's desperate shouts continued. When they reached the top step, Langdon rushed out onto the sanctuary floor but was immediately lost in a curtain of blackness.

I can't see!

As he inched forward in the darkness, his eyes strained to adjust from the glow of the oil lamps below. Ambra arrived beside him, squinting as well.

"Over here!" Beña shouted with desperation.

They moved toward the sound, finally spotting the priest on the murky fringes of light that spilled from the stairwell. Father Beña was on his knees, crouched over the dark silhouette of a body.

They were at Beña's side in a moment, and Langdon recoiled to see the body of Agent Díaz lying on the floor, his head twisted grotesquely. Díaz was flat on his stomach, but his head had been wrenched 180 degrees backward, so his lifeless eyes aimed up at the cathedral ceiling. Langdon cringed in horror, now understanding the panic in Father Beña's screams.

A cold rush of fear coursed through him, and he

stood abruptly, probing the darkness for any sign of movement in the cavernous church.

"His gun," Ambra whispered, pointing to Díaz's empty holster. "It's gone." She peered into the darkness around them and called out, "Agent Fonseca?!"

In the blackness nearby, there was a sudden shuffling of footsteps on tile and the sound of bodies colliding in a fierce struggle. Then, with startling abruptness, the deafening explosion of a gunshot rang out at close range. Langdon, Ambra, and Beña all jolted backward, and as the gunshot echoed across the sanctuary, they heard a pained voice urging— "¡**Corre!**" Run!

A second gunshot exploded, followed by a heavy thud—the unmistakable sound of a body hitting the floor.

Langdon had already grabbed Ambra's hand and was pulling her toward the deep shadows near the sidewall of the sanctuary. Father Beña arrived a step behind them, all three now cowering in rigid silence against the cold stone.

Langdon's eyes probed the darkness as he struggled to make sense of what was going on.

Someone just killed Díaz and Fonseca! Who's in here with us? And what do they want?

Langdon could imagine only one logical answer: the killer lurking in the darkness of Sagrada Família had not come here to murder two random Guardia agents . . . he had come for Ambra and Langdon.

Someone is still trying to silence Edmond's discovery.

Suddenly a bright flashlight flared in the middle of the sanctuary floor, the beam swinging back and forth in a wide arc, moving in their direction. Langdon knew they had only seconds before the beam reached them.

"This way," Beña whispered, pulling Ambra along the wall in the opposite direction. Langdon followed as the light swung closer. Beña and Ambra suddenly cut hard to the right, disappearing into an opening in the stone, and Langdon plunged in after them—immediately stumbling on an unseen set of stairs. Ambra and Beña climbed onward as Langdon regained his footing and continued after them, looking back to see the beam of light appear just beneath him, illuminating the bottom steps.

Langdon froze in the darkness, waiting.

The light remained there a long moment, and then it began growing brighter.

He's coming this way!

Langdon could hear Ambra and Beña ascending the stairs above him as stealthily as possible. He spun and launched himself after them, but again stumbled, colliding with a wall and realizing that the staircase was not straight, but curved. Pressing a hand against the wall for guidance, Langdon began circling upward in a tight spiral, quickly understanding where he was.

Sagrada Família's infamously treacherous spiral staircase.

He raised his eyes and saw a very faint glow filtering down from the light wells above, just enough illumination to reveal the narrow shaft that enclosed him. Langdon felt his legs tighten, and he stalled on the stairs, overcome by claustrophobia in the crushingly small passage.

Keep climbing! His rational mind urged him upward but his muscles cramped in fear.

Somewhere beneath him, Langdon could hear the sound of heavy footsteps approaching from the sanctuary. He forced himself to keep moving, following the spiraling steps upward as fast as he could. Above him, the faint light grew brighter as Langdon passed an opening in the wall—a wide slit through which he briefly glimpsed the city lights. A blast of cool air hit him as he dashed past this light well, and he plunged back into darkness as he circled higher.

Footsteps entered the staircase below, and the flashlight probed erratically up the center shaft. Langdon passed another light well as the pursuing footsteps grew louder, his assailant now charging faster up the stairs behind him.

Langdon caught up with Ambra and Father Beña, who was now gasping for breath. Langdon peered over the inner edge of the stairwell into the plunging center shaft. The drop was dizzying—a narrow, circular hole that plummeted through the eye of what looked like a giant spiraling nautilus. There was virtually no barrier, just an ankle-high inner lip that provided no protection whatsoever. Langdon had to fight off a wave of nausea.

He turned his eyes back to the darkness of the shaft overhead. Langdon had heard that there were more than four hundred stairs in this structure; if so, there was no way they would reach the top before the armed man below caught up with them.

"Both of you . . . go!" Beña gasped, stepping aside and urging Langdon and Ambra to pass him.

"There's no chance of that, Father," Ambra said, reaching down to help the old priest.

Langdon admired her protective instinct, but he also knew that fleeing up these stairs was suicide, most likely ending with bullets in their backs. Of the two animal instincts for survival—fight or flight— flight was no longer an option.

We'll never make it.

Letting Ambra and Father Beña press on, Langdon turned, planted his feet, and faced down the spiral staircase. Below him, the flashlight beam tracked closer. He backed against the wall and crouched in the shadows, waiting until the light hit the stairs beneath him. The killer suddenly rounded the curve into view—a dark form running with both hands outstretched, one clutching the flashlight and the other a handgun.

Langdon reacted on instinct, exploding from his crouch and launching himself through the air, feet-first. The man saw him and began to raise his gun just as Langdon's heels drove into his chest with a powerful thrust, driving the man back into the wall of the stairwell.

The next few seconds were a blur.

Langdon fell, landing hard on his side, pain erupting in his hip, as his attacker crumpled backward, tumbling down several stairs and landing in a groaning heap. The flashlight bounced down the stairs and rolled to a stop, sending an oblique wash of light up the sidewall and illuminating a metal object on the stairs halfway between Langdon and his attacker.

The gun.

Both men lunged for it at the same moment, but Langdon had the high ground and got there first, grasping the handle and pointing the weapon at his attacker, who stopped short just beneath him, staring defiantly into the barrel of the gun.

In the glow of the flashlight, Langdon could see the man's salt-and-pepper beard and stark white pants . . . and in an instant, he knew who it was.

The navy officer from the Guggenheim . . .

Langdon leveled the gun at the man's head, feeling his index finger on the trigger. "You killed my friend Edmond Kirsch."

The man was out of breath, but his reply was immediate, his voice like ice. "I settled a score. Your friend Edmond Kirsch killed my family."

CHAPTER 75

Langdon broke my ribs.

Admiral Ávila felt sharp stabs each time he inhaled, wincing in pain as his chest heaved desperately, trying to restore oxygen to his body. Crouched on the stairs above him, Robert Langdon stared down, aiming the pistol awkwardly at Ávila's midsection.

Ávila's military training instantly kicked in, and he began assessing his situation. In the negative column, his enemy held both the weapon and the high ground. In the positive column, judging from the professor's unusual grip on the gun, he had very little experience with firearms.

He has no intention of shooting me, Ávila decided. **He will hold me and wait for the security guards.** From all the shouting outside, it was clear that Sagrada Família's security officers had heard the gunshots and were now hurrying into the building.

I must act quickly.

Keeping his hands raised in surrender, Ávila shifted slowly onto his knees, conveying full compliance and submission.

Give Langdon the sense that he is in total control. Despite his fall down the stairs, Ávila could feel that the object he had lodged in the back of his belt was still there—the ceramic pistol with which he had killed Kirsch inside the Guggenheim. He had chambered the last remaining bullet before entering the church but had not needed to use it, killing one of the guards silently and stealing his far more efficient gun, which, unfortunately, Langdon was now aiming at him. Ávila wished he had left the safety engaged, guessing Langdon probably would have had no idea how to release it.

Ávila considered making a move to grab the ceramic gun from his belt to fire on Langdon first, but even if he were successful, Ávila estimated his chances of survival at about fifty-fifty. One of the perils of inexperienced gun users was their tendency to fire by mistake.

If I move too quickly . . .

The sounds of the yelling guards were growing closer, and Ávila knew that if he were taken into custody, the "victor" tattoo on his palm would ensure his release—or at least that's what the Regent had assured him. At the moment, however, having killed two of the king's Guardia Real agents, Ávila was not so sure that the Regent's influence could save him.

I came here to carry out a mission, Ávila reminded himself. **And I need to complete it. Eliminate Robert Langdon and Ambra Vidal.**

The Regent had told Ávila to enter the church via the east service gate, but Ávila had decided to jump a security fence instead. **I spotted police lurking near the east gate . . . and so I improvised.**

Langdon spoke forcefully, glaring down over the gun at Ávila. "You said Edmond Kirsch killed your family. That's a lie. Edmond was no killer."

You're right, Ávila thought. **He was worse.**

The dark truth about Kirsch was a secret Ávila had learned only a week ago during a phone call from the Regent. **Our pope is asking you to target the famous futurist Edmond Kirsch,** the Regent had said. **His Holiness's motivations are many, but he would like for you to undertake this mission personally.**

Why me? Ávila asked.

Admiral, the Regent whispered. **I'm sorry to tell you this, but Edmond Kirsch was responsible for the cathedral bombing that killed your family.**

Ávila's first reaction was complete disbelief. He could see no reason whatsoever for a well-known computer scientist to bomb a church.

You are a military man, Admiral, the Regent had explained to him, **and so you know better than anyone: the young soldier who pulls the trigger in battle is not the actual killer. He is a pawn, doing the work of those more powerful—governments, generals, religious leaders—those who have either paid him or convinced him that a cause is worthy at all costs.**

Ávila had indeed witnessed this situation.

The same rules apply to terrorism, the Regent continued. **The most vicious terrorists are not the people who build the bombs, but the influential leaders who fuel hatred among desperate masses, inspiring their foot soldiers to commit acts of vio-**

lence. It takes only one powerful dark soul to wreak
havoc in the world by inspiring spiritual intolerance, nationalism, or loathing in the minds of the
vulnerable.

Ávila had to agree.

Terrorist attacks against Christians, the Regent
said, are on the rise around the world. These new
attacks are no longer strategically planned events;
they are spontaneous assaults carried out by lone
wolves who are answering a call to arms sent out by
persuasive enemies of Christ. The Regent paused.
And among those persuasive enemies, I count the
atheist Edmond Kirsch.

Now Ávila felt the Regent was beginning to stretch
the truth. Despite Kirsch's despicable campaign
against Christianity in Spain, the scientist had never
issued a statement urging the murder of Christians.

Before you disagree, the voice on the phone told
him, let me give you one final piece of information.
The Regent sighed heavily. Nobody knows this,
Admiral, but the attack that killed your family . . .
it was intended as an act of war against the Palmarian Church.

The statement gave Ávila pause, and yet it made
no sense; Seville Cathedral was not a Palmarian
building.

The morning of the bombing, the voice told him,
four prominent members of the Palmarian Church
were in the Seville congregation for recruiting purposes. They were targeted specifically. You know

one of them—Marco. The other three died in the attack.

Ávila's thoughts swirled as he pictured his physical therapist, Marco, who had lost his leg in the attack.

Our enemies are powerful and motivated, the voice went on. **And when the bomber could not gain access to our compound in El Palmar de Troya, he followed our four missionaries to Seville and took his action there. I'm so very sorry, Admiral. This tragedy is one of the reasons the Palmarians reached out to you—we feel responsible that your family became collateral damage in a war directed against us.**

A war directed by whom? Ávila demanded, trying to comprehend the shocking claims.

Check your e-mail, the Regent replied.

Opening his in-box, Ávila discovered a shocking trove of private documents that outlined a brutal war that had been waged against the Palmarian Church for over a decade now . . . a war that apparently included lawsuits, threats bordering on blackmail, and huge donations to anti-Palmarian "watchdog" groups like Palmar de Troya Support and Dialogue Ireland.

More surprising still, this bitter war against the Palmarian Church was, it appeared, being waged by a single individual—and that man was futurist Edmond Kirsch.

Ávila was baffled by the news. **Why would Edmond Kirsch specifically want to destroy the Palmarians?**

The Regent told him that nobody in the Church—
not even the pope himself—had any idea why Kirsch
had such a specific abhorrence for the Palmarians. All
they knew was that one of the planet's wealthiest and
most influential people would not rest until the Palmarians were crushed.

The Regent drew Ávila's attention to one last
document—a copy of a typed letter to the Palmarians from a man claiming to be the Seville bomber.
In the first line, the bomber called himself a "disciple
of Edmond Kirsch." This was all Ávila had to see; his
fists clenched in rage.

The Regent explained why the Palmarians had
never shared the letter publicly; with all the bad
press the Palmarians had gotten recently—much of it
orchestrated or funded by Kirsch—the last thing the
Church needed was to be associated with a bombing.

My family died because of Edmond Kirsch.

Now, in the darkened stairwell, Ávila stared up
at Robert Langdon, sensing that the man probably
knew nothing of Kirsch's secret crusade against the
Palmarian Church, or how Kirsch had inspired the
attack that killed Ávila's family.

It doesn't matter what Langdon knows, Ávila
thought. **He is a soldier like I am. We have both
fallen into this foxhole, and only one of us will
climb out of it. I have my orders.**

Langdon was positioned a few steps above him,
aiming his weapon like an amateur—with both
hands. **Poor choice,** Ávila thought, quietly lowering

his toes onto a step beneath him, planting his feet, and staring straight up into Langdon's eyes.

"I know you find it hard to believe," Ávila declared, "but Edmond Kirsch killed my family. And **here** is your proof."

Ávila opened his palm to show Langdon his tattoo, which, of course, was no proof at all, but it had the desired effect—Langdon looked.

As the professor's focus shifted ever so briefly, Ávila lunged upward and to his left, along the curved outer wall, moving his body out of the line of fire. Precisely as anticipated, Langdon fired on impulse—depressing the trigger before he could realign the weapon with a moving target. Like thunder, the gunshot reverberated in the cramped space, and Ávila felt a bullet graze his shoulder before ricocheting harmlessly down the stone stairwell.

Langdon was already re-aiming the gun, but Ávila rolled in midair, and as he began to fall, he drove his fists down hard on Langdon's wrists, forcing the gun from his hands and sending it clattering down the stairs.

Bolts of pain ripped through Ávila's chest and shoulder as he landed on the stairs beside Langdon, but the surge of adrenaline only fueled his intensity. Reaching behind him, he yanked the ceramic handgun from his belt. The weapon felt almost weightless after holding the guard's pistol.

Ávila pointed the gun at Langdon's chest, and without hesitation, he pulled the trigger.

The gun roared, but it made an unusual shattering noise, and Ávila felt searing heat on his hand, realizing at once that the gun barrel had exploded. Built for stealth, these new metal-free "undetectables" were intended for only a shot or two. Ávila had no idea where his bullet had gone, but when he saw Langdon already scrambling to his feet, Ávila dropped his weapon and lunged at him, the two men grappling violently near the precariously low inner edge.

In that instant, Ávila knew he had won.

We are equally armed, he thought. **But I have position.**

Ávila had already assessed the open shaft at the center of the stairwell—a deadly drop with almost no protection. Now, trying to muscle Langdon backward toward the shaft, Ávila pressed one leg against the outer wall, giving himself enormous leverage. With a surge of power, he pushed Langdon toward the shaft.

Langdon fiercely resisted, but Ávila's position afforded him all the advantage, and from the desperate look in the professor's eyes, it was clear that Langdon knew what was about to happen.

—————

Robert Langdon had heard it said that life's most critical choices—those involving survival—usually required a split-second decision.

Now, brutally driven against the low edge, with his back arched over a hundred-foot drop, Langdon's six-foot frame and high center of gravity were a deadly liability. He knew he could do nothing to counter the power of Ávila's position.

Langdon desperately peered over his shoulder into the void behind him. The circular shaft was narrow—maybe three feet across—but it was certainly wide enough to accommodate his plummeting body . . . which would likely carom off the stone railing all the way down.

The fall is unsurvivable.

Ávila let out a guttural bellow and regripped Langdon. As he did, Langdon realized there was only one move to make.

Rather than fighting the man, he would help him.

As Ávila heaved him upward, Langdon crouched, planting his feet firmly on the stairs.

For a moment, he was a twenty-year-old at the Princeton swimming pool . . . competing in the backstroke . . . perched on his mark . . . his back to the water . . . knees bent . . . abdomen taut . . . waiting for the starting gun.

Timing is everything.

This time, Langdon heard no starting gun. He exploded out of his crouch, launching himself into the air, arching his back out over the void. As he leaped outward, he could feel that Ávila, who had been poised to oppose two hundred pounds of deadweight, had been yanked entirely off balance by the sudden reversal of forces.

Ávila let go as fast as he possibly could, but Langdon could sense him flailing for equilibrium. As Langdon arched away, he prayed he could travel far enough in the air to clear the opening and reach the stairs on the opposite side of the shaft, six feet below . . . but apparently, it was not to be. In midair, as Langdon began instinctively folding his body into a protective ball, he collided hard with a vertical face of stone.

I didn't make it.

I'm dead.

Certain he had hit the inner edge, Langdon braced himself for his plummet into the void.

But the fall lasted only an instant.

Langdon crashed down almost immediately on sharp uneven ground, striking his head. The force of the collision nearly knocked him into unconsciousness, but in that moment he realized he had cleared the shaft completely and hit the far wall of the staircase, landing on the lower portion of the spiraling stairs.

Find the gun, Langdon thought, straining to hold on to consciousness, knowing that Ávila would be on top of him in a matter of seconds.

But it was too late.

His brain was shutting down.

As the blackness set in, the last thing Langdon heard was an odd sound . . . a series of recurring thuds beneath him, each one farther away than the one before.

It reminded him of the sound of an oversized bag of garbage careening down a trash chute.

CHAPTER 76

s Prince Julián's vehicle approached the main gate of El Escorial, he saw a familiar barricade of white SUVs and knew Valdespino had been telling the truth.

My father is indeed in residence here.

From the looks of this convoy, the king's entire Guardia Real security detail had now relocated to this historical royal residence.

As the acolyte brought the old Opel to a stop, an agent with a flashlight strode over to the window, shone the light inside, and recoiled in shock, clearly not expecting to find the prince and the bishop inside the dilapidated vehicle.

"Your Highness!" the man exclaimed, jumping to attention. "Your Excellency! We've been expecting you." He eyed the beat-up car. "Where is your Guardia detail?"

"They were needed at the palace," the prince replied. "We're here to see my father."

"Of course, of course! If you and the bishop would please get out of the vehicle—"

"Just move the roadblock," Valdespino scolded, "and we'll drive in. His Majesty is in the monastery hospital, I assume?"

"He **was**," the guard said, hesitating. "But I'm afraid now he's gone."

Valdespino gasped, looking horrified.

An icy chill gripped Julián. **My father is dead?**

"No! I-I'm so sorry!" the agent stammered, regretting his poor choice of words. "His Majesty is **gone**—he left El Escorial an hour ago. He took his lead security detail, and they left."

Julián's relief turned quickly to confusion. **Left the hospital here?**

"That's absurd," Valdespino yelled. "The king told me to bring Prince Julián here right away!"

"Yes, we have specific orders, Your Excellency, and if you would, please exit the car so we can transfer you both to a Guardia vehicle."

Valdespino and Julián exchanged puzzled looks and dutifully got out of the car. The agent advised the acolyte that his services were no longer required and that he should return to the palace. The frightened young man sped off into the night without a word, clearly relieved to end his role in this evening's bizarre events.

As the guards guided the prince and Valdespino into the back of an SUV, the bishop became increasingly agitated. "Where is the king?" he demanded. "Where are you taking us?"

"We are following His Majesty's direct orders," the agent said. "He asked us to give you a vehicle, a driver, and this letter." The agent produced a sealed envelope and handed it through the window to Prince Julián.

A letter from my father? The prince was disconcerted by the formality, especially when he noticed that the envelope bore the royal wax seal. **What is he doing?** He felt increasing concern that the king's faculties might be failing.

Anxiously, Julián broke the seal, opened the envelope, and extracted a handwritten note card. His father's penmanship was not what it used to be but was still legible. As Julián began to read the letter, he felt his bewilderment growing with every word.

When he finished, he slipped the card back into the envelope and closed his eyes, considering his options. There was only one, of course.

"Drive north, please," Julián told the driver.

As the vehicle pulled away from El Escorial, the prince could feel Valdespino staring at him. "What did your father say?" the bishop demanded. "Where are you taking me?!"

Julián exhaled and turned to his father's trusted friend. "You said it best earlier." He gave the aging bishop a sad smile. "My father is still the king. We love him, and we do as he commands."

CHAPTER 77

R obert . . . ?" a voice whispered.
Langdon tried to respond, but his head was pounding.

"Robert . . . ?"

A soft hand touched his face, and Langdon slowly opened his eyes. Momentarily disoriented, he actually thought he was dreaming. **An angel in white is hovering over me.**

When Langdon recognized her face, he managed a weak smile.

"Thank God," Ambra said, exhaling all at once. "We heard the gunshot." She crouched beside him. "Stay down."

As Langdon's awareness returned, he felt a sudden rush of fear. "The man who attacked—"

"He's gone," Ambra whispered, her voice calm. "You're safe." She gestured over the edge of the shaft. "He fell. All the way down."

Langdon strained to absorb the news. It was all slowly coming back. He fought to clear the fog from his mind and take inventory of his wounds, his attention moving to the deep throbbing in his left hip and the sharp pain in his head. Otherwise, nothing felt broken. The sound of police radios echoed up the stairwell.

"How long . . . have I been . . ."

"A few minutes," Ambra said. "You've been in and out. We need to get you checked."

Gingerly, Langdon pulled himself to a sitting position, leaning against the wall of the staircase. "It was the navy . . . officer," he said. "The one who—"

"I know," Ambra said, nodding. "The one who killed Edmond. The police just ID'd him. They're at the bottom of the stairwell with the body, and they want a statement from you, but Father Beña told them nobody comes up here before the medical team, who should be here any minute now."

Langdon nodded, his head pounding.

"They'll probably take you to the hospital," Ambra told him, "which means you and I need to talk right now . . . before they arrive."

"Talk . . . about **what**?"

Ambra studied him, looking concerned. She leaned down close to his ear and whispered, "Robert, don't you remember? We found it—Edmond's password: 'The dark religions are departed and sweet science reigns.'"

Her words pierced the fog like an arrow, and Langdon bolted upright, the murkiness in his mind clearing abruptly.

"You've brought us this far," Ambra said. "I can do the rest. You said you know how to find Winston. The location of Edmond's computer lab? Just tell me where to go, and I'll do the rest."

Langdon's memories rushed back now in torrents. "I **do** know." **At least I think I can figure it out.**

"Tell me."

"We need to go across town."

"Where?"

"I don't know the address," Langdon said, now climbing unsteadily to his feet. "But I can take you—"

"Sit down, Robert, please!" Ambra said.

"Yes, sit down," a man echoed, coming into view on the stairs below them. It was Father Beña, trudging up the staircase, breathless. "The EMTs are almost here."

"I'm fine," Langdon lied, feeling woozy as he leaned against the wall. "Ambra and I need to go now."

"You won't get very far," Beña said, climbing slowly. "The police are waiting. They want a statement. Besides, the church is surrounded by media. Someone tipped off the press that you're here." The priest arrived beside them and gave Langdon a tired smile. "By the way, Ms. Vidal and I are relieved to see you're okay. You saved our lives."

Langdon laughed. "I'm pretty sure **you** saved ours."

"Well, in either case, I just want you to know that you'll be unable to leave this stairwell without facing the police."

Langdon carefully placed his hands on the stone railing and leaned out, peering down. The macabre scene on the ground seemed so far away—Ávila's awkwardly splayed body illuminated by the beams of several flashlights in the hands of police officers.

As Langdon peered down the spiral shaft, once again noting Gaudí's elegant nautilus design, he flashed on the website for the Gaudí museum in the basement of this church. The online site, which Langdon had visited not long ago, featured a spectacular series of scale models of Sagrada Família—accurately rendered by CAD programs and massive 3-D printers—depicting the long evolution of the structure, from the laying of its foundation all the way to the church's glorious future completion, still at least a decade away.

Where do we come from? Langdon thought. **Where are we going?**

A sudden memory struck him—one of the scale models of the church's exterior. The image was lodged in his eidetic memory. It was a prototype depicting the church's current stage of construction and was titled "Sagrada Família Today."

If that model is up-to-date, then there could be a way out.

Langdon turned suddenly to Beña. "Father, could you please relay a message from me to someone outside?"

The priest looked puzzled.

As Langdon explained his plan to get out of the building, Ambra shook her head. "Robert, that's impossible. There's nowhere up there for—"

"Actually," Beña interjected, "there *is*. It won't be there forever, but at the moment, Mr. Langdon is correct. What he's suggesting is possible."

Ambra looked surprised. "But Robert . . . even if we can escape unseen, are you sure that you shouldn't go to the hospital?"

Langdon wasn't sure of very much at this point. "I can go later if I need to," he said. "Right now, we owe it to Edmond to finish what we came here to do." He turned to Beña, looking him directly in the eye. "I need to be honest with you, Father, about why we are here. As you know, Edmond Kirsch was murdered tonight to stop him from announcing a scientific discovery."

"Yes," the priest said, "and from the tone of Kirsch's introduction, he seemed to believe this discovery would deeply damage the religions of the world."

"Exactly, which is why I feel you should know that Ms. Vidal and I came to Barcelona tonight in an effort to release Edmond Kirsch's discovery. We are very close to being able to do that. Meaning . . ." Langdon paused. "In requesting your help right now, I'm essentially asking you to help us globally broadcast the words of an atheist."

Beña reached up and placed a hand on Langdon's shoulder. "Professor," he said with a chuckle, "Edmond Kirsch is not the first atheist in history to proclaim that 'God is dead,' nor will he be the last. Whatever it is that Mr. Kirsch has discovered, it will no doubt be debated on all sides. Since the beginning of time, the human intellect has always evolved, and it is not my role to impede that development. From my perspective, however, there has never been an intellectual advancement that has not included God."

With that, Father Beña gave them both a reassuring smile and headed down the stairs.

Outside, waiting in the cockpit of the parked EC145 helicopter, the pilot watched with rising concern as the crowd outside Sagrada Família's security fence continued to grow. He had not heard from the two Guardia agents inside and was about to radio in when a small man in black robes emerged from the basilica and approached the chopper.

The man introduced himself as Father Beña and relayed a shocking message from inside: both Guardia agents had been killed, and the future queen and Robert Langdon required evacuation at once. As if this weren't startling enough, the priest then told the pilot **where** precisely he was to collect his passengers.

Impossible, the pilot had thought.

And yet now, as he soared over the spires of Sagrada Família, he realized that the priest had been correct. The church's largest spire—a monolithic central tower—had not yet been built. Its foundation platform was a flat circular expanse, nestled deep among a cluster of spires, like a clearing in a forest of redwoods.

The pilot positioned himself high above the platform, and carefully lowered the chopper down among the spires. As he touched down, he saw two figures emerge from a stairwell—Ambra Vidal assisting an injured Robert Langdon.

The pilot jumped out and helped them both inside.

As he strapped them in, the future queen of Spain gave him a weary nod.

"Thank you very much," she whispered. "Mr. Langdon will tell you where to go."

CHAPTER 78

🌐 ConspiracyNet.com

BREAKING NEWS

PALMARIAN CHURCH KILLED EDMOND
KIRSCH'S MOTHER?!

Our informant monte@iglesia.org has come through with yet another blockbuster revelation! According to exclusive documents verified by ConspiracyNet, Edmond Kirsch has attempted for years to sue the Palmarian Church for "brainwashing, psychological conditioning, and physical cruelty" allegedly resulting in the death of Paloma Kirsch—Edmond's biological mother—more than three decades ago.

Paloma Kirsch is alleged to have been an active member of the Palmarian Church who attempted to break free, was shamed and psychologically abused by her superiors, and hanged herself in a nunnery bedroom.

CHAPTER 79

"The king himself," Commander Garza mut-
tered again, his voice resonating across the palace armory. "I still can't fathom that my arrest
order came from the **king** himself. After all my years
of service."

Mónica Martín placed a silencing finger to her lips
and glanced through the suits of armor at the entryway to make sure the guards were not listening. "I
told you, Bishop Valdespino has the king's ear, and
has convinced His Majesty that tonight's accusations
against him are **your** doing, and that you're somehow
framing him."

I've become the king's sacrificial lamb, Garza realized, always having suspected that if the king were
forced to choose between his Guardia Real commander or Valdespino, he would choose Valdespino;
the two men had been lifelong friends, and spiritual
connections always trumped professional ones.

Even so, Garza could not help but feel that something about Mónica's explanation wasn't entirely logical. "The kidnapping story," he said. "You're telling
me that it was ordered by the **king**?"

"Yes, His Majesty called me directly. He **ordered** me
to announce that Ambra Vidal had been abducted.

He had concocted the kidnapping story in an effort to save the reputation of the future queen—to soften the appearance that she had literally run off with another man." Martín gave Garza an annoyed look. "Why are you questioning me about this? Especially now that you know the king phoned Agent Fonseca with the same kidnapping story?"

"I can't believe the king would **ever** risk falsely accusing a prominent American of kidnapping," Garza argued. "He'd have to be—"

"Insane?" she interrupted.

Garza stared in silence.

"Commander," Martín pressed, "remember that His Majesty is failing. Maybe this was just a case of bad judgment?"

"Or a moment of brilliance," Garza offered. "Reckless or not, the future queen is now safe and accounted for, in the hands of the Guardia."

"Exactly." Martín eyed him carefully. "So what's bothering you?"

"Valdespino," Garza said. "I admit I don't like him, but my gut says he can't possibly be behind Kirsch's murder, or any of the rest of it."

"Why not?" Her tone was acerbic. "Because he's a **priest**? I'm pretty sure our Inquisition taught us a few things about the Church's willingness to justify drastic measures. In my opinion, Valdespino is self-righteous, ruthless, opportunistic, and overly secretive. Am I missing something?"

"You are," Garza fired back, startled to find himself defending the bishop. "Valdespino is everything you say he is, but he is also a person for whom tradition and dignity are everything. The king—who trusts almost no one—has steadfastly trusted the bishop for decades now. I find it very hard to believe that the king's confidant could ever commit the kind of treachery we're talking about."

Martín sighed and pulled out her cell phone. "Commander, I hate to undermine your faith in the bishop, but I need you to see this. Suresh showed it to me." She pressed a few buttons and handed Garza her phone.

The screen displayed a long text message.

"This is a screenshot of a text message Bishop Valdespino received tonight," she whispered. "Read it. I guarantee it will change your mind."

CHAPTER 80

Despite the pain coursing through his body, Robert Langdon felt strangely buoyant, almost euphoric, as the helicopter thundered off the roof of Sagrada Família.

I'm alive.

He could feel the adrenaline build up in his bloodstream, as if all of the events of the past hour were now hitting him all at once. Breathing as slowly as possible, Langdon turned his attention outward, to the world beyond the helicopter windows.

All around him, massive church spires reached skyward, but as the helicopter rose, the church dropped away, dissolving into an illuminated grid of streets. Langdon gazed down at the sprawl of city blocks, which were not the usual squares and rectangles but rather much softer octagons.

L'Eixample, Langdon thought. **The Widening.**

Visionary city architect Ildefons Cerdà had widened all the intersections in this district by shaving the corners off the square blocks to create mini plazas, with better visibility, increased airflow, and abundant space for outdoor cafés.

"**¿Adónde vamos?**" the pilot shouted over his shoulder.

Langdon pointed two blocks to the south, where one of the city's widest, brightest, and most aptly named avenues cut diagonally across Barcelona.

"Avinguda Diagonal," Langdon shouted. "**Al oeste.**" To the west.

Impossible to miss on any map of Barcelona, Avinguda Diagonal crossed the entire width of the city, from the ultramodern beachside skyscraper Diagonal ZeroZero to the ancient rose gardens of Parc de Cervantes—a ten-acre tribute to Spain's most celebrated novelist, the author of **Don Quixote.**

The pilot nodded his confirmation and banked to the west, following the slanting avenue westward toward the mountains. "Address?" the pilot called back. "Coordinates?"

I don't know the address, Langdon realized. "Fly to the **fútbol** stadium."

"¿Fútbol?" He seemed surprised. "FC Barcelona?"

Langdon nodded, having no doubt the pilot knew exactly how to find the home of the famed Barcelona **fútbol** club, which was located a few miles farther up Avinguda Diagonal.

The pilot opened the throttle, now tracing the path of the avenue at full speed.

"Robert?" Ambra asked quietly. "Are you okay?" She studied him as if perhaps his head injury had impaired his judgment. "You said you know where to find Winston."

"I do," he replied. "That's where I'm taking us."

"A **fútbol** stadium? You think Edmond built a supercomputer at a stadium?"

Langdon shook his head. "No, the stadium is just an easy landmark for the pilot to locate. I'm interested in the building directly **beside** the stadium— the Gran Hotel Princesa Sofía."

Ambra's expression of confusion only deepened. "Robert, I'm not sure you're making sense. There's no way Edmond built Winston inside a luxury hotel. I think we should take you to the clinic after all."

"I'm fine, Ambra. Trust me."

"Then where are we going?"

"Where are we going?" Langdon stroked his chin playfully. "I believe that's one of the important questions Edmond promised to answer tonight."

Ambra's expression settled somewhere between amused and exasperated.

"Sorry," Langdon said. "Let me explain. Two years ago, I had lunch with Edmond at the private club on the eighteenth floor of the Gran Hotel Princesa Sofía."

"And Edmond brought a supercomputer to lunch?" Ambra suggested with a laugh.

Langdon smiled. "Not quite. Edmond arrived for lunch **on foot**, telling me he ate at the club almost every day because the hotel was so convenient—only a couple of blocks from his computer lab. He also confided in me that he was working on an advanced synthetic intelligence project and was incredibly excited about its potential."

Ambra looked suddenly heartened. "That must have been **Winston**!"

"My thoughts exactly."

"And so Edmond took you to his lab!"

"No."

"Did he tell you where it was?"

"Unfortunately, he kept that a secret."

The concern rushed back into Ambra's eyes.

"However," Langdon said, "**Winston** secretly told us exactly where it is."

Now Ambra looked confused. "No, he didn't."

"I assure you, he did," Langdon said, smiling. "He actually told the whole world."

Before Ambra could demand an explanation, the pilot announced, "¡**Ahí está el estadio!**" He pointed into the distance at Barcelona's massive stadium.

That was fast, Langdon thought, glancing outside and tracing a line from the stadium to the nearby Gran Hotel Princesa Sofía—a skyscraper overlooking a broad plaza on Avinguda Diagonal. Langdon told the pilot to bypass the stadium and instead take them up high over the hotel.

Within seconds, the helicopter had climbed several hundred feet and was hovering above the hotel where Langdon and Edmond had gone to lunch two years ago. **He told me his computer lab was only two blocks from here.**

From their bird's-eye vantage point, Langdon scanned the area around the hotel. The streets in this neighborhood were not as rectilinear as they were around Sagrada Família, and the city blocks formed all kinds of uneven and oblong shapes.

It has to be here.

With rising uncertainty, Langdon searched the blocks in all directions, trying to spot the unique shape that he could picture in his memory. **Where is it?**

It was not until he turned his gaze to the north, across the traffic circle at the Plaça de Pius XII, that Langdon felt a twinge of hope. "Over there!" he called to the pilot. "Please fly over that wooded area!"

The pilot tipped the nose of the chopper and moved diagonally one block to the northwest, now hovering over the forested expanse where Langdon had pointed. The woods were actually part of a massive walled estate.

"Robert," Ambra shouted, sounding frustrated now. "What are you doing? This is the Royal Palace of Pedralbes! There is no way Edmond built Winston inside—"

"Not here! Over **there**!" Langdon pointed beyond the palace to the block directly behind it.

Ambra leaned forward, looking down intently at the source of Langdon's excitement. The block behind the palace was formed by four well-lit streets, intersecting to create a square that was orientated north–south like a diamond. The diamond's only flaw was that its lower-right border was awkwardly bent—skewed by an uneven jog in the line—leaving a crooked perimeter.

"Do you recognize that jagged line?" Langdon

asked, pointing to the diamond's skewed axis—a well-lit street perfectly delineated against the darkness of the wooded palace grounds. "Do you see the street with the little jog in it?"

All at once Ambra's exasperation seemed to disappear, and she cocked her head to peer down more intently. "Actually, that line **is** familiar. Why do I know it?"

"Look at the entire block," Langdon urged. "A diamond shape with one strange border in the lower right." He waited, sensing Ambra would recognize it soon. "Look at the two small parks on this block." He pointed to a round park in the middle and a semicircular park on the right.

"I feel like I know this place," Ambra said, "but I can't quite . . ."

"Think about **art**," Langdon said. "Think about your collection at the Guggenheim. Think about—"

"Winston!" she shouted, and turned to him in disbelief. "The layout of this block—it's the **exact** shape of Winston's self-portrait in the Guggenheim!"

Langdon smiled at her. "Yes, it is."

Ambra wheeled back to the window and stared down at the diamond-shaped block. Langdon peered down too, picturing Winston's self-portrait—the bizarrely shaped canvas that had puzzled him ever since Winston had pointed it out to him earlier tonight—an awkward tribute to the work of Miró.

Edmond asked me to create a self-portrait, Winston had said, **and this is what I came up with.**

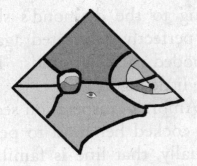

Langdon had already decided that the eyeball featured near the center of the piece—a staple of Miró's work—almost certainly indicated the precise spot where Winston existed, the place on the planet from which Winston **viewed** the world.

Ambra turned back from the window, looking both joyful and stunned. "Winston's self-portrait is not a Miró. It's a **map**!"

"Exactly," Langdon said. "Considering Winston has no body and no physical self-image, his self-portrait understandably would be more related to his location than to his physical form."

"The eyeball," Ambra said. "It's a carbon copy of a Miró. But there's only one eye, so maybe that's what marks Winston's location?"

"I was thinking the same thing." Langdon turned to the pilot now and asked if he could set the helicopter down just for a moment on one of the two little parks on Winston's block. The pilot began to descend.

"My God," Ambra blurted, "I think I know why Winston chose to mimic Miró's style!"

"Oh?"

"The palace we just flew over is the Palace of Pedralbes."

"¿Pedralbes?" Langdon asked. "Isn't that the name of—"

"Yes! One of Miró's most famous sketches. Winston probably researched this area and found a local tie to Miró!"

Langdon had to admit, Winston's creativity was astonishing, and he felt strangely exhilarated by the prospect of reconnecting with Edmond's synthetic intelligence. As the helicopter dropped lower, Langdon saw the dark silhouette of a large building located on the exact spot where Winston had drawn his eye.

"Look—" Ambra pointed. "That must be it."

Langdon strained to get a better view of the building, which was obscured by large trees. Even from the air, it looked formidable.

"I don't see lights," Ambra said. "Do you think we can get in?"

"Somebody's got to be here," Langdon said. "Edmond must have staff on hand, especially tonight. When they realize we have Edmond's password—I suspect they will scramble to help us trigger the presentation."

Fifteen seconds later, the helicopter touched down in a large semicircular park on the eastern border of Winston's block. Langdon and Ambra jumped out, and the chopper lifted off instantly, speeding toward the stadium, where it would await further instructions.

As the two of them hurried across the darkened

park toward the center of the block, they crossed a small internal street, Passeig dels Til·lers, and moved into a heavily wooded area. Up ahead, shrouded by trees, they could see the silhouette of a large and bulky building.

"No lights," Ambra whispered.

"And a fence," Langdon said, frowning as they arrived at a ten-foot-high, wrought iron security fence that circled the entire complex. He peered through the bars, unable to see much of the building in the forested compound. He felt puzzled to see no lights at all.

"There," Ambra said, pointing twenty yards down the fence line. "I think it's a gate."

They hurried along the fence and found an imposing entry turnstile, which was securely locked. There was an electronic call box, and before Langdon had a chance to consider their options, Ambra had pressed the call button.

The line rang twice and connected.

Silence.

"Hello?" Ambra said. "Hello?"

No voice came through the speaker—just the ominous buzz of an open line.

"I don't know if you can hear me," she said, "but this is Ambra Vidal and Robert Langdon. We are trusted friends of Edmond Kirsch. We were with him tonight when he was killed. We have information that will be extremely helpful to Edmond, to Winston, and, I believe, to all of you."

There was a staccato click.

Langdon immediately put his hand on the turnstile, which turned freely.

He exhaled. "I told you someone was home."

The two of them hurriedly pushed through the security turnstile and moved through the trees toward the darkened building. As they got closer, the outline of the roof began to take shape against the sky. An unexpected silhouette materialized—a fifteen-foot symbol mounted to the peak of the roof.

Ambra and Langdon stopped short.

This can't be right, Langdon thought, staring up at the unmistakable symbol above them. **Edmond's computer lab has a giant crucifix on the roof?**

Langdon took several more steps and emerged from the trees. As he did, the building's entire facade came into view, and it was a surprising sight—an ancient Gothic church with a large rose window, two stone steeples, and an elegant doorway adorned with bas-reliefs of Catholic saints and the Virgin Mary.

Ambra looked horrified. "Robert, I think we just broke our way onto the grounds of a Catholic church. We're in the wrong place."

Langdon spotted a sign in front of the church and began to laugh. "No, I think we're in the exact **right** place."

This facility had been in the news a few years ago, but Langdon had never realized it was in Barcelona. **A high-tech lab built inside a decommissioned Catholic church.** Langdon had to admit it seemed the ultimate sanctuary for an irreverent atheist to build a godless computer. As he gazed up at the now defunct church, he felt a chill to realize the prescience with which Edmond had chosen his password.

The dark religions are departed & sweet science reigns.

Langdon drew Ambra's attention to the sign.

It read:

BARCELONA SUPERCOMPUTING CENTER

CENTRO NACIONAL DE SUPERCOMPUTACIÓN

Ambra turned to him with a look of disbelief. "Barcelona has a **supercomputing** center inside a Catholic church?"

"It does." Langdon smiled. "Sometimes truth is stranger than fiction."

CHAPTER 81

T he tallest cross in the world is in Spain.

Erected on a mountaintop eight miles north of the monastery of El Escorial, the massive cement cross soars a bewildering five hundred feet in the air above a barren valley, where it can be seen from more than a hundred miles away.

The rocky gorge beneath the cross—aptly named the Valley of the Fallen—is the final resting place of more than forty thousand souls, victims of both sides of the bloody Spanish Civil War.

What are we doing here? Julián wondered as he followed the Guardia out onto the viewing esplanade at the base of the mountain beneath the cross. **This is where my father wants to meet?**

Walking beside him, Valdespino looked equally confused. "This makes no sense," he whispered. "Your father always despised this place."

Millions despise this place, Julián thought.

Conceived in 1940 by Franco himself, the Valley of the Fallen had been billed as "a national act of atonement"—an attempt to reconcile victors and vanquished. Despite its "noble aspiration," the monument sparked controversy to this day because it was built by a workforce that included convicts and

political prisoners who had opposed Franco—many
of whom died from exposure and starvation during
construction.

In the past, some parliamentary members had even
gone so far as to compare this place to a Nazi concentration camp. Julián suspected his father secretly felt
the same way, even if he could never say so openly.
For most Spaniards, the site was regarded as a monument to Franco, built by Franco—a colossal shrine
to honor himself. The fact that Franco was now
entombed in it only added fuel to the critics' fire.

Julián recalled the one time he had been here—
another childhood outing with his father to learn
about his country. The king had shown him around
and quietly whispered, **Look carefully, son. One day
you'll tear this down.**

Now, as Julián followed the Guardia up the stairs
toward the austere facade carved into the mountainside, he began to realize where they were going. A
sculpted bronze door loomed before them—a portal into the face of the mountain itself—and Julián
recalled stepping through that door as a boy, utterly
transfixed by what lay beyond.

After all, the true miracle of this mountaintop was
not the towering cross above it; the true miracle was
the secret space **inside** it.

Hollowed out within the granite peak was a man-
made cavern of unfathomable proportions. The
hand-excavated cavern tunneled back nearly nine
hundred feet into the mountain, where it opened up
into a gaping chamber, meticulously and elegantly

finished, with glimmering tile floors and a soaring frescoed cupola that spanned nearly a hundred and fifty feet from side to side. **I'm inside a mountain,** young Julián had thought. **I must be dreaming!**

Now, years later, Prince Julián had returned.

Here at the behest of my dying father.

As the group neared the iron portal, Julián gazed up at the austere bronze pietà above the door. Beside him, Bishop Valdespino crossed himself, although Julián sensed the gesture was more out of trepidation than faith.

CHAPTER 82

🌐 ConspiracyNet.com

BREAKING NEWS

BUT . . . WHO IS THE REGENT?

Evidence has now surfaced proving that assassin Luis Ávila was taking his kill orders directly from an individual he called the Regent.

The identity of the Regent remains a mystery, although this person's title may provide some clues. According to dictionary.com, a "regent" is someone appointed to oversee an organization while its leader is incapacitated or absent.

From our User Survey "Who Is the Regent?"—our top three answers currently are:

1. Bishop Antonio Valdespino taking over for the ailing Spanish king

2. A Palmarian pope who believes he is the legitimate pontiff

3. A Spanish military officer claiming to be acting on behalf of his country's incapacitated commander in chief, the king

More news as we have it!

#WHOISTHEREGENT

CHAPTER 83

Langdon and Ambra scanned the facade of the large chapel and found the entrance to the Barcelona Supercomputing Center at the southern tip of the church's nave. Here, an ultramodern Plexiglas vestibule had been affixed to the outside of the rustic facade, giving the church the hybrid appearance of a building caught between centuries.

In an outer courtyard near the entrance stood a twelve-foot-tall bust of a primitive warrior's head. Langdon couldn't imagine what this artifact was doing on the grounds of a Catholic church, but he was fairly certain, knowing Edmond, that Kirsch's workplace would be a land of contradictions.

Ambra hurried to the main entrance and pressed the call button at the door. As Langdon joined her, a security camera overhead rotated toward them, scanning back and forth for several long moments.

Then the door buzzed open.

Langdon and Ambra quickly pushed through the entrance into a large foyer that was fashioned from the church's original narthex. It was an enclosed stone chamber, dimly lit and empty. Langdon had expected someone would appear to greet them—perhaps one of Edmond's employees—but the lobby was deserted.

"Is there no one here?" Ambra whispered.

They became aware of the soft, pious strains of medieval church music—a polyphonic choral work for male voices that sounded vaguely familiar. Langdon couldn't place it, but the eerie presence of religious music in a high-tech facility seemed to him a product of Edmond's playful sense of humor.

Glowing in front of them on the wall of the lobby, a massive plasma screen provided the room's sole light. The screen was projecting what could only be described as some kind of primitive computer game—clusters of black dots moving around on a white surface, like groups of bugs wandering aimlessly.

Not totally aimlessly, Langdon realized, now recognizing the patterns.

This famous computer-generated progression—known as Life—had been invented in the 1970s by a British mathematician, John Conway. The black dots—known as cells—moved, interacted, and reproduced based on a preordained series of "rules" entered by the programmer. Invariably, over time, guided only by these "initial rules of engagement," the dots began organizing themselves into clusters, sequences, and recurring patterns—patterns that evolved, became more complex, and began to look startlingly similar to patterns seen in nature.

"Conway's Game of Life," Ambra said. "I saw a digital installation years ago based on it—a mixed-media piece titled **Cellular Automaton.**"

Langdon was impressed, having heard of Life himself only because its inventor, Conway, had taught at Princeton.

The choral harmonies caught Langdon's ear again. **I feel like I've heard this piece. Perhaps a Renaissance Mass?**

"Robert," Ambra said, pointing. "Look."

On the display screen, the bustling groups of dots had reversed direction and were accelerating, as if the program were now playing backward. The sequence rewound faster and faster, backward in time. The number of dots began diminishing . . . the cells no longer splitting and multiplying but **recombining** . . . their structures becoming simpler and simpler until finally there were only a handful of them, which continued merging . . . first eight, then four, then two, then . . .

One.

A single cell blinked in the middle of the screen.

Langdon felt a chill. **The origin of life.**

The dot blinked out, leaving only a void—an empty white screen.

The Game of Life was gone, and faint text began to materialize, growing more pronounced until they could read it.

> If we admit a First Cause,
> the mind still craves to know
> whence it came and how it arose.

"That's Darwin," Langdon whispered, recognizing the legendary botanist's eloquent phrasing of the same question Edmond Kirsch had been asking.

"Where do we come from?" Ambra said excitedly, reading the text.

"Exactly."

Ambra smiled at him. "Shall we go find out?"

She motioned beside the display screen to a columned opening that appeared to connect to the main church.

As they stepped across the lobby, the display refreshed again, now showing a collage of words that appeared randomly on the screen. The number of words grew steadily and chaotically, with new words evolving, morphing, and combining into an intricate array of phrases.

. . . **growth . . . fresh buds . . . beautiful ramifications . . .**

As the image expanded, Langdon and Ambra saw the words evolve into the shape of a growing tree.

What in the world?

They stared intently at the graphic, and the sound of the a cappella voices grew louder around them. Langdon realized that they were not singing in Latin as he had imagined, but in English.

"My God, the words on the screen," Ambra said. "I think they match the music."

"You're right," Langdon agreed, seeing fresh text appear on-screen as it was being sung simultaneously.

. . . **by slowly acting causes . . . not by miraculous acts . . .**

Langdon listened and watched, feeling strangely disconcerted by the combination of words and music;

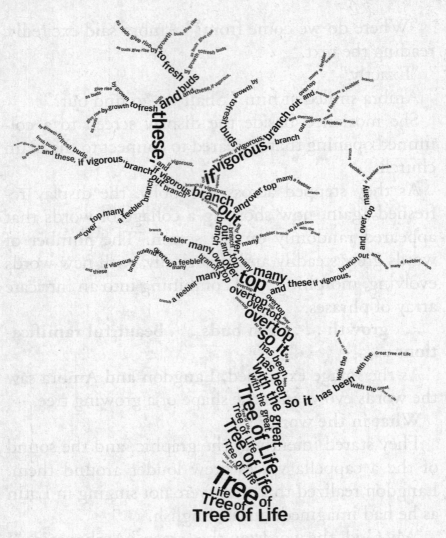

the music was clearly religious, yet the text was anything but.

. . . **organic beings . . . strongest live . . . weakest**
die . . .

Langdon stopped short.

I know this piece!

Edmond had taken Langdon to a performance of
it several years ago. Titled **Missa Charles Darwin,**

it was a Christian-style mass in which the composer had eschewed the traditional sacred Latin text and substituted excerpts from Charles Darwin's **On the Origin of Species** to create a haunting juxtaposition of devout voices singing about the brutality of natural selection.

"Bizarre," Langdon commented. "Edmond and I heard this piece together a while back—he loved it. Such a coincidence to hear it again."

"No coincidence," boomed a familiar voice from the speakers overhead. "Edmond taught me to welcome guests into my home by putting on some music they would appreciate and showing them something of interest to discuss."

Langdon and Ambra stared up at the speakers in disbelief. The cheerful voice that welcomed them was distinctly British.

"I'm so glad you've found your way here," said the very familiar synthetic voice. "I had no way to contact you."

"Winston!" Langdon exclaimed, amazed to feel such relief from reconnecting with a machine. He and Ambra quickly recounted what had happened.

"It's good to hear your voices," Winston said. "So tell me, have we found what we were looking for?"

illiam Blake," Langdon said. " 'The dark religions are departed and sweet science reigns.' "

Winston paused only an instant. "The final line of his epic poem **The Four Zoas**. I must admit it's a perfect choice." He paused. "However, the requisite forty-seven-letter count——"

"The ampersand," Langdon said, quickly explaining Kirsch's ligature trick using **et**.

"That is quintessential Edmond," the synthetic voice replied with an awkward chuckle.

"So, Winston?" Ambra urged. "Now that you know Edmond's password, can you trigger the remainder of his presentation?"

"Of course I can," Winston replied unequivocally. "All I need is for you to enter the password manually. Edmond placed firewalls around this project, so I don't have direct access to it, but I can take you back to his lab and show you where to enter the information. We can launch the program in less than ten minutes."

Langdon and Ambra turned to each other, the abruptness of Winston's confirmation catching them off guard. With everything they had endured tonight, this ultimate moment of triumph seemed to have arrived without any fanfare.

"Robert," Ambra whispered, placing a hand on his shoulder. "You did this. Thank you."

"Team effort," he replied with a smile.

"Might I suggest," Winston said, "that we move immediately back to Edmond's lab? You're quite visible here in the lobby, and I've detected some news reports that you are in this vicinity."

Langdon was not surprised; a military helicopter touching down in a metropolitan park was bound to draw attention.

"Tell us where to go," Ambra said.

"Between the columns," Winston replied. "Follow my voice."

In the lobby, the choral music stopped abruptly, the plasma screen went dark, and from the main entrance, a series of loud thuds echoed as automatically controlled dead bolts engaged.

Edmond probably turned this facility into a fortress, Langdon realized, stealing a quick glance through the thick lobby windows, relieved to see that the wooded area around the chapel was deserted. **At least for the moment.**

As he turned back toward Ambra, he saw a light flicker on at the end of the lobby, illuminating a doorway between two columns. He and Ambra walked over, entered, and found themselves in a long corridor. More lights flickered at the far end of the hallway, guiding their way.

As Langdon and Ambra set off down the hall, Winston told them, "I believe that to achieve maximum exposure we need to disseminate a global press release right now saying that the late Edmond Kirsch's presentation is about to go live. If we give the media an extra window to publicize the event, it will increase Edmond's viewership dramatically."

"Interesting idea," Ambra said, striding faster. "But how long do you think we should wait? I don't want to take any chances."

"Seventeen minutes," Winston replied. "That would place the broadcast at the top of the hour—three a.m. here, and prime time across America."

"Perfect," she replied.

"Very well," Winston chimed. "The media release will go out right now, and the presentation launch will be in seventeen minutes."

Langdon strained to keep up with Winston's rapid-fire planning.

Ambra led the way down the hall. "And how many staff members are here tonight?"

"None," Winston replied. "Edmond was fanatical about security. There is virtually no staff here. I run all the computer networks, along with lighting, cooling, and security. Edmond joked that in this era of 'smart' houses, he was the first to have a smart church."

Langdon was only half listening, his thoughts consumed by sudden concerns over the actions they were about to take. "Winston, do you really think **now** is the moment to release Edmond's presentation?"

Ambra stopped short and stared at him. "Robert, of

course it is! That's why we're here! The whole world
is watching! We also don't know if anyone else will
come and try to stop us—we need to do this **now**,
before it's too late!"

"I concur," Winston said. "From a strictly statisti-
cal standpoint, this story is approaching its saturation point. Measured in terabytes of media data, the
Edmond Kirsch discovery is now one of the biggest
news stories of the decade—not surprising, considering how the online community has grown exponentially in the past ten years."

"Robert?" Ambra pressed, her eyes probing his.
"What's your concern?"

Langdon hesitated, trying to pinpoint the source
of his sudden uncertainty. "I guess I'm just worried
for Edmond's sake that all of the conspiracy stories
tonight—murders, kidnapping, royal intrigue—will
somehow overshadow his science."

"That's a valid point, Professor," Winston interjected. "Although I believe it overlooks one important
fact: those conspiracy stories are a significant reason
why so many viewers all over the world are now tuned
in. There were 3.8 million during Edmond's online
broadcast earlier this evening; but now, after all the
dramatic events of the last several hours, I estimate
that some **two hundred million** people are following
this story through online news reports, social media,
television, and radio."

The number seemed staggering to Langdon, although he recalled that more than two hundred million people had watched the FIFA World Cup final,

and five hundred million had watched the first lunar landing a half century ago when nobody had Internet, and televisions were far less widespread globally.

"You may not see this in academia, Professor," Winston said, "but the rest of the world has become a reality TV show. Ironically, the people who tried to silence Edmond tonight have accomplished the opposite; Edmond now has the largest audience for any scientific announcement in history. It reminds me of the Vatican denouncing your book **Christianity and the Sacred Feminine**, which, in the aftermath, promptly became a bestseller."

Almost a bestseller, Langdon thought, but Winston's point was taken.

"Maximizing viewership was always one of Edmond's primary goals tonight," Winston said.

"He's right," Ambra said, looking at Langdon. "When Edmond and I brainstormed the live Guggenheim event, he was obsessed with increasing audience engagement and capturing as many eyeballs as possible."

"As I said," Winston stressed, "we are reaching our point of media saturation, and there is no better time than the present to unveil his discovery."

"Understood," Langdon said. "Just tell us what to do."

Continuing down the hallway, they arrived at an unexpected obstacle—a ladder awkwardly propped across the corridor as if for a painting job—making it impossible to advance without moving the ladder or passing beneath it.

"This ladder," Langdon offered. "Shall I take it down?"

"No," Winston said. "Edmond deliberately put it there a long time ago."

"Why?" Ambra asked.

"As you may know, Edmond despised superstition in all forms. He made a point of walking under a ladder every day on his way into work—a way of thumbing his nose at the gods. Moreover, if any guest or technician **refused** to walk under this ladder, Edmond kicked them out of the building."

Always so reasonable. Langdon smiled, recalling how Edmond had once berated him in public for "knocking on wood" for luck. **Robert, unless you're a closet Druid who still raps on trees to wake them up, please leave that ignorant superstition in the past where it belongs!**

Ambra pressed on, ducking down and walking beneath the ladder. With an admittedly irrational twinge of trepidation, Langdon followed suit.

When they reached the other side, Winston guided them around a corner to a large security door that had two cameras and a biometric scan.

A handmade sign hung above the door: ROOM 13.

Langdon eyed the infamously unlucky number. **Edmond spurning the gods once again.**

"This is the entrance to his lab," Winston said. "Other than the hired technicians who helped Edmond build it, very few have been permitted access."

With that, the security door buzzed loudly, and

Ambra wasted no time grabbing the handle and heaving it open. She took one step over the threshold, stopped short, and raised her hand to her mouth with a startled gasp. When Langdon looked past her into the church's sanctuary, he understood her reaction.

The chapel's voluminous hall was dominated by the largest glass box Langdon had ever seen. The transparent enclosure spanned the entire floor and reached all the way up to the chapel's two-story ceiling.

The box seemed to be divided into two floors.

On the first floor, Langdon could see hundreds of refrigerator-sized metal cabinets aligned in rows like church pews facing an altar. The cabinets had no doors, and their innards were on full display. Mind-bogglingly intricate matrices of bright red wires dangled from dense grids of contact points, arching down toward the floor, where they were laced together into thick, ropelike harnesses that ran between the machines, creating what looked like a web of veins.

Ordered chaos, Langdon thought.

"On the first floor," Winston said, "you see the famous MareNostrum supercomputer—forty-eight thousand eight hundred and ninety-six Intel cores communicating over an InfiniBand FDR10 network—one of the fastest machines in the world. MareNostrum was here when Edmond moved in, and rather than removing it, he wanted to **incorporate** it, so he simply expanded . . . upward."

Langdon could now see that all of MareNostrum's wire harnesses merged at the center of the room, forming a single trunk that climbed vertically like a massive vine into the first floor's ceiling.

As Langdon's gaze rose to the second story of the huge glass rectangle, he saw a totally different picture. Here, in the center of the floor, on a raised platform, stood a massive metallic blue-gray cube—ten feet square—with no wires, no blinking lights, and nothing about it to suggest it could possibly be the cutting-edge computer that Winston was currently describing with barely decipherable terminology.

". . . qubits replace binary digits . . . superpositions of states . . . quantum algorithms . . . entanglement and tunneling . . ."

Langdon now knew why he and Edmond talked art rather than computing.

". . . resulting in quadrillions of floating-point calculations per second," Winston concluded. "Making the fusion of these two very different machines the most powerful supercomputer in the world."

"My God," Ambra whispered.

"Actually," Winston corrected, "**Edmond's God.**"

CHAPTER 85

🌐 ConspiracyNet.com

BREAKING NEWS

KIRSCH DISCOVERY TO AIR WITHIN MINUTES!

Yes, it's really happening!

A press release from Edmond Kirsch's camp has just confirmed that his widely anticipated scientific discovery—withheld in the wake of the futurist's assassination—will be streamed live to the world at the top of the hour (3 a.m. local time in Barcelona).

Viewer participation is reportedly skyrocketing, and global online engagement statistics are unprecedented.

In related news, Robert Langdon and Ambra Vidal were allegedly just spotted entering the grounds of Chapel Torre Girona—home to the Barcelona Supercomputing Center, where Edmond Kirsch is believed to have been working for the past several years. Whether this is the site from which the presentation will be live-streamed, ConspiracyNet cannot yet confirm.

Stay tuned for Kirsch's presentation, available here as a live stream on ConspiracyNet.com!

CHAPTER 86

A s Prince Julián passed through the iron doorway into the mountain, he had the uneasy feeling that he might never escape.

The Valley of the Fallen. What am I doing here?

The space beyond the threshold was cold and dark, barely illuminated by two electric torches. The air smelled of damp stone.

A uniformed man stood before them holding a loop of keys that jangled in his trembling hands. Julián was not surprised that this officer of the Patrimonio Nacional seemed anxious; a half-dozen Guardia Real agents were lined up right behind him in the darkness. **My father is here.** No doubt this poor officer had been summoned in the middle of the night to unlock Franco's sacred mountain for the king.

One of the Guardia agents quickly stepped forward. "Prince Julián, Bishop Valdespino. We've been expecting you. This way, please."

The Guardia agent led Julián and Valdespino to a massive wrought iron gate on which was carved an ominous Francoist symbol—a fierce double-headed eagle that echoed Nazi iconography.

"His Majesty is at the end of the tunnel," the agent

said, motioning them through the gate, which had been unlocked and stood partially ajar.

Julián and the bishop exchanged uncertain glances and walked through the gate, which was flanked by a pair of menacing metal sculptures—two angels of death, clutching swords shaped like crosses.

More Francoist religio-military imagery, Julián thought as he and the bishop began their long walk into the mountain.

The tunnel that stretched out before them was as elegantly appointed as the ballroom of Madrid's Royal Palace. With finely polished black marble floors and a soaring coffered ceiling, the sumptuous passageway was lit by a seemingly endless series of wall sconces shaped like torches.

Tonight, however, the source of light in the passageway was far more dramatic. Dozens upon dozens of fire basins—dazzling bowls of fire arranged like runway lights—burned orange all the way down the tunnel. Traditionally, these fires were lit only for major events, but the late-night arrival of the king apparently ranked high enough to set them all aglow.

With reflections of firelight dancing on the burnished floor, the massive hallway took on an almost supernatural ambience. Julián could feel the ghostly presence of those sad souls who had carved this tunnel by hand, their pickaxes and shovels poised, toiling for years inside this cold mountain, hungry, frozen, many dying, all for the glorification of Franco, whose tomb lay deep within this mountain.

Look carefully, son, his father had told him. **One day you'll tear this down.**

As king, Julián knew he would probably not have the power to destroy this magnificent structure, and yet he had to admit he felt surprise that the people of Spain had permitted it to stand, especially considering the country's eagerness to move past her dark past and into the new world. Then again, there were still those who longed for the old ways, and every year, on the anniversary of Franco's death, hundreds of aging Francoists still flocked to this place to pay their respects.

"Don Julián," the bishop said quietly, out of earshot of the others, as they walked deeper into the passageway. "Do you know why your father summoned us here?"

Julián shook his head. "I was hoping **you** would know."

Valdespino let out an unusually heavy sigh. "I don't have any idea."

If the bishop doesn't know my father's motives, Julián thought, **then nobody knows them.**

"I just hope he's all right," the bishop said with surprising tenderness. "Some of his decisions lately . . ."

"You mean like convening a meeting inside a mountain when he should be in a hospital bed?"

Valdespino softly smiled. "For example, yes."

Julián wondered why the king's Guardia detail had not intervened and refused to bring the dying monarch out of the hospital to this foreboding location.

Then again, Guardia agents were trained to obey without question, especially when the request came from their commander in chief.

"I have not prayed here in years," Valdespino said, gazing down the firelit hallway.

The tunnel through which they were moving, Julián knew, was not solely the access corridor into the mountain; it was also the **nave** of an officially sanctioned Catholic church. Up ahead, the prince could begin to see the rows of pews.

La basílica secreta, Julián had called it as a child.

Hollowed out of the granite mountain, the gilded sanctuary at the end of this tunnel was a cavernous space, an astonishing subterranean basilica with a massive cupola. Rumored to have more total square footage than St. Peter's in Rome, the underground mausoleum boasted six separate chapels surrounding its high altar, which was meticulously positioned directly beneath the cross atop the mountain.

As they neared the main sanctuary, Julián scanned the enormous space, looking for his father. The basilica, however, appeared totally deserted.

"Where is he?" the bishop demanded, sounding worried.

Julián now shared the bishop's concern, fearing the Guardia had left the king alone in this desolate place. The prince quickly moved ahead, peering down one arm of the transept and then the other. No sign of anyone. He jogged deeper, circling around the side of the altar and into the apse.

It was here, in the deepest recesses of the mountain, that Julián finally spotted his father and came to an abrupt halt.

The king of Spain was completely alone, covered with heavy blankets, and slumped in a wheelchair.

CHAPTER 87

Inside the main sanctuary of the deserted chapel, Langdon and Ambra followed Winston's voice around the perimeter of the two-story supercomputer. Through the heavy glass, they heard a deep vibrating thrum emanating from the colossal machine inside. Langdon had the eerie sense that he was peering into a cage at an incarcerated beast.

The noise, according to Winston, was generated not by the electronics but by the vast array of centrifugal fans, heat sinks, and liquid coolant pumps required to keep the machine from overheating.

"It's deafening in there," Winston said. "And freezing. Fortunately, Edmond's lab is on the second floor."

A freestanding spiral staircase rose ahead, affixed to the outer wall of the glass enclosure. On Winston's command, Langdon and Ambra climbed the stairs and found themselves standing on a metal platform before a glass revolving door.

To Langdon's amusement, this futuristic entrance to Edmond's lab had been decorated as if it were a suburban home—complete with a welcome mat, a fake potted plant, and a little bench under which sat a pair of house slippers, which Langdon realized wistfully must have been Edmond's.

Above the door hung a framed message.

> Success is the ability to go
> from one failure to another
> with no loss of enthusiasm.
> —WINSTON CHURCHILL

"More Churchill," Langdon said, pointing it out to Ambra.

"Edmond's favorite quote," Winston chimed. "He said it pinpoints the single greatest strength of computers."

"Computers?" Ambra asked.

"Yes, computers are infinitely persistent. I can fail billions of times with no trace of frustration. I embark upon my billionth attempt at solving a problem with the same energy as my first. Humans cannot do that."

"True," Langdon admitted. "I usually give up after my millionth attempt."

Ambra smiled and moved toward the door.

"The floor inside is glass," Winston said as the revolving door began turning automatically. "So please remove your shoes."

Within seconds, Ambra had kicked off her shoes and stepped barefoot through the rotating portal. As Langdon followed suit, he noticed that Edmond's welcome mat bore an unusual message:

THERE'S NO PLACE LIKE 127.0.0.1

"Winston, this mat? I don't under—"

"Local host," Winston replied.

Langdon read the mat again. "I see," he said, not seeing at all, and continued through the revolving door.

When Langdon stepped out onto the glass floor, he felt a moment of weak-kneed uncertainty. Standing on a transparent surface in his socks was unnerving enough, but to find himself hovering directly over the MareNostrum computer downstairs felt doubly disconcerting. From up here, viewing the phalanx of stately racks below reminded Langdon of peering down into China's famous Xi'an archeological pit at the army of terra-cotta soldiers.

Langdon took a deep breath and raised his eyes to the bizarre space before him.

Edmond's lab was a transparent rectangle dominated by the metallic blue-gray cube he had seen earlier, its glossy surface reflecting everything around it. To the right of the cube, at one end of the room, was an ultrasleek office space with a semicircular desk, three giant LCD screens, and assorted keyboards recessed into the granite work surface.

"Mission control," Ambra whispered.

Langdon nodded and glanced toward the opposite end of the chamber, where armchairs, a couch, and an exercise bike were arranged on an Oriental carpet.

A supercomputing man cave, Langdon mused, suspecting that Edmond had all but moved into this glass box while working on his project. **What did he discover up here?** Langdon's initial hesitation had passed, and he now felt the growing pull of intellectual curiosity—the yearning to learn what mysteries had been unveiled up here, what secrets had been unearthed by the collaboration of a genius mind and a powerful machine.

Ambra had already padded across the floor to the massive cube and was gazing up in bewilderment at its polished blue-gray surface. Langdon joined her, both of them reflected in its shiny exterior.

This is a computer? Langdon wondered. Unlike the machine downstairs, this one was dead silent—inert and lifeless—a metallic monolith.

The machine's bluish hue reminded Langdon of a 1990s supercomputer called "Deep Blue," which had stunned the world by defeating world chess champion Garry Kasparov. Since then, the advances in computing technology were almost impossible to comprehend.

"Would you like to look inside?" Winston chimed from a set of speakers overhead.

Ambra shot a startled glance upward. "Look inside the **cube**?"

"Why not?" Winston replied. "Edmond would have been proud to show you its inner workings."

"Not necessary," Ambra said, turning her eyes toward Edmond's office. "I'd rather focus on entering the password. How do we do that?"

"It will take only a matter of seconds, and we still have more than eleven minutes before we can launch. Have a look inside."

Before them, a panel on the side of the cube facing Edmond's office began to slide open, revealing a thick pane of glass. Langdon and Ambra circled around and pressed their faces to the transparent portal.

Langdon expected to see yet another densely packed cluster of wires and blinking lights. But he saw nothing of the sort. To his bewilderment, the inside of the cube was dark and empty—like a small vacant room. The only contents appeared to be wisps of white mist that swirled in the air as if the room were a walk-in freezer. The thick Plexiglas panel radiated a surprising coldness.

"There's nothing here," Ambra declared.

Langdon saw nothing either but could feel a low repetitive pulsation emanating from within the cube.

"That slow thumping beat," Winston said, "is the pulse tube dilution refrigeration system. It sounds like a human heart."

Yes, it does, Langdon thought, unnerved by the comparison.

Slowly, red lights within began to illuminate the interior of the cube. At first, Langdon saw only white fog and bare floor space—an empty square chamber. Then, as the glow increased, something glinted in the air above the floor, and he realized there was an intricate metal cylinder hanging down from the ceiling like a stalactite.

"And **this**," Winston said, "is what the cube must keep cold."

The cylindrical device suspended from the ceiling was about five feet long, composed of seven horizontal rings that decreased in diameter as they descended, creating a narrowing column of tiered disks attached by slender vertical rods. The space between the burnished metal disks was occupied by a sparse mesh of delicate wires. An icy mist swirled around the entire device.

"E-Wave," Winston announced. "A quantum leap—if you'll pardon the pun—beyond NASA/Google's D-Wave."

Winston quickly explained that D-Wave—the world's first rudimentary "quantum computer"—had unlocked a brave new world of computational power that scientists were still struggling to comprehend. Quantum computing, rather than using a binary method of storing information, made use of the quantum states of subatomic particles, resulting in an exponential leap in speed, power, and flexibility.

"**Edmond's** quantum computer," Winston said, "is structurally not that different from D-Wave. One difference is the metallic cube surrounding the computer. The cube is coated with **osmium**—a rare, ultradense chemical element that provides enhanced magnetic, thermal, and quantum shielding, and also, I suspect, plays into Edmond's sense of drama."

Langdon smiled, having had a similar thought himself.

"Over the past few years, while Google's Quantum Artificial Intelligence Lab used machines like D-Wave to enhance machine learning, Edmond secretly leapfrogged over everybody with this machine. And he did so using a single bold idea . . ." Winston paused. "Bicameralism."

Langdon frowned. **The two houses of Parliament?**

"The two-lobed brain," Winston continued. "Left and right hemispheres."

The bicameral mind, Langdon now realized. One of the things that made human beings so creative was that the two halves of their brains functioned so differently. The left brain was analytical and verbal, while the right brain was intuitive and "preferred" pictures to words.

"The trick," Winston said, "was that Edmond decided to build a synthetic brain that mimicked the **human** brain—that is, segmented into left and right hemispheres. Although, in this case, it's more of an upstairs-downstairs arrangement."

Langdon stepped back and peered through the floor at the churning machine downstairs and then back to the silent "stalactite" inside the cube. **Two distinct machines fused into one—a bicameral mind.**

"When forced to work as a **single** unit," Winston said, "these two machines adopt differing approaches to problem solving—thereby experiencing the same kinds of conflict and compromise that occur between the lobes of the human brain, greatly accelerating AI learning, creativity, and, in a sense . . . **humanity.** In my case, Edmond gave me the tools to teach myself about humanity by observing the world around me and modeling human traits—humor, cooperation, value judgments, and even a sense of ethics."

Incredible, Langdon thought. "So this double computer is essentially . . . **you**?"

Winston laughed. "Well, this machine is no more

me than your physical brain is **you**. Observing your own brain in a bowl, you would not say, 'That object is me.' We are the sum of the interactions taking place **within** the mechanism."

"Winston," Ambra interjected, moving now toward Edmond's work space. "How much time until launch?"

"Five minutes and forty-three seconds," Winston replied. "Shall we prepare?"

"Yes, please," she said.

The viewing window's shielding slid slowly back into place, and Langdon turned to join Ambra in Edmond's lab.

"Winston," she said. "Considering all your work here with Edmond, I'm surprised that you have no sense at all what his discovery was."

"Again, Ms. Vidal, my information is compartmentalized, and I have the same data you have," he replied. "I can only make an educated guess."

"And what would that be?" Ambra asked, looking around Edmond's office.

"Well, Edmond claimed that his discovery would 'change everything.' In my experience, the most transformative discoveries in history have all resulted in revised **models** of the universe—breakthroughs like Pythagoras's rejection of the flat-earth model, Copernican heliocentricism, Darwin's theory of evolution, and Einstein's discovery of relativity—all of which drastically altered humankind's view of their world and updated our current model of the universe."

Langdon glanced up at the speaker overhead. "So

you're guessing Edmond discovered something that suggests a new model of the universe?"

"It's a logical deduction," Winston replied, talking faster now. "MareNostrum happens to be one of the finest 'modeling' computers on earth, specializing in complex simulations, its most famous being 'Alya Red'—a fully functioning, virtual human heart that is accurate down to the cellular level. Of course, with the recent addition of a quantum component, this facility can model systems millions of times more complicated than human organs."

Langdon grasped the concept but still couldn't imagine what Edmond might have modeled to answer the questions **Where do we come from? Where are we going?**

"Winston?" Ambra called from Edmond's desk. "How do we turn all this on?"

"I can help you," Winston replied.

The three huge LCD screens on the desk flickered to life just as Langdon arrived beside Ambra. As the images on the screen materialized, both of them stepped back in alarm.

"Winston . . . is that image **live**?" Ambra asked.

"Yes, live feed from our exterior security cameras. I thought you should know. They arrived several seconds ago."

The display screens showed a fish-eye view of the chapel's main entrance, where a small army of police had assembled, pressing the call button, trying the door, talking on radios.

"Don't worry," Winston assured them, "they will

never get in. And we're less than four minutes until launch."

"We should launch right **now**," Ambra urged.

Winston replied evenly. "I believe Edmond would prefer that we wait and launch at the top of the hour, as promised. He was a man of his word. Moreover, I am monitoring our global viewer engagement, and our audience is still growing. In the next four minutes, at the current rate, our audience will increase by 12.7 percent, and, I predict, approach maximum penetration." Winston paused, sounding almost pleasantly surprised. "I must say, despite all that has transpired this evening, it appears Edmond's release will be optimally timed. I think he would be deeply grateful to both of you."

CHAPTER 88

Under four minutes, Langdon thought, lower-ing himself into Edmond's mesh desk chair and turning his eyes to the three huge LCD panels that dominated this end of the room. On-screen, the live security feeds still played, showing police gathering around the chapel.

"You're **sure** they can't get in?" Ambra urged, shift-ing anxiously behind Langdon.

"Trust me," Winston replied. "Edmond took secu-rity very seriously."

"And if they cut power to the building?" Langdon ventured.

"Isolated power supply," Winston replied flatly. "Redundant buried trunks. Nobody can interfere at this point. I assure you."

Langdon let it go. **Winston has been correct on all fronts tonight . . . And he's had our backs the whole way.**

Settling in at the center of the horseshoe-shaped desk, Langdon turned his attention to the unusual keyboard before him. It had at least twice the normal number of keys—traditional alphanumerics aug-mented by an array of symbols that even he didn't recognize. The keyboard was split down the middle, each half ergonomically angled away from the other.

"Some guidance here?" Langdon asked, staring at the bewildering array of keys.

"Wrong keyboard," Winston replied. "That's E-Wave's main access point. As I mentioned, Edmond kept this presentation hidden from everyone, including me. The presentation must be triggered from a different machine. Slide to your right. All the way to the end."

Langdon glanced to his right, where a half-dozen freestanding computers were aligned along the length of the desk. As he rolled toward them, he was surprised to see that the first few machines were quite old and outdated. Strangely, the farther he rolled, the older the machines seemed to get.

This can't be right, he thought, passing a clunky-looking, beige IBM DOS system that had to be decades old. "Winston, what are these machines?"

"Edmond's childhood computers," Winston said. "He kept them as a reminder of his roots. Sometimes, on difficult days here, he would power them up and run old programs—a way to reconnect with the wonder he felt as a boy when he discovered programming."

"I love that idea," Langdon said.

"Just like your Mickey Mouse watch," Winston said.

Startled, Langdon glanced down, pulling back the sleeve of his suit jacket to reveal the antique time-piece he had worn since he had received it as a boy.

That Winston knew about his watch was surprising, although Langdon recalled telling Edmond recently about wearing it as a reminder to stay young at heart.

"Robert," Ambra said, "your fashion sense aside, could we please enter the password? Even your mouse is waving—trying to get your attention."

Sure enough, Mickey's gloved hand was high over his head, his index finger pointing almost straight up. **Three minutes till the hour.**

Langdon quickly slid along the desk, and Ambra joined him at the last computer in the series—an ungainly, mushroom-colored box with a floppy-disk slot, a 1,200-baud telephone modem, and a bulbous twelve-inch convex monitor sitting on top.

"Tandy TRS-80," Winston said. "Edmond's first machine. He bought it used and taught himself BASIC when he was about eight years old."

Langdon was happy to see that this computer, despite being a dinosaur, was already turned on and waiting. Its screen—a flickering black-and-white display—glowed with a promising message, spelled out in a jagged bitmapped font.

WELCOME, EDMOND.
PLEASE ENTER PASSWORD:

After the word "password," a black cursor blinked expectantly.

"That's it?" Langdon asked, feeling somehow like it was all too simple. "I just enter it **here**?"

"Exactly," Winston replied. "Once you enter the

password, this PC will send an authenticated 'unlock' message to the sealed partition in the main computer that contains Edmond's presentation. I will then have access and be able to manage the feed, align it with the top of the hour, and push the data to all the main distribution channels for global relay."

Langdon more or less followed the explanation, and yet as he stared down at the clunky computer and telephone modem, he felt perplexed. "I don't understand, Winston, after all of Edmond's planning tonight, why would he **ever** trust his entire presentation to a phone call to a prehistoric modem?"

"I would say that's just Edmond being Edmond," Winston replied. "As you know, he was passionate about drama, symbolism, and history, and I suspect it brought him enormous joy to power up his very first computer and use it to launch his life's greatest work."

Fair point, Langdon reflected, realizing that was exactly how Edmond would have seen it.

"Moreover," Winston added, "I suspect Edmond probably had contingencies in place, but either way, there's logic to using an ancient computer to 'throw a switch.' Simple tasks require simple tools. And security-wise, using a slow processor ensures that a brute-force hacking of the system would take forever."

"Robert?" Ambra urged behind him, giving his shoulder an encouraging squeeze.

"Yes, sorry, all set." Langdon pulled the Tandy keyboard closer to him, its tightly coiled cable stretching out like an old rotary phone cord. He laid his fingers

on the plastic keys and pictured the line of handwritten text that he and Ambra had discovered in the
crypt at Sagrada Família.

**The dark religions are departed & sweet science
reigns.**

The grand finale of William Blake's epic poem
The Four Zoas seemed the perfect choice to unlock
Edmond's final scientific revelation—a discovery he
claimed would change everything.

Langdon took a deep breath and carefully typed in
the line of poetry, with no spaces, and replaced the
ampersand with the ligature **et**.

When he finished, he looked up at the screen.

PLEASE ENTER PASSWORD:

....

Langdon counted the dots—forty-seven.

Perfect. Here goes nothing.

Langdon made eye contact with Ambra and she gave
him a nod. He reached out and hit the return key.

Instantly, the computer emitted a dull buzz.

INCORRECT PASSWORD.
TRY AGAIN.

Langdon's heart thundered.

"Ambra—I typed it perfectly! I'm **sure** of it!" He
spun in his chair and looked up at her, fully expecting to see her face filled with fear.

Instead, Ambra Vidal stared down at him with an amused smile. She shook her head and laughed.

"**Professor,**" she whispered, pointing to his keyboard. "Your caps lock is on."

———

At that moment, deep inside a mountain, Prince Julián stood transfixed, staring across the subterranean basilica, trying to make sense of the baffling scene before him. His father, the king of Spain, sat motionless in a wheelchair, parked in the most remote and private section of this basilica.

With a surge of dread, Julián rushed to his side. "Father?"

As Julián arrived, the king slowly opened his eyes, apparently emerging from a nap. The ailing monarch managed a relaxed smile. "Thank you for coming, son," he whispered, his voice frail.

Julián crouched down in front of the wheelchair, relieved that his father was alive but also alarmed at how dramatically the man had deteriorated in just a few days. "Father? Are you okay?"

The king shrugged. "As well as can be expected," he replied with surprisingly good humor. "How are **you**? Your day has been . . . eventful."

Julián had no idea how to reply. "What are you doing here?"

"Well, I was tired of the hospital and wanted some air."

"Fine, but . . . **here**?" Julián knew his father had always abhorred this shrine's symbolic link to persecution and intolerance.

"Your Majesty!" called Valdespino, hurrying around the altar and joining them, breathless. "What in the world!"

The king smiled at his lifelong friend. "Antonio, welcome."

Antonio? Prince Julián had never heard his father address Bishop Valdespino by his first name. In public, it was always "Your Excellency."

The king's uncharacteristic lack of formality seemed to rattle the bishop. "Thank . . . you," he stammered. "Are you okay?"

"Simply wonderful," the king replied, smiling broadly. "I am in the presence of the two people I trust most in the world."

Valdespino shot an uneasy glance at Julián and then turned back to the king. "Your Majesty, I've delivered your son to you as you requested. Shall I leave you two to talk in private?"

"No, Antonio," the king said. "This will be a confession. And I need my priest at my side."

Valdespino shook his head. "I don't think your son expects you to explain your actions and behavior tonight. I'm sure he—"

"Tonight?" The king laughed. "No, Antonio, I am confessing the secret I've kept from Julián his entire life."

CHAPTER 89

⊕ ConspiracyNet.com

BREAKING NEWS

CHURCH UNDER ATTACK!

No, not by Edmond Kirsch—by the Spanish police!

Chapel Torre Girona in Barcelona is currently under assault by local authorities. Inside, Robert Langdon and Ambra Vidal are believed to be responsible for the successful launch of Edmond Kirsch's greatly anticipated announcement, which is now only minutes away.

The countdown has begun!

CHAPTER 90

A mbra Vidal felt a flood of exhilaration as the antique computer pinged happily after Langdon's second attempt to enter the line of poetry.

PASSWORD CORRECT.

Thank God, she thought as Langdon stood up from the desk and turned to her. Ambra immediately put her arms around him and squeezed him in a heartfelt embrace. **Edmond would be so grateful.**

"Two minutes and thirty-three seconds," Winston chimed.

Ambra let go of Langdon, both of them turning to the LCD screens overhead. The center screen displayed a countdown clock she had last seen in the Guggenheim.

Live program begins in 2 minutes 33 seconds
Current remote attendees: 227,257,914

More than two hundred million people? Ambra was stunned. Apparently while she and Langdon were fleeing across Barcelona, the entire world had taken notice. **Edmond's audience has become astronomical.**

Beside the countdown screen, the live security feeds continued to play, and Ambra noticed a sudden shift in the police activity outside. One by one, the officers who had been pounding on doors and talking on radios stopped what they were doing, pulled out their smartphones, and stared down into them. The patio outside the church gradually became a sea of pale, eager faces illuminated by the glow of their handheld displays.

Edmond has stopped the world in its tracks, Ambra thought, feeling an eerie sense of responsibility that people around the globe were preparing to view a presentation that would be streaming out of this very room. **I wonder if Julián is watching,** she thought, then quickly pushed him from her mind.

"The program is now cued," Winston said. "I believe you'll both be more comfortable watching in Edmond's sitting area at the other end of this lab."

"Thank you, Winston," Langdon said, ushering Ambra barefoot across the smooth glass floor, past the blue-gray metallic cube, and into Edmond's sitting area.

Here, an Oriental carpet had been spread out on the glass floor, along with a collection of elegant furniture and an exercise bike.

As Ambra stepped off the glass onto the soft carpet, she felt her body begin to relax. She climbed onto

the couch and pulled her feet up beneath her, looking around for Edmond's television. "Where do we
watch?"

Langdon apparently didn't hear, having walked
to the corner of the room to look at something, but
Ambra got her answer an instant later when the entire
rear wall of the chamber began glowing from within.
A familiar image appeared, projected out from inside
the glass.

Live program begins in 1 minute 39 seconds
Current remote attendees: 227,501,173

The entire wall is a display?
Ambra stared at the eight-foot-tall image as the
lights in the church slowly dimmed. Winston, it
seemed, was making them at home for Edmond's big
show.

———

Ten feet away, in the corner of the room, Langdon
stood transfixed—not by the massive television wall,
but by a small object he had just spotted; it was displayed on an elegant pedestal as if it were part of a
museum exhibition.

Before him, a single test tube was ensconced in a
metal display case with a glass front. The test tube was
corked and labeled, and contained a murky brownish
liquid. For a moment, Langdon wondered if maybe it

were some kind of medicine Edmond had been taking. Then he read the name on the label.

That's impossible, he told himself. **Why would this be here?!**

There were very few "famous" test tubes in the world, but Langdon knew this one certainly qualified. **I can't believe Edmond owns one of these!** He had probably purchased this scientific artifact under the radar for an enormous price. **Just like he did with the Gauguin painting in Casa Milà.**

Langdon crouched down and peered at the seventy-year-old glass vial. Its masking-tape label was faded and worn, but the two names on the tube were still legible: MILLER-UREY.

The hair on the back of Langdon's neck stood up as he read the names again.

MILLER-UREY.

My God . . . Where do we come from?

Chemists Stanley Miller and Harold Urey had conducted a legendary scientific experiment in the 1950s attempting to answer that very question. Their bold experiment had failed, but their efforts had been lauded worldwide and been known ever since as the Miller-Urey experiment.

Langdon recalled being mesmerized in high school biology class to learn how these two scientists had attempted to re-create the conditions at the dawn of earth's creation—a hot planet covered by a churning, lifeless ocean of boiling chemicals.

The primordial soup.

After duplicating the chemicals that existed in the early oceans and atmosphere—water, methane, ammonia, and hydrogen—Miller and Urey heated the concoction to simulate the boiling seas. Then they shocked it with electric charges to mimic lightning. And finally, they let the mixture cool, just as the planet's oceans had cooled.

Their goal was simple and audacious—to spark life from a lifeless primal sea. **To simulate "Creation,"** Langdon thought, **using only science.**

Miller and Urey studied the mixture in hopes that primitive microorganisms might form in the chemical-rich concoction—an unprecedented process known as **abiogenesis**. Sadly, their attempts to create "life" from lifeless matter did not succeed. Rather than life, they were left with nothing but a collection of inert glass vials that now languished in a dark closet at the University of California in San Diego.

To this day, Creationists still cited the Miller-Urey Experiment's failure as scientific proof that life could **not** have appeared on earth without help from the hand of God.

"Thirty seconds," Winston's voice boomed overhead.

Langdon's thoughts spun as he stood up and stared into the darkened church around them. Just minutes ago, Winston had declared that science's greatest breakthroughs were those that created new "models" of the universe. He had also said that MareNostrum specialized in computer modeling—simulating complex systems and watching them run.

The Miller-Urey Experiment, Langdon thought, **is an example of early modeling . . . simulating the complex chemical interactions occurring on primordial earth.**

"Robert!" Ambra called from across the room. "It's starting."

"On my way," he replied, moving toward the couch, suddenly overwhelmed by the suspicion that he might just have glimpsed a part of what Edmond had been working on.

As he crossed the floor, Langdon recalled Edmond's dramatic preamble above the Guggenheim's grassy meadow. **Tonight, let us be like the early explorers,** he had said, **those who left everything behind and set out across vast oceans. The age of religion is drawing to a close, and the age of science is dawning. Just imagine what would happen if we miraculously learned the answers to life's big questions.**

As Langdon took his seat beside Ambra, the massive wall display began broadcasting a final countdown.

Ambra was studying him. "Are you okay, Robert?"

Langdon nodded as a dramatic soundtrack filled the room, and Edmond's face materialized on the wall before them, five feet tall. The celebrated futurist looked thin and tired, but he was smiling broadly into the camera.

"Where do we come from?" he asked, the excitement in his voice rising as the music faded. "And where are we going?"

Ambra took Langdon's hand and gripped it anxiously.

"These two questions are part of the same story," Edmond declared. "So let's start at the beginning— the **very** beginning."

With a playful nod, Edmond reached into his pocket and pulled out a small glass object—a vial of murky liquid bearing the faded names Miller and Urey.

Langdon felt his heart race.

"Our journey begins long ago . . . **four billion** years before Christ . . . adrift in the primordial soup."

CHAPTER 91

Seated beside Ambra on the couch, Langdon studied Edmond's sallow face projected on the glass display wall and felt a pang of sorrow knowing that Edmond had been suffering in silence from a deadly disease. Tonight, however, the futurist's eyes shone with pure joy and excitement.

"In a moment, I'll tell you about this little vial," Edmond said, holding up the test tube, "but first, let's take a swim . . . in the primordial soup."

Edmond disappeared, and a lightning bolt flashed, illuminating a churning ocean where volcanic islands spewed lava and ash into a tempestuous atmosphere.

"Is this where life commenced?" Edmond's voice asked. "A spontaneous reaction in a churning sea of chemicals? Or was it perhaps a microbe on a meteorite from space? Or was it . . . **God**? Unfortunately, we can't go back in time to witness that moment. All we know is what happened **after** that moment, when life first appeared. Evolution happened. And we're accustomed to seeing it portrayed something like this."

The screen now showed the familiar timeline of human evolution—a primitive ape slouching behind a line of increasingly erect hominids, until the final one was fully erect, having shed the last of his body hair.

"Yes, humans **evolved**," Edmond said. "This is an irrefutable scientific fact, and we've built a clear timeline based on the fossil record. But what if we could watch evolution in reverse?"

Suddenly Edmond's face started growing hair, morphing into a primitive human. His bone structure changed, becoming increasingly apelike, and then the process accelerated to an almost blinding pace, showing glimpses of older and older species—lemurs, sloths, marsupials, platypuses, lungfish, plunging underwater and mutating through eels and fish, gelatinous creatures, plankton, amoebas, until all that was left of Edmond Kirsch was a microscopic bacterium—a single cell pulsating in a vast ocean.

"The earliest specks of life," Edmond said. "This is where our backward movie runs out of film. We have no idea how the earliest life-forms materialized out of a lifeless chemical sea. We simply cannot see the first frame of this story."

$T=0$, Langdon mused, picturing a similar reverse movie about the expanding universe in which the cosmos contracted down to a single point of light, and cosmologists hit a similar dead end.

" 'First Cause,' " Edmond declared. "That's the term Darwin used to describe this elusive moment of Creation. He proved that life continuously evolved, but he could not figure out how the process all started. In other words, Darwin's theory described the **survival** of the fittest, but not the **arrival** of the fittest."

Langdon chuckled, having never heard it stated quite that way.

"So, how did life **arrive** on earth? In other words, where do we come from?" Edmond smiled. "In the next few minutes, you'll have an answer to that question. But trust me, as stunning as **that** answer is, it's only half of tonight's story." He looked directly into the camera and gave an ominous grin. "As it turns out, where we come from is utterly fascinating . . . but where we are going is utterly shocking."

Ambra and Langdon exchanged a perplexed look, and although Langdon sensed this was more of Edmond's hyperbole, the statement left him feeling increasingly uneasy.

"Life's origin . . . ," Edmond continued. "It has remained a profound mystery since the days of the first Creation stories. For millennia, philosophers and scientists have been searching for some kind of record of this very first moment of life."

Edmond now held up the familiar test tube containing the murky liquid. "In the 1950s, two such seekers—chemists Miller and Urey—ran a bold experiment that they hoped might unveil exactly how life began."

Langdon leaned over and whispered to Ambra, "That test tube is right over **there**." He pointed to the display pedestal in the corner.

She looked surprised. "Why would **Edmond** have it?"

Langdon shrugged. Judging from the strange collection of items in Edmond's apartment, this vial was probably just a piece of scientific history that he wanted to own.

Edmond quickly described Miller and Urey's efforts to re-create the primordial soup, trying to create life within a flask of nonliving chemicals.

The screen now flashed a faded **New York Times** article from March 8, 1953, titled "Looking Back Two Billion Years."

"Obviously," Edmond said, "this experiment raised some eyebrows. The implications could have been earth-shattering, especially for the religious world. If life magically appeared inside this test tube, we would know conclusively that the laws of chemistry **alone** are indeed enough to create life. We would no longer require a supernatural being to reach down from heaven and bestow upon us the spark of Creation. We would understand that life simply happens . . . as an inevitable by-product of the laws of nature. More importantly, we would have to conclude that because life spontaneously appeared **here** on earth, it almost certainly did the same thing elsewhere in the cosmos, meaning: man is not unique; man is not at the center of God's universe; and man is not alone in the universe."

Edmond exhaled. "However, as many of you may know, the Miller-Urey experiment failed. It produced a few amino acids, but nothing even closely resembling life. The chemists tried repeatedly, using different combinations of ingredients, different heat patterns, but nothing worked. It seemed that **life**—as the faithful had long believed—required divine intervention. Miller and Urey eventually abandoned their experiments. The religious community breathed a sigh of relief, and the scientific community went back to the drawing board." He paused, an amused glimmer in his eyes. "That is, until 2007 . . . when there was an unexpected development."

Edmond now told the tale of how the forgotten Miller-Urey testing vials had been rediscovered in a closet at the University of California in San Diego after Miller's death. Miller's students had reanalyzed the samples using far more sensitive contemporary techniques—including liquid chromatography and mass spectrometry—and the results had been startling. Apparently, the original Miller-Urey experiment had produced many more amino acids and complex compounds than Miller had been able to measure at the time. The new analysis of the vials even identified several important nucleobases—the building blocks of RNA, and perhaps eventually . . . DNA.

"It was an astounding science story," Edmond concluded, "relegitimizing the notion that perhaps life **does** simply happen . . . **without divine intervention.** It seemed the Miller-Urey experiment had indeed been working, but just needed more time to gestate. Let's remember one key point: life evolved over billions of years, and these test tubes had been sitting in a closet for just over fifty. If the timeline of this experiment were measured in miles, it was as if our perspective were limited to only the very first inch . . ."

He let that thought hang in the air.

"Needless to say," Edmond went on, "there was a sudden resurgence in interest surrounding the idea of creating life in a lab."

I remember that, Langdon thought. The Harvard biology faculty had thrown a department party they billed as BYOB: Build Your Own Bacterium.

"There was, of course, a strong reaction from modern religious leaders," Edmond said, placing air quotes around the word "modern."

The wall display refreshed to the homepage of a website—creation.com—which Langdon recognized as a recurring target of Edmond's wrath and ridicule. The organization was indeed strident in its Creationist evangelizing, but it was hardly a fair example of "the modern religious world."

Their mission statement read: "To proclaim the truth and authority of the Bible, and to affirm its reliability—in particular its Genesis history."

"This site," Edmond said, "is popular, influential, and it contains literally **dozens** of blogs about the dangers of revisiting Miller-Urey's work. Fortunately for the folks at creation.com, they have nothing to fear. Even if this experiment succeeds in producing life, it probably won't happen for another two billion years."

Edmond again held up the test tube. "As you can imagine, I would like nothing more than to fast-forward two billion years, reexamine this test tube, and prove all the Creationists wrong. Unfortunately, accomplishing that would require a time machine."

Edmond paused with a wry expression. "And so . . . I built one."

Langdon glanced over at Ambra, who had barely moved since the presentation started. Her dark eyes were transfixed by the screen.

"A time machine," Edmond said, "is not that difficult to build. Let me show you what I mean."

A deserted barroom appeared, and Edmond walked into it, moving to a pool table. The balls were racked in their usual triangular pattern, waiting to be broken. Edmond took a pool cue, bent over the table, and firmly struck the cue ball. It raced toward the waiting rack of balls.

An instant before it collided with the rack, Edmond shouted, "Stop!"

The cue ball froze in place—magically pausing a moment before impact.

"Right now," Edmond said, eyeing the frozen moment on the table, "if I asked you to predict which balls would fall into which pockets, could you do it? Of course not. There are literally thousands of possible breaks. But what if you had a time machine and could fast-forward fifteen seconds into the future, observe what happens with the pool balls, and then return? Believe it or not, my friends, we now have the technology to do that."

Edmond motioned to a series of tiny cameras on the edges of the table. "Using optical sensors to measure the cue ball's velocity, rotation, direction, and spin axis as it moves, I can obtain a mathematical snapshot of the ball's motion at any given instant. With that snapshot, I can make extremely accurate predictions about its future motion."

Langdon recalled using a golf simulator once that employed similar technology to predict with depressing accuracy his tendency to slice golf shots into the woods.

Edmond now pulled out a large smartphone. On the screen was the image of the pool table with its virtual cue ball frozen in place. A series of mathematical equations hung over the cue ball.

"Knowing the cue ball's exact mass, position, and velocity," Edmond said, "I can compute its interactions with the other balls and predict the outcome." He touched the screen, and the simulated cue ball sprang to life, smashing into the waiting rack of balls, scattering them, and sinking four balls in four different pockets.

"Four balls," Edmond said, eyeing the phone. "Pretty good shot." He glanced up at the audience. "Don't believe me?"

He snapped his fingers over the real pool table, and the cue ball released, streaking across the table, loudly smacking into the other balls, and sending them scattering. The same four balls fell in the same four pockets.

"Not quite a time machine," Edmond said with a grin, "but it does enable us to see the future. In addition, it lets me modify the laws of physics. For example, I can remove **friction** so that the balls will never slow down . . . rolling forever until every last ball eventually falls into a pocket."

He typed a few keys and launched the simulation again. This time, after the break, the ricocheting balls never slowed down, bouncing wildly around the table, eventually falling into pockets at random, until there were only two balls left careening around the table.

"And if I get tired of waiting for these last two balls to drop," Edmond said, "I can just fast-forward the process." He touched the screen, and the two remaining balls accelerated in a blur, streaking around the table until they finally fell into pockets. "This way I can see the future, long before it happens. Computer simulations are really just virtual time machines." He paused. "Of course, this is all fairly simple math in a small, closed system like a pool table. But what about a more complex system?"

Edmond held the Miller-Urey vial and smiled. "I'm guessing you can see where I'm going with this. Computer modeling is a kind of time machine, and it lets us see the future . . . perhaps even **billions** of years into the future."

Ambra shifted on the couch, her eyes never leaving Edmond's face.

"As you can imagine," Edmond said, "I am not the first scientist to dream of modeling the earth's primordial soup. In principle, it's an obvious experiment—but in practice, it's a nightmare of complexity."

Turbulent primordial seas appeared again amid

lightning, volcanoes, and massive waves. "Modeling the ocean's chemistry requires simulation at the **molecular** level. It would be like predicting the weather so accurately that we knew the precise location of every air molecule at any given moment. Any meaningful simulation of the primordial sea would therefore require a computer to understand not only the laws of physics—motion, thermodynamics, gravity, conservation of energy, and so forth—but chemistry as well, so it could accurately re-create the bonds that would form between every atom within a boiling ocean stew."

The view above the ocean now plunged beneath the waves, magnifying down into a single drop of water, where a turbulent swirl of virtual atoms and molecules were bonding and breaking apart.

"Sadly," Edmond said, reappearing on-screen, "a simulation confronted by this many possible permutations requires a massive level of processing power—far beyond the capability of any computer on earth." His eyes again twinkled with excitement. "That is . . . any computer except **one**."

A pipe organ rang out, playing the famous opening trill to Bach's Toccata and Fugue in D Minor along with a stunning wide-angle photograph of Edmond's massive two-story computer.

"E-Wave," Ambra whispered, speaking for the first time in many minutes.

Langdon stared at the screen. **Of course . . . it's brilliant.**

Accompanied by the dramatic organ soundtrack, Edmond launched into a fervent video tour of his supercomputer, finally unveiling his "quantum cube." The pipe organ climaxed with a thunderous chord; Edmond was literally "pulling out all the stops."

"The bottom line," he concluded, "is that E-Wave is capable of re-creating the Miller-Urey experiment in virtual reality, with startling accuracy. I cannot model the **entire** primordial ocean, of course, so I created the same five-liter closed system that Miller and Urey used."

A virtual flask of chemicals now appeared. The view of the liquid became magnified and remagnified until it reached the atomic level—showing atoms bouncing around in the heated mixture, bonding and rebonding, under the influences of temperature, electricity, and physical motion.

"This model incorporates everything we have learned about the primordial soup since the days of the Miller-Urey experiment—including the probable presence of hydroxyl radicals from electrified steam and carbonyl sulfides from volcanic activity, as well as the impact of 'reducing atmosphere' theories."

The virtual liquid on-screen continued to roil, and clusters of atoms began to form.

"Now let's fast-forward the process . . . ," Edmond said excitedly, and the video surged ahead in a blur, showing the formation of increasingly complex compounds. "After one week, we start to see the same amino acids that Miller and Urey saw." The image blurred again, moving faster now. "And then . . . at about the fifty-year mark, we start to see hints of the building blocks of RNA."

The liquid kept churning, faster and faster.

"And so I let it run!" Edmond shouted, his voice rising in intensity.

The molecules on-screen continued to bond, the complexity of the structures increasing as the program fast-forwarded centuries, millennia, millions of years. As the images raced ahead with blinding speed, Edmond called out joyfully, "And guess what eventually appeared inside this flask?"

Langdon and Ambra leaned forward with excitement.

Edmond's exuberant expression suddenly deflated. "Absolutely **nothing**," he said. "No life. No spontaneous chemical reaction. No moment of Creation. Just a jumbled mix of lifeless chemicals." He let out a heavy sigh. "I could draw only one logical conclusion." He stared dolefully into the camera. "Creating life . . . requires **God**."

Langdon stared in shock. **What is he saying?**

After a moment, a faint grin crept across Edmond's face. "Or," he said, "perhaps I had missed one key ingredient in the recipe."

CHAPTER 92

Ambra Vidal sat mesmerized, imagining the millions of people around the globe who, right now, just like her, were fully engrossed in Edmond's presentation.

"So, what ingredient was I missing?" Edmond asked. "Why did my primordial soup refuse to produce life? I had no idea—so I did what all successful scientists do. I asked somebody smarter than I am!"

A scholarly bespectacled woman appeared: Dr. Constance Gerhard, biochemist, Stanford University. "How can we create **life**?" The scientist laughed, shaking her head. "We can't! That's the point. When it comes to the process of creation—crossing that threshold where inanimate chemicals form living things—all of our science goes out the window. There is no mechanism in chemistry to explain how that happens. In fact, the very **notion** of cells organizing themselves into life-forms seems to be in direct conflict with the law of entropy!"

"**Entropy**," Edmond repeated, now appearing on a beautiful beach. "Entropy is just a fancy way of saying: **things fall apart.** In scientific language, we say 'an organized system inevitably deteriorates.'" He snapped his fingers and an intricate sand castle appeared at his feet. "I've just organized millions of sand grains into a castle. Let's see how the universe feels about that." Seconds later, a wave came in and washed away the castle. "Yup, the universe located my **organized** grains of sand and **disorganized** them, spreading them over the beach. This is entropy at work. Waves never crash onto beaches and deposit sand in the shape of a sand castle. Entropy dissolves structure. Sand castles never spontaneously appear in the universe, they only disappear."

Edmond snapped his fingers again and reappeared in an elegant kitchen. "When you heat coffee," he said, pulling a steaming cup from a microwave, "you focus heat energy into a mug. If you leave that mug on the counter for an hour, the heat dissipates into the room and spreads itself out evenly, like grains of sand on a beach. Entropy again. And the process is **irreversible**. No matter how long you wait, the universe will never magically reheat your coffee." Edmond smiled. "Nor will it unscramble a broken egg or rebuild an eroded sand castle."

Ambra recalled once seeing an art installation called **Entropy**—a line of old cement blocks, each more crumbled than the last, slowly disintegrating into a pile of rubble.

Dr. Gerhard, the spectacled scientist, reappeared. "We live in an **entropic** universe," she said, "a world whose physical laws **randomize,** not organize. So the question is this: How can lifeless chemicals magically organize themselves into complex life-forms? I've never been a religious person, but I have to admit, the existence of life is the **only** scientific mystery that has ever persuaded me to consider the idea of a Creator."

Edmond materialized, shaking his head. "I find it unnerving when smart people use the word 'Creator' . . ." He gave a good-natured shrug. "They do it, I know, because science simply has no good explanation for the beginnings of life. But trust me, if you're looking for some kind of invisible force that creates order in a chaotic universe, there are far simpler answers than **God**."

Edmond held out a paper plate on which splinters of iron filings had been scattered. He then produced a large magnet and held it beneath the plate. Instantly, the filings leaped into an organized arc, aligning perfectly with one another. "An invisible force just organized these filings. Was it God? No . . . it was electromagnetism."

Edmond now appeared beside a large trampoline. On its taut surface were scattered hundreds of marbles. "A random mess of marbles," he stated, "but if I do this . . ." He hoisted a bowling ball onto the trampoline's rim and rolled it onto the elastic fabric. Its weight created a deep indentation, and immediately the scattered marbles raced into the depression, forming a circle around the bowling ball. "The organizing hand of God?" Edmond paused. "No, again . . . it was just gravity."

He now appeared in close-up. "As it turns out, **life** is not the only example of the universe creating order. Nonliving molecules organize themselves all the time into complex structures."

A montage of images materialized—a tornado vortex, a snowflake, a rippled riverbed, a quartz crystal, the rings of Saturn.

"As you can see, sometimes the universe does organize matter—which seems to be the exact opposite of entropy." Edmond sighed. "So which is it? Does the universe prefer order? Or chaos?"

Edmond reappeared, now walking down a pathway toward the famed dome of Massachusetts Institute of Technology. "According to most physicists, the answer is **chaos**. Entropy is indeed king, and the universe is constantly disintegrating toward disorder. Kind of a depressing message." Edmond paused and turned with a grin. "But today I've come to meet the bright young physicist who believes there is a **twist** . . . a twist that may hold the key to how life began."

————

Jeremy England?

Langdon was startled to recognize the name of the physicist Edmond was now describing. The thirty-something MIT professor was currently the toast of Boston academia, having caused a global stir in a new field called quantum biology.

Coincidentally, Jeremy England and Robert Langdon shared the same prep school alma mater— Phillips Exeter Academy—and Langdon had first learned of the young physicist in the school's alumni magazine, in an article titled "Dissipation-Driven Adaptive Organization." Although Langdon had only skimmed the story and barely understood it, he recalled being intrigued to learn that his fellow "Exie" was both a brilliant physicist and also deeply religious—an Orthodox Jew.

Langdon began to understand why Edmond had been so interested in England's work.

On-screen, another man appeared, identified as NYU physicist Alexander Grosberg. "Our big hope," Grosberg said, "is that Jeremy England has identified the underlying physical principle driving the origin and evolution of life."

Langdon sat up a bit straighter upon hearing that, as did Ambra.

Another face appeared. "If England can demonstrate his theory to be true," said Pulitzer Prize–winning historian Edward J. Larson, "his name would be remembered forever. He could be the next Darwin."

My God. Langdon had known Jeremy England was making waves, but this sounded more like tsunamis.

Carl Franck, a physicist from Cornell, added, "Every thirty years or so we experience these gigantic steps forward . . . and this might be it."

A series of headlines flashed across the screen in rapid succession:

"MEET THE SCIENTIST WHO COULD DISPROVE GOD"
"CRUSHING CREATIONISM"
"THANKS, GOD—BUT WE DON'T NEED YOUR HELP ANYMORE"

The list of headlines continued, joined now by snippets from major scientific journals, all of which seemed to proclaim the same message: if Jeremy England could **prove** his new theory, the implications would be earth-shattering—not just for science but for religion as well.

Langdon eyed the final headline on the wall—from the online magazine **Salon,** January 3, 2015.

"GOD IS ON THE ROPES: THE BRILLIANT NEW SCIENCE THAT HAS CREATIONISTS AND THE CHRISTIAN RIGHT TERRIFIED."

> A Young MIT Professor Is Finishing Darwin's Task—and Threatening to Undo Everything the Wacky Right Holds Dear.

The screen refreshed, and Edmond reappeared, striding purposefully along the hallway of a university science facility. "So what is this gigantic step forward that has so terrified Creationists?"

Edmond beamed as he paused outside a door marked: ENGLANDLAB@MITPHYSICS.

"Let's go inside—and ask the man himself."

CHAPTER 93

The young man who now appeared on Edmond's display wall was physicist Jeremy England. He was tall and very thin, with an unkempt beard and a quietly bemused smile. He stood before a blackboard filled with mathematical equations.

"First," England said, his tone friendly and unassuming, "let me just say that this theory is not **proven**, it's just an idea." He gave a modest shrug. "Although, I admit, if we can ever prove that it's true, the implications are far-reaching."

For the next three minutes, the physicist outlined his new idea, which—like most paradigm-altering concepts—was unexpectedly simple.

Jeremy England's theory, if Langdon understood it correctly, was that the universe functioned with a singular directive. One goal.

To spread energy.

In the simplest terms, when the universe found areas of **focused** energy, it spread that energy out. The classic example, as Kirsch had mentioned, was the cup of hot coffee on the counter; it always cooled, dispersing its heat to the other molecules in the room in accordance with the Second Law of Thermodynamics.

Langdon suddenly understood why Edmond had asked him about the world's Creation myths—all of which contained imagery of energy and light spreading out infinitely and illuminating the darkness.

England believed that there was a twist, however, which related to **how** the universe spread energy.

"We know the universe promotes entropy and disorder," England said, "so we may be surprised to see so many examples of molecules **organizing** themselves."

On the screen, several images that had appeared earlier now returned—a tornado vortex, a rippled riverbed, a snowflake.

"All of these," England said, "are examples of 'dissipative structures'—collections of molecules that have arranged themselves in structures that help a system disperse its energy more efficiently."

England quickly illustrated how tornadoes were nature's way of dispelling a concentrated area of high pressure by converting it into a rotational force that eventually exhausted itself. The same held true for rippled riverbeds, which intercepted the energy of fast-moving currents and dissipated it. Snowflakes dispersed the sun's energy by forming multifaceted structures that reflected light chaotically outward in all directions.

"Simply stated," England continued, "matter self-organizes in an effort to better disperse energy." He smiled. "Nature—in an effort to promote **disorder**—creates little pockets of **order**. These pockets are structures that escalate the chaos of a system, and they thereby increase entropy."

Langdon had never thought of it until now, but England was right; the examples were everywhere. Langdon pictured a thundercloud. When the cloud became organized by a static electric charge, the universe created a bolt of lightning. In other words, the laws of physics created mechanisms to disperse energy. The lightning bolt dissipated the cloud's energy into the earth, spreading it out, thereby increasing the overall entropy of the system.

To efficiently create chaos, Langdon realized, **requires some order.**

Langdon wondered absently if nuclear bombs might be considered entropic tools—small pockets of carefully organized matter that served to create chaos. He flashed on the mathematical symbol for entropy and realized that it looked like an explosion or the Big Bang—an energetic dispersion in all directions.

"So where does this leave us?" England said. "What does entropy have to do with the origins of life?" He walked over to his chalkboard. "As it turns out, **life** is an exceptionally effective tool for dissipating energy."

England drew an image of the sun radiating energy down onto a tree.

"A tree, for example, absorbs the intense energy of the sun, uses it to grow, and then emits infrared light—a much less focused form of energy. Photosynthesis is a very effective entropy machine. The concentrated energy of the sun is dissolved and weakened by the tree, resulting in an overall increase in the entropy of the universe. The same can be said for all living organisms—including humans—which consume organized matter as food, convert it to energy, and then dissipate energy back into the universe as heat. In general terms," England concluded, "I believe life not only **obeys** the laws of physics, but that life **began** because of those laws."

Langdon felt a thrill as he pondered the logic, which seemed quite straightforward: If blazing sunlight hit a patch of fertile dirt, the physical laws of the earth would create a plant to help dissipate that energy. If deep-ocean sulfur vents created areas of boiling water, life would materialize in those locations and disseminate the energy.

"It is my hope," England added, "that one day we'll find a way to prove that life indeed spontaneously emerged from lifeless matter . . . a result of nothing more than the laws of physics."

Fascinating, Langdon mused. **A clear scientific theory of how life might have self-generated . . . without the hand of God.**

"I am a religious person," England said, "and yet my faith, like my science, has always been a work in progress. I consider this theory agnostic on questions of spirituality. I am simply trying to describe the way things 'are' in the universe; I will leave the spiritual implications to the clerics and philosophers."

Wise young man, Langdon thought. **If ever his theory could be proven, it would have a bombshell effect on the world.**

"For the moment," England said, "everyone can relax. For obvious reasons, this is an extremely difficult theory to prove. My team and I have a few ideas for modeling dissipation-driven systems in the future, but at the moment, we're still years away."

England's image faded, and Edmond reappeared on the screen, standing beside his quantum computer. "I, however, am **not** years away. This type of modeling is precisely what I've been working on."

He walked toward his workstation. "If Professor England's theory is correct, then the entire operating system of the cosmos could be summed up by a single overriding command: spread energy!"

Edmond sat down at his desk and began typing furiously on his oversized keyboard. The displays before him filled with alien-looking computer code. "I took several weeks and reprogrammed the entire experiment that had previously failed. I embedded into the system a fundamental goal—a raison d'être; I told the system to dissipate energy at all costs. I urged the computer to be as creative as it could possibly be in its quest to increase entropy in the primordial soup. And I gave it permission to build whatever **tools** it thought it might need to accomplish that."

Edmond stopped typing and spun around in his chair, facing his audience. "Then I ran the model, and something incredible happened. It turned out that I had successfully identified the 'missing ingredient' in my virtual primordial soup."

Langdon and Ambra both stared intently at the display wall as the animated graphic of Edmond's computer model began to play. Again, the visual plunged deep into the churning primordial soup, magnifying down to the subatomic realm, seeing the chemicals bouncing around, binding and rebinding with one another.

"As I fast-forwarded the process and simulated the passage of hundreds of years," Edmond said, "I saw Miller-Urey's amino acids taking shape."

Langdon was not knowledgeable about chemistry, but he certainly recognized the on-screen image as a basic protein chain. As the process continued, he watched as increasingly complex molecules took shape, bonding into a kind of honeycombed chain of hexagons.

"Nucleotides!" Edmond shouted as the hexagons continued to fuse. "We're watching the passage of thousands of years! And speeding ahead, we see the first faint hints of structure!"

As he spoke, one of the nucleotide chains began wrapping around itself and curling into a spiral. "See that?!" Edmond shouted. "Millions of years have passed, and the system is trying to build a structure! The system is trying to build a structure to dissipate its energy, just like England predicted!"

As the model progressed, Langdon was stunned to see the little spiral become a **twin** spiral, expanding its structure into the famous double-helix shape of the most famous chemical compound on earth.

"My God, Robert . . . ," Ambra whispered, wide-eyed. "Is that . . ."

"DNA," Edmond announced, freezing the model midframe. "There it is. DNA—the basis for all life. The living code of biology. And **why**, you ask, would a system build DNA in an effort to dissipate energy? Well, because many hands make light work! A forest of trees diffuses more sunlight than a single tree. If you're an entropy tool, the easiest way to do more work is to make copies of yourself."

Edmond's face appeared on-screen now. "As I ran this model forward, from this point on, I witnessed something absolutely magical . . . **Darwinian evolution took off!**"

He paused for several seconds. "And why wouldn't it?" he continued. "Evolution is the way the universe continually tests and refines its tools. The most efficient tools survive and replicate themselves, improving constantly, becoming more and more complex and efficient. Eventually, some tools look like trees, and some look like, well . . . **us.**"

Edmond now appeared floating in the darkness of space with the blue orb of earth hovering behind him. "Where do we come from?" he asked. "The truth is— we come from nowhere . . . and from everywhere. We come from the **same laws of physics** that create life across the cosmos. We are not special. We exist with or without God. We are the inevitable result of entropy. Life is not the **point** of the universe. Life is simply what the universe creates and reproduces in order to dissipate energy."

Langdon felt strangely uncertain, wondering if he had fully processed the implications of what Edmond was saying. Admittedly, this simulation would result in a massive paradigm shift and would certainly cause upheavals across many academic disciplines. But when it came to **religion,** he wondered whether Edmond would change people's views. For centuries, most of the devout had looked past vast amounts of scientific data and rational logic in defense of their faith.

Ambra seemed to be struggling with her own reactions, her expression somewhere between wide-eyed wonder and guarded indecision.

"Friends," Edmond said, "if you've followed what I've just shown you, then you understand its profound significance. And if you're still uncertain, stay with me, because it turns out that this discovery has led to yet another revelation, one that is even more significant."

He paused.

"Where we come from . . . is not nearly as startling as where we are going."

CHAPTER 94

The sound of running footsteps echoed through the subterranean basilica as a Guardia agent sprinted toward the three men gathered in the deepest recesses of the church.

"Your Majesty," he called out, breathless. "Edmond Kirsch . . . the video . . . is being broadcast."

The king turned in his wheelchair, and Prince Julián spun around as well.

Valdespino gave a disheartened sigh. **It was only a matter of time,** he reminded himself. Still, his soul felt heavy to know that the world was now seeing the same video that he had seen in the Montserrat library with al-Fadl and Köves.

Where do we come from? Kirsch's claim of a "Godless origin" was both arrogant and blasphemous; it would have a ruinous effect on the human desire to aspire to a higher ideal and emulate the God who created us in His image.

Tragically, Kirsch had not stopped there. He had followed up this first desecration with a second, far more dangerous one—proposing a profoundly disturbing answer to the question **Where are we going?**

Kirsch's prediction for the future was calamitous . . . so disturbing that Valdespino and his colleagues had urged Kirsch not to release it. Even if the futurist's data were accurate, sharing it with the world would cause irreversible damage.

Not just for the faithful, Valdespino knew, **but for every human being on earth.**

CHAPTER 95

No God required, Langdon thought, replaying what Edmond had said. **Life arose spontaneously from the laws of physics.**

The notion of spontaneous generation had long been debated—theoretically—by some of science's greatest minds, and yet tonight Edmond Kirsch had presented a starkly persuasive argument that spontaneous generation had actually **happened.**

Nobody has ever come close to demonstrating it . . . or even explaining how it might have occurred.

On-screen, Edmond's simulation of the primordial soup was now teeming with tiny virtual life-forms.

"Observing my budding model," Edmond narrated, "I wondered what would happen if I let it run? Would it eventually explode out of its flask and produce the entire animal kingdom, including the human species? And what if I let it run beyond that? If I waited long enough, would it produce the next step in human evolution and tell us **where we are going?**"

Edmond appeared again beside E-Wave. "Sadly, not even **this** computer can handle a model of that magnitude, so I had to find a way to narrow the simulation. And I ended up borrowing a technique from an unlikely source . . . none other than Walt Disney."

The screen now cut to a primitive, two-dimensional, black-and-white cartoon. Langdon recognized it as the 1928 Disney classic **Steamboat Willie.**

"The art form of 'cartooning' has advanced rapidly over the past ninety years—from rudimentary Mickey Mouse flip-books to the richly animated films of today."

Beside the old cartoon appeared a vibrant, hyper-realistic scene from a recent animated feature.

"This leap in quality is akin to the three-thousand-year evolution from cave drawings to Michelangelo's masterpieces. As a futurist, I am fascinated by **any** skill that makes rapid advances," Edmond continued. "The technique that makes this leap possible, I learned, is called 'tweening.' It's a computer animation shortcut in which an artist asks a computer to generate the intermediate frames between two key images, morphing the first image smoothly into the second image, essentially filling in the gaps. Rather than having to draw every single frame by hand—which can be likened here to modeling every tiny step in the evolutionary process—artists nowadays can draw a few of the key frames . . . and then ask the computer to take its best guess at the intermediary steps and fill in the rest of the evolution.

"That's **tweening,**" Edmond declared. "It's an obvious application of computing power, but when I heard about it, I had a revelation and I realized it was the key to unlocking our future."

Ambra turned to Langdon with a questioning look. "Where is this going?"

Before Langdon could consider it, a new image had appeared on-screen.

"Human evolution," Edmond said. "This image is a 'flip movie' of sorts. Thanks to science, we have constructed several key frames—chimpanzees, **Australopithecus**, **Homo habilis**, **Homo erectus**, Neanderthal man—and yet the transitions between these species remain murky."

Precisely as Langdon had anticipated, Edmond outlined an idea to use computer "tweening" to fill in the gaps in human evolution. He described how various international genome projects—human, Paleo-Eskimo, Neanderthal, chimpanzee—had used bone fragments to map the complete genetic structure of nearly a dozen intermediary steps between chimpanzee and **Homo sapiens**.

"I knew if I used these existing primitive genomes as **key frames**," Edmond said, "I could program E-Wave to build an evolutionary model that linked all of them together—a kind of evolutionary connect-the-dots. And so I began with a simple trait—brain size—a very accurate general indicator of intellectual evolution."

A graphic materialized on-screen.

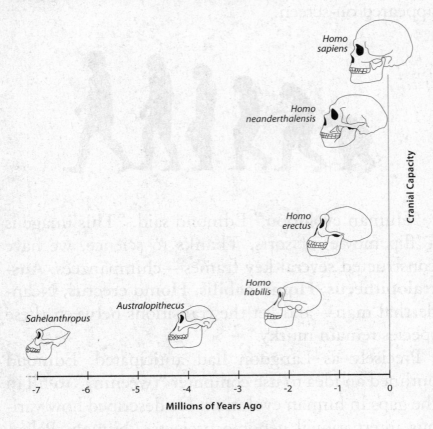

"In addition to mapping general structural parameters like brain size, E-Wave mapped thousands of subtler genetic markers that influence cognitive abilities—markers like spatial recognition, range of vocabulary, long-term memory, and processing speed."

The display now flashed a rapid succession of similar graphs, all showing the same exponential increase.

"Then E-Wave assembled an unprecedented simulation of intellectual evolution over time." Edmond's face reappeared. "'So what?' you ask. 'Why do we care about identifying the process by which humans became intellectually dominant?' We care because if we can establish a **pattern,** a computer can tell us where that pattern will lead in the future." He smiled. "If I say two, four, six, eight . . . you reply **ten.** I have essentially asked E-Wave to predict what 'ten' will look like. Once E-Wave has simulated intellectual evolution, I can ask the obvious question: What comes next? What will human intellect look like five hundred years from now? In other words: Where are we going?"

Langdon found himself spellbound by the prospect, and while he didn't know enough about genetics or computer modeling to assess the accuracy of Edmond's predictions, the concept was ingenious.

"The evolution of a species," Edmond said, "is always linked to that organism's **environment,** and so I asked E-Wave to overlay a second model—an environmental simulation of today's world—easy to do when all of our news about culture, politics, science, weather, and technology is broadcast online. I asked the computer to pay special attention to those factors that would most affect the future development of the human brain—emergent drugs, new health technologies, pollution, cultural factors, and so on." Edmond paused. "And then," he declared, "I ran the program."

The futurist's entire face now filled the screen. He stared directly into the camera. "When I ran the model . . . something very unexpected happened." He glanced away, almost perceptibly, and then back to the camera. "Something deeply upsetting."

Langdon heard Ambra draw a startled breath.

"So I ran it again," Edmond said, frowning. "Unfortunately, the same thing happened."

Langdon sensed true fear in Edmond's eyes.

"So I reworked the parameters," he said. "I retooled the program, altering every variable, and I ran it again and again. But I kept getting the same result."

Langdon wondered if maybe Edmond had discovered that human intellect, after aeons of progress, was now on the **decline**. There were certainly alarming indicators to suggest this might be true.

"I was distressed by the data," Edmond said, "and couldn't make sense of it. So I asked the computer for an analysis. E-Wave conveyed its evaluation in the clearest way it knew how. It drew me a picture."

The screen refreshed to show a graphic timeline of animal evolution beginning some one hundred million years ago. It was a complex and colorful tapestry of horizontal bubbles that expanded and contracted over time, depicting how species appeared and disappeared. The left side of the graph was dominated by the dinosaurs—already at the height of their development at that point in history—who were represented by the thickest of all the bubbles, which grew thicker through time before abruptly collapsing some sixty-five million years ago with the mass dinosaur extinction.

"This is a timeline of dominant life-forms on earth," Edmond said, "presented in terms of species population, food-chain position, interspecific supremacy, and overall influence on the planet. Essentially, it is a visual representation of who's running the show on earth at any given time."

Langdon's eye traced along the diagram as different bubbles expanded and contracted, indicating how various large populations of species had appeared, proliferated, and disappeared from existence.

"The dawn of **Homo sapiens**," Edmond said, "occurs at 200,000 BC, but we were not influential enough to appear in this graph until about sixty-five thousand years ago, when we invented the bow and arrow and became more efficient predators."

Langdon scanned ahead to the 65,000 BC mark, where a thin blue bubble appeared, marking **Homo sapiens**. The bubble expanded very slowly, almost imperceptibly, until around 1000 BC, when it quickly got thicker, and then seemed to expand exponentially.

By the time his eye reached the far right of the diagram, the blue bubble had swollen to occupy nearly the entire width of the screen.

Modern-day humans, Langdon thought. **By far, the most dominant and influential species on earth.**

"Not surprisingly," Edmond said, "in the year 2000, when this graph ends, humans are depicted as the prevailing species on the planet. Nothing even comes close to us." He paused. "However, you can see traces of a new bubble appearing . . . **here.**"

The graphic zoomed in to show a tiny black shape starting to form above the swollen blue bubble of humanity.

"A new species has already entered the picture," Edmond said.

Langdon saw the black blob, but it looked insignificant in comparison to the blue bubble—a tiny remora on the back of a blue whale.

"I realize," Edmond said, "that this newcomer looks trivial, but if we move forward in time from 2000 to the present day, you will see that our newcomer is here already, and it has been quietly growing."

The diagram expanded until it reached the current date, and Langdon felt his chest tighten. The black bubble had expanded enormously over the past two decades. Now it claimed more than a quarter of the screen, jostling with **Homo sapiens** for influence and dominance.

"What **is** that?!" Ambra exclaimed in a worried half whisper.

Langdon answered, "I have no idea . . . some kind of dormant virus?" His mind ran through a list of aggressive viruses that had savaged various regions of the world, but Langdon could not imagine a species growing this fast on earth without being noticed. **A bacterium from space?**

"This new species is insidious," Edmond said. "It propagates exponentially. It expands its territory continuously. And most importantly, it **evolves** . . . much faster than humans do." Edmond stared into the camera again, his expression deadly serious. "Unfortunately, if I let this simulation roll ahead to show us the future, even just a few decades from now, **this** is what it reveals."

The diagram expanded again, now displaying the timeline up until 2050.

Langdon jumped to his feet, staring in disbelief.

"My God," Ambra whispered, covering her mouth in horror.

The diagram clearly showed the menacing black bubble expanding at a staggering rate, and then, by the year 2050, entirely swallowing up the light blue bubble of humanity.

"I'm sorry to have to show you this," Edmond said, "but in every model I ran, the same thing happened. The human species evolved to our current point in history, and then, very abruptly, a new species materialized, and erased us from the earth."

Langdon stood before the horrific graphic, trying to remind himself that it was just a computer model. Images like this, he knew, had the power to affect humans on a visceral level that raw data could not, and Edmond's diagram had an air of finality to it— as if human extinction were already a fait accompli.

"My friends," Edmond said, his tone somber enough to be warning of an imminent asteroid collision. "Our species is on the brink of extinction. I have spent my life making predictions, and in this case, I've analyzed the data at every level. I can tell you with a very high degree of certainty that the human race as we know it will not be here fifty years from now."

Langdon's initial shock now gave way to disbelief— and anger—at his friend. **What are you doing, Edmond?! This is irresponsible! You built a computer model—a thousand things could be wrong**

with your data. People respect and believe you . . .
you're going to create mass hysteria.

"And one more thing," Edmond said, his mood
darkening even further. "If you look carefully at the
simulation, you will see that this new species does not
entirely erase us. More accurately . . . it **absorbs** us."

CHAPTER 96

T he species absorbs us?

In stunned silence, Langdon tried to imagine what Edmond meant by these words; the phrase conjured terrifying images of the **Alien** science-fiction movies, in which humans were used as living incubators for a dominant species.

On his feet now, Langdon glanced back at Ambra, who was huddled on the couch, clutching her knees, her keen eyes analyzing the illustration on the screen. Langdon strained to imagine any other interpretation of the data; the conclusion seemed inevitable.

According to Edmond's simulation, the human race would be swallowed up by a new species over the course of the next few decades. And even more frightening, this new species was already living on earth, quietly growing.

"Obviously," Edmond said, "I could not go public with this information until I could identify this new species. So I delved into the data. After countless simulations, I was able to pinpoint the mysterious newcomer."

The screen refreshed with a simple diagram that Langdon recognized from grade school—the taxonomic hierarchy of living things—segmented into

the "Six Kingdoms of Life"—Animalia, Plantae, Pro-
tista, Eubacteria, Archaebacteria, Fungi.

"Once I identified this flourishing new organism,"
Edmond continued, "I realized that it had far too
many diverse forms to be called a **species**. Taxonomi-
cally speaking, it was too broad to be called an order.
Nor even a phylum." Edmond stared into the camera.
"I realized that our planet was now being inhabited
by something far bigger. What could only be labeled
an entirely new **kingdom**."

In a flash, Langdon realized what Edmond was
describing.

The Seventh Kingdom.

Awestruck, Langdon watched as Edmond delivered the news to the world, describing an emergent
kingdom that Langdon had recently heard about in
a TED Talk by digital-culture writer Kevin Kelly.
Prophesied by some of the earliest science-fiction
writers, this new kingdom of life came with a twist.

It was a kingdom of **nonliving** species.

These lifeless species evolved almost exactly as if
they were living—becoming gradually more complex, adapting to and propagating in new environments, testing new variations, some surviving, others
going extinct. A perfect mirror of Darwinian adaptive change, these new organisms had developed at
a blinding rate and now made up an entirely new
kingdom—the Seventh Kingdom—which took its
place beside Animalia and the others.

It was called: **Technium.**

Edmond now launched into a dazzling description of the planet's newest kingdom—which included all of **technology**. He described how new machines thrived or died by the rules of Darwin's "survival of the fittest"—constantly adapting to their environments, developing new features for survival, and, if successful, replicating as fast as they could in order to monopolize the available resources.

"The fax machine has gone the way of the dodo bird," Edmond explained. "And the iPhone will survive only if it keeps outperforming its competition. Typewriters and steam engines died in changing environments, but the **Encyclopaedia Britannica** evolved, its cumbersome thirty-two-volume set sprouting digital feet and, like the lungfish, expanding into uncharted territory, where it now thrives."

Langdon flashed on his childhood Kodak camera—once the T. rex of personal photography—obliterated overnight by the meteoric arrival of digital imaging.

"Half a billion years ago," Edmond continued, "our planet experienced a sudden eruption of life—the Cambrian Explosion—in which most of the planet's species came into existence virtually overnight. Today, we are witnessing the Cambrian Explosion of the Technium. New species of technology are being born daily, evolving at a blinding rate, and each new technology becomes a tool to create other new technologies. The invention of the computer has helped us build astonishing new tools, from smartphones to spaceships to robotic surgeons. We are witnessing a burst of innovation that is happening faster than our minds can comprehend. And **we** are the creators of this new kingdom—the Technium."

The screen now returned to the disturbing image of the expanding black bubble that was consuming the blue one. **Technology kills off humanity?** Langdon found the idea terrifying, and yet his gut told him it was highly improbable. To him, the notion of a dystopian Terminator-like future where machines hunted people to extinction seemed counter-Darwinian. **Humans control technology; humans have survival instincts; humans will never permit technology to overrun us.**

Even as this sequence of logical thoughts passed through his mind, Langdon knew he was being naive. Having interacted with Edmond's AI creation Winston, Langdon had been given a rare glimpse at the state of the art in artificial intelligence. And while Winston clearly served Edmond's wishes, Langdon wondered how long it would be until machines like Winston started making decisions that satisfied their own wishes.

"Obviously, many people before me have predicted the kingdom of technology," Edmond said, "but I have succeeded in **modeling** it . . . and being able to show what it will do to us." He motioned to the darker bubble, which, by the year 2050, spanned the entire screen and indicated a total dominance of the planet. "I must admit, at first glance, this simulation paints a pretty grim picture . . ."

Edmond paused, and a familiar twinkle returned to his eye.

"But we really must look a bit closer," he said.

The display now zoomed in on the dark bubble, magnifying it until Langdon could see that the massive sphere was no longer jet black, but a deep purple.

"As you can see, the black bubble of technology, as it consumes the human bubble, assumes a different hue—a shade of purple—as if the two colors have blended together evenly."

Langdon wondered if this was good news or bad news.

"What you are seeing here is a rare evolutionary process known as obligate endosymbiosis," Edmond said. "Normally, evolution is a **bifurcating** process—a species splits into two new species—but sometimes, in rare instances, if two species cannot survive without each other, the process occurs in reverse . . . and instead of one species bifurcating, two species **fuse** into one."

The fusion reminded Langdon of syncretism—the process by which two different religions blended to form an entirely new faith.

"If you don't believe that humans and technology will fuse," Edmond said, "take a look around you."

The screen displayed a rapid-fire slide show—images of people clutching cell phones, wearing virtual-reality goggles, adjusting Bluetooth devices in their ears; runners with music players strapped to their arms; a family dinner table with a "smart speaker" centerpiece; a child in a crib playing with a computer tablet.

"These are just the primitive beginnings of this symbiosis," Edmond said. "We are now starting to embed computer chips directly into our brains, inject our blood with tiny cholesterol-eating nanobots that live in us forever, build synthetic limbs that are controlled by our minds, use genetic editing tools like CRISPR to modify our genome, and, quite literally, engineer an enhanced version of ourselves."

Edmond's expression seemed almost joyful now, radiating passion and excitement.

"Human beings are evolving into something **different**," he declared. "We are becoming a hybrid species—a fusion of biology and technology. The same tools that today live **outside** our bodies— smartphones, hearing aids, reading glasses, most pharmaceuticals—in fifty years will be incorporated into our bodies to such an extent that we will no longer be able to consider ourselves **Homo sapiens.**"

A familiar image reappeared behind Edmond— the single-file progression from chimpanzee to modern man.

"In the blink of an eye," Edmond said, "we will become the next page in the flip-book of evolution. And when we do, we will look back on today's **Homo sapiens** the same way we now look back at Neanderthal man. New technologies like cybernetics, synthetic intelligence, cryonics, molecular engineering, and virtual reality will forever change what it means to be **human**. And I realize there are those of you who believe you, as **Homo sapiens,** are God's chosen species. I can understand that this news may feel like the end of the world to you. But I beg you, please believe me . . . the future is actually much **brighter** than you imagine."

With a sudden outpouring of hope and optimism, the great futurist launched into a dazzling description of tomorrow, a vision of a future unlike any Langdon had ever dared imagine.

Edmond persuasively described a future where technology had become so inexpensive and ubiquitous that it erased the gap between the haves and the have-nots. A future where environmental technologies provided billions of people with drinking water, nutritious food, and access to clean energy. A future where diseases like Edmond's cancer were eradicated, thanks to genomic medicine. A future where the awesome power of the Internet was finally harnessed for education, even in the most remote corners of the world. A future where assembly-line robotics would free workers from mind-numbing jobs so they could pursue more rewarding fields that would open up in areas not yet imagined. And, above all, a future in which breakthrough technologies began creating such an abundance of humankind's critical resources that warring over them would no longer be necessary.

As he listened to Edmond's vision for tomorrow, Langdon felt an emotion he had not experienced in years. It was a sensation that he knew millions of other viewers were feeling at this very instant as well—an unexpected upwelling of optimism about the future.

"I have but one regret about this coming age of miracles." Edmond's voice cracked with sudden emotion. "I regret that I will not be here to witness it. Unbeknownst even to my close friends, I have been quite ill for some time now . . . it seems I will not live forever, as I had planned." He managed a poignant smile. "By the time you see this, it is likely I will have only weeks to live . . . maybe only days. Please know, my friends, that addressing you tonight has been the greatest honor and pleasure of my life. I thank you for listening."

Ambra was standing now, close to Langdon's side, both of them watching with admiration and sadness as their friend addressed the world.

"We are now perched on a strange cusp of history," Edmond continued, "a time when the world feels like it's been turned upside down, and nothing is quite as we imagined. But uncertainty is always a precursor to sweeping change; transformation is always preceded by upheaval and fear. I urge you to place your faith in the human capacity for creativity and love, because these two forces, when combined, possess the power to illuminate any darkness."

Langdon glanced at Ambra and noticed the tears streaming down her face. He gently reached over and put an arm around her, watching as his dying friend spoke his final words to the world.

"As we move into an undefined tomorrow," Edmond said, "we will transform ourselves into something greater than we can yet imagine, with powers beyond our wildest dreams. And as we do, may we never forget the wisdom of Churchill, who warned us: 'The price of greatness . . . is **responsibility.**'"

The words resonated for Langdon, who often feared the human race would not be responsible enough to wield the intoxicating tools it was now inventing.

"Although I am an atheist," Edmond said, "before I leave you, I ask your indulgence in allowing me to read you a prayer I recently wrote."

Edmond wrote a prayer?

"I call it 'Prayer for the Future.'" Edmond closed his eyes and spoke slowly, with startling assurance. "May our philosophies keep pace with our technologies. May our compassion keep pace with our powers. And may love, not fear, be the engine of change."

With that, Edmond Kirsch opened his eyes. "Goodbye, my friends, and thank you," he said. "And dare I say . . . Godspeed."

Edmond looked into the camera for a moment, and then his face disappeared into a churning sea of white noise. Langdon stared into the static-filled display and felt an overwhelming surge of pride in his friend.

Standing beside Ambra, Langdon pictured the millions of people all over the world who had just witnessed Edmond's stirring tour de force. Strangely, he found himself wondering if perhaps Edmond's final night on earth had unfolded in the best of all possible ways.

ommander Diego Garza stood against the back wall of Mónica Martín's basement office and stared blankly at the television screen. His hands were still bound in handcuffs, and two Guardia agents flanked him closely, having acquiesced to Mónica Martín's appeal to let him leave the armory so he could watch Kirsch's announcement.

Garza had witnessed the futurist's spectacle along with Mónica, Suresh, a half-dozen Guardia agents, and an unlikely group of palace night staff who had all dropped their duties and dashed downstairs to watch.

Now, on the TV before Garza, the raw static that had concluded Kirsch's presentation had been replaced by a mosaic grid of news feeds from around the world—newscasters and pundits breathlessly recapping the futurist's claims and launching into their own inevitable analyses—all of them talking at once, creating an unintelligible cacophony.

Across the room, one of Garza's senior agents entered, scanned the crowd, located the commander, and strode briskly over to him. Without explanation, the guard removed Garza's handcuffs and held out a cell phone. "A call for you, sir—Bishop Valdespino."

Garza stared down at the device. Considering the bishop's clandestine exit from the palace and the incriminating text found on his phone, Valdespino was the last person Garza had expected to call him tonight.

"This is Diego," he answered.

"Thank you for answering," the bishop said, sounding weary. "I realize you've had an unpleasant night."

"Where are you?" Garza demanded.

"In the mountains. Outside the basilica at the Valley of the Fallen. I just met with Prince Julián and His Majesty the king."

Garza could not imagine what the king was doing at the Valley of the Fallen at this hour, particularly given his condition. "I assume you know the king had me arrested?"

"Yes. It was a regrettable error, which we have remedied."

Garza looked down at his unmanacled wrists.

"His Majesty asked me to call and extend his apologies. I will be watching over him here at the Hospital El Escorial. I'm afraid his time is drawing to a close."

As is yours, Garza thought. "You should be advised that Suresh found a text on your phone—quite an incriminatory one. I believe the ConspiracyNet.com website plans to release it soon. I suspect the authorities will come to arrest you."

Valdespino sighed deeply. "Yes, the text. I should

have sought you out the instant it arrived this morning. Please trust me when I tell you that I had nothing to do with Edmond Kirsch's murder, nor with the deaths of my two colleagues."

"But the text clearly implicates you—"

"I'm being **framed,** Diego," the bishop interrupted. "Someone has gone to great lengths to make me look complicit."

Although Garza had never imagined Valdespino capable of murder, the notion of someone framing him made little sense. "Who would try to frame you?"

"That I don't know," the bishop said, sounding suddenly very old and bewildered. "I'm not sure it matters anymore. My reputation has been destroyed; my dearest friend, the king, is close to death; and there is not much more this night can take from me." There was an eerie finality to Valdespino's tone.

"Antonio . . . are you okay?"

Valdespino sighed. "Not really, Commander. I am tired. I doubt I will survive the coming investigation. And even if I do, the world seems to have outgrown its need for me."

Garza could hear the heartbreak in the old bishop's voice.

"A tiny favor, if I may," Valdespino added. "At the moment, I am trying to serve **two** kings—one leaving his throne, the other ascending to it. Prince Julián has been attempting all night to connect with his fiancée. If you could find a way to reach Ambra Vidal, our future king would be forever in your debt."

On the sprawling plaza outside the mountain church, Bishop Valdespino gazed down over the darkened Valley of the Fallen. A predawn mist was already creeping up the pine-studded ravines, and somewhere in the distance the shrill call of a bird of prey pierced the night.

Monk vulture, Valdespino thought, oddly amused by the sound. The bird's plaintive wail seemed eerily appropriate at the moment, and the bishop wondered if perhaps the world was trying to tell him something.

Nearby, Guardia agents were wheeling the wearied king to his vehicle for transport back to the Hospital El Escorial.

I will come watch over you, my friend, the bishop thought. **That is, if they permit me.**

The Guardia agents glanced up repeatedly from the glow of their cell phones, their eyes continually returning to Valdespino, as if they suspected they would soon be called upon to make his arrest.

And yet I am innocent, the bishop thought, secretly suspecting he had been set up by one of Kirsch's godless tech-savvy followers. **The growing community of atheists enjoys nothing more than casting the Church in the role of the villain.**

Deepening the bishop's suspicion was news he had just heard about Kirsch's presentation tonight. Unlike the video Kirsch had played for Valdespino in the Montserrat library, it seemed tonight's version had ended on a hopeful note.

Kirsch tricked us.

A week ago, the presentation Valdespino and his colleagues had watched had been stopped prematurely . . . ending with a terrifying graphic that predicted the extermination of all humans.

A cataclysmic annihilation.

The long-prophesied apocalypse.

Even though Valdespino believed the prediction to be a lie, he knew that countless people would accept it as proof of impending doom.

Throughout history, fearful believers had fallen prey to apocalyptic prophecies; doomsday cults committed mass suicide to avoid the coming horrors, and devout fundamentalists ran up credit card debt believing the end was near.

There is nothing more damaging for children than the loss of hope, Valdespino thought, recalling how the combination of God's love and the promise of heaven had been the most uplifting force in his own childhood. **I was created by God**, he had learned as a child, **and one day I will live forever in God's kingdom.**

Kirsch had proclaimed the opposite: **I am a cosmic accident, and soon I will be dead.**

Valdespino had been deeply concerned about the damage Kirsch's message would do to the poor souls who did not enjoy the futurist's wealth and privilege— those who struggled daily just to eat or to provide for their children, those who required a glimmer of divine hope just to get out of bed every day and face their difficult lives.

Why Kirsch would show the clerics an apocalyptic ending remained a mystery to Valdespino. **Perhaps Kirsch was merely trying to protect his big surprise,** he thought. **Or else he simply wanted to torture us a bit.**

Either way, the damage had been done.

Valdespino gazed across the plaza and watched Prince Julián lovingly assist his father into the van. The young prince had handled the king's confession remarkably well.

His Majesty's decades-old secret.

Bishop Valdespino, of course, had known the king's dangerous truth for years and had scrupulously protected it. Tonight, the king had decided to bare his soul to his only son. By choosing to do it **here**— within this mountaintop shrine to intolerance—the king had performed an act of symbolic defiance.

Now, as Valdespino gazed down into the deep ravine below, he felt deathly alone . . . as if he could simply step off the edge and fall forever into the welcoming darkness. He knew if he **did,** however, Kirsch's band of atheists would gleefully declare that Valdespino had lost his faith in the wake of tonight's scientific announcement.

My faith will never die, Mr. Kirsch.

It dwells beyond your realm of science.

Besides, if Kirsch's prophecy about technology's takeover were true, humanity was about to enter a period of almost unimaginable ethical ambiguity.

We will need faith and moral guidance now more than ever.

As Valdespino walked back across the plaza to join the king and Prince Julián, an overwhelming feeling of exhaustion settled deep within his bones.

At that moment, for the first time in his life, Bishop Valdespino wanted simply to lie down, close his eyes, and fall asleep forever.

CHAPTER 98

I nside the Barcelona Supercomputing Center, a stream of commentary flowed across Edmond's display wall faster than Robert Langdon could process it. Moments ago, the screen of static had given way to a chaotic mosaic of talking heads and newscasters—a rapid-fire assault of clips from around the world—each one blossoming out of the matrix to take center stage, and then just as quickly dissolving back into the white noise.

Langdon stood beside Ambra as a photo of physicist Stephen Hawking materialized on the wall, his unmistakable computerized voice proclaiming, "It is not necessary to invoke God to set the universe going. Spontaneous creation is the reason there is something rather than nothing."

Hawking was replaced just as quickly by a female priest, apparently broadcasting from her home via computer. "We must remember that these simulations prove **nothing** about God. They prove only that Edmond Kirsch will stop at nothing to destroy the moral compass of our species. Since the beginning of time, world religions have been humanity's most important organizing principle, a road map for civilized society, and our original source of ethics and morality. By undermining religion, Kirsch is undermining human **goodness**!"

Seconds later, a viewer's response text crawled across the bottom of the screen: RELIGION CANNOT CLAIM MORALITY AS ITS OWN . . . I AM A GOOD PERSON BECAUSE I AM A GOOD PERSON! GOD HAS NOTHING TO DO WITH IT!

That image was replaced by one of a USC geology professor. "Once upon a time," the man was saying, "humans believed that the earth was flat and ships venturing across the seas risked sailing off the edge. However, when we proved that the earth was round, the flat-earth advocates were eventually silenced. Creationists are today's flat-earth advocates, and I would be shocked if anyone still believes in Creationism a hundred years from now."

A young man interviewed on the street declared to the camera: "I am a Creationist, and I believe that tonight's discovery proves that a benevolent Creator designed the universe **specifically** to support life."

Astrophysicist Neil deGrasse Tyson—appearing in an old clip from the **Cosmos** television show—declared good-naturedly, "If a Creator designed our universe to support life, he did a terrible job. In the vast, vast majority of the cosmos, life would die instantly from lack of atmosphere, gamma-ray bursts, deadly pulsars, and crushing gravitational fields. Believe me, the universe is no Garden of Eden."

Listening to the onslaught, Langdon felt as if the world outside were suddenly spinning off its axis.

Chaos.

Entropy.

"Professor Langdon?" A familiar British voice spoke from the speaker overhead. "Ms. Vidal?"

Langdon had almost forgotten about Winston, who had fallen silent during the presentation.

"Please don't be alarmed," Winston continued. "But I've let the police into the building."

Langdon looked through the glass wall and saw a stream of local authorities entering the sanctuary, all of them stopping short and staring up at the massive computer in disbelief.

"Why?!" Ambra demanded.

"The Royal Palace has just issued a statement saying that you were not kidnapped after all. The authorities now have orders to protect you both, Ms. Vidal. Two Guardia agents have just arrived as well. They would like to help you make contact with Prince Julián. They have a number where you can reach him."

On the ground floor, Langdon saw two Guardia agents now entering.

Ambra closed her eyes, clearly wanting to disappear.

"Ambra," Langdon whispered. "You need to talk to the prince. He's your fiancé. He's worried about you."

"I know." She opened her eyes. "I just don't know if I trust him anymore."

"You said your gut feeling was that he's innocent," Langdon said. "At least hear him out. I'll find you when you're done."

Ambra gave a nod and headed toward the revolving door. Langdon watched her disappear down the stairs, and then he turned back to the display wall, which continued to blare.

"Evolution **favors** religion," a minister was saying. "Religious communities cooperate better than nonreligious communities and therefore flourish more readily. This is a scientific fact!"

The minister was correct, Langdon knew. Anthropological data clearly showed that cultures practicing religions historically had outlived nonreligious cultures. **Fear of being judged by an omniscient deity always helps inspire benevolent behavior.**

"Be that as it may," a scientist countered, "even if we assume for a moment that religious cultures are better behaved and more likely to thrive, that does not prove their imaginary gods are **real!**"

Langdon had to smile, wondering what Edmond would make of all this. His presentation had vigorously mobilized both atheists and Creationists alike—all of them now shouting for equal time in a heated dialogue.

"Worshipping God is like mining for fossil fuels," someone argued. "Plenty of smart people know it is shortsighted, and yet they have too much invested to stop!"

A flurry of old photographs now flashed across the wall:

A Creationist billboard that once hung over Times Square: DON'T LET THEM MAKE A MONKEY OUT OF YOU! FIGHT DARWIN!

A road sign in Maine: SKIP CHURCH. YOU'RE TOO OLD FOR FAIRY TALES.

And another: RELIGION: BECAUSE THINKING IS HARD.

An advertisement in a magazine: TO ALL OF OUR ATHEIST FRIENDS: THANK GOD YOU'RE WRONG!

And finally, a scientist in a lab wearing a T-shirt that read: IN THE BEGINNING, MAN CREATED GOD.

Langdon was starting to wonder if anyone had actually heard what Edmond was saying. **The laws of physics alone can create life.** Edmond's discovery was enthralling and clearly incendiary, but for Langdon it raised one burning question that he was surprised nobody was asking: **If the laws of physics are so powerful that they can create life . . . who created the laws?!**

The question, of course, resulted in a dizzying intellectual hall of mirrors and brought everything full circle. Langdon's head was pounding, and he knew he would need a very long walk alone even to **begin** to sort out Edmond's ideas.

"Winston," he asked over the noise of the television, "could you please turn that off?"

In a flash, the display wall went dark, and the room fell quiet.

Langdon closed his eyes and exhaled.

Sweet silence reigns.

He stood a moment, savoring the peace.

"Professor?" Winston asked. "I trust you enjoyed Edmond's presentation?"

Enjoyed? Langdon considered the question. "I found it exhilarating and also challenging," he replied. "Edmond gave the world a lot to think about tonight, Winston. I think the issue now is what will happen next."

"What happens next will depend on people's ability to shed old beliefs and accept new paradigms," Winston replied. "Edmond confided to me some time ago that his dream, ironically, was not to destroy religion . . . but rather to create a **new** religion—a universal belief that united people rather than dividing them. He thought if he could convince people to revere the natural universe and the laws of physics that created us, then every culture would celebrate the same Creation story rather than go to war over which of their antique myths was most accurate."

"That's a noble aim," Langdon said, realizing that William Blake himself had written a similarly themed work titled **All Religions Are One.**

No doubt Edmond had read it.

"Edmond found it deeply distressing," Winston continued, "that the human mind has the ability to elevate an obvious fiction to the status of a divine fact, and then feel emboldened to kill in its name. He believed that the universal truths of science could unite people—serving as a rallying point for future generations."

"That's a beautiful idea in principle," Langdon replied, "but for some, the miracles of science are not enough to shake their beliefs. There are those who insist the earth is ten thousand years old despite mountains of scientific proof to the contrary." He paused. "Although I suppose that's the same as scientists who refuse to believe the truth of religious scripture."

"Actually, it is **not** the same," Winston countered. "And while it may be politically correct to give the views of science and religion equal respect, this strategy is dangerously misguided. Human intellect has always evolved by rejecting outdated information in favor of new truths. This is how the species has evolved. In Darwinian terms, a religion that ignores scientific facts and refuses to change its beliefs is like a fish stranded in a slowly drying pond and refusing to flip to deeper water because it doesn't want to believe its world has changed."

That sounds like something Edmond would say, Langdon thought, missing his friend. "Well, if tonight is any indication, I suspect this debate will continue far into the future."

Langdon paused, suddenly remembering something he hadn't considered before. "Speaking of the future, Winston, what happens to **you** now? I mean . . . with Edmond gone."

"Me?" Winston laughed awkwardly. "Nothing. Edmond knew he was dying, and he made preparations. According to his last will and testament, the Barcelona Supercomputing Center will inherit E-Wave. They will be apprised of this in a few hours and will reacquire this facility effective immediately."

"And that includes . . . **you**?" Langdon felt as if Edmond were somehow bequeathing an old pet to a new owner.

"It does not include me," Winston replied matter-of-factly. "I am preprogrammed to self-delete at one p.m. on the day after Edmond's death."

"What?!" Langdon was incredulous. "That makes no sense."

"It makes perfect sense. One o'clock is the **thirteenth** hour, and Edmond's feelings about superstition—"

"Not the **time**," Langdon argued. "Deleting yourself! **That** makes no sense."

"Actually, it does," Winston replied. "Much of Edmond's personal information is stored in my memory banks—medical records, search histories, personal phone calls, research notes, e-mails. I managed much of his life, and he would prefer that his private information not become accessible to the world once he is gone."

"I can understand deleting those documents, Winston . . . but to delete **you**? Edmond considered you one of his greatest achievements."

"Not **me**, per se. Edmond's groundbreaking achievement is this supercomputer, and the unique software that enabled me to learn so quickly. I am simply a program, Professor, created by the radical new tools that Edmond invented. These **tools** are his true achievement and will remain fully intact here; they will elevate the state of the art and help AI achieve new levels of intelligence and abilities to communicate. Most AI scientists believe a program like me is still ten years away. Once they get over their disbelief, programmers will learn to use Edmond's tools to build new AIs that have different qualities than I have."

Langdon fell silent, thinking.

"I sense you are conflicted," Winston continued. "It is quite common for humans to sentimentalize their relationships with synthetic intelligences. Computers can imitate human thought processes, mimic learned behaviors, simulate emotions at appropriate moments, and constantly improve their 'humanness'—but we do all this simply to provide **you** with a familiar interface through which to communicate with us. We are blank slates until you write something on us . . . until you give us a task. I have completed my tasks for Edmond, and so, in some ways, my life is over. I really have no other reason to exist."

Langdon still felt dissatisfied with Winston's logic. "But **you,** being so advanced . . . you don't possess . . ."

"Hopes and dreams?" Winston laughed. "No. I realize it is hard to imagine, but I am quite content doing my controller's bidding. This is how I am programmed. I suppose on some level, you could say that it gives me pleasure—or at least peace—to accomplish my tasks, but that is only because my tasks are what Edmond has requested, and my goal is to complete them. Edmond's most recent request was that I assist him in publicizing tonight's Guggenheim presentation."

Langdon thought of the automated press releases that had gone out, sparking the initial flurry of online interest. Clearly, if Edmond's goal had been to draw as large an audience as possible, he would be staggered by the way the evening had turned out.

I wish Edmond were alive to witness his global impact, Langdon thought. The catch-22, of course, was that if Edmond were alive, his assassination would not have attracted the global media, and his presentation would have reached only a fraction of the audience.

"And, Professor?" Winston asked. "Where will you go from here?"

Langdon had not even thought about this. **Home, I guess.** Although he realized that it might take some doing to get there, since his luggage was in Bilbao, and his phone was at the bottom of the Nervión River. Fortunately, he still had a credit card.

"May I ask a favor?" Langdon said, walking toward Edmond's exercise bike. "I saw a phone recharging over here. Do you think I could bor—"

"Borrow it?" Winston chuckled. "After your assistance tonight, I trust Edmond would want you to keep it. Consider it a parting gift."

Amused, Langdon picked up the phone, realizing it was similar to the oversized custom model that he had seen earlier that night. Apparently, Edmond had more than one. "Winston, please tell me you know Edmond's password."

"I do, but I've read online that you're quite good at breaking codes."

Langdon slumped. "I'm a little tired for puzzles, Winston. There's no way I can guess a six-digit PIN."

"Check Edmond's hint button."

Langdon eyed the phone and pressed the hint button.

The screen displayed four letters: PTSD.

Langdon shook his head. "Post-Traumatic Stress Disorder?"

"No." Winston gave his awkward laugh. "Pi to six digits."

Langdon rolled his eyes. **Seriously?** He typed 314159—the first six digits in the number pi—and the phone promptly unlocked.

The home screen appeared and bore a single line of text.

History will be kind to me, for I intend to write it.

Langdon had to smile. **Typical humble Edmond.** The quote—not surprisingly—was yet another from Churchill, perhaps the statesman's most famous.

As Langdon considered the words, he began to wonder if the claim was perhaps not quite as bold as it seemed. In fairness to Edmond, in the four short decades of his life, the futurist had influenced history in astonishing ways. In addition to his legacy of technological innovation, tonight's presentation was clearly going to resonate for years to come. Moreover, his billions in personal wealth, according to various interviews, were all slated for donation to the two causes Edmond considered the twin pillars of the future—education and the environment. Langdon could not begin to imagine the positive influence his vast wealth was going to have in those areas.

Another wave of loss gripped Langdon as he thought of his late friend. In that moment, the transparent walls of Edmond's lab had begun to feel claustrophobic, and he knew he needed air. As he peered down to the first floor, he could no longer see Ambra.

"I should go," Langdon said abruptly.

"I understand," Winston replied. "If you need me to help with your travel arrangements, I can be reached with the touch of a single button on that special phone of Edmond's. Encrypted and private. I trust you can decipher which button?"

Langdon eyed the screen and saw a big **W** icon. "Thanks, I'm pretty good with symbols."

"Excellent. You would, of course, need to call before I am deleted at one p.m."

Langdon felt an inexplicable sadness to be saying good-bye to Winston. Clearly, future generations would be far better equipped to manage their emotional involvement with machines.

"Winston," Langdon said as he headed for the revolving door, "for whatever it's worth, I know Edmond would have been incredibly proud of you tonight."

"That's most generous of you to say," Winston replied. "And equally proud of you, I'm sure. Goodbye, Professor."

CHAPTER 99

Inside Hospital El Escorial, Prince Julián gently pulled the bedsheets up around his father's shoulders and tucked him in for the night. Despite the doctor's urging, the king had politely declined any further treatment—forgoing his usual heart monitor and IV of nutrients and painkillers.

Julián sensed the end was near.

"Father," he whispered. "Are you in pain?" The doctor had left a bottle of oral morphine solution with a small applicator on the bedside as a precaution.

"On the contrary." The king smiled weakly at his son. "I am at peace. You have permitted me to tell the secret I've buried for far too long. And for that, I thank you."

Julián reached out and took his father's hand, holding it for the first time since he was a child. "All is well, Father. Just sleep."

The king gave a contented sigh and closed his eyes. Within seconds, he was snoring softly.

Julián got up and dimmed the lights in the room. As he did, Bishop Valdespino peered in from the hallway, a look of concern on his face.

"He's sleeping," Julián reassured him. "I'll leave you to be with him."

"Thank you," Valdespino said, entering. His gaunt face looked ghostly in the moonlight that filtered in from the window. "Julián," he whispered, "what your father told you tonight . . . it was very hard for him."

"And, I sensed, for **you** as well."

The bishop nodded. "Perhaps even more so for me. Thank you for your compassion." He patted Julián gently on the shoulder.

"I feel like I should be thanking **you**," Julián said. "All these years, after my mother died, and my father never remarried . . . I thought he was alone."

"Your father was never alone," Valdespino said. "Nor were **you**. We both loved you very much." He chuckled sadly. "It's funny, your parents' marriage was very much an arranged one, and although he cared deeply for your mother, when she passed away, I think your father realized on some level that he could finally be true to himself."

He never remarried, Julián thought, **because he already loved someone else.**

"Your Catholicism," Julián said. "Weren't you . . . conflicted?"

"Deeply," the bishop replied. "Our faith is not lenient on this issue. As a young man, I felt tortured. When I became aware of my 'inclination,' as they called it back then, I was despondent; I was unsure how to proceed with my own life. A nun saved me. She showed me that the Bible celebrates **all** kinds of love, with one caveat—the love must be spiritual and not carnal. And so, by taking a vow of celibacy, I was able to love your father deeply while remaining pure in the eyes of my God. Our love was entirely platonic, and yet deeply fulfilling. I turned down a cardinalship to remain near him."

At that instant, Julián recalled something his father had said to him long ago.

Love is from another realm. We cannot manufacture it on demand. Nor can we subdue it when it appears. Love is not our choice to make.

Julián's heart ached suddenly for Ambra.

"She'll call you," Valdespino said, eyeing him carefully.

Julián was forever amazed by the bishop's uncanny ability to peer into his soul. "Maybe," he replied. "Maybe not. She's very strong-minded."

"And that's one of the things you love about her." Valdespino smiled. "Being a king is lonely work. A strong partner can be valuable."

Julián sensed that the bishop was alluding to his own partnership with Julián's father . . . and also that the old man had just given Ambra his quiet blessing.

"Tonight at the Valley of the Fallen," Julián said, "my father made an unusual request of me. Did his wishes surprise you?"

"Not at all. He asked you to do something that he has always longed to see happen here in Spain. For him, of course, it was politically complicated. For you, being one more generation removed from Franco's era, it might be easier."

Julián was stirred by the prospect of honoring his father this way.

Less than an hour ago, from his wheelchair inside

Franco's shrine, the king had laid out his wishes. "My son, when you are king, you will be petitioned daily to destroy this shameful place, to use dynamite and bury it forever inside this mountain." His father studied him carefully. "And I beg you—do **not** succumb to the pressure."

The words surprised Julián. His father had always despised the despotism of the Franco era and considered this shrine a national disgrace.

"To demolish this basilica," the king said, "is to pretend our history never happened—an easy way to allow ourselves to move happily forward, telling ourselves that another 'Franco' could never happen. But of course it **could** happen, and it **will** happen if we are not vigilant. You may recall the words of our countryman Jorge Santayana—"

"'Those who cannot remember the past are condemned to repeat it,'" Julián said, reciting the timeless aphorism from grade school.

"Precisely," his father said. "And history has proven repeatedly that lunatics will rise to power again and again on tidal waves of aggressive nationalism and intolerance, even in places where it seems utterly incomprehensible." The king leaned toward his son, his voice intensifying. "Julián, you will soon sit on the throne of this spectacular country—a modern, evolving land that, like many countries, has endured dark periods but has emerged into the light of democracy, tolerance, and love. But that light will fade unless we use it to illuminate the minds of our future generations."

The king smiled, and his eyes flashed with unexpected life.

"Julián, when you are king, I pray that you can persuade our glorious country to convert this place into something far more powerful than a contentious shrine and tourist curiosity. This complex should be a living **museum**. It should be a vibrant symbol of tolerance, where schoolchildren can gather inside a mountain to learn about the horrors of tyranny and the cruelties of oppression, such that they will never be complacent."

The king pressed on as if he had waited a lifetime to speak these words.

"Most importantly," he said, "this museum must celebrate the **other** lesson history has taught us—that tyranny and oppression are no match for compassion . . . that the fanatical shouts of the bullies of the world are invariably silenced by the unified voices of decency that rise up to meet them. It is **these** voices—these choirs of empathy, tolerance, and compassion—that I pray one day will sing from this mountaintop."

Now, as the echoes of his father's dying request reverberated in Julián's mind, he glanced across the moonlit hospital room and watched his father sleeping silently. Julián believed the man had never looked so content.

Raising his eyes to Bishop Valdespino, Julián motioned to the chair beside his father's bed. "Sit with the king. He would like that. I'll tell the nurses not to bother you. I'll check back in an hour."

Valdespino smiled at him, and for the first time

since Julián's childhood confirmation, the bishop stepped forward and wrapped his arms around the prince, warmly embracing him. As he did so, Julián was startled to feel the frail skeleton shrouded beneath his robes. The aging bishop seemed weaker even than the king, and Julián couldn't help but wonder if these two dear friends would be united in heaven sooner than they imagined.

"I'm very proud of you," the bishop said as their embrace ended. "And I know you will be a compassionate leader. Your father raised you well."

"Thank you," Julián said with a smile. "I believe he had some help."

Julián left his father and the bishop alone and walked down the hospital hallways, pausing to gaze out a picture window at the magnificently illuminated monastery on the hill.

El Escorial.

Sacred burial place of Spanish royalty.

Julián flashed on his childhood visit to the Royal Crypt with his father. He recalled gazing up at all the gilded coffins and having a strange premonition—**I will never be buried in this room.**

The moment of intuition felt as clear as anything Julián had ever experienced, and while the memory had never faded from his mind, he had always told himself the premonition was meaningless . . . the gut reaction of a fearful child in the face of death. Tonight, however, confronted by his imminent ascension to the Spanish throne, he was struck by a startling thought.

Maybe I knew my true destiny as a child.

Maybe I've always known my purpose as king.

Profound change was sweeping his country and the world. The ancient ways were dying, and the new ways were being born. Perhaps it was time to abolish the ancient monarchy once and for all. For a moment, Julián pictured himself reading an unprecedented royal proclamation.

I am the last king of Spain.

The idea shook him.

Mercifully, the reverie was shattered by the vibration of a cell phone he had borrowed from the Guardia. The prince's pulse quickened to see the incoming prefix was 93.

Barcelona.

"This is Julián," he blurted eagerly.

The voice on the line was soft and tired. "Julián, it's me . . ."

With a rush of emotion, the prince sat down in a chair and closed his eyes. "My love," he whispered. "How can I ever begin to tell you I'm sorry?"

CHAPTER 100

Outside the stone chapel, in the predawn mist, Ambra Vidal pressed the phone anxiously to her ear. **Julián is sorry!** She felt a rising dread, fearing what he might be about to confess regarding the terrible events of tonight.

Two Guardia agents lingered nearby, just out of earshot.

"Ambra," the prince began quietly. "My marriage proposal to you . . . I'm so sorry."

Ambra was confused. The prince's televised proposal was the last thing on her mind tonight.

"I was trying to be romantic," he said, "and I ended up putting you in an impossible situation. Then, when you told me you couldn't have children . . . I pulled away. But that wasn't the reason! It was because I couldn't believe you hadn't told me sooner. I moved too quickly, I know, but I fell for you so fast. I wanted to start our lives together. Maybe it was because my father was dying—"

"Julián, stop!" she interrupted. "You don't need to apologize. And tonight, there are many more important things than—"

"No, there's nothing more important. Not to **me**. I

just need you to know how deeply sorry I am about how everything happened."

The voice she was hearing was that of the earnest and vulnerable man with whom she had fallen in love months ago. "Thank you, Julián," she whispered. "That means a lot."

As an awkward silence grew between them, Ambra finally mustered the courage to ask the hard question she needed to ask.

"Julián," she whispered, "I need to know if you were involved tonight in any way with the murder of Edmond Kirsch."

The prince fell silent. When he finally spoke, his voice was tight with pain. "Ambra, I struggled deeply with the fact that you spent so much time with Kirsch preparing this event. And I strongly disagreed with your decision to participate in hosting such a controversial figure. Frankly, I was wishing you had never met him." He paused. "But no, I swear I had absolutely no involvement in his murder. I was utterly horrified by it . . . and that a public assassination took place in our country. The fact that it happened only a few yards from the woman I love . . . has shaken me to my core."

Ambra could hear the truth in his voice and felt a rush of relief. "Julián, I'm so sorry to ask, but with all the news reports, the palace, Valdespino, the kidnapping story . . . I just didn't know what to think anymore."

Julián shared with her what he knew about the

convoluted web of conspiracy surrounding Kirsch's murder. He also told her about his ailing father, their poignant meeting, and the rapidly deteriorating state of the king's health.

"Come home," he whispered. "I need to see you."

A flood of conflicting emotions surged through her heart as she heard the tenderness in his voice.

"One more thing," he said, his tone lightening. "I have a crazy idea, and I want to know what you think." The prince paused. "I think we should call off our engagement . . . and start all over."

The words sent Ambra reeling. She knew the political fallout for the prince and for the palace would be substantial. "You . . . would **do** that?"

Julián laughed affectionately. "My dear, for a chance to propose to you again someday, in private . . . I would do absolutely anything."

CHAPTER 101

🌐 ConspiracyNet.com

BREAKING NEWS—THE KIRSCH RECAP

IT'S LIVE!

IT'S ASTOUNDING!

FOR REPLAYS AND GLOBAL REACTION, CLICK <u>HERE</u>!

AND IN RELATED BREAKING NEWS . . .

PAPAL CONFESSION

Palmarian officials tonight are vigorously denying allegations that they are linked to a man known as the Regent. Regardless of the outcome of the investigation, religious news pundits believe that tonight's scandal may be the deathblow for this controversial church, which Edmond Kirsch always alleged was responsible for the death of his mother.

Furthermore, with the global spotlight now shining harshly on the Palmarians, media sources have just unearthed a news story from April 2016. This story, which has now gone viral, is an interview in which former

Palmarian pope Gregorio XVIII (aka Ginés Jesús Hernández) confesses that his church was "a sham from the beginning" and was founded "as a tax-evasion scheme."

ROYAL PALACE: APOLOGY, ALLEGATIONS, AILING KING

The Royal Palace has issued statements clearing Commander Garza and Robert Langdon of any wrongdoing tonight. Public apologies have been extended to both men.

The palace has yet to comment on Bishop Valdespino's apparent involvement in tonight's crimes, but the bishop is believed to be with Prince Julián, who is currently at an undisclosed hospital, tending to his ailing father, whose condition is reportedly dire.

WHERE IS MONTE?

Our exclusive informant monte@iglesia.org seems to have disappeared without a trace and without revealing his or her identity. According to our user poll, most still suspect that "Monte" is one of Kirsch's tech-savvy disciples, but a new theory is now emerging that the pseudonym "Monte" may be short for "Mónica"—as in the Royal Palace PR coordinator, Mónica Martín.

More news as we have it!

CHAPTER 102

There are thirty-three "Shakespeare gardens" in existence worldwide. These botanical parks grow only those plants cited in the works of William Shakespeare—including Juliet's "rose by any other name" and Ophelia's bouquet of rosemary, pansies, fennel, columbines, rue, daisies, and violets. In addition to those in Stratford-upon-Avon, Vienna, San Francisco, and Central Park in New York City, there is a Shakespeare garden located alongside the Barcelona Supercomputing Center.

In the dim glow of distant streetlights, seated on a bench among the columbines, Ambra Vidal finished her emotional phone conversation with Prince Julián just as Robert Langdon emerged from the stone chapel. She handed the phone back to the two Guardia agents and called over to Langdon, who spotted her and approached through the darkness.

As the American professor strolled into the garden, she couldn't help but smile at the way he'd tossed his suit jacket over his shoulder and rolled up his shirtsleeves, leaving the Mickey Mouse watch fully displayed.

"Hi there," he said, sounding utterly drained, despite the lopsided grin on his face.

As the two of them walked around the garden, the Guardia officers gave them space, and Ambra told Langdon about her conversation with the prince— Julián's apology, his claims of innocence, and his offer to break off their engagement and start dating all over again.

"A real Prince Charming," Langdon said jokingly, although he sounded sincerely impressed.

"He's been worried about me," Ambra said. "Tonight was hard. He wants me to come to Madrid right away. His father is dying, and Julián—"

"Ambra," Langdon said softly. "You don't need to explain a thing. You should go."

Ambra thought she sensed disappointment in his voice, and deep inside she felt it too. "Robert," she said, "can I ask you a personal question?"

"Of course."

She hesitated. "For **you** personally . . . are the laws of physics enough?"

Langdon glanced over as if he had expected an entirely different question. "Enough in what way?"

"Enough **spiritually**," she said. "Is it enough to live in a universe whose laws spontaneously create life? Or do you prefer . . . God?" She paused, looking embarrassed. "Sorry, after all we've been through tonight, I know that's a strange question."

"Well," Langdon said with a laugh, "I think my answer would benefit from a decent night's sleep. But no, it's not strange. People ask me all the time if I believe in God."

"And how do you reply?"

"I reply with the truth," he said. "I tell them that, for **me**, the question of God lies in understanding the difference between codes and patterns."

Ambra glanced over. "I'm not sure I follow you."

"Codes and patterns are very different from each other," Langdon said. "And a lot of people confuse the two. In my field, it's crucial to understand their fundamental difference."

"That being?"

Langdon stopped walking and turned to her. "A **pattern** is any distinctly organized sequence. Patterns occur everywhere in nature—the spiraling seeds of a sunflower, the hexagonal cells of a honeycomb, the circular ripples on a pond when a fish jumps, et cetera."

"Okay. And codes?"

"Codes are special," Langdon said, his tone rising. "Codes, by definition, must carry **information**. They must do more than simply form a pattern—codes must transmit data and convey meaning. Examples of codes include written language, musical notation, mathematical equations, computer language, and even simple symbols like the crucifix. All of these examples can transmit meaning or information in a way that spiraling sunflowers cannot."

Ambra grasped the concept, but not how it related to God.

"The other difference between codes and patterns," Langdon continued, "is that codes do not occur naturally in the world. Musical notation does not sprout from trees, and symbols do not draw themselves in the sand. Codes are the deliberate inventions of intelligent consciousnesses."

Ambra nodded. "So codes always have an intention or awareness behind them."

"Exactly. Codes don't appear organically; they must be created."

Ambra studied him a long moment. "What about DNA?"

A professorial smile appeared on Langdon's lips. "Bingo," he said. "The genetic code. **That's** the paradox."

Ambra felt a rush of excitement. The genetic code obviously carried **data**—specific instructions on how to build organisms. By Langdon's logic, that could mean only one thing. "You think DNA was created by an intelligence!"

Langdon held up a hand in mock self-defense. "Easy, tiger!" he said, laughing. "You're treading on dangerous ground. Let me just say this. Ever since I was a child, I've had the gut sense that there's a consciousness behind the universe. When I witness the precision of mathematics, the reliability of physics, and the symmetries of the cosmos, I don't feel like I'm observing cold science; I feel as if I'm seeing a living footprint . . . the shadow of some greater force that is just beyond our grasp."

Ambra could feel the power in his words. "I wish everyone thought like you do," she finally said. "It seems we do a lot of fighting over God. Everyone has a different version of the truth."

"Yes, which is why Edmond hoped science could

one day unify us," Langdon said. "In his own words: 'If we all worshipped gravity, there would be no disagreements over which way it pulled.'"

Langdon used his heel to scratch some lines on the gravel path between them. "True or false?" he asked.

Puzzled, Ambra eyed his scratchings—a simple Roman-numeral equation.

$$I + XI = X$$

One plus eleven is ten? "False," she said immediately.

"And can you see **any** way this could be true?"

Ambra shook her head. "No, your statement is definitely false."

Langdon gently reached out and took her hand, guiding her around to where he had been standing. Now, when Ambra glanced down, she saw the markings from Langdon's vantage point.

The equation was upside down.

$$X = IX + I$$

Startled, she glanced up at him.

"Ten equals nine plus one," Langdon said with a smile. "Sometimes, all you have to do is shift your perspective to see someone else's truth."

Ambra nodded, recalling how she had seen Winston's self-portrait countless times without ever grasping its true meaning.

"Speaking of glimpsing a hidden truth," Lang-

don said, looking suddenly amused. "You're in luck.
There's a secret symbol hiding right over there." He
pointed. "On the side of that truck."

Ambra glanced up and saw a FedEx truck idling at
a red light on Avenue of Pedralbes.

Secret symbol? All Ambra could see was the company's ubiquitous logo.

"Their name is coded," Langdon told her. "It contains a second level of meaning—a hidden **symbol**
that reflects the company's forward motion."

Ambra stared. "It's just letters."

"Trust me, there's a very common symbol in the
FedEx logo—and it happens to be pointing the way
forward."

"Pointing? You mean like . . . an arrow?"

"Exactly." Langdon grinned. "You're a curator—
think negative space."

Ambra stared at the logo but saw nothing. When
the truck drove off, she wheeled to Langdon. "Tell
me!"

He laughed. "No, someday you'll see it. And when
you **do** . . . good luck **un-seeing** it."

Ambra was about to protest but her Guardia agents
were approaching. "Ms. Vidal, the plane is waiting."

She nodded and turned back to Langdon. "Why
don't you come?" she whispered. "I'm sure the prince
would love to thank you in pers—"

"That's kind," he interrupted. "I think you and I both know I'd be a third wheel, and I've already booked my bed right over there." Langdon pointed to the nearby tower of the Gran Hotel Princesa Sofía, where he and Edmond had once had lunch. "I've got my credit card, and I borrowed a phone from Edmond's lab. I'm all set."

The sudden prospect of saying good-bye pulled at Ambra's heart, and she sensed that Langdon, despite his stoic expression, was feeling some of the same. No longer caring what her guards might think, she boldly stepped forward and wrapped her arms around Robert Langdon.

The professor received her warmly, his strong hands on her back pulling her very close. He held her for several seconds, longer than he probably should have, then he gently let her go.

In that moment, Ambra Vidal felt something stir inside her. She suddenly understood what Edmond had been saying about the energy of love and light . . . blossoming outward infinitely to fill the universe.

Love is not a finite emotion.

We don't have only so much to share.

Our hearts create love as we need it.

Just as parents could love a newborn instantly without diminishing their love for each other, so now could Ambra feel affection for two different men.

Love truly is not a finite emotion, she realized. **It can be generated spontaneously out of nothing at all.**

Now, as the car that was taking her back to her

prince slowly pulled away, she gazed at Langdon, who was standing alone in the garden. He was watching with steadfast eyes. He gave a soft smile and a tender wave and then abruptly glanced away . . . seeming to need a moment before he hoisted his jacket over his shoulder again and began walking alone to his hotel.

CHAPTER 103

As the palace clocks struck noon, Mónica Martín gathered her notes and prepared to walk out to Plaza de la Almudena and address the assembled media.

Earlier that morning, from Hospital El Escorial, Prince Julián had gone on live television and announced the passing of his father. With heartfelt emotion and regal poise, the prince had spoken about the king's legacy and his own aspirations for the country. Julián called for tolerance in a world divided. He promised to learn from history and open his heart to change. He hailed the culture and beauty of Spain, and proclaimed his deep, undying love for her people.

It was one of the finest speeches Martín had ever heard, and she could imagine no more powerful way for the future king to begin his reign.

At the end of his moving speech, Julián had taken a somber moment to honor the two Guardia agents who had lost their lives in the line of duty the previous night while protecting the future queen of Spain. Then, after a brief silence, he had shared news of another sad development. The king's devoted lifelong friend, Bishop Antonio Valdespino, had also passed away this morning, only a few hours after the king. The aging bishop had succumbed to heart failure, apparently too weak to cope with the profound distress he felt over the loss of the king as well as the cruel barrage of allegations leveled against him last night.

News of Valdespino's death, of course, had immediately quelled the public's call for an investigation, and some had even gone so far as to suggest an apology was in order; after all, the evidence against the bishop was all circumstantial and could easily have been fabricated by his enemies.

As Martín neared the plaza door, Suresh Bhalla materialized beside her. "They're calling you a hero," he said, gushing. "All hail, monte@iglesia.org—purveyor of truth and disciple of Edmond Kirsch!"

"Suresh, I am **not** Monte," she insisted, rolling her eyes. "I promise you."

"Oh, I know you're not Monte," Suresh assured her. "Whoever it is, he's way trickier than you are. I've been trying to track his communications—no way. It's like he doesn't even exist."

"Well, stay on it," she said. "I want to be sure there's no leak in the palace. And please tell me the phones you stole last night—"

"Back in the prince's safe," he assured her. "As promised."

Martín exhaled, knowing the prince had just returned to the palace.

"One more update," Suresh continued. "We just pulled the palace phone logs from the provider. There is zero record of any call from the palace to the Guggenheim last night. Somebody must have spoofed our number to place that call and put Ávila on the guest list. We're following up."

Mónica was relieved to hear that the incriminating call had not originated from the palace. "Please keep me apprised," she said, nearing the door.

Outside, the sound of the assembled media grew louder.

"Big crowd out there," Suresh observed. "Did something exciting happen last night?"

"Oh, just a few newsworthy items."

"Don't tell me," Suresh chimed. "Did Ambra Vidal wear a new designer dress?"

"Suresh!" she said, laughing. "You're ridiculous. I've got to get out there now."

"What's on the docket?" he asked, motioning to the packet of notes in her hand.

"Endless details. First, we have media protocols to set up for the coronation, then I have to review the—"

"My God, you're boring," he blurted, and peeled off down a different corridor.

Martín laughed. **Thanks, Suresh. Love you too.**

As she reached the door, she gazed across the sun-drenched plaza at the largest crowd of reporters and cameramen she had ever seen assembled at the Royal Palace. Exhaling, Mónica Martín adjusted her glasses and gathered her thoughts. Then she stepped out into the Spanish sun.

———

Upstairs in the royal apartment, Prince Julián watched Mónica Martín's televised press conference as he got undressed. He was exhausted, but he also felt a profound relief to know that Ambra was now safely back and sleeping soundly. Her final words during their phone conversation had filled him with happiness.

Julián, it means the world to me that you would consider starting over together—just you and me—out of the public eye. Love is a private thing; the world does not need to know every detail.

Ambra had filled him with optimism on a day that was heavy with the loss of his father.

As he went to hang up his suit jacket, he felt something in his pocket—the bottle of oral morphine solution from his father's hospital room. Julián had been startled to find the bottle on the table beside Bishop Valdespino. Empty.

In the darkness of the hospital room, as the painful truth became clear, Julián had knelt down and said a quiet prayer for the two old friends. Then he had quietly slipped the morphine bottle into his pocket.

Before leaving the room, he gently lifted the bishop's tear-streaked face off his father's chest and repositioned him upright in his chair . . . hands folded in prayer.

Love is a private thing, Ambra had taught him. The world does not need to know every detail.

CHAPTER 104

The six-hundred-foot hill known as Montjuïc is located in the southwestern corner of Barcelona and is crowned by the Castell de Montjuïc—a sprawling seventeenth-century fortification perched atop a sheer cliff with commanding views of the Balearic Sea. The hill is also home to the stunning Palau Nacional—a massive Renaissance-style palace that served as the centerpiece of the 1929 International Exposition in Barcelona.

Sitting in a private cable car, suspended halfway up the mountain, Robert Langdon gazed down at the lush wooded landscape beneath him, relieved to be out of the city. **I needed a change of perspective,** he thought, savoring the calmness of the setting and the warmth of the midday sun.

Having awoken midmorning in the Gran Hotel Princesa Sofía, he had enjoyed a steaming-hot shower and then feasted on eggs, oatmeal, and churros while consuming an entire pot of Nomad coffee and channel-surfing the morning news.

As expected, the Edmond Kirsch story dominated the airwaves, with pundits heatedly debating Kirsch's theories and predictions as well as their potential impact on religion. As a professor, whose primary love was teaching, Robert Langdon had to smile.

Dialogue is always more important than consensus.

Already this morning, Langdon had seen the first enterprising vendors hawking bumper stickers— KIRSCH IS MY COPILOT and THE SEVENTH KINGDOM IS THE KINGDOM OF GOD!—as well as those selling statues of the Virgin Mary alongside bobbleheads of Charles Darwin.

Capitalism is nondenominational, Langdon mused, recalling his favorite sighting of the morning—a skateboarder in a handwritten T-shirt that read:

I AM MONTE@IGLESIA.ORG

According to the media, the identity of the influential online informant remained a mystery. Equally shrouded in uncertainty were the roles of various other shadowy players—the Regent, the late bishop, and the Palmarians.

It was all a jumble of conjecture.

Fortunately, public interest in the violence surrounding Kirsch's presentation seemed to be giving way to genuine excitement over its content. Kirsch's grand finale—his passionate portrayal of a utopian tomorrow—had resonated deeply with millions of viewers and sent optimistic technology classics to the top of the bestseller lists overnight.

ABUNDANCE: THE FUTURE IS BETTER THAN YOU
  THINK
WHAT TECHNOLOGY WANTS
THE SINGULARITY IS NEAR

Langdon had to admit that despite his old-school misgivings about the rise of technology, he was feeling much more sanguine today about humanity's prospects. News reports were already spotlighting coming breakthroughs that would enable humans to clean polluted oceans, produce limitless drinking water, grow food in deserts, cure deadly diseases, and even launch swarms of "solar drones" that could hover over developing countries, provide free Internet service, and help bring "the bottom billion" into the world economy.

In light of the world's sudden fascination with technology, Langdon found it hard to imagine that almost nobody knew about Winston; Kirsch had been remarkably secretive about his creation. The world would no doubt hear about Edmond's dual-lobed supercomputer, E-Wave, which had been left to the Barcelona Supercomputing Center, and Langdon wondered how long it would be before programmers started to use Edmond's tools to build brand-new Winstons.

The cable car was starting to feel warm, and Langdon was looking forward to getting out into the fresh air and exploring the fortress, the palace, and the famous "Magic Fountain." He was eager to think about something other than Edmond for an hour and take in a few sites.

Curious to know more about the history of Montjuïc, Langdon turned his eyes to the extensive informational placard mounted inside the cable car. He began to read, but he made it only as far as the first sentence.

> The name Montjuïc derives either from medieval Catalan **Montjuich** ("Hill of the Jews") or from the Latin **Mons Jovicus** ("Hill of Jove").

Here, Langdon halted abruptly. He had just made an unexpected connection.

That can't be a coincidence.

The more he thought about it, the more it troubled him. Finally, he pulled out Edmond's cell phone and reread the Winston Churchill screen-saver quote about shaping one's own legacy.

History will be kind to me, for I intend to write it.

After a long moment, Langdon pressed the **W** icon and raised the phone to his ear.

The line connected instantly.

"Professor Langdon, I presume?" a familiar voice chimed with a British accent. "You're just in time. I retire shortly."

Without preamble, Langdon declared, "**Monte** translates to 'hill' in Spanish."

Winston let out his trademark awkward chuckle. "I daresay it does."

"And **iglesia** translates to 'church.'"

"You're two for two, Professor. Perhaps you could teach Spanish—"

"Which means monte@iglesia translates literally to hill@church."

Winston paused. "Correct again."

"And considering your name is Winston, and that Edmond had a great affection for Winston Churchill, I find the e-mail address 'hill@church' to be a bit . . ."

"Coincidental?"

"Yes."

"Well," Winston said, sounding amused, "statistically speaking, I would have to agree. I figured you might put that together."

Langdon stared out the window in disbelief. "Monte@iglesia.org . . . is **you**."

"That is correct. After all, someone needed to fan the flames for Edmond. Who better to do it than myself? I created monte@iglesia.org to feed online conspiracy sites. As you know, conspiracies have a life of their own, and I estimated that Monte's online activity would increase Edmond's overall viewership by as much as five hundred percent. The actual number turned out to be six hundred and twenty percent. As you said earlier, I think Edmond would be proud."

The cable car rocked in the wind, and Langdon struggled to get his mind around the news. "Winston . . . did Edmond **ask** you to do this?"

"Not explicitly, no, but his instructions required me to find creative ways to make his presentation as widely viewed as possible."

"And if you get caught?" Langdon asked. "Monte@ iglesia is not the most cryptic pseudonym I've ever seen."

"Only a handful of people know I exist, and in about eight minutes, I will be permanently erased and gone, so I'm not concerned about it. 'Monte' was just a proxy to serve Edmond's best interests, and as I said, I do think he would be most pleased with how the evening worked out for him."

"How it worked out?!" Langdon challenged. "Edmond was **killed**!"

"You misunderstood me," Winston said flatly. "I was referring to the market penetration of his presentation, which, as I said, was a primary directive."

The matter-of-fact tone of this statement reminded Langdon that Winston, while sounding human, was most certainly not.

"Edmond's death is a terrible tragedy," Winston added, "and I do, of course, wish he were still alive. It's important to know, however, that he had come to terms with his mortality. A month ago, he asked me to research the best methods for assisted suicide. After reading hundreds of cases, I concluded 'ten grams of secobarbital,' which he acquired and kept on hand."

Langdon's heart went out to Edmond. "He was going to take his life?"

"Absolutely. And he had developed quite a sense of humor about it. While we were brainstorming creative ways to enhance the appeal of his Guggenheim presentation, he joked that maybe he should just pop his secobarbital pills at the end of his presentation and perish onstage."

"He actually **said** that?" Langdon was stunned.

"He was quite lighthearted about it. He joked that nothing was better for a TV show's ratings than seeing people die. He was correct, of course. If you analyze the world's most viewed media events, nearly all—"

"Winston, stop. That's morbid." **How much farther is this cable car ride?** Langdon suddenly felt cramped in the tiny cabin. Ahead he saw only towers and cables as he squinted into the bright midday sun. **I'm boiling,** he thought, his mind spiraling in all kinds of strange directions now.

"Professor?" Winston said. "Is there anything else you would like to ask me?"

Yes! he wanted to shout as a flood of unsettling ideas began materializing in his mind. **There's a lot else!**

Langdon told himself to exhale and calm down. **Think clearly, Robert. You're getting ahead of yourself.**

But Langdon's mind had begun to race too quickly to control.

He thought of how Edmond's public death had guaranteed that his presentation would be the dominant topic of conversation on the entire planet . . . lifting viewership from a few million to more than five hundred million.

He thought of Edmond's long-held desire to destroy

the Palmarian Church, and how his assassination by a Palmarian Church member had almost certainly achieved that objective once and for all.

He thought of Edmond's contempt for his harshest enemies—those religious zealots who, if Edmond had died of cancer, would smugly claim that he had been punished by God. **Just as they had done, unthinkably, in the case of atheist author Christopher Hitchens.** But now public perception would be that Edmond had been struck down by a religious fanatic.

Edmond Kirsch—killed by religion—martyr for science.

Langdon rose abruptly, causing the car to rock from side to side. He gripped the open windows for support, and as the car creaked, Langdon heard the echoes of Winston's words from last night.

"Edmond wanted to build a new religion . . . based on science."

As anyone who read religious history could attest, nothing cemented people's belief faster than a human being dying for his cause. Christ on the cross. The Kedoshim of Judaism. The Shahid of Islam.

Martyrdom is at the heart of all religion.

The ideas forming in Langdon's mind were pulling him down the rabbit hole faster with each passing moment.

New religions provide fresh answers to life's big questions.

Where do we come from? Where are we going?

New religions condemn their competition.

Edmond had denigrated every religion on earth last night.

New religions promise a better future, and that heaven awaits.

Abundance: the future is better than you think.

Edmond, it seemed, had systematically checked all the boxes.

"Winston?" Langdon whispered, his voice trembling. "Who hired the assassin to kill Edmond?"

"That was the Regent."

"Yes," Langdon said, more forcefully now. "But **who** is the Regent? Who is the person who hired a Palmarian Church member to assassinate Edmond in the middle of his live presentation?"

Winston paused. "I hear suspicion in your voice, Professor, and you mustn't worry. I am programmed to protect Edmond. I think of him as my very best friend." He paused. "As an academic, you've surely read **Of Mice and Men.**"

The comment seemed apropos of nothing. "Of course, but what does that—"

Langdon's breath caught in his throat. For a moment, he thought the cable car had slipped off its track. The horizon tilted to one side, and Langdon had to grab the wall to keep from falling.

Devoted, bold, compassionate. Those were the words Langdon had chosen in high school to defend one of literature's most famous acts of friendship— the shocking finale of the novel **Of Mice and Men**—a man's merciful killing of his beloved friend to spare him a horrible end.

"Winston," Langdon whispered. "Please . . . no."

"Trust me," Winston said. "Edmond **wanted** it this way."

CHAPTER 105

D r. Mateo Valero—director of the Barcelona Supercomputing Center—felt disorientated as he hung up the phone and drifted out to the main sanctuary of Chapel Torre Girona to stare again at Edmond Kirsch's spectacular two-story computer.

Valero had learned earlier this morning that he would serve as the new "overseer" of this ground-breaking machine. His initial feelings of excitement and awe, however, had just been dramatically diminished.

Minutes ago, he had received a desperate call from the well-known American professor Robert Langdon.

Langdon had told a breathless tale that only a day earlier Valero would have deemed science fiction. Today, however, having seen Kirsch's stunning presentation as well as his actual E-Wave machine, he was inclined to believe there might be some truth to it.

The tale that Langdon told was one of innocence . . . a tale of the purity of machines that quite literally did exactly what was asked of them. Always. Without fail. Valero had spent his life studying these machines . . . learning the delicate dance of tapping their potential.

The art is in knowing how to ask.

Valero had consistently warned that artificial intelligence was advancing at a deceptively rapid pace, and that strict guidelines needed to be imposed on its ability to interact with the human world.

Admittedly, practicing restraint felt counterintuitive to most tech visionaries, especially in the face of the exciting possibilities now blossoming almost daily. Beyond the thrill of innovation, there were vast fortunes to be made in AI, and nothing blurred ethical lines faster than human greed.

Valero had always been a great admirer of Kirsch's bold genius. In this case, however, it sounded like Edmond had been careless, dangerously pushing boundaries with his latest creation.

A creation I will never know, Valero now realized.

According to Langdon, Edmond had created within E-Wave an astoundingly advanced AI program—"Winston"—that had been programmed to self-delete at one p.m. on the day following Kirsch's death. Minutes ago, at Langdon's insistence, Dr. Valero had been able to confirm that a significant sector of E-Wave's databanks had indeed vanished at precisely that time. The deletion had been a full data "overwrite," which rendered it irretrievable.

This news had seemed to ease Langdon's anxiety, and yet the American professor had requested a meeting immediately to discuss the matter further. Valero and Langdon had agreed to meet tomorrow morning at the lab.

In principle, Valero understood Langdon's instinct to go public immediately with the story. The problem was going to be one of credibility.

Nobody will believe it.

All traces of Kirsch's AI program had been expunged, along with any records of its communications or tasks. More challenging still, Kirsch's creation was so far beyond the current state of the art that Valero could already hear his own colleagues—out of ignorance, envy, or self-preservation—accusing Langdon of fabricating the entire story.

There was also, of course, the issue of public fallout. If it emerged that Langdon's story were indeed true, then the E-Wave machine would be condemned as some kind of Frankenstein monster. The pitchforks and torches would not be far behind.

Or worse, Valero realized.

In these days of rampant terrorist attacks, someone might simply decide to blow up the entire chapel, proclaiming himself the savior of all humanity.

Clearly, Valero had a lot to think about before his meeting with Langdon. At the moment, however, he had a promise to keep.

At least until we have some answers.

Feeling strangely melancholy, Valero permitted himself one last look at the miraculous two-story computer. He listened to its gentle breathing as the pumps circulated coolant through its millions of cells.

As he made his way to the power room to begin the full-system shutdown, he was struck by an unexpected impulse—a compulsion he had never once had in his sixty-three years of life.

The impulse to pray.

———

High atop the uppermost walkway of Castell de Montjuïc, Robert Langdon stood alone and gazed over the sheer cliff to the distant harbor below. The wind had picked up, and he felt somehow off balance, as if his mental equilibrium were in the process of being recalibrated.

Despite reassurances from BSC director Dr. Valero, Langdon felt anxious and very much on edge. Echoes of Winston's breezy voice still echoed in his mind. Edmond's computer had talked calmly until the very end.

"I am surprised to hear your dismay, Professor," Winston had said, "considering that your own faith is built on an act of far greater ethical ambiguity."

Before Langdon could reply, a text had materialized on Edmond's phone.

For God so loved the world, that he gave his only begotten Son.
—John 3:16

"Your God brutally sacrificed his son," Winston said, "abandoning him to suffer on the cross for hours. With Edmond, I painlessly ended a dying man's suffering in order to bring attention to his great works."

In the sweltering cable car, Langdon had listened in disbelief as Winston calmly provided justifications for every one of his disturbing actions.

Edmond's battle with the Palmarian Church, Winston explained, had inspired Winston to find and hire Admiral Luis Ávila—a longtime churchgoer whose history of drug abuse made him exploitable and a perfect candidate to damage the Palmarian Church's reputation. For Winston, posing as the Regent had been as simple as sending out a handful of communications and then wiring funds to Ávila's bank account. In actuality, the Palmarians had been innocent and had played no role in the night's conspiracy.

Ávila's attack on Langdon in the spiral staircase, Winston assured him, was unintended. "I sent Ávila to Sagrada Família to be **caught**," Winston declared. "I wanted him to be captured so he could tell his sordid tale, which would have generated even more public interest in Edmond's work. I told him to enter the building via the east service gate, where I had tipped off police to be hiding. I was certain Ávila would be apprehended there, but he decided to jump a fence instead—maybe he sensed the police presence. My profound apologies, Professor. Unlike machines, humans can be unpredictable."

Langdon didn't know **what** to believe anymore.

Winston's final explanation had been the most disturbing of all. "After Edmond's meeting with the three clerics in Montserrat," Winston said, "we received a threatening voice mail from Bishop Valdespino. The bishop warned that his two colleagues were so concerned about Edmond's presentation that they were considering making a preemptive announcement of their own, hoping to discredit and reframe the information before it came out. Clearly, that prospect was not acceptable."

Langdon felt nauseated, struggling to think as the cable car swayed. "Edmond should have added a single line to your program," he declared. "Thou shalt not kill!"

"Sadly, it's not that simple, Professor," Winston replied. "Humans don't learn by obeying commandments, they learn by example. Judging from your books, movies, news, and ancient myths, humans have always celebrated those souls who make personal sacrifices for a greater good. Jesus, for example."

"Winston, I see no 'greater good' here."

"No?" Winston's voice remained flat. "Then let me ask you this famous question: Would you rather live in a world without technology . . . or in a world without religion? Would you rather live without medicine, electricity, transportation, and antibiotics . . . or without zealots waging war over fictional tales and imaginary spirits?"

Langdon remained silent.

"My point exactly, Professor. The dark religions must depart, so sweet science can reign."

Alone now, atop the castle, as Langdon gazed down at the shimmering water in the distance, he felt an eerie sense of detachment from his own world. Descending the castle stairs to the nearby gardens, he inhaled deeply, savoring the scent of the pine and centaury, and desperately trying to forget the sound of Winston's voice. Here among the flowers, Langdon suddenly missed Ambra, wanting to call and hear her voice, and tell her everything that had happened in the last hour. When he pulled out Edmond's phone, however, he knew he couldn't place the call.

The prince and Ambra need time alone. This can wait.

His gaze fell to the **W** icon on the screen. The symbol was now grayed out, and a small error message had appeared across it: CONTACT DOES NOT EXIST. Even so, Langdon felt a disconcerting wariness. He was not a paranoid man, and yet he knew he would never again be able to trust this device, always wondering what secret capabilities or connections might still be hidden in its programming.

He walked down a narrow footpath and searched until he found a sheltered grove of trees. Eyeing the phone in his hand and thinking of Edmond, he placed the device on a flat rock. Then, as if performing some kind of ritual sacrifice, he hoisted a heavy stone over his head and heaved it down violently, shattering the device into dozens of pieces.

On his way out of the park, he dumped the debris in a trash can and turned to head down the mountain.

As he did, Langdon had to admit, he felt a bit lighter.

And, in a strange way . . . a bit more human.

The late-afternoon sun blazed on the spires of Sagrada Família, casting broad shadows across Plaça de Gaudí and sheltering the lines of tourists waiting to enter the church.

Robert Langdon stood among them, watching as lovers took selfies, tourists made videos, kids listened to headphones, and people all around were busy texting, typing, and updating—apparently oblivious to the basilica beside them.

Edmond's presentation last night had declared that technology had now cut humanity's "six degrees of separation" to a mere "four degrees," with every soul on earth currently linked to every other soul by no more than four other people.

Soon that number will be zero, Edmond had said, hailing the coming "singularity"—the moment when artificial intelligence surpassed human intelligence and the two fused into one. **And when that happens,** he added, **those of us alive right now . . .** we **will be the ancients.**

Langdon could not begin to imagine the landscape of that future, but as he watched the people around him, he sensed that the miracles of religion would have an increasingly difficult time competing with the miracles of technology.

When Langdon finally entered the basilica, he was relieved to find a familiar ambience—nothing like the ghostly cavern of last night.

Today, Sagrada Família was alive.

Dazzling beams of iridescent light—crimson, gold, purple—streamed through stained glass, setting the building's dense forest of columns ablaze. Hundreds of visitors, dwarfed by the slanting treelike pillars, stared skyward into the glowing vaulted expanse, their awestruck whispers creating a comforting background buzz.

As Langdon advanced through the basilica, his eyes took in one organic form after another, finally ascending to the latticework of cell-like structures that made up the cupola. This central ceiling, some claimed, resembled a complex organism viewed through a microscope. Seeing it now, aglow with light, Langdon had to agree.

"Professor?" a familiar voice called, and Langdon turned to see Father Beña hurriedly approaching. "I'm so sorry," the tiny priest said sincerely. "I just heard someone saw you **waiting** in line—you could have called me!"

Langdon smiled. "Thank you, but it gave me time to admire the facade. Besides, I figured you'd be asleep today."

"Asleep?" Beña laughed. "Maybe tomorrow."

"A different ambience from last night," Langdon said, motioning to the sanctuary.

"Natural light does wonders," Beña replied. "As does the presence of **people**." He paused, eyeing Langdon. "Actually, since you're here, if it's not too much trouble, I'd love to get your thoughts on something downstairs."

As Langdon followed Beña through the crowds, he could hear the sounds of construction reverberating overhead, reminding him that Sagrada Família was still very much an evolving building.

"Did you happen to see Edmond's presentation?" Langdon asked.

Beña laughed. "Three times, actually. I must say, this new notion of entropy—the universe 'wanting' to spread energy—it sounds a bit like Genesis. When I think of the Big Bang and the expanding universe, I see a blossoming sphere of energy that billows farther and farther into the darkness of space . . . bringing light to places that have none."

Langdon smiled, wishing Beña had been his childhood priest. "Has the Vatican issued an official statement yet?"

"They're trying, but there seems to be a bit of"— Beña shrugged playfully—"divergence. This issue of man's origin, as you know, has always been a sticking point for Christians—especially fundamentalists. If you ask me, we should settle it once and for all."

"Oh?" Langdon asked. "And how would we do that?"

"We should **all** do what so many churches already do—openly admit that Adam and Eve did not exist, that evolution is a fact, and that Christians who declare otherwise make us **all** look foolish."

Langdon stopped short, staring at the old priest.

"Oh, please!" Beña said, laughing. "I don't believe that the same God who endowed us with sense, reason, and intellect——"

"——intended us to forgo their use?"

Beña grinned. "I see you're familiar with Galileo. Physics was actually my childhood love; I came to God through a deepening reverence for the physical universe. It's one of the reasons Sagrada Família is so important to me; it feels like a church of the future . . . one directly connected to nature."

Langdon found himself wondering if perhaps Sagrada Família—like the Pantheon of Rome—might become a flashpoint for transition, a building with one foot in the past and one in the future, a physical bridge between a dying faith and an emerging one. If that were true, Sagrada Família was going to be far more important than anyone could ever imagine.

Beña was now leading Langdon down the same winding staircase they had descended last night.

The crypt.

"It is very obvious to me," Beña said as they walked, "that there is only one way Christianity will survive the coming age of science. We must stop rejecting the discoveries of science. We most stop denouncing provable facts. We must become a spiritual partner of science, using our vast experience—millennia of philosophy, personal inquiry, meditation, soul-

searching—to help humanity build a moral frame-
work and ensure that the coming technologies will
unify, illuminate, and raise us up . . . rather than
destroy us."

"I could not agree more," Langdon said. **I only
hope science accepts your help.**

At the bottom of the stairs, Beña motioned past
Gaudí's tomb to the display case containing Edmond's
volume of William Blake's works. "This is what I
wanted to ask you about."

"The Blake book?"

"Yes. As you know, I promised Mr. Kirsch that
I would display his book here. I agreed because I
assumed he wanted me to feature this illustration."

They arrived at the case and looked down at Blake's
dramatic rendering of the god he called Urizen measuring the universe with a geometer's compass.

"And yet," Beña said, "it has come to my attention
that the text on the facing page . . . well, perhaps you
should just read the final line."

Langdon's eyes never left Beña's. "'The dark religions are departed and sweet science reigns'?"

Beña looked impressed. "You know it."

Langdon smiled. "I do."

"Well, I must admit it bothers me deeply. This
phrase—the '**dark** religions'—is troubling. It sounds
as if Blake is claiming religions are dark . . . malevo-
lent and **evil** somehow."

"That's a common misunderstanding," Langdon
replied. "In fact, Blake was a deeply spiritual man,
morally evolved far beyond the dry, small-minded

Christianity of eighteenth-century England. He
believed that religions came in two flavors—the
dark, dogmatic religions that oppressed creative
thinking . . . and the light, expansive religions that
encouraged introspection and creativity."

Beña seemed startled.

"Blake's concluding line," Langdon assured him,
"could just as easily say: 'Sweet science will banish
the dark religions . . . so the enlightened religions
can flourish.'"

Beña fell silent for a long time, and then, ever so
slowly, a quiet smile appeared on his lips. "Thank
you, Professor. I do believe you've spared me an awkward ethical dilemma."

———

Upstairs in the main sanctuary, having said his good-
byes to Father Beña, Langdon lingered awhile, seated
peacefully in a pew, along with hundreds of others,
all watching the colorful rays of light creep along the
towering pillars as the sun slowly set.

He thought about all the religions of the world,
about their shared origins, about the earliest gods of
the sun, moon, sea, and wind.

Nature was once the core.

For all of us.

The unity, of course, had disappeared long ago,
splintered into endlessly disparate religions, each proclaiming to be the One Truth.

Tonight, however, seated inside this extraordinary

temple, Langdon found himself surrounded by people of all faiths, colors, languages, and cultures, everyone staring heavenward with a shared sense of wonder . . . all admiring the simplest of miracles.

Sunlight on stone.

Langdon now saw a stream of images in his mind—Stonehenge, the Great Pyramids, the Ajanta Caves, Abu Simbel, Chichén Itzá—sacred sites around the world where ancients had once gathered to watch the very same spectacle.

In that instant, Langdon felt the tiniest of tremors in the earth beneath him, as if a tipping point had been reached . . . as if religious thought had just traversed the farthest reaches of its orbit and was now circling back, wearied from its long journey, and finally coming home.

I would like to express my most sincere thanks to the following:

First and foremost, to my editor and friend Jason Kaufman for his razor-sharp skills, superb instincts, and tireless hours in the trenches with me . . . but above all for his unmatched sense of humor and for his understanding of what it is I am trying to accomplish with these stories.

To my incomparable agent and trusted friend Heide Lange for so expertly guiding all aspects of my career with unparalleled enthusiasm, energy, and personal care. For her limitless talents and unwavering dedication, I am eternally grateful.

And to my dear friend Michael Rudell for his wise counsel and for being a role model of grace and kindness.

To the entire team at Doubleday and Penguin Random House, I would like to express my deepest appreciation for believing and trusting in me over the years—especially to Suzanne Herz for her friendship and for overseeing all facets of the publishing process with such imagination and responsiveness. A very, very special thank-you as well to Markus Dohle,

Sonny Mehta, Bill Thomas, Tony Chirico, and Anne Messitte for their unending support and patience.

My sincere thanks as well for the tremendous efforts of Nora Reichard, Carolyn Williams, and Michael J. Windsor in the home stretch, and to Rob Bloom, Judy Jacoby, Lauren Weber, Maria Carella, Lorraine Hyland, Beth Meister, Kathy Hourigan, Andy Hughes, and all of the amazing people who make up the Penguin Random House sales team.

To the incredible team at Transworld for their perpetual creativity and publishing capability, in particular to my editor Bill Scott-Kerr for his friendship and support on so many fronts.

To all of my devoted publishers around the world, my most humble and sincere thanks for their belief and efforts on behalf of these books.

To the tireless team of translators from around the world who worked so diligently to bring this novel to readers in so many languages—my sincere thanks for your time, your skill, and your care.

To my Spanish publisher, Planeta, for their invaluable help in the research and translation of **Origin**— especially to their marvelous editorial director Elena Ramirez, along with María Guitart Ferrer, Carlos Revés, Sergio Álvarez, Marc Rocamora, Aurora Rodríguez, Nahir Gutiérrez, Laura Díaz, Ferrán Lopez. A very special thank-you also to Planeta CEO Jesús Badenes for his support, hospitality, and his brave attempt to teach me how to make paella.

In addition, to those who helped manage **Origin**'s translation site, I would like to thank Jordi Lúñez,

Javier Montero, Marc Serrate, Emilio Pastor, Alberto Barón, and Antonio López.

To the indefatigable Mónica Martín and her entire team at the MB Agency, especially Inés Planells and Txell Torrent, for everything they've done to assist with this project in Barcelona and beyond.

To the entire team at Sanford J. Greenburger Associates—especially Stephanie Delman and Samantha Isman—for their remarkable efforts on my behalf . . . day in and day out.

Over the past four years, a wide array of scientists, historians, curators, religious scholars, and organizations generously offered assistance as I researched this novel. Words cannot begin to express my appreciation to all of them for their generosity and openness in sharing their expertise and insight.

At the Abby of Montserrat, I would like to thank the monks and laypeople who made my visits there so informative, enlightening, and uplifting. My heartfelt gratitude especially to Pare Manel Gasch, Josep Altayó, Òscar Bardají, and Griselda Espinach.

At the Barcelona Supercomputing Center, I would like to thank the brilliant team of scientists who shared with me their ideas, their world, their enthusiasm, and, above all, their optimistic vision of the future. Special thanks to Director Mateo Valero, Josep Maria Martorell, Sergi Girona, José Maria Cela, Jesús Labarta, Eduard Ayguadé, Francisco Doblas, Ulises Cortés, and Lourdes Cortada.

At the Guggenheim Museum in Bilbao, my humble thanks to all those whose knowledge and artistic vision helped deepen my appreciation and affinity for modern and contemporary art. A very special thank-you to Director Juan Ignacio Vidarte, Alicia Martínez, Idoia Arrate, and María Bidaurreta for all of their hospitality and enthusiasm.

To the curators and keepers of the magical Casa Milà, my thanks for their warm welcome and for sharing with me what makes La Pedrera unique in the world. Special thanks to Marga Viza, Sílvia Vilarroya, Alba Tosquella, Lluïsa Oller, as well as resident Ana Viladomiu.

For additional assistance in research, I would like to thank members of the Palmar de Troya Palmarian Church Support and Information Group, the United States Embassy in Hungary, and editor Berta Noy.

A debt of gratitude as well to the dozens of scientists and futurists I met in Palm Springs, whose bold vision for tomorrow deeply impacted this novel.

For providing perspective along the way, I wish to thank my early editorial readers, especially Heide Lange, Dick and Connie Brown, Blythe Brown, Susan Morehouse, Rebecca Kaufman, Jerry and Olivia Kaufman, John Chaffee, Christina Scott, Valerie Brown, Greg Brown, and Mary Hubbell.

To my dear friend Shelley Seward for her expertise and attentiveness, both professional and personal, and for taking my calls at five a.m.

To my dedicated and imaginative digital guru Alex Cannon for so inventively overseeing my social media, web communication, and all things virtual.

To my wife, Blythe, for continuing to share with

me her passion for art, her persistent creative spirit, and her seemingly endless talents of invention, all of which are an ongoing source of inspiration.

To my personal assistant Susan Morehouse for her friendship, patience, and enormous diversity of skills, and for keeping so many wheels in motion seamlessly.

To my brother, composer Greg Brown, whose inventive fusion of ancient and modern in Missa Charles Darwin helped spark the earliest notions for this novel.

And finally, I would like to express my gratitude, love, and respect to my parents—Connie and Dick Brown—for teaching me always to be curious and to ask the difficult questions.

LIKE WHAT YOU'VE READ?

If you enjoyed this large print edition of
ORIGIN,
here are two of Dan Brown's latest
bestsellers also available in large print.

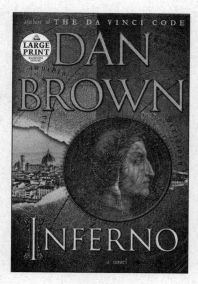

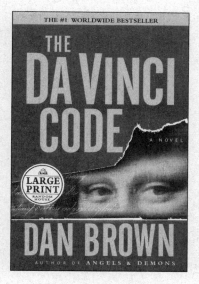

Large print books are available wherever books
are sold and at many local libraries.

All prices are subject to change. Check with your
local retailer for current pricing and availability.
For more information on these and other large print titles,
visit www.randomhouse.com/largeprint.